"The first quality that is needed is audacity."

—Winston Churchill

CHURCHILL'S SECRET AGENT

CHURCHILL'S SECRET AGENT

MAX AND LINDA CIAMPOLI

B

BERKLEY BOOKS, NEW YORK

THE BERKLEY PUBLISHING GROUP
Published by the Penguin Group
Penguin Group (USA) Inc.
375 Hudson Street, New York, New York 10014, USA
Penguin Group (Canada), 90 Eglinton Avenue East, Suite 700, Toronto, Ontario M4P 2Y3, Canada
(a division of Pearson Penguin Canada Inc.)
Penguin Books Ltd., 80 Strand, London WC2R 0RL, England
Penguin Group Ireland, 25 St. Stephen's Green, Dublin 2, Ireland (a division of Penguin Books Ltd.)
Penguin Group (Australia), 250 Camberwell Road, Camberwell, Victoria 3124, Australia
(a division of Pearson Australia Group Pty. Ltd.)
Penguin Books India Pvt. Ltd., 11 Community Centre, Panchsheel Park, New Delhi—110 017, India
Penguin Group (NZ), 67 Apollo Drive, Rosedale, North Shore 0632, New Zealand
(a division of Pearson New Zealand Ltd.)
Penguin Books (South Africa) (Pty.) Ltd., 24 Sturdee Avenue, Rosebank, Johannesburg 2196,
South Africa

Penguin Books Ltd., Registered Offices: 80 Strand, London WC2R 0RL, England

This is a work of fiction. Names, characters, places, and incidents either are the product of the authors' imagination or are used fictitiously, and any resemblance to actual persons, living or dead, business establishments, events, or locales is entirely coincidental. The publisher does not have any control over and does not assume any responsibility for author or third-party websites or their content.

CHURCHILL'S SECRET AGENT

A Berkley Book / published by arrangement with the authors

PRINTING HISTORY
Berkley premium edition / December 2010

Copyright © 2010 by Max Ciampoli and Linda Ciampoli.
Cover photo art by Alin Popescu. Cover design by Rich Hasselberger.
Interior text design by Kristin del Rosario.

ISBN: 978-0-425-22975-0

BERKLEY®
Berkley Books are published by The Berkley Publishing Group,
a division of Penguin Group (USA) Inc.,
375 Hudson Street, New York, New York 10014.
BERKLEY® is a registered trademark of Penguin Group (USA) Inc.
The "B" design is a trademark of Penguin Group (USA) Inc.

PRINTED IN THE UNITED STATES OF AMERICA

10 9 8 7 6 5 4 3 2 1

I dedicate this book to my mother,
who I never stopped loving
and who I know never stopped loving me.
I always wanted her to be proud of me.
Had she known what I did, I believe she would have been.

Max Ciampoli

ACKNOWLEDGMENTS

I especially would like to pay tribute to my wife, Linda, because without her my story would never have been written or translated.

I am forever grateful to my dear tutor and all the Jesuit brothers who made of me the man I became.

To my godfather, I express my appreciation for arranging my reintroduction to Winston Churchill.

To Mr. Churchill, who afforded me the opportunity to do my part in bringing freedom back to the world.

Finally, my heart is full of gratitude as I thank the Allies; the French, German, and all other European Resistance groups; the Freemasons; the Gypsies; and all those individuals who risked their lives to help defeat the Third Reich.

—MAX CIAMPOLI

I would like to thank my beloved Max, most importantly for his heroic efforts that contributed to the survival of the Jewish people and to civilization as we know it, and also for enduring my repeated questioning about the very things he wanted to forget but, of course, couldn't.

To Brian Davis, for his varied and creative contributions and enduring belief in Max and me since the mid-1990s. To Laurie Roberts, who never said "no" when we needed her computer advice or her point of view.

Heartfelt thanks to Nancy Ellis, now our most cherished agent and friend, who has done so much more than could ever be expected of an agent. And to Natalee Rosenstein, vice president and senior executive editor; Michelle Vega, associate editor; and all those at The Berkley Publishing Group for breathing life into Max's story.

Particular thanks for Ed Breslin's significant editorial contribution, and to my dear friend Victoria Branch for her valuable editing assistance.

To CEO-Space, where we met Tim Trainor and Brad Scobey, who have encouraged us in our endeavors since 2007. It is also where we had the good fortune to meet publicist Jill Lublin and author Dina Dove, who kindly introduced us to our literary agent.

Gratitude to Alex Kloske and Mick McGovern for their invaluable support and meaningful suggestions. Through their interviews of Max, I gained deeper insight into the ramifications of what Max had accomplished.

To my friend Leo Hettich, to Brother Matthew Cunningham and Rev. Monsignor Roger Roensch, who all helped us procure a copy of Max's baptismal certificate from the Vatican. A special thank-you to Sister Agnes Faleono of the Vatican, who was not only efficient but kind.

To the Department of French at UCLA, whose professors taught me the basics of the language and made it possible for me to go to the University of Bordeaux.

Deep appreciation goes to Rev. Dr. Sandy Jacob, Rev. Liza Chapen, Circle's Edge Center for Spiritual Living, Kathy Hunter, Michael Adler, and *all* of our cherished friends whose support never wavered throughout this incredible journey.

Finally, profound thanks to my husband for always loving me unconditionally.

—LINDA CIAMPOLI

CONTENTS

INTRODUCTION

I was only a seventeen-year-old French boy at the time this story begins. Now I am well into my ninth decade, and a lifetime has passed since I helped strike down the greatest force for evil the world had ever known.

A graduate of the Jesuit lycée in Nice, I had entered the university intending to become a dentist. Though I loved school, there were rumblings that war was imminent, and I wanted to defend my country. An influential friend was able to get me into the Chasseurs Alpins, even though I was underage. Because of a special military course that I had taken at the lycée, I soon found myself serving as a lieutenant in the French army's elite Alpine infantry on skis. Then catastrophe struck.

The Nazis invaded and overran my beloved country. The French military was swiftly crushed, resulting in unequivocal surrender. France lay prostrate and defeated. Chaos reigned. Collaboration was pervasive, something I could not comprehend. I told my men to find a way to Algeria or even to England if they could. *I* would never surrender nor consider defeat. Rather, I would find a way to fight the enemy until my beautiful country was free once more.

I assessed my options and decided to return to the south of France where I'd grown up as the son of a successful Monte Carlo nightclub owner. Though I hated my Fascist, abusive father, my dear godfather, a brilliant architect, lived nearby in Cap d'Antibes. I decided to pay him a visit.

As it happened, Winston Churchill used to vacation frequently on the Côte d'Azur in a villa close to my godfather's house. During my boyhood, I often saw him sitting outdoors in front of his easel, paintbrush in hand and cigar between his lips. It was there we first met. Mr. Churchill had a great love for France: The climate, beauty, language, sophistication, cuisine, and nightlife provided a welcome respite from the hubbub of London and the stresses of politics.

When I told my godfather how furious I was that France had lost the war before my troop even had the chance to do battle and how determined I was to defeat the Nazis, he not only listened—he took me seriously. Though I didn't know where to go or what to do next, my godfather sat thinking. That was when the great idea came to him. He would call his friend Winston Churchill.

Before I knew it, I was on my way to England, not even realizing how well prepared I already was for my destiny. Thanks to my childhood tutor, a retired Austrian colonel, I spoke fluent German and Italian. This strict but very kind man had also taught me to ski, ride a horse, fence, and wrestle Greco-Roman style. I was five when he showed me how to shoot with a special rifle that he had made especially for me. By his fine example, he also taught me ethics, morals, and manners. In short, thanks to my tutor and my subsequent studies at the Jesuit lycée, I was already a gentleman as well as an officer—though still so very young—when I arrived in England. Subsequently, Mr. Churchill and the British special forces training school would transform me into a spy, an operative, and a warrior.

I spent the next four years as a secret agent, crisscrossing Europe, in and out of the shadowy world of espionage. I worked in an era when audacity, determination, and ingenuity counted more than age. I saved lives, and I took them. I was determined to liberate France and do my part in the fight for world freedom.

I was a spy.

What follows is my story.

PART ONE

THE BEGINNING

Never, never, never quit.
—WINSTON CHURCHILL

ONE

Training

Mr. Churchill's secretary greeted me at the door. The driver took my luggage inside. "Mr. Churchill is not here to welcome you and asked me to get you settled in. Your godfather has called several times asking that we call him when you arrive. Mr. Churchill has suggested that you select one of two rooms on the ground level with a view of the pond. He'll return within the next few days. He said to make yourself at home and to ask me for anything you need or want."

Her French was quite good. She was a short, plain woman who looked to be in her sixties. She seemed kind though rather reserved. She escorted me to the rooms. I selected the room on the left, which had more character and already had a bed in place. It looked to have been an artist's studio before. I later found paintbrushes and a palette in a storage trunk. The other room was a library with floor-to-ceiling bookshelves. Both rooms had lovely fireplaces made of brick.

After I put my things away, I went upstairs to the secretary's office. "Would it be possible to have some logs for the fireplace? The room is damp and a little musty."

"Of course, I'll have someone take care of it."

"If you don't mind, madame, I'm rather hungry. Would you have something to eat, perhaps some soup and bread?"

She stood up from her desk. "Certainly. Just follow me to the kitchen."

The kitchen was large but very gloomy and had a large, rustic rough-hewn table in the center. There was a bench on one side and chairs on the other. The room was cold, though not as cold as the rest of the house. When anyone spoke, their voice resounded off the walls. I was extremely tired but hungry, as usual.

The secretary talked to the two women who were in the kitchen, apparently asking one of them about something to eat for me.

"Monsieur, there is potato soup, a beef pot-au-feu, goat cheese, and of course, fresh bread. For dinner, they plan to prepare chicken in cream sauce over rice. They usually prepare a formal dinner because we never know when the prime minister will arrive unexpectedly from London. I think you'll find that we are always well stocked with excellent food."

Changing the subject, she said, "I'll send someone

down to light the fireplaces in both rooms and leave you extra logs. That will take care of the humidity problem."

"Thank you, madame. Will you tell the servants that I would like the pot-au-feu, goat cheese, and bread? And will you please thank them for me?" Feeling intense hunger pangs, I added, "And tell them that I will be pleased to have the chicken in cream sauce as soon as it's ready."

She relayed to them what I said, and the three women chuckled, I'm sure, at my youthful appetite. "I'd like to go change and get comfortable in my new surroundings. Would someone be so kind as to bring me the meal in my room?"

"Certainly, monsieur," the secretary replied.

I went downstairs, and a few minutes later there was a knock on the door. The younger of the two servants had arrived already with a tray of food that she placed on the table in the library. As soon as she left, I sat down and devoured it all. Though the beef was boiled and under-seasoned, it was good to have something hot to eat. The cheese was rich and creamy, and the bread was fresh and crusty. I wanted to finish eating so that I could sleep a little.

I hadn't slept since leaving France. I had waited half a day in Geneva for the airplane to Casablanca, then waited endlessly in the Casablanca airport for the plane to England. Once in England, I waited a long time yet again for the car to pick me up. The journey had been lengthy and sleepless.

After eating, I collapsed on top of the bed and fell

asleep. I slept soundly for three or four hours and woke up refreshed. The room was warm and cozy now. *It must be time for dinner,* I thought, as I put on my uniform jacket and climbed the stairs. I didn't want to miss dinner. I loved chicken prepared in fresh cream sauce with mushrooms. I appreciated the time and effort it took to prepare this dish.

As I passed the secretary's office, I saw her still working at her desk. "Excuse me, madame. Since Mr. Churchill apparently will not be here for dinner this evening, would you care to join me?"

"Thank you, but no, monsieur," she said. "The prime minister would not approve of that. Anyway, I have so much work to complete while he is away. When he's here, he's often dictating letters to catch up with the mountains of correspondence that pile up during his absence."

She paused and smiled, then continued, "You'll see what a wonderful man he is. He has already told me about you. Just so you'll know, when he's here, he often follows a certain routine. He gets up before dawn every day and goes out to talk to the horses. Then he comes back to his office where he reads his correspondence and several newspapers. He loves to take long walks in the forest. He appreciates the beauty of nature and the fresh country air. This place gives him the quiet he needs. He goes for walks even when it's foggy or rainy. When he returns, he goes to his office to write notes and make calls. Sometimes, he nods off while writing. You'll see that he basically follows this routine every day when he's here, but most of the time he stays in London."

One of the servants came to her office to tell her they would be serving my dinner in the small library next to my room and that the gardener had rebuilt the fires in both rooms. I bid her good evening and went downstairs to have dinner.

The guest library was spacious. There was a small table with four chairs, a tufted brown leather couch and armchair next to which sat a wooden radio and a gramophone. On the other side of the couch was an end table holding a lamp with a large oval green lampshade under which a big ashtray nestled. An area rug covered the center of the room on top of the parquet floor. Dark draperies framed the window that looked out over the pond. Had I chosen this room, they probably would have brought the bed in from the adjacent room, or perhaps there were extra beds in another part of the house. Dinner was on the table, and everything was under bell. Since the only heating in the house was from fireplaces, the rooms remained cold unless the fireplaces were lit.

Before I sat down, I lifted up one bell, and to my great surprise, the whole chicken, sprinkled with paprika, was swimming in the cream. Hmm. I had expected it to be cut in pieces and served over rice. And the chicken looked small. Would it be enough? I lifted another bell and found what smelled so good—the rice in cream sauce with wild mushrooms. On another plate, I found Jerusalem artichokes and on the last were baked Rennet apples. I couldn't resist and took a bite of apple right away. Savoring the taste, I sat down. There was a half loaf of country bread and a bottle of white wine on the table. By the time I was finished, nothing was left. There was clearly an excellent cook in the kitchen.

I went to the bathroom to take a shower before going to bed, but it was so cold that I decided just to go to sleep instead. I needed to catch up on all the sleep I had lost during my trip. I put on my pajamas and gratefully got under the warm blankets. Before I knew it, I fell asleep.

When I awoke, it was still dark. I went to the bathroom to take a shower. The water was nice and hot and felt wonderful. I hadn't had a shower for three days. I dressed in my uniform, my hat, and coat and went out on the terrace. It was just before dawn. I saw the gardener. When he saw me, he picked up a bundle of wood and brought it to my room. As he lit the fire, there was a knock on the door. I opened it to a man who spoke to me in Italian.

"*Buongiorno*, Lieutenant. It's a pleasure to meet you. My name is Hughes. Mr. Churchill and I have just arrived from London. He has gone to his room to get some sleep and has asked me to show you around. Would you like to have your breakfast first?"

"Nice meeting you, Hughes. I ate well last night, so breakfast can wait awhile. I would love to see the property."

Though his Italian was broken, I understood him well. Before leaving the room, he said, "You can only receive two stations on this old radio: one in English and the other from the Belgium Congo. So, I'm sure you'll be tuning in to Radio Brazzaville from Africa because it's in French. Would you like to start our tour at the stables? I've heard you're quite a horseman."

"I'd love to see the stables."

"After breakfast, Mr. Churchill will be up to receiving you, I am sure."

There were four horses, and he introduced me to each one by name. They looked like cavalry horses to me. We took a short walk around the property and returned to the house.

"I'll have breakfast sent to your room," he told me as he left.

I turned the radio on and found the French-speaking station. About twenty minutes later, there was a knock on the door. I opened it and the younger servant placed my meal on the table. It smelled so good. There was a large pot of hot chocolate. Under one bell was an omelette with mushrooms and lamb brains accompanied by lyonnaise potatoes. Under another was toast with fresh butter, and under the third was a baked apple with whipped cream.

I finished breakfast and went out on the terrace. The view was superb in spite of the light fog. There was a forest in the distance, and in front of me white swans were playing together on the pond. On the far side, a couple of black swans elegantly floated together. This was the first time I had ever been to England, and I was enchanted.

Hughes came to get me. "It's too early to see the prime minister. Let me take you for a ride in the buggy."

"That sounds wonderful."

We went to the stables, and he hooked two horses to the carriage. We left the property to take a look at the surrounding area. It was lovely. We returned about an hour later. He summoned the gardener and had him take care of the horses as he escorted me to the secretary's office, where he left us alone.

"Mr. Churchill is on the telephone right now, but he suggested you wait in his office while he finishes the call," she said. "Please, follow me." We went into his office, right next to hers. "Have a seat," she offered. As I sat down, he looked up. He was just as I remembered him, though, of course, a little older. I don't know what he said to the person on the line because he spoke in English, but he hung up almost immediately.

He addressed the secretary. "We can forget about the dictation for now," he said in French, obviously to be polite for my benefit. As she turned to leave, Mr. Churchill got up slowly from his desk, slightly hunched, his arm raised to shake my hand as he approached me in what looked like slow motion. He didn't grasp my hand, but rather just placed his palm on mine. He began in a natural joking manner, "Lieutenant, you have gotten taller since I saw you last in Cap d'Antibes. Let me think. You must have been five or six years old. You didn't have a beard back then. Your godfather warned me that you now had a beard and were no longer wearing short pants."

He chuckled, then continued, "Welcome to England. This is your new home for now. While you're here, I want you to enjoy our magnificent countryside. Please ride the horses. I know you'll enjoy them. I'm sorry that I must excuse myself right away. I have important meetings in London to prepare for, one at the Admiralty and another at Scotland Yard. I'll be back in a few days, but in the meantime, I'll arrange to send you to our special forces training school. You'll be kept quite occupied, I assure you."

We talked for a short while. Then he said, "*À bientôt*, I'll see you again soon. I leave you in the good hands of my trusted secretary. Ask her for anything you need."

Biding my time at the delightful property, I began a ritual of riding every day. Hughes or the gardener would have my horse saddled and ready to go each morning. One day, on my return, the secretary was waiting to talk to me.

"We're going to send you to a camp for some specialized training," she announced. "We have your first mission waiting for you, Lieutenant, but it has certain requirements you must be prepared for. So, pack your bag. The driver will be here in two hours."

Precisely two hours later, one of the women military drivers was waiting in front of the house. I climbed into the small car. We drove for hours to a camp located near a Royal Air Force base. This training camp was totally secret, the entire circumference protected by guard dogs. To enter, the imprint of an individual's right hand needed to be on record. In addition, a special identification card was required in order to gain access. Once on file, a person only had to put his or her right hand into a machine to be immediately identified. Only then were they permitted to enter. This method was much more secure than individual fingerprints. My hand imprint was taken, and I was issued an identification card to be kept on file.

After a rigorous week's training, I received a message that Mr. Churchill was sending a car to pick me up. When I arrived back at his estate, he greeted me with great enthusiasm. "Now we're going to get some work done. In the morning, an officer will give you the details of the task at hand, but I'll give you the general parameters right now. The day after tomorrow, you have an appointment to see the dentist."

"But my teeth are fine. I don't need to see a dentist, monsieur."

"Yes, you do. You'll return to camp. A nurse will come to pick you up at your quarters. The dentist will take an imprint of your teeth. He will then drill a hole in one of your molars and make a cap in gold to put on the tooth. There will be space for a pill inside. At camp you'll be trained how to chew to avoid knocking the cap off, as well as how to take it off with the tip of your tongue should the need arise. If you are captured and think you might talk, remove the pill and chew it. I warn you that if you accidentally knock it off, you'll be dead in seconds. The pill is pure cyanide, *mon petit*."

* * *

The next day I took it easy, taking leisurely walks around the property. Late in the afternoon, a driver came to take me back to camp. When I arrived, I went to dinner with a French-speaking officer who explained the process I would be going through and the subsequent training required. He then accompanied me to my room. The next morning, a driver dressed in the typical gray uniform of the English women auxiliaries (the French called them "little mice" because of this gray attire) came to get me at my quarters and brought me to the dentist's office located on the far side of the camp. She was very nice, as they all were, but she didn't communicate much. How could she? Very few of them spoke other languages, so we had no way to really talk.

I went directly into the dentist's office. He pointed to a chair and I sat down. He didn't speak French, Italian, or German, so things were very quiet until he turned the drill on. He gestured that I should open my mouth and then gave me a shot. When my mouth was deadened, he began drilling out the third molar from the back on the top right side of my mouth. When he finished, he put in a temporary filling and then indicated that I should leave.

The following morning, I was picked up and taken to his office, again escorted by a "little mouse." This time the dentist gave me several shots to deaden the area and then removed the nerve. The following day, the nurse came for me yet again. The dentist worked for a very long time and finished by taking an imprint of my teeth.

I didn't return to see him for about a week. Then, once again, a lady in gray picked me up and drove me back to his office. More drilling. Finally, the day of my last scheduled visit, the dentist placed a pill inside the tooth, though not a cyanide pill, and put the gold cap in place. A liaison officer picked me up at his office and took me to the officers' mess hall where we began our new training—how to keep the pill in place, yet accessible, should I need to use it. Breakfast was being served. This was the only time of day that I enjoyed English food. Every other meal at the camp was tasteless.

Basically, that was my life for a couple of weeks. The only times I was allowed out of my quarters were the trips to the dentist and the forays into the mess hall. To entertain myself, I listened to the radio: the BBC in French and Radio Brazzaville.

The lesson I learned in the dining room was vitally important: how to eat without knocking against the tooth so hard as to lose the cap. The cap needed to be loose enough to remove at will with my tongue but tight enough to stay in place.

I had never thought my tongue would be in training for dexterity when I came to England. The absurdity of this thought had me laughing within myself.

I returned to the dentist several times during my tongue-training period to either loosen or tighten the cap. Obviously, it was critical that it fit just right. Three times a day, I was escorted to the mess hall to practice. No one from the outside went anywhere in this camp without an escort.

One Saturday, I was interrupted during breakfast. A soldier beckoned that I come with him. We arrived at an office, and the soldier said, "Mr. Churchill," as he handed me the receiver.

"Allo," I said.

"Hello, my boy. I hear you're making excellent progress. If it's not too foggy tomorrow, I'll send a driver to pick you up at four thirty in the morning to bring you to my country home. I want to go hunting, and I have no one to go with. We'll shoot pheasant."

Not waiting for an answer, he hung up.

T W O

The Hunt

There was just a hint of fog when the car picked me up in the morning. When we arrived at the estate, Mr. Churchill was ready to go. We spent the entire day together. He shot two pheasant, and I brought down one.

"We'll sample the day's 'profits' this evening," he said. "The cook prepares the pheasant stuffed with a chestnut, plum, and bitter orange-peel dressing." That evening, the two of us finished all three pheasant. It was a memorable meal.

Sunday, Churchill's private game warden accompanied us on the hunt. We left before the sun came up. Two hunting dogs accompanied us, a beautiful Irish setter and a Brittany from France. We relied mostly on the Brittany, as the setter got overanxious when he smelled the pheasant in the brush. We walked at a very slow pace so as to sneak up on them, but the setter, in his anxiety, often moved too early and scared the pheasant away before they were in shooting range. The law specified that one had to wait until the bird was airborne before shooting. When the birds took flight, they took off in a zigzag pattern, so it was best to shoot immediately after they took to the air. This setter would rarely fail to set them to flight before the right time, but I loved him anyway. He was simply gorgeous.

I was so taken by this dog that I later bought myself one at the completion of one of my missions and left him at my father's property in Drap, France. He was stunning, his long reddish coat falling almost to the ground. Marcello, the caretaker, called him "Knick" for Knickerbocker, one of my father's clubs in Monaco where he had worked as a dishwasher. When I next visited the property, Marcello recounted a sad tale: "I decided to give Knick a bath, not long after he came to live here. He was still very nervous about the change of environment, so nervous that he had a heart attack while I was bathing him and died. I am so sorry, Monsieur Marc." I was saddened by the loss, but Marcello was deeply affected. Knick had filled the emptiness of his solitary life on the isolated property.

While we were on our Sunday hunt, Mr. Churchill shared some interesting information with me. "There are rumors circulating that General Catroux, the governor of Indonesia, has arrived in London and wants me to consider his case that since he outranks Charles de Gaulle, he should take the leadership of the Free French in England. This should be an interesting conversation."

* * *

After a couple of days, I returned to the special forces camp to continue my training. Now that the tooth was in place, the next part of the training program began. It was varied, and I loved it. Much of the content was how to avoid being detected by the enemy. Like a ninja, I dressed in black and learned how to blend in with nature and with the night, to adopt the forms of my surroundings. "Become the tree, the bush, the hill," I learned. "Take any form *except* that of a human being."

I worked alone with the instructor. He gave me phosphorus pills so that I would have better night vision. There were electronic dummies that shot infrared rays as soon as they detected a human presence. "You're dead," the instructor said to me over and over again. I worked at this until I was able to move about undetected.

There were dummies of plywood, camouflaged according to the color of what ground material they were in, whether sand, moss or dirt. These dummies lay flat on the ground and when stepped upon would suddenly bounce up.

I repeated my instructions back to my teacher. "You'll give me a rubber knife. I am to stab the enemy or slit his throat, and quickly move on. If I stab a vital organ or successfully slit his throat, a red light will come on. If I don't, there will be no light, and you'll say 'You're dead,' and I'll start over again."

Learning to kill was a lot easier than I expected. The training numbed me to the fact that I was ending a human life. I learned how to kill using pressure points only, how to strangle someone with a wire, and how to use a blow dart. The blow dart took me a long time to master.

"What am I doing wrong?" I asked my instructor. "I can't seem to make a bull's-eye once, much less accomplish it one hundred percent of my tries. That's what I must do to pass, right?"

"Yes, it is, monsieur. You'll get it eventually."

I learned Morse code using a light or a tapper. I was taught the universal military signs used in combat, which replaced voice communication. I was trained to throw a knife accurately. I lifted weights daily to build myself up even more and ran an hour a day with about sixty pounds of sand on my back, up and down all sorts of terrain.

I perfected the Greco-Roman fighting that I had learned from my tutor as a child. I was taught how to throw a grenade and how to shoot a machine gun. "Do not waste ammunition," my instructor emphasized. He showed me how to effectively destroy an objective with "plastics," a crude type of explosive.

I went underwater with another instructor who showed me how to blow up my intended target with a form of explosive made of putty. I learned to swim long distances holding my breath, to breathe through a reed, and to dive with scuba equipment, concentrating on using as little oxygen as possible.

All this training was one on one. At the camp, there were research laboratories creating James Bond–ish types of apparatus like a camera hidden in the button of a jacket or overcoat, a camera that could be activated in the mouth by clicking the shutter with the tongue, a ring that would emit a dart to instantly put an enemy to sleep, another ring that had a small needle inside, which would kill the adversary instantly with curare. There were land mines created that resembled horse droppings and blowguns with curare-tipped arrows developed in South America that killed instantly.

After the completion of the course, as I was leaving camp, I realized that I had enjoyed the training immensely, but I hadn't learned to parachute from an airplane yet. I knew that I couldn't go on a mission until I learned how to jump from a plane, unless they planned to take me to Europe by boat. I was growing increasingly anxious to go on my first mission, but instead one of the gray mice drove me to Mr. Churchill's house, which was, in fact, feeling more and more like home to me each time I returned.

THREE

Learning to Parachute

The staff at the estate seemed pleased to have me back. I changed my clothes and went out to the stables to visit the horses. Mr. Churchill was in London. Soon I fell back into my routine of riding every day and eating exceptionally well.

Days later, the prime minister returned and summoned me to his office. He seemed preoccupied, but I had correctly anticipated what was coming. "Now that you have finished your training and have your first gold tooth, I am going to send you to learn to parachute jump."

He must be a mind reader, I thought.

"You'll go to the mountains of Scotland where there is a specialized training camp. You'll have a Scottish instructor who speaks French. I've been told he's as big as a mountain. They say he can lift five hundred pounds like nothing. That sounds like a bit of an exaggeration, so let me know if it's true. You'll be under his tutelage, so you'll learn to jump well."

I arrived by plane at a military airfield and was picked up by several men, one of whom, a sergeant, was enormous. They all climbed out of a small bus-like vehicle and welcomed me enthusiastically. Their exuberance was so different from the English reserve. I sat behind the sergeant who was scrunched next to the driver.

If people had watched all of us big men climb into this little car, they would have doubled over in fits of laughter. The big Scot turned and began speaking to me in French. The others were speaking animatedly in English, so I understood nothing of what they said.

"I'm in charge of your training, and you'll be an expert when I finish with you."

It took hours to get to the camp in the Highlands. It was well guarded and surrounded by wire fencing topped with barbed wire. Located on a very large, flat graded area surrounded by mountains, the camp had barracks that were simple one-story dormitories. The mess hall was small for a military base, seating only a couple hundred people. There were only about twenty men at lunch when we arrived. The two of us left the others behind talking and went to get something to eat. We found a quiet place to sit down alone. He took a flask from his pocket and poured two glasses. "Let's toast your arrival." I sniffed it first and then drank. It was an excellent scotch. The food was simple but tasty. During my stay, I remember we ate a lot of potatoes, soup, and lamb and generally drank beer, tea, or milk. Strangely, I don't remember there being any coffee or water, but there must have been.

After lunch, a woman driver took us to a nearby valley. We drove past soldiers who were crawling on their bellies under barbed-wire fences. Others were shooting just above the barbed wire making sure the trainees kept their bodies low.

"I was informed that you've already had all the basic training you need in the French military, so we'll just concentrate on jumping," he told me. As we descended into the valley, the sergeant pointed toward a freestanding tower about five stories high. "That's the small tower where you'll start learning to jump tomorrow." He then indicated to the driver to continue up the mountain. Against a cliff was another tower about ten stories high. "When you're ready, you'll be driven to this tower to practice."

"We'll start training tomorrow, but now we'll go back to the base and pick up overalls, leggings, boots, and a protective helmet for you."

After picking up the equipment, he showed me the barracks, my cot, and a locker to put my things in. The showers and bathroom were on the other side of the barracks, not far from where his cot was located. It took me no time to put my things away, and then we walked over to the mess hall to have dinner. We talked quite a while afterward. His mother was a professor of French at the university. When we returned to the barracks, everyone was already asleep. "See you in the morning," he said, and walked to the far side of the large room.

Early the next day, before dawn, the siren sounded and everyone got up, showered, dressed, and went to the mess hall for breakfast. The room was packed. The sergeant and I ate a big breakfast, including hot cereal, eggs, potatoes, ham, and toast. He talked a lot. I mostly listened. As we exited the dining room, there was a car and driver waiting for us. It was raining. Actually, it rained most of the time I was there.

I climbed the stairs up the tower, and he followed me. Inside, there was a soldier who normally gave the instruction. The sergeant showed me how to get into the harness that was attached to the parachute. The chute was loose, not tightly packed like it would be on a real jump from a plane. At the practice facility, the parachute was connected by a cable to the top of the tower. We walked outside onto the platform, about the size of a small room. There were two handrails leading to the end of the platform from which I was to jump.

"You'll place your body like this," he said while shifting his body sideways at the end of the platform. "Then you'll just let your body fall over the side. There is no cord to pull like there will be when you jump from a plane. The parachute will fully open when it feels the weight of your body," he said. He went back down the stairs to wait for me at the bottom.

The soldier gave me the signal, and I jumped. It was a shock to feel the jolt when the chute stopped my fall.

Then my feet hit the ground hard. The sergeant came over to me, slapped me on the back, and asked, "So how'd you like it?" Though it really had hurt my thighs when the straps around them were pulled suddenly extra tight by the force of the chute opening, and though the landing had roughly jarred my whole body, I simply responded, "That was nothing. Why don't we go to the tall tower now?"

He laughed. "Let's finish the day out here. We'll go to the other tower tomorrow."

I jumped a few more times. Then the car took us back for lunch. I didn't share with him the pain I felt throughout my body, though I'm certain he knew. With those chutes, I'm sure no one experienced a pain-free jump when they were learning. You just got used to the way it felt. That afternoon, we returned to the tower. I took another few jumps, and then we called it a day. He showed me where the release cord would be and explained how and when to pull it in a real jump. The chute itself would be prepacked. We changed into dry clothes, had a beer, and then went to have dinner.

The next morning, my thighs were black and blue from the day before. They ached, but it didn't matter to me. Very soon I'd be on my first mission.

After breakfast, a driver picked us up at the mess-hall door. It was not the same driver, though it was a woman again. The drivers were always women in Scotland, too. She drove us to the taller tower.

The landing area below the big tower was different from the first, smaller tower. Rather than being horizontal, it was sloped away from the cliff. Before going up, the sergeant demonstrated how to roll. I already knew what he showed me from previous training, but I was polite and just listened. After landing, I would roll about twelve meters or so, right shoulder first. Then the soldier in the tower would crank the chute back up, and I'd get ready to jump again.

I stayed a couple of weeks, practicing these techniques. The first time I actually jumped from an airplane would be the day of my first mission. That experience I'll never forget—the feeling of jumping into the nothingness, the limitless darkness. I wasn't scared, but I felt butterflies in my stomach. I remember the fall took my breath away. The ground rushed at me so fast, and I forced myself to wait longer than I wanted before I pulled the cord. So as not to drift too much, one must wait till the last moment to pull it. Since all my jumps would be at night, I would always take phosphorus pills beginning a few days before to improve my night vision. Today, nothing would get me to jump from an airplane again.

On the flight back to England from the secret jumping camp in the Highlands, my body still ached from all the practice jumps, but I ignored the pain. I just kept wondering what Mr. Churchill had in store for me.

PART TWO

BEHIND ENEMY LINES

In Defeat: Defiance.

—WINSTON CHURCHILL

FOUR

Spying in Africa

The following week, Mr. Churchill called me into his office. "You are about to embark on your first mission," he announced.

A feeling of excitement instantly filled my being.

"You'll be with seven others posing as tourists. We'll fly you to Turkey from where you'll leave on a sailboat to do reconnaissance on the Red Sea. The owner of the sailboat is Turkish, a very successful carpet dealer by profession. He has volunteered to help us in any way he can. Since Turkey is neutral, and he is extremely influential, we should encounter no problems. He can sail almost anywhere he wants without being bothered."

Shortly thereafter, I was on my way. I was so eager to get started that the plane trip from England to Turkey seemed even longer than it was. We made one stop in

Casablanca to refuel and then headed for Istanbul. The carpet dealer came to the airport to pick me up. Somehow he figured out who I was and introduced himself. We talked as we walked to his car. The chauffeur took my duffel bag and opened the doors for us.

From this moment, I was introduced to a culture that I could not have imagined. As we approached his house, he pointed it out on a hill in the distance.

"That's a palace, not a home," I remember thinking. The building was immense, enclosed by a high wall finished with elaborate grillwork with gates of wrought iron enhanced by gold filigree. This magnificent piece of architecture looked like a magic castle out of a fairy tale. It was perfectly opulent.

A man came out of the guardhouse to open the gates for us. The driver pulled the car in and drove along an avenue bordered by palm trees at the end of which was a *rond-point* where the car pulled up to the grand entrance of the mansion. Statues of lions framed the staircase of red and black marble that led up to the front door.

Two servants opened the doors of the entry, revealing a Roman-style mosaic fountain at the far end. On either side was a salon, each displaying extraordinary carpets on the floors and on the walls. He invited me to sit down in the salon on the left. The furniture had been fashioned from splendid exotic wood, carved by hand and inlaid with mother of pearl. The furnishings reflected his fine taste and a sense of quality and design, although it was somewhat extravagant.

As soon as we sat down, two young girls draped in

fine, semitransparent dresses came to serve us tea. He excused himself for a moment and returned with a wallet filled with American, French, and British currency.

"This will be for any expenses you incur on the voyage," he said. "I won't be going. My captain will take you to Africa. He has all the documents you'll need to go anywhere you choose." We chatted for a while and finished our tea. "Let's go," he said. "I'll accompany you to the port."

The quay where his boat was docked was not far from the house. When we arrived, we got out of the car and I saw my first yawl, a two-masted English nineteen-meter Olson custom-made of mahogany that was painted black.

"This is a splendid boat," I complimented him. "The bloodred sails add to its beauty." One of the sails was partially unfurled to stabilize the boat. The decks were made of teak and the boat itself was an extraordinary work of art, shining exquisitely in the sun. Unforgettable!

The boat flew the Turkish flag. We "tourists" were the crew and the others were already on board when we arrived. He introduced me to the captain and the other travelers. The captain spoke French.

"I wish you good sailing," my charming host said with a smile as he waved good-bye.

From Istanbul, we sailed the Black Sea, passing between Greece and Turkey. We stopped at Cypress for supplies and then traveled through the Suez Canal and on to the Red Sea. Passing the Sudan and Djibouti, we went

through the Gulf of Aden and continued on to Madagascar, where we picked up a British agent who posed
as our photographer. From Madagascar, we had strong
winds. We traveled at about eleven knots with only a six-
meter sail.

"We'll return to Djibouti," the agent/photographer
told me, "where we'll stop and feign engine problems.
This is where we want to start gathering information
and taking photos because it's filled with Germans, German sympathizers, and Vichy French." With the help of
a crane, we removed the engine and took it apart on the
dock. Since we all had tourist visas, we were able to travel
freely.

"In Ethiopia, we'll find a guide to take us on camelback to Addis Ababa. All along the way, I'll take photos
of all of you with the 'scenery' of German and Italian
forces in the background. In Addis Ababa, we'll rent cars
and drive throughout Ethiopia, Somalia, the Sudan—all
around Africa, secretly taking photos of enemy troops."

The information we gathered in the summer of 1940
was vital because Churchill needed to know the German and Italian troop concentration and location. The
Italians, already in their colony of Eritrea, planned to
cross the border of the Sudan and Kenya. They had two
brigades, four cavalry units, a dozen tanks, and about
6,600 men ready to attack a post in the Sudan protected
by 300 British soldiers.

The agent explained to me, "The British officer, Major
General William Platt, is commander in charge of the
Sudan. He has only three infantry battalions to defend

the entire region based at Khartoum, Trinkitat, and at the port of the Sudan, about a hundred and sixty kilometers to the north of Eritrea. Seeing how slowly the Italians are advancing, I don't think the major general needs to attack at this time, although I believe he'll need to occupy several more posts on the border.

"The Duke d'Aosta is the governor-general and supreme commander of Italian East Africa and Ethiopia. Most important, he is a double agent working for the Allies. The port of Djibouti, although a French colony, remains a free port. The English want to maintain a low profile in the area because they don't want to incite the Germans to invade the port. Djibouti offers too much temptation to the Axis powers.

"The Duke d'Aosta has no confidence in the existing treaty between France and the Axis powers, so he has decided to occupy a large part of English Somalia. He wants to keep the Germans from invading Djibouti. The situation, as it stands, is quite favorable to him, and he doesn't want the Germans to infringe on his power in Africa."

An English battalion called the Second Black Watch had been sent to further slow down the Italian advance. The Italian forces were composed of twenty-six battalions, including tanks and artillery. A small corps of Somalians, mounted on camels, was holding the pass called Tug Argan, near the port of Berbera, against the Italian forces. Major General Godwin-Austen arrived to relieve the Somalians' miraculous effort but would eventually have to withdraw his forces to Berbera.

The intelligence we compiled proved helpful to the English. As the result of our observations, Great Britain sent reinforcements in large numbers. Three divisions were formed from six thousand British infantry for the Sudan. East Africa soon witnessed the arrival of twenty-eight thousand men on the side of England that included the Fourth and Fifth Indian Divisions. The two divisions participated in an extraordinary and brilliant attack on the advancing Italians in Africa. A squadron of tanks was sent from the Fourth Royal Tank Division to reinforce existing troops in defense of the Sudan.

The tides of war turned in January 1941, with a determined British campaign to drive the Italians out of East Africa. Eritrea was successfully invaded by the Indian forces from Sudan, and South African and East African troops from Kenya attacked Italian Somaliland. The next month, the British advanced into Ethiopia.

By spring of 1941, Mr. Churchill arranged for Emperor Haile Selassie, currently in exile in England, to return to Ethiopia with the intention of restoring him to power at Addis Ababa. This action enabled the emperor to promptly take the reins of leadership, which greatly boosted morale. The united effort of the British and the native Ethiopians succeeded much more quickly than expected because Italian troops suffered very heavy losses. Instead of facing nineteen thousand men, the English encountered only eight thousand.

The Duke d'Aosta, gallant soldier that he was, agreed

to surrender to the English under honorable terms. Great numbers of Italians were taken prisoner, including all forces in southwest Ethiopia. Some Italian resistance continued on till November of 1941, followed by a guerrilla war that lasted through 1943.

Thus, the Italian presence in Ethiopia and Mussolini's African empire came to its end. The summer before the Duke's surrender, our group, having gathered the information we needed, returned to Djibouti to pick up our boat with its engine repaired. We all returned to Turkey, and from there the British agent and I flew to England to report what we had discovered to Mr. Churchill. While on the flight, I reflected, "I certainly didn't do much, but perhaps this was just a test mission for me. What is important is that we accomplished our goal."

FIVE

Motorcycling in Europe

Mr. Churchill was on the phone when I entered his office. "They even bombed Buckingham Palace," he bellowed into the receiver. "Our Londoners are adapting to living in this state of being perpetually attacked. The bombardments are night and day and are concentrated especially in central London and along the docks of the river Thames. The Blitz is obliterating supply warehouses and factories. London is in flames. The Luftwaffe is targeting other cities besides London, though at this time, we are getting the brunt of its attacks. But I tell you now, the Nazis will eventually learn that our people are courageous and steadfast. Their morale will not be broken."

He hung up the phone and got right to the point.

"Marc, I'm going to send you on a mission to determine the location of German divisions deployed in Europe— how many there are, where they are concentrated, and in what direction they are headed. We'll determine certain military operations based on the information you'll gather.

"I'm going to order a motorcycle with a sidecar for you. I've already talked to the designer of the equipment in our research lab. We will have a camera installed in the nose of the sidecar, and on the handlebars you'll have the shutter-release button to take photos. The evidence you'll gather will allow us to identify the divisions of German tanks and trucks according to their matriculation letters and numbers. In this way, we'll know where the German garrisons are."

The bombing of Buckingham Palace had infuriated the prime minister. He wanted more intelligence, and he wanted it now. He continued on, explaining my assignment: "You'll be traveling through Europe under the guise of a reporter for a Swiss gastronomic magazine. You'll wear a badge with the Swiss flag on it identifying you as a reporter. The right people at the magazine will have the information necessary to verify your story. You'll have appropriate identification and additional papers proving you are doing this particular article under sanction of the Swiss government.

"We'll deliver the motorcycle and papers to you in Turkey. You'll begin your interviews in Bulgaria and complete them in Trento, Italy. Then you'll go to Switzerland, from there you can send us the film in a diplomatic pouch. Be sure to label where you took each photo and what direction the units were traveling."

With that statement, our meeting ended. Fully briefed, I was immediately dispatched.

I was parachuted to the north of Brignoles in the Var region of France. Two members of *Combat* drove me to the Hotel Cavalière, located between Le Lavandou and Saint-Tropez. All was arranged in advance. The owner of the hotel was also an agent working for the English.

"There is a message for you that a submarine is coming from Gibraltar that will wait near the Îles d'Hyères, off the southeast coast," he told me. "At the appropriate time, we'll take you to a sailboat that will take you out to sea to meet the sub."

I checked into a room that had a lovely view of the sea. I took all my meals at the hotel so that I would be there when it was time to leave. After several days, around midnight, there was a knock on my door. It was the hotel owner. "*En route, monsieur!* The sailboat will pick you up in an hour or two and will take you to the submarine," he announced.

On our way to the dock, he explained, "I have your Swiss documents, including letters of introduction and correspondence between the magazine and restaurants in Bulgaria, Greece, Italy, and other countries. These documents and letters verify your contract as a freelance writer for the Swiss magazine and its relationship with the countries you are to visit. Your focus will be on the gastronomic preferences of each country. You'll need to cover a lot of ground during the eight weeks allotted for your research on this article. Here are several letters of credit that you will need to cash in the banks of each country to cover your expenses," he said as he handed me the letters. "Here is the list of our agents assigned to you in every country who will serve as your interpreters/photographers. Each one is fluent in the language of the country and in French. In the report, you will note the date and location of the restaurant reviewed and accompany it with photos taken by the local agent. Of course, you know about the photos and reports that England is really interested in."

This writing assignment created an excellent cover that was crucial to the secrecy of our mission because the local authorities of each country were dominated by the Gestapo. There were also Russian spies that had infiltrated the different countries years earlier who were interested in any unusual activity or outside person visiting the countries I was to visit. We could trust no one. Suspicious eyes were everywhere. The interviews had been set up in spite of these dangers.

"Inside this leather bag, I have all the official papers for the motorcycle, including the matriculation number, your Geneva license plate, and gas coupons for each country through which you'll be traveling. *Bonne chance.*"

The sailboat brought me out to the submarine. After I boarded, the vessel submerged and headed toward

Turkey. We followed the west coast of Turkey north until we reached the Dardanelles straits. A rubber boat brought me to land where I was picked up by a car from the British Embassy that took me to the carpet merchant's house on the outskirts of Istanbul, the same man whose sailboat we had used on the mission to Djibouti.

"Welcome back," he said, greeting me with a smile as one of his servants brought me to where he was seated in his living room. Cordially, he offered me coffee or tea, as is the custom. As we talked, he kidded me, "One time a sailboat, now a motorcycle. What type of locomotion will it be next time?" He had a wonderful, lighthearted way about him. After our coffee, we descended to the entry where his chauffeur was waiting in the car to take us into the city where the motorcycle was being kept in a garage for me. There, he had it filled up with gas and filled four extra gas cans for me to take in the sidecar.

It was a superb French motorcycle, a Gnome & Rhône painted brilliant red with a white chassis. There was a pinstripe on each side, red where it was painted white and white where it was painted red. There were Swiss flags painted on the fender and on the back of the sidecar that had a windshield and wipers. Its interior was upholstered in red leather while the motorcycle's three seats were covered with white leather. The sidecar had a convertible top of a heavy white, waterproof fabric. The Gnome & Rhône was known for its very powerful four-cylinder engine, 1400cc, which was horizontally mounted and totally enclosed. Only two cylinders were exposed on each side. The starter was a pedal. It took one's entire strength to start it because of the extraordinary compression. I weighed about 225 pounds at the time and I needed every ounce of that to jump on the pedal to get the engine to turn over. It had four speeds plus reverse. The sidecar could be motorized in low gear in case of snow or mud. In the nose of the sidecar was a *hublot*, a window behind which the camera had been installed.

"May I take a ride with you?" the carpet dealer asked excitedly.

"Of course. Climb on behind me." He got on, and I gave him the time of his life. He had a memorable ride despite his fear, never having been on a motorcycle before.

"Regrettably, you're leaving again very soon, I understand," he said as he got off. "Perhaps when you come again, you'll have some time to stay awhile and get to know my daughters. Then you could marry one or two."

"And why not three?" I retorted jokingly. I didn't know if he was serious, and I did not dare ask.

I stayed with him two or three days, waiting for further instructions from the British Embassy in Istanbul. I got glimpses of two of his lovely daughters several times as they passed through the grand salon to the area where his wives passed their time. I never met his wives, nor was I introduced to his daughters. When he was at work, I took the motorcycle out for rides in and around the city.

Late one afternoon, a messenger came with a letter for me that explained the route I was to take and the safe houses along the way. It also listed the agents who would serve as both translator and photographer in each city where an interview was to take place and how to contact each of them. My first destination was Burgas, Bulgaria, a port on the Black Sea.

That night at dinner, I told my host, "I'll be leaving first thing in the morning."

"I'm sorry to see you leave, Michel." My nom de guerre was Michel Carbonell. "I've enjoyed your company. What time do you want to have breakfast?"

"About seven o'clock. I'd like to get started early."

Once I got into Bulgaria, I began seeing troops, though not a lot of them. I started taking photos right away, making mental notes of their locations and direction they were traveling. When I arrived in Burgas, I went directly to the safe house where I was expected. They contacted my translator/photographer, who came to the house and then arranged an interview and a tasting menu with the scheduled restaurant owners the following day. All went smoothly. It was really quite simple. I gave the agent my list of questions to ask. He translated the answers, and I took notes. Afterward he took photos of the restaurant owners and me and the food they had presented.

Next I traveled east to Plovdiv. On the roads I saw light activity that I photographed and noted. After the same sort of interview in Plovdiv, I left for Sofia. I took a lot of pictures because there was a large military presence along the way. I was really enjoying the motorcycle, but the roads were really terrible. Whenever possible, I would ride in the middle of the road to avoid the grooves previously made by heavy truck travel. Even on these heavily rutted roads, the Gnome & Rhône handled like a dream.

In the evenings, in my room at the safe houses, I gathered my exposed film together and made written notes. In the larger cities, curfew was in effect and I could not travel across the city after certain hours. This had an effect on the times of my interviews and my travel plans.

From Sofia, I continued on to Skopje and then to Thessaloniki, a large port in Macedonia. The roads were not quite as rough as they had been in Bulgaria. The safe house owners always contacted the translators who met me and set up interviews and tastings at the restaurants. Interviews, photos, and meals or tastings became quite routine for me. The people were usually quite cordial and anxious to please. My agent contacts would take me to banks when I needed money and to gas stations when I needed to fill up my tank and my gas cans. All went surprisingly smoothly.

My next stop was Volos, in Greece, a beautiful seaside city. Immediately after the restaurant interview, I got on the road headed toward Lamia. My contacts in Greece proved to be just as thorough as those before them had been. I really enjoyed the Greek tastings, but on the way to Athens I began to feel sick. I didn't know whether it was the sun or the food, but I needed to recuperate. I stayed in a safe house in Khalkis for a couple of days before continuing on to Athens.

After wrapping up my assignments in Athens, I headed to Ioannina in northern Greece. I got along very well with the charming restaurant owner who invited me to stay on the premises in a room above the restaurant for an additional night. Since the trip was tiring, traveling so many kilometers each day in the heat, I decided a day off was well deserved before leaving for Albania.

After my day's rest, I left early in the morning, heading northwest to the Albanian port of Vlorë, where I had another interview scheduled. On the way, I encountered a large concentration of troops. I took extensive photos with my sidecar camera and jotted down notes that evening. The restaurant interview was more interesting this time because the owner spoke some French, and I was able to ask the questions myself. I appreciated her cooking and conversation and enjoyed the process so much more being able to interact with her myself. I left the next day and headed northeast toward Dubrovnik, Croatia, where I stayed overnight in a safe house. No interviews were scheduled.

I had a leisurely breakfast the next morning before taking the road toward Belgrade, Serbia, where I had my next appointment. Along the way, I photographed troop concentrations in Croatia and Serbia. These troops were primarily Italian. My final meeting in Croatia took place in Zagreb. Though the restaurant owner was especially eager to please, I left as soon as I could, anxious to get to Italy where the roads would be better and where I'd be able to communicate.

Once I crossed the border, the roads were terrific. Now I could really enjoy this fine machine. I passed through Trieste and continued to Trento for my final interview. That was fun because I enjoyed speaking Italian and loved Italian cooking. Again, the process was more interesting because, since I spoke the language, I was able to conduct the interview myself while my photographer took the photos. I remember that the restaurant owner served saltimbocca, a stuffed veal that was delicious. She was an older woman and confided in my photographer that she was afraid of me. She thought I was a German spy working out of Switzerland, and she didn't want me to stay in her safe house.

"But I don't have another place for him to stay, *signora*," my photographer said, trying to reason with her.

"Don't worry, *signore*. He can stay the night with me and my boy," the cook offered.

"Thank you, *signora*," I responded. "I gratefully accept."

Though I had fallen in love with riding my motorcycle, I was very pleased that the next day would be the last leg of my journey. I had gathered the data that Mr. Churchill needed and was ready to go home. All in all, the trip was quite an ordeal physically and psychologically. There was the ever-present tension of possibly being stopped by the Gestapo. My anxiety on this score increased when I started seeing Italian troops because I knew the Italians were sharp. But good fortune smiled on me. I was never stopped and never questioned.

After arriving in Berne, a long day's ride from Trento, I wrote my report and gave it to the vice-consul of the American Embassy to forward to England. My photos and notes furnished the information needed so desperately by Mr. Churchill regarding the concentration, locations, and travel directions of the troops.

Then I took the short ride to Lausanne to stay at the hotel school, a safe house where I often would stay throughout the war. I called my contact in Geneva and asked him to take the train to come see me, not explaining why I didn't want him to take his car.

I met him on the station platform the next day when he arrived. "Hello, Monsieur Toby. I have something to show you." He followed me to where I had parked the Gnome & Rhône.

"Where did you get this beauty?" he asked as he looked her over. He was really impressed.

"The British asked me to do a little road trip for them. I'm finished with it now. It's yours to use until you turn it back to the British."

"You're kidding!" he replied in astonishment, thrilled. I invited him to join me for a drink before he headed back to Geneva.

We walked across the street to a café. As soon as we sat down, I began enthusiastically, "I know you're going to love this motorcycle." I told him how it had handled across eastern Europe, and then we talked motorcycles for quite a while. Then I asked him, "So, how do I get back to England, Toby?"

"I'll arrange a seat on a Turkish flight for you to Morocco and from there, a flight to England. You'll be back in the cool weather before you know it."

SIX

Youth Camps in France

"I want you to gain access to the youth camps to find out if they are pro-Nazi," Mr. Churchill began. "Your mission is to infiltrate the youth camps at Hyères in the Massif des Maures and Die in the department of Drôme. You need to be extremely wary of the French Militia and the German Gestapo in this part of France. You'll be posing as a wholesale textile representative when you land, and you'll change identities after that. Good luck, *mon petit*, and come back safe and sound with the information we need."

This mission sounded more involved to me. I believed I was gaining Mr. Churchill's confidence. After the occupation, the Germans required that male children in unoccupied France go to youth camps, build blockhouses to defend the coasts of France, or go to work for the Germans in their occupied territories.

It was only a few days later when I parachuted near a pine forest in the Maures region of France. I quickly hid my parachute under some rocks. I had been flown out of England and had changed planes in Gibraltar.

I was well dressed in a brown double-breasted suit, felt hat, tie, trench coat, and the most beautiful pair of crocodile shoes I have ever owned. The clothing all had French labels, but the shoes were Bally, made in Switzerland. As a well-to-do textile representative, I had for my main customers hotels and hospitals. While on the plane, I had looked through my briefcase to familiarize myself with the paperwork and the textile samples inside. They were very convincing, as was the fine, well-used briefcase I had been given. Everything indicated that I was successful and that I'd been in the profession for quite a while. This last detail would not have worked had I not looked much older than I actually was. After all, at the time I was barely eighteen years old.

I went to the road and started walking toward Cannes. A while after sunrise, I caught a bus to Nice and then transferred to another bus to Monaco. In Monaco, I was supposed to get new identification papers. I was going to be a horse breeder by the name of Michel Carbonell. The question came to me, why didn't I start off as a horse breeder instead of having to change professions?

I would never know because I certainly would not ask. That wouldn't have been acceptable.

Once in Monaco, I decided to go see Monsieur Dalembert, the Monte Carlo chief of detectives who lived on the rue Grimaldi near the place Sainte-Dévote. I had known him since I was a child.

"Bonjour, monsieur," I said when he opened the door. Of course, he didn't recognize me. "Do you remember me? I am Monsieur Franck's son." He was shocked to see me and invited me in. We sat down in the salon and started to talk. He said casually, "I haven't seen your parents for a long time. They moved to their apartment in Nice, from what I understand."

Since I knew directly from Mr. Churchill that Monsieur Dalembert was working for the English, I explained to him that I was on a mission. "Monsieur, I need to go to the youth camp in Hyères. Do you think it safer to take the train or take a limousine with my friend Pierre?"

He considered my question for a moment and then responded, "Let me think about this. Would you care for a glass of lemonade or an aperitif?"

"No, monsieur, but I thank you all the same."

He got himself a drink, and we resumed our conversation. "I have an idea," he said after a while. "I have some friends in Bandol. I would like to surprise my wife by visiting them. If we take you in our car, she will not suspect my intentions. The man we will visit is a dear friend from childhood who has retired from his post as the chief of French customs."

I had had a feeling that he would want to be helpful, because of my relationship with him over the years and from the fine reputation he had always maintained. "You are very kind, monsieur. Thank you so much. I need to wait to receive new identification. That will take two or three days. Will that be convenient for you and your wife?"

"Of course, and you're welcome to stay with us, if you like."

The day after I received my new identity, we left Monte Carlo about four in the morning in his 1937 black Delage. Mr. Dalembert drove, his wife sat next to him, and I sat in the backseat.

The mistral wind was relentless that day. We took our time on the road because of its gale force. In the early afternoon, we stopped in San Rafael to wait for the wind to die down. When it finally did, we took to the road again in the direction of Saint-Tropez, where we stopped for a bite to eat. After a late lunch, we took the National Route 98 to Hyères, where they dropped me off at the youth camp. We said our adieus, and the Dalemberts headed toward Bandol, the surprise visit still a secret from Madame.

I entered the camp and went directly to the office to introduce myself as Michel Carbonell to the commander in charge.

"I've been expecting you, monsieur," he said. "You'll have the rank of *chef de chantiers*, and you'll be in charge of transportation, horses, and supplies. Everything comes to the camp from Toulon. You'll take the horse-drawn supply wagons to and from the city, picking up everything we need." One of his assistants took me to the supply office to get my uniforms, which consisted of a short-sleeved shirt, shorts, a beret, and short, lace-up boots. Then, the assistant escorted me to the barracks.

The next day, I met two officers, one of whom was from Saint-Florent, Corsica. Burly and tough, yet extremely nice, he was a typical Corsican. We got on very well. The other officer left us to ourselves since we were so engrossed in conversation with each other.

"You know, I went to the island of Corsica when I was five or six years old," I told him. "I went underwater diving with a few other children using the aqualungs developed for us by Monsieur Cousteau, Jacques' father. We were able to stay underwater over five minutes!" (This device was the precursor to the aqualungs later used in submarines to provide a means of escape for the men inside should they be hit by the enemy.)

"The trip was organized by my tutor, I'm sure, without my father's knowledge," I explained, "because my father would have been opposed to my having a good time. It's an experience I'll treasure forever. My tutor didn't have an aqualung, but he put a mask on and caught langoustes with his hands," I described with boyish glee. "Mr. Cousteau and my tutor both showed us a lot of love and caring," I added, my eyes unexpectedly filling with tears.

"Mr. Cousteau's house was in Cap d'Ail. One of my friends, Nadine Dabron, lived a few doors away from him with her family," I told him. I was a bit surprised at myself since I rarely shared personal information this way with anyone. I had an unusually good feeling about this man.

The Corsican was finally able to get a word in. "You know my homeland," he said with pride.

"Yes, I do, and I absolutely love it," I responded.

"In a few days, I'll have some time off. Would you like to accompany me to Corsica?" he asked, excitedly. It pleased him, I'm sure, that I loved his island so much. "If you want to, I am sure that I can arrange it with the commander," he said eagerly.

"My father is a friend of General Weygand. They are both pro-Pétain. So many think Pétain is pro-German, but I know for a fact it isn't true!" he added, vehemently. "But that's beside the point. What I'm saying is that my father could arrange for our leaves of absence if you'd like to join me. Anyway, think about it. Right now, let me show you the transportation unit and the rest of the camp. We've been waiting for your arrival for a couple of days now, Carbonell."

As I walked with him, he explained, "There are more than a thousand boys here. Our commander wants you to take charge of two very special horses. They are on loan to the camp from a gentleman who comes to visit them every day. They are Shires, about five years old, and so enormous"—he gestured, reaching his hand as high as he could—"that I can barely touch their withers." He added excitedly, "You'll see how full of life they are!"

We arrived at a stone building where the horses were kept. There were twenty-two pairs of carriage horses. At the end of the aisle were two immense brown horses with feathery white hair on their lower legs. They were in a separate set of stalls built especially for them because of their size.

"Aren't they beautiful?" he exclaimed in awe, though he knew them quite well.

"Yes, they're extraordinary!"

"I'll show you how to harness them," he said as he led me toward their stalls. He haltered one as I watched, then told me to put a halter on the other one and follow him. We tied them to big iron rings attached to the wall. Then we went to the tack room to get the headstalls with blinders and their harnesses, which we brought back to where the horses were tied.

"I'll be right back," he told me as he scurried off. A few minutes later, he returned with a double-sided two-meter ladder. As he climbed up, he explained, "First, I'll put the headstall on the horse that will be on the left. Don't worry about a thing. Though they're enormous, they are very well trained. Today, just to be on the safe side, I'll tack up both of them. The one that goes on the right is the more docile of the two. Now, watch how I put the harness on."

All my attention was focused on what he did. When he finished, he said, "See that big wagon over there, the one about five meters long with the meter-and-a-half wheels in back?" I nodded. "Take your horse to the right side, and I'll take mine to the left. Walk a ways in front of the wagon and stop, and I'll do the same. Then I'll back my horse in first. Then you do the same thing."

I did as he said. The horses were totally docile. "Now we'll finish the bridling process. We must first lay the reins gently on their backs. If we pick up the reins, they will start to prance animatedly because they love to go. Keep in mind the importance of keeping the brakes on while you're hooking them up."

"I checked already. The brakes are on."

"Now slowly take the reins in your hand without pulling and get up into the wagon."

I was very careful, but as soon as I took the reins in hand, the horses started prancing. Their feet were enormous. I was a little nervous, but I didn't let it show. The Corsican got up on the left side of the wagon. At the same time I climbed up on the right.

"Take it easy, Carbonell. You'll get used to it. Now, gradually release the brake and go straight ahead."

Very, very slowly, I released the brake so as not to disturb these giants any more than I already had. As I did, the horses calmed down and began walking forward as they felt the wheels begin to turn. They increased their pace slightly as we left the stone stable.

"What an extraordinary feeling," I said.

"Let the reins lie on their backs and raise them gently

from time to time. Now, they're at a nice walk. If you keep doing the same thing, they'll walk all the way to Toulon. To trot, take the slack out of the reins and pull a little."

"I've never felt anything like this before. I can feel an enormous amount of controlled energy inside them."

"Pass me the reins and I'll show you how to turn left and right."

I passed him the reins very gently. We were still at the walk. He pulled on the left reins, and we started going left. The horse on the left was the leader. As he pulled more and more on the left reins, the wagon pivoted in place. "Let me show you what to do to turn right." With all the reins together in his two hands, he made a sort of twisting motion with his right hand, which caused his left hand to make a kind of pull on the bit of the horse on the left. Reacting to the movement of the bit, the horse on the left pushed the horse on the right toward the right, creating a pivot to the right.

"They are amazing," I said as he handed me all the reins.

"Now do what I did." I was able to do the same thing. This was such a thrill for me, as I had never driven more than one horse at a time. After I had straightened the horses up, he asked, "Do you see the field in front of us? These are two rugby fields. Brace yourself by putting your feet on the footrest in front of you. Don't be afraid now," he cautioned. "I'm going to give the horses a voice command. Hold the reins firmly, but give and take as they extend the trot." He called each by name. Their ears turned back to listen. Then he shouted, "Eu, ah! Eu, ah!" and the horses moved out with extraordinary speed.

"Straight ahead, Carbonell. Pull and release, pull and release," he instructed. "That's it. That's it." I had the impression I was a gladiator behind these grand horses in a chariot race at the coliseum in Rome. "Do you think they're going fast?" the Corsican queried. As I nodded, he took the reins from my hands. He let them fall once and then again on the horses' backs, and they took off with astonishing speed. I had never felt anything like this. After a short while, he slowed them down to a walk and turned them toward the stable.

When we arrived, he looked at me and said, "Now you're an expert. I'll leave you to your horses. When you put them away, start with the left. Give each of them a bucket of barley and a half bucket of carob when they're cooled off." That said, he left. I untacked the horses, brushed them, let them dry, and gave them their reward. After the barley and carob, I gave them each a generous portion of hay.

Before daybreak the next morning, there was a knock on my door. I got up and opened it. A man was standing at attention.

"At ease," I said.

"I have orders to relate to you from the commander

to get your horses ready to go to Toulon. You are to pick up four barrels of wine, each containing four hundred and fifty liters, and bring them back to camp. When you return, you are to deliver them to the steward in charge of the storeroom. He said to stop at the barracks and get four men to help you harness the horses to the same wagon you drove yesterday."

"Thank you. You're dismissed." I then readied myself for the day ahead. I was excited to drive the two Shires again.

When the horses and wagon were ready to go, one of the officers gave me the written orders, which included the route to take. I read, "Turn left when leaving the camp and take the coast road in the direction of Car- queranne to avoid the center of town. Turn toward the village of La Seyne and pass it. Take the direction, Six- Fours-les-Plages. Go to the wine merchant in town. When the barrels are loaded, return directly to camp."

I got my horses ready. I was in heaven as I brushed, tacked, and hooked them up. We arrived without inci- dent. I gave my order to the merchant, and he sent some men out to load and secure the massive barrels on the wagon. While they were loading, I unhitched the horses and brought them to the fountain to drink. I removed the hay I had brought in the wagon and fed them near the fountain. The loading took about two hours.

Two gendarmes and a mailman came out from the wine merchant's, each holding a glass of wine. The mail- man looked at the horses, then looked at me and said,

"It's a pleasure to see these two big guys." He turned to the gendarmes. "These are the two horses that Monsieur Deleau bought before the war. I saw them when they were little—only two meters tall! I never saw them work. Look at this load! Probably more than a thousand liters of wine, plus the barrels, plus the wagon!" he exclaimed.

I proudly responded, as if they were my own, "Messieurs, now that the wagon is loaded, I am going to hook them up. It's the first day that I'm working with them. They're extraordinary. It is a privilege to drive them."

They watched as I attached the horses. "Look, the wagon is on a downslope. Watch as I release the brake—they will hold the entire load with the strength of their hind ends. And they are so calm, docile, and willing." The three of them marveled at this display of strength and talent. "Messieurs, I must hurry now because I must get back to camp. I wish you a good day and hope to see you again."

I arrived at camp after a smooth, syncopated trot all the way back. I went directly to the storeroom where I unhooked my horses, leaving the wagon in front of the steward's office. I then brushed, fed, and put the boys away for the night. For about a week, I worked with this pair transporting hay and straw. Then I went to see the priest who was my contact and told him that I thought my work at this camp was finished. I asked him to request my transfer to Die.

Several days later, the commander asked me to his

quarters. He told me that he had received orders for my transfer to the camp at Die. I left that same afternoon. I immediately missed my two giants. Even now, after all these years, I still miss them.

SEVEN

Courage on Parade

I really liked the city of Die. I knew it from my childhood. It was nestled in a wide, green valley in the department of Drôme at the foot of Glandasse, an impressive mountain of granite towering nearly one thousand five hundred meters above the city.

I arrived by train and asked directions to the youth camp from one of the railroad men. "Turn left at the street in front of the train station. Go straight. It's not far. You will see the French flag flying above the barracks," he told me. I followed his directions and soon found myself in front of a tall iron gate guarded by a sentry.

I said to him, "I'm the new officer in charge of transportation, Michel Carbonell. Will you announce my arrival to your commander?"

He immediately went to the phone inside the guard-house, then returned and opened the gate. "Go straight ahead," he said, pointing the way, "and you will see the commander's office."

I entered the camp. It was about six in the evening. In the distance, about four hundred and fifty meters from the entrance, I saw an officer walking toward me. To my surprise, as he approached, I recognized the stripes on his uniform. This was the commander. I thought it strange that the commander himself would come out to meet me.

"Are you Michel Carbonell?" he asked.

"*Oui, mon commandant,*" I replied, as I came to attention. A car drove up next to us.

"I'm late. Get in the car with me," he ordered.

The driver got out and opened the door for the commander. I walked to the other side. A moment later, he was there to open my door. The car was a Citroën, front-wheel drive and camouflaged in green and brown paint with the flag of the camp flying from the middle of the front bumper.

"Drive us to my home and hurry," he told the driver. Then he turned to me and said, "My wife is waiting for us. She's an excellent cook, originally from Montélimar," he boasted. "I'm sure you know that the region is renowned for its cuisine."

I thought to myself, *Why is he taking me to his home? This is peculiar.*

The commander continued, "I assure you, you will

eat well this evening. She may have prepared a *boeuf en daube* or, perhaps, a *boeuf mironton*. That's my favorite. I am certain about dessert, however, because she made it yesterday. I had to turn the crank on the ice-cream maker. A rich vanilla. And, of course, she being from Montélimar, the home of nougat, there will be pieces of nougat sprinkled on the top."

We had to stop in the old part of the city because six oxen were crossing the very narrow road in front of the car, and there was no way to go around them. While we were waiting, the commander turned to me and said, "Let me give you the facts about the camp here in Die. But before talking about that, I must tell you that my friend, the commander of the camp at Hyères told me about you. He said that you were assigned to his camp by a general whose name he did not want to divulge. By the way, he congratulates you on your dexterity in handling the two Shires. Now, about our camp. We produce wood coal. We have more than twenty-eight hundred young men. My boys are extremely well disciplined. We have parade-ground review every morning followed by intense exercise. Then the men return to their barracks, shower, dress in uniform, and present the flag. After that, they go to breakfast. That is how we start our day."

At the commander's home, his charming wife greeted us and told us immediately that she had indeed prepared what promised to be an incredible *boeuf en daube*. The commander beamed with pride. We had a long, enjoyable dinner ending with rich vanilla ice cream covered with decadent nougat. Madame loved to cook, which was evident from the fine meal she had created. After dinner, we adjourned to the salon for espresso and cognac. The commander and I savored a good smoke, taking pleasure in puffing on our pipes filled with fine prewar tobacco. The three of us enjoyed a lovely visit.

"Years ago, I was an officer in the foreign legion," the commander said, "and I'm now enjoying being a leader to these boys. Carbonell, you'll be in charge of the stables, which are located in the center of the old city. We bought and converted warehouses into stables to accommodate the large number of horses we need. The two-story granite building takes up a square block. We use the second floor for hay and straw storage. We have eighteen teams of horses and forty oxen that work at the camp. Our work is to cut trees that are often in areas difficult to access. We deliver them to a sawmill where they are cut to size for the manufacture of coal made from wood. Only hardwood trees, such as oak, walnut, and chestnut, are cut down for this purpose."

We talked of the German occupation and the sad state of affairs in the world. Late that evening, the driver took me back to the camp.

The next day, the commander called me into his office. "Next Sunday, I want you to organize and participate in a camp parade that will go straight through the center of town," he announced.

No time to waste. I began to organize the event so that everyone could participate, one way or another. To head up the parade, I would place a group of five hundred boys who would march and sing following their choirmaster. The others would march in military formation behind them. I delegated four wagons to be filled with hay and pulled by teams of horses. Six pairs of oxen with their handlers would follow. I chose to mount a Poitevin, a very hefty, well-muscled horse that would be pulling an enormous tree trunk behind him. Since this would make a lot of dust, I placed the two of us at the end of the parade. I would ride him bareback. I fell for him immediately because he loved to do his job. He would make a big fuss if others were chosen instead of him to work on any particular day.

The following Sunday after lunch, we paraded through the town. The marching song the boys sang astounded me. These are the words, roughly translated: "Three Germans in a wheelbarrow, alee, alee, oh. Alee, alee, oh, oh, eh. Three Germans in a wheelbarrow, alee, alee, oh. Alee, alee, oh, eh. They fell into the manure, alee, alee, oh, oh, eh." As they marched through the town, the boys repeated the entire song over and over again. They sang loudly with great enthusiasm, and they enunciated clearly. It was quite daring, given the occupation of France.

The pièce de résistance was that the parade happened to block a national route. At the intersection sat two cars filled with Nazis. Certainly, no one had planned that. The cars had to wait for the end of the parade before continuing. The Germans even saluted the boys as the French and camp flags passed them. Fortunately, they didn't understand the words of the song.

When we returned to camp, the commander and all the barracks' leaders celebrated. Red wine was served to all in great profusion. I didn't care for red wine at the time, so I didn't drink with them. Instead, I went to my room and wrote my report. Within the report, I stated, "Based on the camp's performance today, I believe that the leaders of the camp are truly dedicated to Free France and *not* to the France of the Vichy government."

When I saw the commander the next day, he told me that Pétain had given him permission to sing this song in the parade. "Pétain told me, 'As long as the Germans don't catch on, I'll take the entire responsibility. If someone does understand, I'll take care of it, somehow. The burden will not be on your shoulders.' I feel it's good for the morale of the young men," the commander added.

In the weeks that followed, I chose to stay at the camp to await word from Mr. Churchill. The commander at Die had learned from his friend at Hyères that the English had planted me in the youth camps to find out if the camps were under the influence of Vichy. I had quickly realized the opposite was true. Both commanders were resolutely pro–Free French and would gladly put themselves at the disposition of the English should there be any need for help or information of any kind.

Later in the war, they would help us place great numbers of Jewish children, whom we would provide with false baptismal certificates. During the winter, the very severe winter when the snow level in the valleys could rise to eleven meters, the commanders would keep the Jewish children inside the barracks where they would be lodged and fed until homes could be found that would accept them.

While I was at Die, the French minister Reynaud was forced to resign by Minister Laval. Laval was more Nazi than the Nazis. In one of his speeches, he said something to this effect: "I have just had a meeting with Hitler, and I will cause the Jews who live in France to disappear. I swear that these contemptible creatures will be wiped from the face of the earth. And I order all my militia to exterminate the dirty race with due dispatch."

During my time at the camp, the commander and I continued to get along quite well. His wife took great pleasure in putting weight on me, and I greatly enjoyed the process. She prepared the first fox pâté I ever ate. This fox was captured in the month of September when foxes are almost drunk from eating grapes off the vines. I never forgot this pâté, and later in life when I became an established chef, I prepared many fox pâtés myself using her recipe.

Having found out what Mr. Churchill needed to know, and having hidden in my suitcase a coded version of the full report, I took the train from Nice to Monte Carlo, where I stayed with friends from childhood. The next day, I got in touch with my contact who would smuggle my full report to London and also let the English know that I was ready for my next mission.

Gold Bullion

When I arrived in Monte Carlo, I called friends of my mother, Monsieur and Madame Mastrangelo. They owned a bank in the galerie Charles III, a property leased to them by my father, an influential man, but generally disliked.

Madame Mastrangelo answered the phone. "Don't call your parents," she warned me. "I'm afraid your father will turn you in to the Gestapo. He and your mother are not in Monte Carlo anymore. They were forced to leave Monaco because of your father's unpopular Fascist politics. They're now living in their apartment in Nice. Marc, why don't you stay with us while you're in the area?"

"That is very kind of you, madame. Would it be convenient if I came over now?"

"Yes, of course. Come right over."

Before dinner that evening Monsieur Mastrangelo told me he had a friend, Monsieur Dabron, who owned a bank in Tarbes. "You know his daughter, Marc. Do you remember Nadine? When you were youngsters, you went diving with Monsieur Cousteau. They are neighbors of his in Cap d'Ail where they have a vacation home. Before the war, they used to rent their home to English tourists who visited for months at a time. Now, because of the German occupation, they are considering moving permanently to Cap d'Ail.

"As you know, Tarbes is presently in the Free Zone under control of Pétain. Monsieur Dabron's real name is Dabronowski. The family is Jewish, originally from Poland. Their eyes are open to the danger approaching. You should see Nadine now, Marc. She has become a real beauty. She could pass as a double for the actress Michèle Morgan. She has the same nose and eyes, but is younger and more vibrant."

We talked for a while before he suddenly asked me, "Would you happen to know anyone who could obtain a travel visa to go from Monte Carlo to Lourdes? It would be for a pilgrimage for my wife."

"Yes, I do. I have a good friend in Beausoleil who has a limousine service. You could hire one of his chauffeurs to drive your Rolls. You and your wife would be in good hands."

My friend, Pierre Embalier, owned a three-story garage that was the largest on the Riviera. His business was maintaining and storing cars as well as providing chauffeured limousines to destinations throughout France and beyond.

"That sounds good to me. Do you think it would be possible to have the chauffeur with us for about two weeks?"

"Why not? Everything is possible, monsieur." I could sense that he wasn't telling me what was really going on, but I didn't question or press him in any way.

Then, he said, "Marc, I know I can trust you. The real reason for this trip is the German occupation. If they are successful in taking the rest of France, Monsieur Dabron is concerned that since he is Jewish, they will confiscate his bank and everything he owns. He would like to find a way to transfer all his wealth to my bank in Monte Carlo. The Germans must respect the borders of the principality of Monaco as stipulated in the Geneva Pact. Dabron has a lot of gold bullion to transport, all cast in bricks."

"So, if the car has a breakdown, or if there is a road-block or a search by the militia, do you have a plan on how to keep the gold from being discovered?"

"No. I didn't think of that," Mastrangelo replied. "If this happens, what should we do, Marc?"

"Exactly how many bricks does he have?"

"I don't know, but I can find out."

"Let me know. I think I can figure something out, but I must know the weight and how many gold bricks need to be transferred."

"Why is that?" he asked.

"I must know the volume of space that I need to hide them in."

"I understand. I'll call Dabron right away."

He went to his office. When he returned, he said that he had left a message with the butler to have Dabron call back.

"Shall we have dinner now?" Mastrangelo suggested, gesturing toward the dining room. While we were dining, I said to his wife, "Madame, would you call my mother to find out if everything is all right without saying I am here?"

"Certainly, Marc. I'll call her in the morning. That's the time of day I can usually reach her."

The telephone rang. Mastrangelo picked it up in the dining room. It was Monsieur Dabron returning his call. They were on the phone for a few minutes.

"Marc, it is not only Dabron's gold. His bank does business with many industrialists, and he wants to include their gold in the transfer as well. He says that the bricks are small. He had them reduced from one kilo to two hundred fifty grams each. There are between nine hundred and one thousand kilos of gold bars. He thought this size would be easier to transport in briefcases. But now that we've talked, I think that is too risky. I realize that time is of the essence. Do you have any ideas?"

"Let me think about it for a while, monsieur."

We adjourned to the living room. As I sat and considered, the answer came to me.

"Eureka," I shouted. "I found the solution! May I use the phone to call my friend in Beausoleil?"

While handing me the phone, Mastrangelo turned to

his wife and said, "I knew he would find a way. Do you remember when Marc's father was so angry because after only three months of study Marc could speak German rather well and refused to speak to him in French? And remember the time we took Marc to the hospital because Franck was so frustrated that he beat him and broke his nose? Remember how stoic the little one was? Always courageous, always determined and bright—not at all like his father."

A bit embarrassed, I asked, "May I call Pierre from the study?"

"Of course, go right ahead."

When I returned to the living room, I said, "After speaking with Pierre, there is a drawback to my plan. It will take four or five trips to get the job done. That will not be inexpensive."

Mastrangelo called Dabron. "My friend, it will be pricey but possible. Marc needs to know where the gold bars are located. Let me put him on the phone."

"Thank you for helping me out of this predicament, Monsieur Marc. The bars are in my basement. My home is twenty-five kilometers south of Tarbes in a village called Bagnères-de-Bigorre. My property is heavily wooded, so it will be easy to load the gold without being seen. What is your plan?"

"Monsieur Dabron, you need to melt the gold bars again. Pierre can have his employees remove the bumpers, front and back, and make molds in plaster. The molds will need to be filled with the melted gold. Then the bumpers will need to be replaced by the gold bumpers and sprayed with black enamel to match the paint on the car." ·

"That's ingenious!" he responded.

"Do you still have the means to melt the gold? And are those who did the work for you discreet?"

"The man is a Polish Jew who works and lives at my home. He never leaves the property because he has no papers. He is more than discreet. Thank you, thank you, monsieur. We will come to Cap d'Ail in a few days to prepare the move to our villa. I'll bring my wife and daughter. You and I can make detailed plans then, if that is all right with you and your friend."

"That will be fine, monsieur. Until then," I said, and handed the phone back to Monsieur Mastrangelo.

Two days later, Monsieur Dabron called to say that they had arrived in Cap d'Ail, and he had made reservations the following day for lunch at the Hôtel de Paris in Monte Carlo. The Mastrangelo's chauffeur took us in their largest black Rolls limousine (they owned three) to the hotel. We were only a few minutes away. They sat in the backseat, and I sat behind the driver in the seat that folded down. The chauffeur stopped in front of the hotel. The porter opened the door, and I got out first.

"Tanga!" I exclaimed as I climbed out of the car. He looked at me quizzically. "I'm Marc, Franck Crovetto's son. Don't you remember?"

As the recognition came into his eyes, he responded,

"Monsieur Marc. It has been so long! What are you doing here?"

Tanga was an impressive, tall man with very dark, beautiful ebony skin, a man of imposing stature from Cameroon. He was wearing a beautiful cream-colored uniform with red and gold epaulettes. Celebrities from all over the world knew who he was. Everyone who was anyone knew Tanga. I had known him, his wife, and little boy since I was three years old but had seen him last when I was fourteen.

I said, "Why, Monsieur Tanga, I am here on holiday." Bowing his head, he greeted Monsieur and Madame Mastrangelo as they got out of the car.

We climbed the white marble steps, entered the foyer, and turned right toward the dining room. We told the maître d' that we were meeting the Dabrons, and he took us to one of the outdoor balconies where they were already seated. Mastrangelo was right. Nadine was a beautiful young woman—certainly the most beautiful girl on the French Riviera, in my opinion. We all greeted one another and sat down at the table in the plush, comfortable chairs that afforded a wonderful view of the casino and of the renowned jewelers, Van Cleef & Arpels. Monsieur Mastrangelo ordered a magnum of Lanson brut, an excellent champagne. I don't think I ever saw him drink any other besides Lanson.

Being at the Hôtel de Paris reminded me of the days when my tutor and I would eat lunch together at this restaurant. When the waiter returned and asked me what

I wanted, I ordered my favorite dishes. To start, I would have a seared foie gras in a white truffle sauce. For my entrée, a cold half langouste with mayonnaise prepared at tableside. For dessert, I knew what I wanted. While the others were ordering, I motioned for the maître d' to come to the table.

"You weren't here when I came as a young boy. I would always order a chocolate soufflé made from Marquise de Sévigné chocolate. Would it be possible to make that for me?"

"I will talk to the executive chef, monsieur, and return right away."

"Oh, will you ask Monsieur Vitalli to come over if he has the time?"

"Certainly, monsieur. I'll ask the chef to come to the table."

Nadine was shy and hadn't known what to order when the waiter had asked her.

"Why don't you order what I did? I guarantee you, it will be excellent," I told her. She agreed, and I ordered for her. When the maître d' returned, he said that the kitchen would be able to oblige my request and that the chef would come over momentarily.

"Nadine, shall we share the soufflé?" She nodded her assent.

"Will you split it at the table for us?" I asked the maître d'.

"*Oui, monsieur.*"

Monsieur Vitalli, a renowned executive chef, approached our table.

"*Bonjour, monsieur.* Do you remember me?" He looked at me with no recollection in his eyes. He himself looked much the same in his chef's toque, though, of course, a bit older.

"I'm afraid I don't, monsieur," he replied apologetically.

"I used to come with my tutor when I was a little boy. My father owned the Knickerbocker . . ."

"Oh my God. You're Franck's son. I would never have guessed. You're a man now. How time does pass. It's so good to see you again. And Monsieur and Madame Mastrangelo, it is so nice to see you," he said, recognizing the biggest banker in town.

"I would like to introduce you to my friends, Monsieur and Madame Dabron and their daughter, Nadine."

"It is a pleasure. I welcome you. If there is anything special I can have prepared for you, do not hesitate to ask," he said cordially. He stayed a few minutes longer and then excused himself to return to his kitchen.

I had never developed a taste for champagne, so I ordered bottles of Vittel water for Nadine and me. The two of us had a wonderful time, reminiscing about when we were children. The meal was superb. Of course, the place brought back fond memories. My tutor had been so wonderful to me.

I asked the *chef de rang* to bring me a telephone. When it was placed on the table, I asked the operator to connect me to Pierre Embalier's Limousine Service in Beausoleil. "Pierre, we'll be there within the hour." I had already alerted him to expect us in the afternoon.

After lunch, the chauffeur took us to Pierre's garage, and Monsieur Dabron and his family followed in their car. We went straight ahead on the avenue du Casino, passing the boulevard des Moulins. On the right was the Pâtisserie Pasquier next to the Barclay Bank. We continued to the place de la Crémaillère, where we turned left. In front of us was the Service de Limousine de Pierre Embalier, a three-story building with 252 individual boxes in which you could lock and store your car. Each box was hermetically sealed so that no dust would get on the car. How clearly I remember it all.

I introduced everyone. "Marc already told me what you want to do," Pierre began. "It is possible, but only at night, in the garage at my home. We don't want to draw suspicion to what we are doing. Marc tells me that you will need to make four or five trips. I would suggest that we make ten molds, five of each bumper. What we will do is transport the molds to your home in Bagnères-de-Bigorre, melt the gold in the molds, wait until the gold solidifies, remove the gold bumpers from the molds, reinstall the two bumpers on the limousine, spray them with the black lacquer, and then, underneath the chassis, find several places to put gold bars, drill, screw them in, and paint them black also. That's it. Then we'll leave for Monaco. The only obstacle is that when you arrive in Monaco, you will have to wait for the delivery of the original bumpers from Bagnères-de-Bigorre, which may take two or three days. Then we will reinstall the bumpers, and you can return home. You'll have to continue doing this, of course, until all the gold is in Monaco."

Monsieur Mastrangelo interjected, "I would like to drive, if you don't mind, monsieur."

"That is absolutely fine with me," Pierre replied.

"It sounds like a good plan. Start making the molds as soon as you can," Dabron told Pierre.

That next day, my contact called me at Monsieur Mastrangelo's house and asked that we meet in the lobby of the Hôtel de Paris at 9 P.M. He told me to look for a man in a gray suit wearing a white carnation. I borrowed Madame's car and met him there, spotting him immediately. He handed me an envelope that contained my orders, wished me good luck and left. I opened the envelope and learned that I was to go to Paris. Then I returned to the Mastrangelos, thanked them for my stay, and told them I would be leaving in the morning.

"We thank you for helping the Dabrons. And you are welcome to stay with us whenever you like, Marc."

"I know you'll stay in touch with my mother, madame. You are her dearest friend. Please let her know how much I love her."

"I will, Marc. I'll make sure she knows. Keep in touch, and let us know that you are safe."

NINE

Maxim's

"Madame Monique, I need to infiltrate a location such as Maxim's to collect intelligence," I told the owner of the beauty salon whose business was across the street from the famous Paris restaurant on the rue Royale. She was very active in the French underground, and I knew she would help in any way she could.

"We want to gather information from high-ranking German officers and influential officials who now make up the greater part of Maxim's clientele. These types have vital knowledge that we could certainly use. We expect, because they are in a relaxed social situation, we can somehow pry useful data out of them. You know the owners well, I've been told. Do you think you can help us?"

"Let me talk to them and see what I can do," she offered. "Come by my salon at the same time tomorrow."

Prior to seeing her, I had asked Monsieur Plantier, chief of police of Monte Carlo, to help me out with procuring an identity card. He was able to get away from Monaco for a few days and said he would meet me in Paris. That evening, I had arranged to meet him and a friend of mine from childhood, Vadim, in front of the famous cabaret and restaurant Le Boeuf sur le Toit. It was opening night at the cabaret for a good friend of Vadim's who had a two-week contract at Le Boeuf. She was also an acquaintance of mine from childhood. Before the war, Yolanda had sung at the Knickerbocker, my father's cabaret, a hot spot frequented by celebrities, royalty, diplomats, and politicians from all over the world.

Yolanda was an excellent singer and entertainer who had many friends, especially in artistic circles. Of course, Plantier knew her, too. Everybody knew everybody, or at least just *about* everybody, in the small city of Monte Carlo.

Vadim was the son of an accomplished tennis player my tutor played doubles with. They had played at Saint Roman, the tennis club of Monte Carlo, where I took lessons, too. Later, Vadim had become a member of the Troupe des Ballets Russes of Monte Carlo.

Yolanda was so surprised. She recognized Plantier, but I had to tell her who I was. I didn't look at all like the child she had known so long ago. I told her and Vadim not to use my name. We stayed for both performances. She introduced us to some of her friends, including Jean Marais and Jean Cocteau, both well known in the artistic world. We all had supper together after her second performance, but time got away from us, and owing to the 11 P.M. curfew, a friend of Cocteau's who lived nearby invited us to stay at her place. Anyone found in the street after eleven at night could be arrested by the Germans for being out after curfew. So we piled into her miniscule apartment, which had barely enough space to fit us all. Most of us stood or sat on the floor. We talked, debated, drank, and smoked all night. In the meantime, my mind was working on what could be done at Maxim's because I had faith that Monique was going to be able to get us in.

"Monsieur Cocteau, do you know a few technicians and electricians I could use for a small project, men that can be trusted?" I asked him when I got him aside for a few moments.

"Yes, I have several who work for me. Let me know what you need. I'll be glad to help out." He didn't even ask what I needed them for.

We left early the next morning after the long, sleepless night. All we needed to move about the city was a *carte d'identité*. The photo identity card that Plantier had procured for me stated I was Yves Marsan, a citizen of Monaco. He had also brought an international driving permit as a secondary identification. Marsan was really a citizen of Monaco and was my age. It was a good thing that I had left Plantier photos the last time he had helped me out because he had needed them to have these two forms of identity forged.

The fresh air and open space felt good after being crammed into those close quarters. "Is your hotel far from here, monsieur?" I asked him.

"It's a pretty good distance, near the place de l'Étoile. We can get a bicycle-taxi or take the métro, if you like."

"If you wouldn't mind, I'd prefer to walk. That will give us some time alone. I'd like to share some private information with you."

"Certainly, that would be fine."

On the way to Plantier's hotel, I told him that I was meeting someone that afternoon who was going to try to get me access to Maxim's to use as a means of spying on the Germans.

"If I can be of any help whatsoever, I don't want you to hesitate to ask," he told me.

"Just by getting me the false identity saying I'm a citizen of Monaco, you have done more than I could have hoped for. It relieves me of worry for my own safety here in Paris."

When we arrived at the hotel, I booked a room as well. "I need to shower and get some sleep before my appointment this afternoon, and I'm sure you're tired as well."

"I'm exhausted. I'm not young like you are. Shall we have dinner after your rendezvous?"

"I don't know what time that will be, but I'll be in touch. If you get hungry, don't wait for me."

When I arrived at Monique's shop, she said, "I have everything arranged. Let's go across the street."

She introduced me to the manager and owners of

the restaurant. I explained some of my thoughts, and they shared theirs. "You'll be well paid by the English government," I told them, not knowing if that made a difference or not, but Mr. Churchill had told me to inform them. "I need to make arrangements and develop some plans to install a system of microphones attached to recording devices. I've found some safe technicians to help us."

"And I know some women who will help us encourage the Germans to talk," Monique added.

Maxim's was singular in its expression of extraordinary luxuriousness within a setting that was full of mystery. The lighting itself was a work of art, dim in some areas, brighter in others. The walls were padded in silk, partially covered with sumptuous draperies over draperies, some brocade and others thick velvet gracefully hung in dramatic swags, accented with gold fringe and pulled back with cords from which tassels hung. Adding to the opulence of the private rooms and alcoves were thick Persian rugs. Here and there, impressive mirrors framed in twenty-four-carat gold reflected the exclusive clientele that graced the restaurant, now dominated by influential Germans.

"I've been considering how to put the operation into place. Would it be possible for me to work as maître d' on the second floor?" I asked the owners. "That way I can direct those who I feel will be the most helpful to the private salons or alcoves that are bugged. I can discreetly ask if they want us to provide female companionship.

We will have some of Monique's friends preselected and coached to lead the conversation to our topics of interest," I told them.

"Yes, we can work that out," one of them responded.

We returned to Monique's shop. "An idea came to me," she blurted out. "I can organize parties to which I'll invite diplomats from different countries. I'll encourage them to invite German officers and French Militia members. I have quite an exclusive clientele at my salon that I can draw from, you know. I also know many women I can recruit to help us. Many are widowed because of the war. Others have husbands interned in Germany or Poland in forced labor camps. Several who are Jewish have husbands in concentration camps. These women are totally dedicated to terminating the Nazi occupation of Europe. Many will go to any length to help." She was excited about her inspiration.

I contacted Cocteau, and he sent me the men I needed and some of the equipment. Once the intelligence system was in place, I became maître d' and interacted with the German clientele. Most Germans of the upper echelon would have rather died than miss coming to Maxim's if they were in Paris. It was an exclusive restaurant in those days, as it still is today, and wasn't far from German headquarters.

A few days later Monique introduced us to the wonderful women willing to help. Monsieur Plantier spent a few days with me to help select our people before returning home. I trusted his judgment and experience as the long-standing chief of police of Monte Carlo.

The scheme worked beautifully. Many women were able to continue the relationships established at Maxim's and were thus in position to maintain the influx of intelligence. Monique was responsible for coding and sending the data collected to England. Her friends used their feminine wiles for the Allied cause to furnish us with more secrets than we had even hoped for. These women were true patriots.

After a few weeks, I passed the job on to my successor, who would continue to gather information at Maxim's and help set up other locations popular with high-ranking Germans for the duration of the war.

I got in touch with my contact in Paris, who said I needed to make my way to England via Lisbon, Portugal. He gave me the locations of several safe houses and people who could help me. I decided I would pass through the south of France on the way.

Some years later, in 1947, I was traveling to Le Havre to take a ship to New York. I stopped in Paris to visit Monique and to get a haircut and my beard trimmed in her men's salon upstairs before leaving for the United States. The salon was there, but she wasn't. I talked to the manager, who confided, "During the war, Monique was caught by the Germans, questioned interminably, and finally blinded by the lights they used in her interrogations.

Of course, she doesn't work anymore, but she is still the owner and we are still in touch every evening."

"I am so sorry." I was deeply moved and somewhat shaken by this news. "Will you give her this package and letter for me?" I had written a letter of thanks for her enormous contribution and enclosed my 9-millimeter Lugar as a memento of the times. "I am sorry I cannot stay to go visit her, but I must take a train this afternoon for Le Havre. Please express to Monique my deep regrets for her loss. I will never forget her and her friends' sacrifices. What they did is etched in my mind forever."

TEN

Jews for Sale

Once I reached the south of France, I decided to go to a restaurant I knew in La Turbie whose owner I had known for many years. I was staying with a priest at a church in a nearby village. As I was eating lunch, the owner came over to me.

"I have a dilemma, Monsieur Marc," he said, "and I need some advice." He knew we both shared the same outlook about Germans occupying France. "What can I do?" He was really agitated about something.

"Do about what?" I asked.

"I learned that a customer of mine who is pro-Nazi intends to go to the militia headquarters in Nice to report a camp in the woods nearby where two hundred fifty to three hundred Jewish refugees are hiding along with some French partisans. I must find a way to stop him."

"Tell me more."

"This man is really angry because his son told him about this camp where he's helping out. The father is anti-Semitic, so that did not sit too well with him. On top of that, the boy has fallen in love with a Jewish girl he met at the camp and plans to marry her. The father is vehemently opposed to Christians marrying Jews, of course."

"What he doesn't know is that several other local residents and I take care of feeding these refugees and providing for their medical needs. If he knew, he wouldn't be frequenting my establishment. He has been bragging that he intends to denounce the whole group to the militia in Nice. I don't know what to do to protect them."

"But his son is at the camp," I said. "He risks losing his son if he reports the camp. Doesn't he understand that?"

"That's the point. He wants to get rid of the Jews and his Jew-loving son. He feels he'll take care of both problems at once."

"Does he know that it is likely his son will be killed?" I asked, incredulous.

"I'm afraid he does. He's a Jew-hating fanatic and believes his son is better off dead than married to a Jewish girl. Can you help?"

"Yes, I believe I can," I replied as I began to feel the heat of anger rising within me.

"If you'd like to meet him, he stops at my bar almost every night and gets drunk before going home. He lives close by, only two or three kilometers away."

* * *

That evening I returned to his restaurant. Most of the tables outside were occupied. As I entered, I saw a man seated alone at a table, holding a glass of red wine. I looked over at the owner behind the bar. He nodded slightly, indicating that this was the man.

I went up to the bar. "I'll have a bottle of red wine, please," I said to the owner. He opened a bottle and poured a glass for me. I picked up the bottle and glass and walked over to the table next to the man and sat down. After a few minutes, I opened the conversation.

"Excuse me, monsieur. I'm going to Nice tomorrow, but I don't know the address of the place where I need to go. I'm not from around here. Do you know Nice at all?"

"Where is it you're going?"

"I want to go to the militia headquarters, but I'm not familiar with the city, and it's so big. I have no idea how to find it. Would you know?"

"Not exactly but I can tell you it's near the center of town. But this is such a coincidence. I happen to be going there myself tomorrow. I'm a member of the militia," he said proudly. "Why do you want to go? Do you want to join?"

"Yes, I do," I lied enthusiastically.

"Good man," he said. "You can come with me tomorrow. I'm going to take my car."

"That is kind of you. I really appreciate it," I responded. "May I pour you a glass of wine?"

He nodded. "Why thank you." He took a big gulp

and finished his glass, and I poured him another. He drank it down, and I filled his glass again.

"Wonderful. We'll go together," I said. I thought to myself that I'd better get him drunk because I needed to subdue him tonight, and he was very well built. This way, I'd make it easier on myself.

We continued talking, and I continued pouring. With each pause in the conversation, he downed a glass of wine until the bottle was empty.

"Would you mind doing me a favor?" he asked, slurring his words.

"Yes, of course. What can I do for you?"

He was having a lot of difficulty expressing himself. "Would you mind doing me a big favor?"

"I already said yes. What's the favor?"

"Between militia men, after all," he slurred, with a grin on his face.

"Whatever it is, it would be my pleasure."

"My farm is about three kilometers away. You see, I drank a little too much. I don't know if I can make it home alone. You can stay at my house if you'd like, but I really need some help getting there."

"Certainly, I understand."

We got up and stumbled out into the night together like two drunks. It was around nine or nine thirty when we began walking toward his home. I asked myself how I was going to get rid of him. About ten minutes later, it came to me. "I need to go to the bathroom," I said.

"Don't worry about a thing," he responded. "I know of a stable for sheep nearby. The French shepherds use it when they stop with their herds on the way to Italy for the winter to find more grass. Then, on the way back, in the summer they stop there again."

Shortly afterward, he announced, "Here we are. I'll come with you. I really have to go, too."

As we took refuge to relieve ourselves, it started to rain. The entry to the large stone stable was very low. It could hold well over a hundred sheep. As we entered, I noticed the trap into which the sheep's urine would run so they wouldn't have to sleep in it. The hole was covered with a boulder.

As we both urinated, I suggested, "We can stay in the shelter for a while until the rain lightens up."

"That's a good idea," he managed to say.

Then I asked, "Do you know if there are any Jews in the area?"

He fell for it. "Those dirty Jews! They're everywhere! Even here. There's a bunch of them hiding in this very forest. There are a lot of them in Nice, too. When we catch them, we sell them to the Nazis for a hundred francs a head," he said proudly. "That's why I'm going to Nice tomorrow. I'm going to collect a bundle of money for a whole camp of Jews! But that's not the only reason. My son has been bewitched by a Jewish girl and wants to marry her. I can't understand it. I won't accept it. It's just not done."

"You mean, your own son is in the camp?"

"Can you believe it? He joined them. He takes himself for a Jew now. It's his own fault that he'll be arrested with the rest of them."

CHURCHILL'S SECRET AGENT   93

"You only have one problem," I said as I pulled out the Colt .45 from my belt and pointed it at him. "Get on your knees," I ordered. He looked at me, not comprehending. I hit him on the side of the head with the pistol. He fell to the ground that was covered with sheep droppings. "I said get on your knees, you dirty beast."

He was so drunk. He began to cry and blubber like the coward he was. "Don't hurt me, don't hurt me," he pleaded.

"It won't hurt," I explained. "It will be over much too quickly. I don't think you understand that it is not right to sell human beings. Listen carefully to what I have to say. In the name of Free France, I condemn you to death."

"No," he said, "you don't have the right."

"Enough of this useless chatter. Say your final prayers and consider what you were about to do. You have thirty seconds. And don't move. If you do, I'll shoot you in the shoulder, and that *will* hurt and cause you to suffer before you die. So say your prayers and ask forgiveness and die worthy of being a man."

Suddenly I realized that I'd better get on with it and waste no more time. You just never knew when an interruption might arise. I had to take advantage of the opportunity at hand. The rain was not letting up but coming down harder and harder. "Have you finished your prayers? Finished crying? I'm sure you don't find anything to reproach yourself for. Am I correct?"

He looked at me, stunned.

I put the Colt .45 on the center of his forehead and pulled the trigger. The bullet went through his head.

The explosion resonated throughout the enclosed stable, reverberating off the stone walls. The effect was like that of an echo chamber.

I was relieved that it was over. I removed the stone from the well that drained the stable of urine. I pulled the dead man by his feet across the opening and then dropped him headfirst down the well shaft. I replaced the large stone and started back to the hotel next to the restaurant whose owner had put me on to this scoundrel. As I walked through the dark rainy night, I felt so good inside that I had saved all those people from probable death. But there was no time to dwell on it. I knew I now had to make my way to Portugal as soon as I possibly could. Before leaving in the morning, I would need to reach my British contact in Nice.

A few years later, after the end of the war, the gendarmes came to see me at the Eden-Roc, a luxury hotel in the south of France that was serving as a hospital for officers and where I was recovering from an injury.

"A body was found in a *bergerie* near La Turbie," one of them began. "When we asked around to see if anyone knew what had happened, the owner of the restaurant explained the circumstances and named you as the person responsible. Is that so?"

"Yes, it is."

"Please read and sign the statement we have prepared, if you find it accurate."

Since it was true, I signed it. The policemen thanked

me and left. That was the last time anyone mentioned the incident to me.

From La Turbie I made my way to Lisbon, where I would contact the appropriate people to get back to England. The city was a major destination for refugees, especially Jewish families, from all parts of Europe trying to escape Nazi tyranny. Their desperation was palpable. Another aspect of the city's changing climate was the continual influx of spies. Intrigue reigned as their numbers increased from Russia, England, Germany, Italy, France, Spain, and elsewhere. Spies from the world over either mingled or cautiously avoided one another. Lisbon was teeming with secrets, schemes, and conspiracies. The enemy was unidentifiable. No one could be trusted. Everyone was spying on everyone else. If it hadn't been so serious, it would have been comical.

A couple of days later, compliments of the British, I embarked on a fishing trawler that took me and a number of Jewish refugees to England. The others were already on board when I arrived dockside. The trip took a long time because we had to avoid the path of the German submarines. As soon as we arrived in port, I made a telephone call to Mr. Churchill's secretary.

"I'm in England and ready to be picked up," I said, happy to hear her familiar voice.

A couple of hours later, a car driven by a woman soldier came to take me to the prime minister's residence. On the way to my safe haven, I hoped that Mr. Churchill would have time to go hunting. I could use the relax-ation. Then again, I thought, maybe he would have a mission for me right away. In any case, I breathed easier now that I was back in England and my mission had been completed successfully.

ELEVEN

Josephine

While on a long ride on one of Mr. Churchill's horses, I thought about how much I loved to be out in nature, just my horse and me. I was enjoying the long, relaxed days alone in the countryside while Mr. Churchill was engaged with his wartime responsibilities in London. But this restful interlude did not last long.

The prime minister returned the following week and called me to his office. "I haven't seen you for such a long time, *mon petit*," he said as he took me in his arms. "It makes me happy to see you here and to be able to speak French with you. By the way, I commend you on the plan you formulated at Maxim's. When the war is over, you and I will have to pay them a visit. We must thank them for their invaluable assistance in defeating the Germans, and we must show our appreciation to the salon owner as well. One day, we'll have a lot to celebrate," he said with resolve.

"I love your devotion to getting rid of the Hitler regime," he added. "I love your posture and your allure. You represent what we call in Great Britain a true gentleman. You seem to be at ease in any milieu. That serves us well."

I was too embarrassed to respond. Anyway, I didn't know what to say. I was just pleased to be useful, but I wanted to do something more, something definitive.

"I hope you've been sleeping well and enjoying your rest because it's time for you to leave on an important mission. The United States has fifty-three bombers in mothballs that we desperately need for our Royal Air Force. We are alone in this fight against the Nazis. Not only do we need these planes, but we need more arms and more supplies to conquer the Germans. They are much better equipped than we are. Every time the Nazis bomb London, we must retaliate immediately and with precision."

At the time, neither the United States nor Canada was willing to get involved in the war. "Marc, I need you to go to France to talk to a very influential person that I met years ago in Monte Carlo at your father's club. She could be crucial to our obtaining these airplanes. We need to convince some financiers and influential industrialists in the United States to sell us these bombers. I know the U.S. wants to remain neutral; however, if we don't get them, I fear for the future of the world."

He sighed and nodded, emphasizing the seriousness

of what he was about to confide. "You'll go to her home. She lives in the countryside, about two hundred kilometers north of Toulouse. I want you to talk to her and explain how critical the situation is. Tell her that each time we are attacked, it is imperative that we counterattack. We cannot continue doing so if we don't increase our airpower. We have lost too many airplanes, and we do not have the means to produce them quickly enough. It is vital that we obtain these American planes so we can destroy the German arms factories and war production machine." Churchill didn't say why he chose me for the mission, but I would figure that out later.

I responded, "I'm ready. When do I leave?"

"Through personal contacts in France, I've arranged your cover. You are on the books of a company that buys and sells farm animals and through selective breeding improves the breed quality. Your specialty is cows. You can increase the quantity of their milk production. Your title is "*négociant de bestiaux*," a farm animal salesman. Your region is nonoccupied France. Everything is well organized, with people in the industry claiming to have known you for years, those for whom you work and have worked, and those who will unequivocally stand up for your good reputation in the industry. Your biggest concern, as always, will be the French Militia. The pro-Nazi movement is growing and they are treacherous, as you already know. Good luck, Marc, and may God be with you. My secretary will give you all the details tomorrow." Before I left his office, he gave me another hug.

* * *

The next day, his secretary gave me the particulars. "Monsieur Marc, you will be dropped in the vicinity of Brive-la-Gaillarde in the Gers department of France. You will have a Peugeot 304 at your disposition and plenty of coupons for gasoline. Your name will again be Michel Carbonell. All papers confirming your identity will be in the car. Only Mr. Churchill and I know about this mission. Do not trust anyone else. The German Fifth Column is everywhere. We know that many of them have been in England for years and are in powerful positions. They are doctors, lawyers, and politicians. We never know who we are truly talking to. They established themselves well before the war started, from the time when Hitler was first forming his Nazi party."

The departure was planned for a night with no moon, with takeoff set for 11:30 P.M. I boarded a small, slow-moving but very quiet and light airplane, one most often used for observation. For the longer range necessary with this mission, an additional gas tank had been installed. The frame of the airplane was built of wood, covered with canvas, and painted with an aluminum paint to waterproof it. As little metal as possible was used in the body to avoid detection from radar.

After we were in the air about ten minutes, I handed the pilot our flight plan. We were to head south from England, avoiding the coast of France. Then we would head toward Arcachon on the coast and go inland toward

Périgueux where the partisans of *Combat* would be waiting for me. Hours later, I spotted what I was trained to detect.

"There are the fires," I said to the pilot. There were always three fires placed in an arrowlike arrangement to indicate the direction of the wind. The pilot lifted one wing and was able to get a bit more elevation. He landed beautifully, coming to a stop before the end of the field, which was about 150 meters long. Fortunately, he made a soft landing, as this type of plane, owing to its light construction, can take very little shock.

At the field, hundreds of men and women, most of them Basques, were armed heavily with Steins (9-millimeter machine guns), hunting rifles, and grenades. All were there to protect me. They quickly threw dirt on the fires, and I was directed toward a narrow dirt road where a truck was waiting. Three members of the Resistance were in the back of the truck. One of them had a bazooka. I got in next to the driver, who turned on the ignition but not the headlights. It was around three in the morning. He told me, "Curfew is at eleven. We have to be extremely careful. No lights. The French Militia is vicious in our region. If they spot us, we'll be imprisoned." A short while later, the truck came to a halt. "This is your destination for tonight, monsieur. Be ready at eleven tomorrow morning. We'll pick you up." They left me at a nearby farm where the woman of the house and her two children were awaiting my arrival.

"Come into the kitchen and sit down. I've prepared a little something for you to eat," she offered cordially.

I sat down at a lovely, traditional rectangular chestnut table where each place had a bowl carved into the wood, country-style. At this type of table, no plates were used. The "bowls" were simply wiped clean after the meal. The fireplace was at the far end of the kitchen/family room. Made of massive granite, it took up the entire wall. There were two stone benches inside the fireplace that provided a wonderful place to warm up on winter mornings. Each bench could easily seat two people. The ceiling was supported lengthwise by two tremendous chestnut beams. Each of these was supported by two beams on either end of the ceiling. On the table was a welcome spread: rye bread; Reblochon cheese, a rarity in the area (from the Haute-Savoie region); and a bottle of Bordeaux.

After I finished the special meal, the farmer's wife showed me to my room, located on the mezzanine and overlooking the enormous room below. There were three other bedrooms down the hall. I fell asleep right away, only to be awakened a couple of hours later by the whispering of her two young boys. Both were dressed for school in white shirts and navy blue short pants covered by aprons. They wore lace-up shoes with long navy blue socks. The two stared at me in awe. They were so excited to have "the spy" in their home.

When on a mission, I often slept in my trousers, so I had only to finish dressing fully. I put on my disguise: a long-sleeved shirt, a virgin-wool ecru pullover sweater, a beige angora scarf that could easily be wrapped around my neck three times, a cap from Auvergne, short boots, and socks. I "brushed" my teeth with soap and the end of the towel, washed up, and combed my hair. I was letting my beard grow so there was no need to shave. The two boys each grabbed a hand and pulled me downstairs.

"Voilà l'officier anglais, Maman!" the older of the two shouted. They evidently thought I was a British officer. "Come and eat," the older boy said to me. "Our mother has already prepared breakfast."

They were so adorable. The staircase steps were very narrow—just fine for the two excited little ones, but at the speed they were pulling me, I was having a hard time keeping myself from falling. Finally, I just whisked each boy up in the air by putting my arms straight up, and I arrived safely at the ground level with a giggling boy hanging at the end of each arm.

The two of them pulled me toward the table. I sat down and was immediately sandwiched by the two kids. The bread was warm, the block of butter (about a kilo and a half) had just been removed from the churn, and the mirabelle plum jam was the best I had ever eaten. I generously buttered the bread and dipped it in my bowl of café au lait, made from barley and chicory and lightened with fresh cream. I took a second helping of bread with a mound of fresh jam piled on top. This was to be a memorable breakfast. I started to get up from the table, but the lady of the house stopped me. "Monsieur, I have fresh apple beignets for you," she said. They were sprinkled with powdered sugar, and she served them with a bowl of fresh cream. Extraordinary.

The kids began to pull on me. "Monsieur, come help us milk the cows. We've been eating for so long that we're late. The truck that collects the milk cans will be here soon!" Smiling, I hurried out with them to the barn to take care of the twelve beautiful Holsteins. The cows smelled so good. They were impeccably clean. Each cow gave about nine liters of milk. The three of us completed the job in no time at all. I milked five cows in the time that it took their little hands to milk three each. Then the two kids milked the last one. They kidded me, laughing, "For a grown-up, you sure milk slowly."

We filled the three milk containers with one bucket at a time, dumping the bucket of milk in after finishing each cow. We loaded them into a wheelbarrow that the two boys pushed to the side of the road. Then we placed the milk containers in an old bathtub into which flowed fresh and icy underground spring water.

Unexpectedly, the truck that I had ridden in the night before appeared, followed by the Peugeot that I was to drive. It was eight o'clock in the morning, not eleven.

"Are you ready?" the driver of the truck shouted. I nodded. "Get into the car on the passenger's side." A woman was at the driver's wheel.

"I'll just grab a few things inside the house," I said. I hardly had time to say thank you and good-bye to the dear people. I jumped into the car, and we drove off immediately, taking the road toward Brive-la-Gaillarde.

I turned for a last look at the family. I noticed the sad little eyes of the two boys, each one wrapped in an arm of their mother, standing in front of the farmhouse.

The truck took the lead. The road was dusty and filled with potholes. After four or five hours, the driver said to me, "After this curve, on the right, you will see a fifteenth-century château. It is called Les Milandes. As you will see, it's surrounded by a forest and rolling pastureland. It's located to the northwest of Toulouse and overlooks Castelnaud-Fayrac, next to the Dordogne River."

The truck came to a stop in front of the estate, and the car stopped directly behind it. From the passenger's side of the truck emerged one of the men from the previous evening. He motioned to the Peugeot driver to go ahead, and the driver of the truck honked the horn four times.

The entrance to the estate was a dirt road lined on both sides by plane trees, *platanes*. Arriving in front of the chateau, the car came to a stop on the cobblestone directly in front of the impressive entrance.

The driver of the car got out, handed me the keys, and jumped into the truck. The truck pulled away. No one said another word. When I reached the top of the front steps, I found the door partially open. I called out, "Is anyone home?"

Two small hands appeared on the edge of the door, pulling it open. The servant said, "Come in, monsieur. Madame is expecting you." She led me to the salon.

A woman was seated on the Empire-style red velvet couch. She wore long pants of white shantung, which hugged her body from slender waist to knee and from there flared out on the sumptuous red velvet. Through the sheer long-sleeved white blouse, I could see her beautiful black skin. She was smiling.

I could not believe my eyes! My throat tightened. I couldn't say a word. I knew this woman! She jumped up, seeing me suddenly lose all color in my face.

"Do you feel all right, monsieur? Would you like a glass of water?" Her very short hair was worn tight against her head like Rudolph Valentino, parted on the side. I tried to bring myself under control so that I could tell her I was all right, but I could not utter a sound. This was such a shock. I wanted to say, "Do you remember me?" but nothing came out. Again, she asked, "Please, may I get you some water?" This time I nodded, thinking that the water might help me speak. She hurriedly left the room.

Meanwhile, I flashed back to the time when I was four years old. This woman held such a special place in my memory. She flew back into the room with a glass of water in hand and gave it to me. Elegant in her every movement, she darted about like a firefly. I took a couple of sips of water and glanced her way. She looked very concerned.

This bearded young man, not yet nineteen years old, suddenly felt again just like that little boy of four. The extraordinary entertainer standing before my eyes had been a guest in my parents' home for three or four months while she entertained at my father's nightclub. She had always treated me so kindly, calling me "*mon petit bonhomme*," my little young man. I also had fond memories of her little black Pekinese, "Minuit," who would lie on my lap for hours on end, licking my hands and arms.

When I was able to pull myself together, I looked at her directly and began to sing, "*J'ai deux amours: mon pays et Paris*" (I have two loves: my country and Paris). That was her special song. While looking into her eyes, I added, just as she had in my youth, "*Et vous aussi*." (That's what she added to the song when she sang it to me, "And you, too.")

She looked at me. It was obvious that there was no recognition. Smiling quizzically, Josephine Baker responded, "Oh, they didn't give me a password. '*Et vous aussi*'—is that the password? Or do I know you?"

I answered with unusual tenderness in my voice, "You know me, mademoiselle. I am your *petit bonhomme*, but I haven't seen you since I was four years old in Monte Carlo."

She approached me saying, "Oh my God! Of course, I see it now. You are Franck and Celeste's son. Now I see the resemblance to your mother. You have her smile. You've grown up, but you still have that unforgettable, sincere smile of your dear mother," she said, as her eyes filled with tears. "Come, come over here and kiss me."

She began sobbing as she held me in her arms. After some time, we both regained our composure. How times had changed since then!

"I've thought of you so often," she said kindly. "You were the most polite and considerate child I have ever met. I know that must have come from the education of your tutor. I'm certain you didn't learn it from your father. And you undoubtedly have your mother's big heart," she said wistfully. She had always cared a lot for my mother. We reminisced. My mind was flooded with memories. During those few months, she had given me the affection, the hugs and kisses, and attention that my mother was forbidden to give me. From Josephine, during that brief period, I had received the mothering and nurturing that I had longed for.

My mother had been ripped away from my life when she was forced to stop breast-feeding me when I had reached the age of eighteen months. After that, my father would allow her no more contact with me. I never understood why he wouldn't let us be together, and I hated him for this as well as for so many other things.

"I was expecting an English spy," she said. "I never thought I would meet *you* again after all these years. They told me that the agent would be staying here for a week or two. What should I call you? I don't want to say anything wrong."

Memories, words, and feelings were all jumbled together inside me. I felt like that love-starved little boy again. Dryly, I said, "My name is Michel Carbonell. I was born in Oran, Algeria, on November 21, 1922. I sell farm animals."

Josephine took my hand in hers. I melted inside. We sat together talking on the couch for a long time, remembering the days long ago in Monaco. (Now, as I write this decades later, I have tears in my eyes. But back in those days, I rarely showed my emotion. I experienced so little tenderness in my life until these recent years with my wife. Recalling these memories and expressing them on paper moves me deeply.)

I started to take in the décor of the room. The exquisite antique furniture would have made any collector jealous.

"Before we eat lunch, I want to introduce you to my family," Josephine announced. We walked into the next room, the grand salon, which was impressive, to say the least. The stone fireplace was immense. Inside was a door leading down to an underground room and secret passageway that led out of the château. Of course, I would use it should I need a quick escape.

"I used the room to hide British pilots who were shot down while trying to help the French defend themselves. We were able to get them all back to England safely."

As we entered the grand salon, I stopped abruptly. There, on the parquet floor, head resting inside the fireplace, one of the members of the family, Agathe, a python that was six meters in length, was introduced to me. Josephine saw the look in my eyes.

"Most people have that special look when they first meet Agathe," she said, very endearingly. "She just loves the little breeze that comes up from the passageway. That's her favorite spot."

"What do you feed her?"

"She loves chicken. I have them killed fresh for her. She swallows them whole, feathers and all. Just one will nourish her for an entire week."

We walked to the other side of the room. "I want you to meet Hannibal." The stunning green, blue, and yellow parrot was sitting on a platform just outside his cage. He seemed to understand English and French, but most of the time he spoke English, and I didn't understand a word when he did. Josephine opened the window and said to Hannibal, "*Appelle* Bozo. Call Bozo." Hannibal called out, "Bozo, Bozo." A beautiful Great Dane came running at full speed toward the terrace. Josephine took Hannibal, opened the door to the terrace, placed the bird on Bozo's collar, and said to me, "They're going to go for a walk. Let's go with them."

In the distance, behind the château, was a large carriage house with a door for each vehicle. There were several doors. Inside, she had two limos, a Citroën Rosalie and a horse carriage. Three servants lived on the second floor of the building, but the gardener didn't live on the property. Behind the carriage house was another garage in which a small truck was parked. In a big cage, next to the garage, was a chimpanzee with two white mice for company. In the stable, there were two black and white cows and several black and white pigs. Josephine called out to Bozo and said in French, "Let's take Hannibal back to the house and have lunch."

"My cook has today off. Let's go to the kitchen and I'll make some sandwiches. Would you like *jambon de Bayonne* or *des rillettes*?

"Both," I replied, as we walked to the kitchen. "Do you have some butter for the ham sandwich?"

I felt so at ease with her, and I never felt comfortable with people. "Of course," she said, "and I even have some apples for the shredded pork spread." I put together my own sandwiches, and she made one for herself along with a salad for both of us. Then she poured two glasses of rich milk. We sat down at one end of the huge, farm-style table and enjoyed our lunch together. Finishing her second glass of milk, she said laughingly, "With all the milk I drink, I should be as white as snow by now."

"Oh, *non!* You are magnificent as you are." I shuddered at the thought of her not having her beautiful black skin. She smiled affectionately. Her smile lit up the room.

"After lunch, I usually take a nap, but sometimes I don't wake till four or five in the morning. If I'm still asleep when you get up, just help yourself to whatever you want to eat. My room is in the right wing on the second floor. There is a lovely tower room in the left wing ready for you. Most of the servants are off on Sunday, so you'll have to fend for yourself." She let the dog out, locked the doors, and I went upstairs to find my room.

*   *   *

It wasn't just a room. It encompassed the entire tower. The Roman-style bathtub looked inviting, but I chose the Louis XIV canopy bed and went right to sleep. A while later, I heard some noise in the grand salon. I quietly went down the stairs to investigate. I peeked through the door of the great room. There, I saw a hysterical scene. The gardener was pulling the python by the tail in the direction of the terrace door.

"Do you need some help?" I asked, amused by the sight. "Yes, that would be wonderful. Agathe always spends the night outside. When she is hungry, I have no problem because I can just hold a chicken in front of her, and she follows me to the terrace. Today, she just wants to sleep because she had her chicken yesterday, so food doesn't interest her in the least."

The two of us grabbed Agathe by the tail and pulled. It took us a good fifteen minutes to get her out. I was wide awake now.

"Would you like some help feeding the animals?" I asked. At first, the man refused but finally relented when I told him how much pleasure it would give me to help. The two of us fed the "family" and all the farm animals. Afterward, I came back inside and went directly to the kitchen. I went in the walk-in refrigerator and saw a side of lamb hanging. I cut myself four thick double-boned chops, helped myself to three potatoes out of which I made French fries, covering them with four fresh whipped egg yolks. I finished my meal with another glass of milk and was well satisfied.

I took some of the leftover fries with me and took a walk down to see the goats and sheep. There, in the barn, I found the gardener at the coal stove cooking corn and bran together for the pigs. After filling their trough, he said good-bye and climbed into his carriage, clucking to the horse to begin his journey home. I returned to the kitchen, took a bottle of milk and a glass, grabbed a kerosene lamp, and returned to my room.

TWELVE

The Code of *Combat*

It was still dark outside when I woke up. That night I had had the luxury of sleeping without clothes on because I felt relatively safe in the château. I got dressed and lit the kerosene lamp to find my way down to the kitchen. There, I found the cook busily at work.

"*Bonjour, monsieur.* Did you have a good night's sleep?" Not waiting for a response, she continued, "And Madame, did she sleep well?"

"I slept well, thank you," I answered, abruptly. "I don't know about Madame." I did not appreciate her audacity or insinuation.

She realized and said, "Oh, excuse me, monsieur." She sounded apologetic and seemed slightly embarrassed. She quickly changed the subject, "What would you like for breakfast, monsieur?"

"What do you have?" I asked, letting go of my indignation. After all, Josephine was a mother figure to me, and anyway, an employee should not be making such insinuations about her employer.

"Oh, there is white sausage and blood sausage. I could fix you an omelette, duck eggs, goose eggs—"

"Stop right there," I exclaimed. "I'll have two goose eggs, soft-boiled, served in the shell, with a lot of bread and butter and a bowl of café au lait."

"Would you like to eat in the dining room or in the kitchen, monsieur?"

"The kitchen is just fine."

Then she had another thought. "Oh, I forgot to tell you that I also have fresh chicken liver, if you would like me to sauté some for you. I always have them on hand for Madame. Most mornings, she has a liver and *champignons de Paris* omelette after her half-grapefruit."

As she was saying this, Josephine entered the kitchen. "*Bonjour, tout le monde!*" she sang out. "And you, *mon petit bonhomme*, did you sleep well?" Before I could answer, the cook said in a sarcastic tone, "He's not so little!" I was fairly tall, broad-shouldered and had a thirty-four-inch waistline. My thighs were quite muscled and almost as large as my waist. I weighed about 225 pounds, mostly muscle.

"You have a big mouth," Josephine said, scolding the cook. "Nobody asked you for your opinion!" She was furious at her insolence. "Serve us in the dining room," she said curtly, and then turned toward me. "*Venez, mon petit,*" she said, beckoning for me to come with her to the dining room.

After we were both seated, the cook brought in our breakfast. We had barely begun eating when Josephine said, "When we've finished, you'll have to tell me what those English have on their minds. If they'll let you stay with me an extra week, the answer is yes before you ask," she said sweetly.

Immediately, I jumped at the opportunity. I began talking to her about my mission. I told her that the English wanted her to help the cause by using her influence with certain big industrialists in Saint Louis and Chicago to convince them to allow Great Britain to purchase fifty-three bomber planes, currently in storage, to use against the Germans.

"There is a civilian crew ready to take delivery at any time, anywhere in the United States," I told her. "They'll have cash in hand to complete the purchase. All U.S. emblems and unnecessary instruments will be removed before leaving the United States so as not to conflict with the U.S. Neutrality Act." I became impassioned when I spoke of my mission; completing it successfully was of the highest priority for the war effort.

Josephine smiled and said, "Consider it done, *mon petit*. I will contact my friends and get you an answer." Still smiling, she continued, "Why did they happen to choose *you* to come see me? Do you think it was destiny?"

"*Ma chère madame*, I also was wondering about that, and I think I know why. My godfather must have talked to Mr. Churchill and told him that you had a soft place in your heart for me, if I'm not being too bold. It may be that I had a better chance than anyone else of convincing you to help us."

"Perhaps that is so. But something bothers me," she said. "I should not get in touch with my friends by telephone or by mail. It's just too risky."

I thought for a moment, then responded, "I think I have the solution. If you're available, we can go together to send a telegram."

"Oh, no! That is just as dangerous, *mon petit!*"

"No, listen to me," I said. "It's very simple. We'll take your car or mine and go to the American Consulate in Lyon. From there, we can send a message in code that can be deciphered upon receipt by the appropriate government agency and then forwarded to your friends. We'll tell them to send their answer back to the U.S. agency and direct the agency to code and forward the reply to Mr. Churchill. In that way none of you will be in danger. You just need to compose the message and make a list of your friends' names, addresses, and phone numbers so that each can be contacted."

As she considered what I said, I boldly asked, "So, shall we take your car or mine?"

As she got up, she responded, "Let's get ready and make that decision after we finish dressing. Come upstairs to the room next to mine, open the armoire, and choose whatever clothing you want. That's my lover's closet and you're just about his size. It looks like his shoes might fit as well," she added. "Take the suitcase on the bottom of the armoire and fill it up. Don't forget socks and underwear," she added, in a motherly way. Besides discussing my mission, we had reminisced for quite a while. It was already ten thirty in the morning. As we climbed the stairs she said, "Let's take a picnic lunch with us and take my car. I've decided that I want to drive. It will relax me. All this intrigue makes me tense."

I was ready first and decided to wait in the library. I knew that her pet python would be in the grand salon, and I wasn't fond of snakes. Within the hour, she came into the library looking for me. She looked extraordinary in her elegant, form-fitting white suit, made of fine silk. She was such a sensual woman. It was evident she was not wearing anything underneath. She also wore long white gloves and a fashionable large-brimmed white hat. Everything looked superb next to her smooth, dark skin.

From her boyfriend's wardrobe, I had selected olive green riding pants, a white long-sleeved shirt, a white wool sweater, and an olive green ascot. I also took a very smart green and black houndstooth riding jacket adorned with solid silver buttons in the shape of boars' heads that I accented with a black silk *pochette* in the breast pocket. Black leather boots completed my attire. We went to the garage, and she chose the 1935 Renault limousine, a Viva Stella, to make the trip.

We arrived in Lyon at five thirty in the afternoon. The city was in the Free Zone. We went to the consulate, but it was already closed. "Let's go to La Mère Brossard for dinner!" she eagerly suggested. This was a restaurant well known throughout Europe. I nodded enthusiastically in agreement. I was always ready to eat in those days—especially to eat well, though I never imagined it would lead to my becoming an executive chef years later in America. "After that, if you like, we could go to the movie theater. It will be too early to go to sleep," she added.

The restaurant was close by, so we were there in no time. Inside we were greeted warmly by Madame Brossard. "Mademoiselle Baker, you've arrived so early. We don't have your table ready yet. Please take a seat at the bar. May I offer you both aperitifs and some escargots as an appetizer?"

At that moment, I realized that Josephine had planned to eat here in advance. "It is always good to see you, madame. May we have two absinthes, please?"

"Certainement, mademoiselle," she said as she went toward the kitchen to place the appetizer order.

We went into the bar and sat down at a small round table. Though it was early, a few other tables were occupied. One table of three men aroused my suspicions. An accordionist was entertaining, playing the songs of Edith Piaf. When the entertainer saw *the* Josephine Baker enter the room, he got up, reverently bowed, and began playing some songs from Josephine's repertoire. Everybody turned, and seeing Josephine, they all stood up and applauded. She was well appreciated in France and throughout Europe.

I leaned over and whispered in her ear, "Go to Madame Brossard and ask her if she knows the three men sitting to our left." She graciously thanked the audience and left to talk to Madame. As she left, two of the three men got up and walked toward the men's room. I thought to myself, *They want to know if she's up to something.* Josephine saw them get up, too. Instead of asking for Madame Brossard in the dining room, she went directly into the kitchen, where she found Madame directing her cooks. Josephine described the three men to her, and Madame knew them well. They were members of the pro-Nazi Militia. Josephine returned to our table and told me what she had found out. The two men returned to their table immediately afterward.

Moments later, Madame Brossard came to our table in the bar. "Your table is ready in the dining room," she said. We followed her to a table next to the window. Famous as her restaurant was, Madame Brossard always maintained a very simple décor.

"Would you like your standing order, mademoiselle?" she asked Josephine. "Of course," she replied in anticipation. Then Madame turned to me and asked what I wanted.

"What do you suggest?" I asked.

"I received fresh frog legs this morning. May I prepare them for you *à la Provençale*?"

"Absolutely," I replied, "but would you ask the cook to deglaze them in absinthe?"

"Of course," she responded, and vanished.

A few minutes later, she reappeared with another couple who had also been sitting in the bar. She seated them at a table that had just become available. There were only about fifteen tables in the entire room, and they were all occupied.

Just then, one of the three militiamen came into the dining room shouting, "This is not right. We were here before both of those couples! Don't you know who we are? We control Lyon!"

Hands on her hips, Madame replied calmly, "It is you who don't know who you are dealing with!" The man abruptly turned on his heel, got his two friends from the bar, walked through the restaurant, opened the door, and slammed it behind them. Madame Brossard, not seeming to pay any special attention to the incident, simply turned around and went back to the kitchen. There was a waiter at the other couple's table already, taking their order.

Another waiter brought the main course to our table. We had finished our escargots earlier in the bar. On my plate were six large frog legs, covered with chunky tomato sauce. The dish was prepared to perfection. I finished my entrée before Josephine finished hers and asked if I could taste one of her quenelles. She cut a piece with her fork and, reaching across the table, placed it in my mouth.

"*C'est delicieux!* I think I'll order some." This was Madame Brossard's specialty, known the world over by anyone who really knew food, *les quenelles de brochet*. The pike, a freshwater fish coming from Lake Geneva, is poached in its own broth and finished in the oven in a béchamel sauce. These dumplings were exquisitely light and really delicious.

"Since you're going to order the quenelles, I'll order the frog legs. I didn't dare ask you to taste one, you were devouring them with such gusto." She motioned to the waiter, placed the order, and asked him to bring us two more absinthes.

"Ask *la mère Brossard* to come to the table when you place the order," she said to the waiter. He returned a few moments later.

"Madame Brossard had to leave for a few minutes," he said. I'll send her to your table as soon as she returns. It won't be too long, I'm sure." He poured an absinthe for each of us, then turned and left the room.

Josephine got up, took her chair and placed it next to mine on the other side of the table, and sat down again. "Now, let's drink to victory, your good health, and your safe return. And," she said, "I want you to promise to invite me to your wedding whenever and wherever that might be!" She took me by the hand as we toasted, each taking a sip from our glasses. This was an extraordinarily touching moment for me. She really knew how to move me emotionally, though one wouldn't have known from my countenance.

Memories of my childhood suddenly filled my head: my mother who was forbidden to have any contact with me, who was brutally beaten by the father I despised, and this woman who had offered me kindness then as she did now. I took a long sip of absinthe to squelch my feelings.

*   *   *

When Madame Brossard returned, she came directly to our table and began making conversation, asking me where I was from and what I did for a living. I was more than well trained for this type of exchange. Amicably, I answered her questions, telling her that I dealt in farm animals, especially cows, and specialized in improving breeds so that they would give more milk. I told her that I was a regional representative for my company, covering the entire south of France.

"Stop, stop," she said, laughing. "I know much more than you think."

By this time, the dining room was completely empty. Only the three of us remained at our little table. "No more secrets, mademoiselle and monsieur." She called out to one of the waiters, saying, "Lock all the doors. We are going to celebrate. The restaurant is closed to the public. Call everyone from the kitchen. Let's join together in saluting Free France!"

Fifteen employees came into the dining room and surrounded our table. Josephine sat there, wide-eyed, holding my hand in hers, not daring to utter a word. Madame Brossard said to the same waiter, "Now, go open the back door. Ask my bodyguards to join us."

When everyone was gathered together, she turned toward us with her whole staff behind her and said, "Let me introduce ourselves. We are a part of the group *Combat*, and I am in charge. There are many members here in Lyon. The group from Brive-la-Gaillarde met you when you arrived from England," she said addressing me. "We were put on alert because we did not know if you would be going to Brive-la-Gaillarde or coming to us. When mademoiselle asked me if I knew who those three men were in the bar, I followed my instincts and went with my men to take care of the three before they had the chance to take care of us. We took them to the docks, killed them, and pushed them into the river.

"Now that everything is out in the open, may I bring dessert for mademoiselle and monsieur?" she asked, gaily. Perhaps, *crèpes Suzette aux poires* for you both?"

"*Certainement!* And I want two portions. You've made me very hungry, madame. And champagne for everyone, especially Madame Brossard!" Josephine shouted.

Immediately, Madame responded, "No, no! The champagne is on me! And the dinner as well! If you wish to pay for a meal, come back tomorrow night, and I'll prepare for you a *grand dîner gastronomique*. And, mademoiselle, take my private number. Call me when monsieur has left. We can be at your disposal to provide protection should the need arise."

Josephine gladly took her number. In those times, one never knew when a certain need might arise. The room was charged with a wonderful electrifying energy. We toasted and drank to *la victoire*.

"I want to reassure you, mademoiselle, that your special relationship with monsieur will be entirely safe with us. We don't want your life to be put in jeopardy. The code of *Combat* keeps the incidence of traitors very low. As you certainly know monsieur, our code is to kill any member of the group suspected of treason along with their entire family. So you know your secret is safe with us."

After the joyous celebration, we excused ourselves and drove to the hotel. It was late. Josephine decided not to go to the movies after all. She was full of questions about the spy business.

"Is it true what Madame Brossard said regarding the code of *Combat*?"

"Yes, it is. Unfortunately, probably fifty percent of the time the member is not guilty, but the chance can't be taken that a traitor lives and endangers the lives of others as well as the cause."

The next day I walked to the American Consulate and sent Josephine's message, instructing the officer in charge that the message was to be directed to the appropriate U.S. agency, and as soon as the response was received, it was to be coded and forwarded to the British prime minister.

When Josephine woke up late that afternoon, I told her that I had to leave in the morning for Gibraltar. She insisted on coming with me, suggesting that at the Spanish border I could pose as her driver, making our border crossing that much easier. This proved to be true. A few days later we passed customs with no problem due to her celebrity throughout Europe. We reached Gibraltar two days later. Since Josephine slept much of the trip, I drove straight through taking very few breaks.

Josephine was immediately recognized when we

entered the sumptuous Hotel Excelsior in Gibraltar. The concierge rushed over to welcome her and before we knew it, we were checked in and settled in our rooms. Both tired from the long trip, we went to sleep early.

First thing in the morning, I went to the military base. "May I see the officer in charge?" I asked the guard. Neither the guard nor the officer spoke French or Italian. I tried to make the officer comprehend that I needed a message coded and sent to England right away. Not understanding, he called the commander, who came out to see who this visitor was. I explained to him, "This message is extraordinarily urgent and needs to be coded and forwarded immediately to Winston Churchill."

The commander had a perplexed look on his face, but he heard "Winston Churchill" and got on the phone while indicating that I should take a seat. Soon, another officer came in who could communicate with me in French. I gave him the message to send to Mr. Churchill's secretary, which was, "Call me at the commander's office at the base in Gibraltar. If I don't hear from you within an hour, I will return to my hotel and call you from the lobby at noon."

No call came for me, so I went back to the hotel. I had the operator place the call for me while I waited next to the phone in the lobby.

The phone rang. "Great news! The U.S. has accepted," the secretary shouted. "In four days, our pilots will pick up the bombers and fly them to Halifax. We'll arrange a flight for you back to England. Mr. Churchill will fill you in on your next mission as soon as you arrive."

I went to Josephine's room to tell her of my imminent departure. Sadness filled the afternoon as we talked away the precious hours. Around five o'clock, there was a knock on her door. It was the concierge. "Monsieur, there is a military driver waiting in front of the hotel for you."

"Thank you. Please tell him I'll be down within half an hour." After a tear-filled good-bye, I pulled myself away to go to my room to pack.

I put all the clothes that I had borrowed in the suitcase and placed it at Josephine's door. The few things that were mine fit into my duffel bag. I left the hotel, jumped into the idling jeep, and was driven to the air base. The pilot was waiting for me in a fighter plane.

THIRTEEN

Escape by Submarine

"And how was our beautiful Josephine?" Mr. Churchill asked, but didn't wait for the answer. "It was a real coup to get those planes, Marc. Great work. Now we're back on good footing. I have a little time, so tell me the details of the mission."

I began my account with the shock of finding Josephine as my contact for the assignment. He smiled faintly as he puffed on his cigar and continued to listen intently. Suddenly he broke in, "Now I have a challenge for you in La Turbie, *mon petit*. Since you know the area well, we want you to come up with a plan to liberate the Royal Air Force pilots being held there in prison."

He was right. I was totally familiar with the area. For four years, from the age of three, I had ridden horses almost every day in the hills around La Turbie with my tutor. The stables were located in nearby Mont Agel, less than an hour from Monte Carlo. After our ride, my tutor and I would often have breakfast at the restaurant, the only one in the village, located on the Grande Place. I remembered the restaurant owner. I also knew the village carpenter, the firemen, and the priest.

"I fear if we wait too much longer, these pilots will be sent to the German forced labor camps set up by Todt Company. There are thirty-six British pilots who have been chosen for immediate return out of the one hundred fifty English military men imprisoned there. That is all we can accommodate at this time. Here is the list. We will have a submarine at your disposition for the trip back to England."

Two nights later I was parachuted into the Paillon Valley not far from my father's property called *le domaine des Croves* in Drap. From there, shortly after daybreak, having buried my parachute, I made my way toward La Turbie on foot using several shortcuts, passing through Laghet, a tiny village of ten homes, only a few kilometers away. Dressed in a business suit and posing as a textile representative from Lille, I had all my false papers in order. When I arrived in La Turbie, I went directly to the restaurant whose owner I remembered so well. I spotted him as soon as I entered, but, of course, he did not recognize a six-foot-tall "little Marc" with a full beard. There were quite a few customers having lunch at the time.

As soon as he was free, I approached him. I gave him a few hints, and he realized who I was. After talking about the old days for a while, I broached other topics.

"Do you know the chief engineer for bridges and roadways?" I asked. "I heard that his son fled to Algeria recently."

"Yes, of course, I do. He eats lunch here every day. They're Jewish, you know. That's why his son left the country. It's certainly not good to be Jewish right now in France. I'll introduce you. He's out on the terrace right now having coffee."

The owner accompanied me out to the terrace to make the introduction and immediately returned inside to attend to his other customers. I'd been informed that this restaurant owner and others he knew in the village could be trusted. That is why I was able to be so open in my conversation. The man at the table stood up to shake my hand and asked me to join him. I sat down and quickly came to the point.

"I know you can be trusted," I said. "I know that your son left the country a couple of months ago to go to Algeria. If you and your wife would like to join him, I can provide the means. I am in La Turbie to liberate thirty-six RAF pilots being held in the fortress. I am sure that the plans for the fortress's interior are accessible to you. I would like your help."

"Of course, I'll help you. And we would like nothing more than to join our son, but I would have helped anyway. I can make you a general sketch here on the ground. I'll draw you an exact map of the interior later."

He took a twig and began. "The tunnel is here. There are two iron grill separations that block the sewers here and here. Let me think. You will need an acetylene torch to remove the doors to open the way for escape. I know six young men who work together in the boiler room who could be of help. They are all sixteen or seventeen years old."

I said to him, "You realize they'll all eventually be sent to forced labor camps for the Todt Company where they'll be building fortifications for the Germans on the coast of France. To avoid that, I'll provide passage for them out of France in exchange for their assistance. Will you ask the boys if they'll agree to help us?"

"Of course, I will."

I continued, "The priest in Laghet can send a message to London that the plan is in the process of being formulated and that we will contact them in a few days when we're ready for the proposed escape. I'll be in touch with you, monsieur." I got up, shook hands, and left.

All six young men jumped at the chance to help with the escape and were thrilled at the opportunity to get out of France. They would also go to Algeria. They knew all too well what their future held as long as France was occupied.

The man brought me the diagrams, and I formulated the plan. The boys agreed to start the next night. They cut through the ground-level iron grate closure. That would allow access to the sewer. While four of them stood guard outside, the other two went in to cut the second iron closure. They rotated their shifts, always two inside doing the work with the acetylene torch while four stayed out to provide cover. Once they finished, they propped the grates up in place so no one would notice that they were cut.

As soon as the job was completed, I went to talk to the priest. "Contact London and tell them we are ready to implement our plan." Within a couple of days, I received the message to execute the escape the following Sunday night.

Early Sunday evening, I dressed like a priest and went to the restaurant. I sat down at a table on the terrace located on the square directly across from the prison where I could keep an eye on the entrance. While waiting and watching, I sipped on my beer, one I especially liked that was produced in Monaco. If I saw anything out of the ordinary, I would blow my nose several times in succession to warn the partisan lookouts.

At about eight in the evening, three Germans sat down at the adjacent table and ordered red wine. Then they started talking to me. I was affable but pulled out the handkerchief from my pocket, just in case. The whole plan might have to be canceled if they did anything at all to provoke suspicion. I was hoping they would just go away and not put the escape plan into jeopardy. They left after about an hour, and I was relieved.

I looked at my watch. Nine o'clock. If all went according to schedule, I'd leave at nine thirty, and the plan would go into action. At nine thirty exactly, I got up and left. I took my bicycle that I had parked in front of the restaurant and nonchalantly pushed it toward the church. Nothing had happened that had indicated any sort of problem. As I walked along, two local farmers passed me on their bicycles.

I went over the plan in my head. These farmers were the two partisans who would be guides for the escaping aviators. They would lead the aviators to the submarine waiting for them at Cap Martin. The six boys who helped with the grills and the chief engineer of bridges and roadways and his wife would be leaving, too, but by other means. We only had room for the thirty-six aviators on the submarine.

I followed the partisans, staying a reasonable distance behind, and then put my bicycle in the bushes near the fortress. About twenty more partisans were hiding there. My part in the mission complete, I left the guides and partisans behind. I walked toward the old, out-of-service funicular that connected La Turbie and Beausoleil and began walking along the tracks toward Beausoleil, which was not far away.

On my way, I heard the sirens go off. I could see in my mind what was going on. Everyone was scattering in all directions, creating as much confusion as possible, and the aviators were being swept away to Cap Martin where the submarine was waiting.

* * *

Once in Beausoleil, I headed toward my friend Pierre's home. Since his garage was on the way, I stopped there first, even though it was late Sunday evening. I went to the back door, knocked, and walked in. There was Pierre, working in the office. This man worked seven days a week. He had had no idea that I was coming. Still dressed as a priest, I quickly identified myself.

"Pierre, c'est moi, Marc."

"I have eyes. What do you need, my friend?"

"Start up a car. I need to leave right away."

Because he already knew the work I was doing, he moved quickly and didn't ask any questions. He started up a 1935 green Packard limousine, and within minutes we were on the road toward Paris. This would be about an eleven-hour trip. Pierre had all the necessary exit visas because he provided chauffeured limousines for the Germans. I expected no problems. It was invaluable to have a friend like Pierre in my life, especially in my line of work.

Once we arrived in Paris, I asked, "Would you take me to Maxim's? I'm to meet a contact at the restaurant to arrange another mission." When we arrived, I said, "Thank you, dear friend, and have a safe journey home."

"Think nothing of it," he said with a smile.

Intimate knowledge of the area of operation around La Turbie had been indispensable once again. Later, I learned that fourteen of the pilots were shot while fleeing, and other prisoners were killed or recaptured during the escape attempt. Not many got away. The engineer, his wife, and the six boys were waiting at Cap Martin for further instructions. Because of the heavy losses, the submarine offered passage to them all. The six boys gratefully accepted this rare opportunity, as did the engineer and his wife, and they all departed for England.

I met with my contact at Maxim's. "The plans have been changed," he said. "You need to return to England for some special training for your next mission in Martinique."

"What is going on in Martinique?"

"I don't know, but they want you back in England as soon as possible."

"I just let my transportation go. Can you help get me to Portugal?"

"I'll see what I can do. Come with me to a safe house where you can stay the night."

FOURTEEN

Martinique

"I have an extremely important assignment for you, *mon petit*," Mr. Churchill explained to me solemnly. "You and fifteen other men will go by submarine to Martinique. North of the capital, Fort-de-France, at Saint-Pierre, the Gestapo has files stored on all persons suspected of being spies or double agents. These are originals and, we hope, are the only copies. They are being stored on the second floor of the fortress. You'll depart from a base in the north of Scotland. The voyage will take several weeks. You will travel submerged during daylight hours, surfacing only at night. You'll coordinate with the locals who will help by drugging the guards at the fortress. You'll destroy the documents by blowing up the building, and then you'll return by submarine to England."

Churchill had assembled a commando group that included three Canadians and about a dozen Poles and Slavs, all of whom spoke French since Martinique was a French-speaking island. The next day, after an early morning flight to Glasgow, we were driven to northern Scotland, arriving after nightfall. A rubber boat was sent from the vessel to pick us up. Our task force was lodged in the torpedo room at the nose of the submarine.

I'm going to vomit, I thought, as I entered the space we would be living in while at sea. The smell, I'll never forget—it was like putrefying rats. We were "housed" next to the batteries. The twin stenches of acid and gas combined diabolically. The entire English submarine was worn out and very dirty. *This sub should be refurbished or retired,* I thought, reviled by the smell and the filth. *And how will I tolerate being cooped up like this?* I asked myself, not sharing my initial anxiety with anyone.

I had an extremely negative physical reaction to the environment, bordering on phobia. Not only did the enclosed quarters bother me, but the odors made me feel continuously sick. I urged myself to focus on something else but found the circumstances unbearable. I directed myself silently to somehow put up with it. Looking around, I noticed that most of the men just seemed to accept this dreadful situation. Of course, I was comparing their external appearance to my inner reactions. Still, I told myself, "If they can take it, Marc, so can you."

I had a continual internal dialogue, hour by hour, day by day. Today, seven decades later, as I reflect, I really don't know how I did it. My reaction was so intense that it seems impossible to have put up with it. I certainly could not do it today, but I was young and resilient back then, and I drew encouragement from the others. I felt so much admiration for those who just accepted the confinement.

The voyage began on the surface of the North Sea. The commander was Australian. He was abrupt, inconsiderate, and pretentious. After he put us in the torpedo room, he commanded, "You'll stay here unless otherwise ordered." Occasionally, during the change of shift, he allowed us to go on the bridge, four at a time. Otherwise, we were not allowed to leave the torpedo room until we arrived in Martinique.

In the room were eight torpedoes, two of them loaded and ready to go. The space was very limited. I slept in a scrunched fetal position because there wasn't enough legroom to stretch out. I considered myself fortunate, though, because some of the men could not even lie down. My spot was across from the sink, next to the locked, watertight door that connected the torpedo room to the rest of the ship.

As you can imagine, the voyage was long and agonizing. The room was dimly lit. The minutes crawled by. Dealing with the claustrophobia was challenging. "We'll be there soon," the Canadians kept assuring me. I guess I didn't hide my malady very well. They kindly tried to distract me by talking about their lives back home.

I vaguely remember what we ate. We always had hard crackers available. Mealtime, we were brought a choice of hot porridge or diced, boiled potatoes mixed with salted herring. I had never tasted anything like this mixture before, and it was hard to get accustomed to. But I ate what I could when I didn't feel too nauseous. There was something else they served, but for the life of me, I can't tell you what it was. It was a grayish liquid with lumps of something in it and had no seasoning. I thought to myself that it must be leftover dishwater with floating garbage added in chunks. That, I couldn't eat. We were given mess tins and forks and spoons to eat with. They were gathered and cleaned after each meal.

There were a few buckets for elimination purposes placed next to the sink where we could wash our hands and faces. No one washed anything else, so you can imagine how the stench intensified day by day in those closed quarters. Each morning, one of the sailors came to pick up the buckets and replace them with empty ones. That was our life day after endless day.

After many long weeks, traveling only at night, we slipped into the bay of Fort-de-France and took two rubber boats to the island. Under the cover of darkness, we rowed ashore. Once on land, I became terribly seasick.

"I've lost my sense of balance," I told my French Canadian companions in between bouts of vomiting. "I feel like the ground is moving under me like on a boat," I explained. These feelings lasted several hours before I was able to feel in control of my body again.

Martinique, a department of France, was officially under control of the collaborationist Vichy government from 1940 to 1943. We were met by the Martiniquais partisans who were anti-Vichy. They lodged us in their huts, dressed us in their colorful clothing, and gave us leather sandals to wear. They let us use their showers (probably in self-defense) and fed us well. We were treated like kings. What a contrast from life on the submarine!

The people of Martinique are a physically beautiful people, elegant and graceful. They reminded me of the people of Cameroon, with lighter complexions. They were sincere and loving—simply precious human beings. It took a while to get my appetite back again on the island, but it returned. "This is for you from the British," I said as I handed the leader a fabric sack filled with money that Churchill had given me. "This will cover any expenses and then some," I assured him. "Our sole purpose is to destroy all the documents being stored here. Your suggestions are welcome as we develop a strategy."

The partisan replied, "I'll take you tonight to have a look at the fortress where all the dossiers are being kept." That evening, he showed us the target area from a safe distance. "As you can see, the German contingent guarding the building is minimal," the leader pointed out. "They really expect nothing to happen here."

We went back to the village and began talking. "I've formulated a plan," he said. "Tell me what you think. Since the island's occupation, life has been joyless and grim. We are generally a happy people. Everyone would welcome a celebration just for the sake of having a good time and forgetting about the war. We'll have the locals put on a festival and invite everyone on the island, including the French Militia and the Gestapo. The party will last for three days around the clock. As the days pass, the enemy will let down their guard. The first day, we'll focus on food, music, and dance. The next, we'll offer alcohol in abundance. We'll have our women entertain the Gestapo and Militia and help them drink to their heart's delight. The final day, we'll place sleeping potion in the drinks and bottles of wine. Only our partisans will know, and they will avoid or feign drinking. Once everyone is asleep, you'll easily be able to do what you need to inside the fortress."

My commando comrades and I discussed the strategy. One of the Canadians summed it up. "The soldiers are stuck on this island with little to do except guard the building. The party will be a welcome distraction for everyone. The three days will give them time to strengthen their trust in the locals. When they determine nothing negative is happening, they'll begin to drop their defenses. It sounds like a great plan to me."

We all agreed and made our plans for entering the

building through the air vents on the roof. That would provide easy access. When we located the files, we would liberally place the bombs, more than enough to blow them all sky high.

The party started well and went on as scheduled, growing in intensity each day. The Martiniquais knew how to have a good time and bring joy to all. By the third night, all the guards and those not involved in the mission were sound asleep.

Our group went into the fortress and planted the bombs, all on timed detonators. When the explosives went off, the entire fortress went up in flames. No one was hurt because none of the guards were close to the building. We didn't want them to blame the civilians, so we left a note accompanied by a small English flag saying, "The British have blown up all your documents and records for the good of the world. The day will come when you will understand why we needed to do this."

By the time the bombs went off, we had already rowed back to the submarine, but we saw the blaze in the distance. I climbed aboard with the others. Once on the bridge, you could say I became totally irrational. "I can't go in," I insisted, "I just can't. There has to be another way."

My Canadian comrades helped change my mind. I was strong, and I fought hard. Finally, they took me by the seat of my pants and pushed me down the stairs headfirst where the others were ready to pull me in.

Returning to the sub was a mental and physical ordeal for me. So, too, was the cramped, smelly, and unsanitary trip back across the Atlantic, most of it spent submerged except for brief respites on the surface each night. That's when we usually got to gulp a little clean night air and stretch our bodies out. When we reached the submarine base in northern Scotland, I almost fell to the ground and kissed it, so relieved was I to be out of that hellhole.

Back at Churchill's estate, I entered his office. He wore his glasses halfway down his nose. He reminded me of a witch, so I had an internal laugh at his expense. I felt sure that he had been debriefed thoroughly on the Martinique mission and might well taunt me about my aversion to underwater travel.

"Ah, there you are," he said as I came in. "I want to share with you the results of your mission. As far as we know, those were original files you destroyed, and according to our intelligence, there are no duplicates. Congratulations on a mission well done, Marc. I would have joined you on your little vacation," he added with a twinkle in his eye, "but I wouldn't have had my cigars and cognac to enjoy, cooped up on the sub as you were. I decided it was a better choice for me to stay here in England."

He chuckled. "Rest up for a few days, and then I'll tell you about your next mission in France. You'll be parachuting outside Lyon. In the meantime, enjoy the cuisine, the horses, and the abundance of air. You deserve some time off, *mon petit*."

I was right. He had heard about my difficulty aboard the submarine. It was his jocularity that gave him away. This mission is forever emblazoned in my memory. I have never overcome my aversion for submarines—especially old, smelly English ones.

FIFTEEN

Riding the Rails

I am totally clear and focused on one thing: Jump. My preparations are complete. All is in perfect order. Now, assume a comfortable but braced position next to the door. I see the pilot's hand signal. I jump into the blackness. I'm freefalling. I start counting: one, two, three . . . until I reach twelve. It seems like forever. I pull the cord. The sudden jolt shudders through my body. The parachute has opened, and I'm floating. I know I have no control, so I let myself be guided by the air currents. I can do nothing else.

Suddenly I hit the ground, hard. I focus on my right shoulder as I let my body go absolutely limp. I roll and roll, finally coming to a stop. I'm surrounded by men, the partisans of Combat. I've arrived safely, outside Lyon.

* * *

As the partisans helped me out of my parachute, the leader said, "All plans have changed. Churchill says it's vital you get to Vienna as soon as you can."

As we walked toward a vehicle, still a little taken aback by the last-minute change, I told the partisan, "I don't have any identity papers. I can't travel to Vienna without papers. Can you get me forgeries?"

"We don't have the resources right now, monsieur. I don't know how we can help you." He seemed troubled that he couldn't get me out of this predicament. They took me to a safe house where they fed me and put me up for the night. As I lay in bed, I concentrated on finding a solution. Eventually, I came up with a plan, perhaps a little far-fetched, but it was all I could come up with. I would go to Vienna by train.

While in France and Switzerland, it might be possible to ride in the brake room in the last car. Once in Nazi-occupied Austria, however, I would travel on the underside frame between the wheels. To accomplish this, I would have to squeeze my almost six-foot-tall, muscled body between the bottom of the boxcar and the top of the axle and crossbars. There would be barely enough space, but I really thought I could do it. My back would go along the top of the axle, and my arms and legs would fit along the crossbars. I would have to be careful to always wear gloves so that my hands would not freeze to the iron. I understood that I would be totally exposed to the cold weather conditions, but I really believed it would work. In France, I would have a lot of support because railroad employees were usually anti-Nazi. I knew they would help me along the way.

The next day, my contact in Lyon put me in touch with the stationmaster who came to meet me at the safe house. I told him my plan and added I would need the schedules of freight trains going toward Vienna.

His face clouded over, and then, after a pause, he warned, "I agree, it is possible, but beyond France and Switzerland, you'll have no more railroad contacts to help you. And from the Swiss border you'll have about seven hundred kilometers to reach Vienna. That will be extremely difficult as, I'm sure you realize, you'll have to jump off the train before every bridge and before every station. You'll be climbing up and down mountains, crossing streams or rivers, and finding your way around towns infested with Germans. Then, you'll have to find a place where the train is going slow enough to get on again. It's very risky. I'm sure you'll have enormous challenges, but you certainly look fit enough to get the job done. I'll bring you the schedules, and I wish you good luck."

One stop before the main station in Lyon, I got on a freight train and climbed up to the brake room tower at the rear. It was in the open air, and I got filthy, but at least I did not have to squeeze myself underneath the train yet. The brakeman only came to the caboose when the terrain was descending. While he was there, I stayed out of his way so he could do his work. Since we were traveling in the Free Zone, I didn't have to get off at all in France.

Just before crossing into Switzerland, I jumped off. Across the rugged terrain, I found my way to Chancy where I had an excellent contact at the hotel/brasserie. The Swiss helped us a lot; they also helped the Germans a lot. This particular couple, the owners of a small hotel, could be trusted. Mr. Churchill paid them well.

It was after dark when I arrived at the brasserie. I entered through the storage room where deliveries were received. Madame was in the kitchen. She greeted me and went to get her husband. They knew me well because I had passed this way many times before on the way to Lausanne, where I often hid in an excellent hotel school. I could sleep there any time, have my meals, and even take hotel courses if I wanted. I took many fine courses there, which greatly helped my career opportunities after the war.

The owners brought me up to a guest room. The wife stayed to help clean me up with cleanser. The grime was black and extremely thick, especially on my face, neck, ears, and scalp. After her scrubbing, my forehead felt like it was on fire, but at least I was white again. Mercifully, I was able to shower after she finished. They laid out clothes for me on the bed while I was washing up. It felt wonderful to be totally clean and to put on fresh clothes. The husband brought me dinner in my room.

"Monsieur, I need to stay one night only," I told him. "In the morning, I need you to take me to Geneva and introduce me to the train stationmaster, if that's possible."

"Of course, I can do that," he said. "Until tomorrow morning. Good night."

That night, I slept like a baby. I felt safe at their hotel. I got up early to wash and dress. The wife brought me a baguette, butter, and café au lait to the room. Then, her husband came to get me, and we left right away.

At the train station, we met with the *chef de gare*. I told him my plan. "I'll arrange for you to pose as a government employee working in the Swiss postal car that is attached to the *train bleu*," he proposed. "I'll have a complete postal uniform brought to my office right away. What are your sizes?" I gave him larger sizes so that I could put the uniform on over my own clothes. When it arrived, I slipped into it at the back of his office. Then, he handed me a small bag of food for the short trip across Switzerland.

"Thank you, monsieur. That is very kind of you," I said as I took the package.

It proved to be a delightful, problem-free trip. I got off the Swiss train just before the Austrian border and hid the uniform under some rocks. I successfully avoided the border guards by climbing the mountainous terrain far away from the official border crossing. Then I had to find the rail tracks again and a station. In Austria, the real challenges of the journey would begin.

That night I waited close to the tracks just beyond the station. "Here's the train approaching. It's moving slowly enough to get on now," I said to myself. "I'll lie down on my stomach next to the track and let a few cars pass before making my move. I don't want to place myself too close to the front nor too close to the back because that's where the cars are more likely to be checked by the Nazis. The timing has to be right so I can roll over on my back onto the tracks after the wheels go by." I got ready to make my move. Before leaving France, I had bought high-quality gloves so that my hands wouldn't freeze to the rods.

At the propitious moment, I rolled onto the track. "Now, Marc, count the cars as they run over you. Study their understructures as they pass: one, two, three, four, five, six, seven, eight—now!" I told myself. I grabbed onto the rods with my hands, arms, legs, and feet and pulled myself up and then, while the train was still moving slowly, I wedged myself in between the bottom of the boxcar and the rods of the frame. It was harder than I imagined it would be. "Thank you, dear Jesuits, for the great shape I'm in," I said as I squeezed myself between frame and car. Because of my intense physical training with them for seven years, my muscled upper arms were the size of most men's thighs, and my thighs were enormous. I was exceptionally strong.

I scooted my body down to where the rods came to a V and joined the axle. That V supported my lower back; however, there were other challenges to contend with. Every time the train went over a point where two rails were joined, there was a sound like "ba-da-du, ba-da-du," and the train shook. "Your body can't take that, Marc. Pull it up, pull it up," I demanded, encouraging myself. With my hands and arms, I pulled my torso up at each seam to avoid the painful jarring of my back. Although my legs and torso had pretty good support, I did not dare relax the muscles of my upper body. I had to keep tensed up so as not to fall. The train shook a lot, and I could feel every bump acutely.

Before each station, I had to get off because at those scheduled stops the trains were searched by German patrols, as I've already mentioned. As soon as I heard the brakes, I turned my body over, still holding on with my feet, legs, and hands about sixty centimeters above the track. Then, all at once, I would let go and let the train pass over me. Next, I would quickly run for cover and wait for nightfall to find my way around the village or town to the other side of the station.

Before every bridge, the train would also brake. That was my signal to drop to the tracks. I would get off, hide, and wait for dark if it wasn't night already. Then I would climb down the mountain, into the deep valleys, often cross a river or a stream, and climb up the other side. I was usually bruised and often bloody from the time I spent hanging from, and dropping off, the underbelly of the train. It was extremely helpful that I loved to climb. The mountains of Austria are tall and difficult to scale. After each arduous detour, I would catch the next train on the same track and continue my journey, not knowing the exact destination of that particular train. The trip from Lyon to Vienna took me between six and eight weeks.

During that time, I had to find food and water. The only way I could do this was to steal from farms along the way. I had to risk my life by taking rabbits, chickens, eggs, water, whatever I could get my hands on, while on foot. During the daytime, I would find safe places to sleep and recover my strength. Sometimes I would even make a little fire to cook a rabbit or a chicken. At night, I would look for more food and water.

It's hard to explain just how much tenacity this journey required. What got me through was total dedication to my goal. For strength I would repeat to myself, "We will rid the world of Nazi tyranny. My beautiful France will be free again."

I must say that this was, without doubt, the most difficult task I had to accomplish during the war. It was extremely wearing, physically and mentally. Many times, I found myself on a train heading in the wrong direction. You can imagine how distressing this was since I knew it was vital that I get to Vienna. In retrospect, it was miraculous that I was able to arrive alive and in one piece.

Just before the Vienna station, I dropped onto the track and ran to hide for the last time. I knew the place I needed to find, just not how to get there. At all costs, I had to avoid any confrontation with the authorities.

It was extraordinarily dangerous for me to be traveling with no papers, especially in a large city governed by Nazis. If stopped, I would certainly be put in prison.

I was totally exhausted. It was early morning, and the temperature was below freezing. "Come on, body, cooperate. You must move," I tried to persuade myself to go forward, as I got on my feet. "You can move. Don't pay attention to the cold or the pain," I commanded.

All my muscles, my back, my arms and legs—everything ached. I needed to find my way to the Château de Schönbrunn, as my contact was the castle's guard. There was no choice. I had to risk asking directions from one of the railroad employees. I saw an older man, about sixty years old, walking away from the station along the tracks. Many Austrians, especially the older generation, were not Nazis. So I addressed him in German and asked him the location of the château. As usual, luck was in my favor. "It's in the same direction as my home, where I'm headed right now. Walk along with me, if you like," he offered.

I don't know what he thought of this dirty, ragged traveler, but he said nothing about my appearance. In fact, he talked very little as we took the road toward his house. We saw no pedestrians on the way and only a few cars and trucks. I was so dirty that I must have looked like a coal miner just coming off shift. My clothing was probably even dirtier than I was, full of soot and smoke from the coal burned by the train for fuel.

I was concerned that sunrise would soon come.

"Perhaps you'll join me for coffee at the house," the man suggested. "Well, it's not really coffee," he added. "We can't get any. We make a warm drink from grilled grain. I'm sure you're familiar with it. And right now, we have no milk to add because of food rationing."

We continued walking. Then, in the distance, I spotted the silhouette of the château. It was immense. It resembled the Château de Versailles but on a smaller scale.

"Thank you, monsieur, for your kind offer, but I must continue on," I told him, and gave a slight wave of my hand. I was anxious to get there before the sun came up and wanted to avoid any unexpected encounter. I needed to be hidden from any prying eyes. I had no desire to be prey for the Nazis.

Once I reached the château, I tried to open the shutters of a window and found them unlocked. I pushed the window, and to my surprise, it opened but not easily. I pressed on it and realized that the heavy drapes inside were preventing it from fully opening. I steadily applied pressure until the window opened wide enough for me to climb in. Then, I quietly closed and locked the window.

I peeked through the draperies and my eyes grew wide with amazement. I was in a sumptuously decorated, enormous ballroom. I silently crossed the room toward a door that I soundlessly cracked open. I felt like a burglar. There was a grand hallway with numerous doors. Closing the ballroom door behind me, I moved cautiously down the hall and tried one of the doors. It opened, revealing a magnificent bedroom suite, complete with a grand canopy bed. "Ah, this is perfect," I said to myself. It was time for me to rest although the room felt like an icebox. I crawled underneath the bed and instantly fell asleep.

SIXTEEN

The Barber of Vienna

Suddenly, I awoke. I listened as heavy footsteps coming down the hall grew louder. Then the door opened. A man entered who was dressed as a guard. He was whistling softly to himself the tune that the partisans would often sing. *This must be my contact,* I thought. Trusting my instinct, I began whistling the same tune as I came out from under the bed. As I crawled out, I saw a huge smile illuminating the guard's face.

"I've been waiting and watching for you for weeks. What took you so long?" I must have looked awful because before I could respond he said, "Come, come and wash up. I can't even see your face. There's no one else in the château. I'll find you something clean to put on. Tomorrow or the day after, I'll accompany you to your rendezvous. I have a motorcycle. But for now, follow me. I'll tell you more about your new contact later."

He brought me to a utility room filled with brooms, mops, and the like. And there it was—a sink with running water! This was going to be delightful.

"There are clean towels in the cabinet," he said. "I'll go get you some overalls and something to eat."

"If it's possible, could you find me some handkerchiefs? My nose is full of soot. And I could also use a comb and some sort of medicated cream for my lips. They're terribly dry and cracked. I appreciate all your help."

The air was so cold, though certainly not as cold as it had been under the trains. It was just that now I had time to reflect, and, stiff, cold, and sore from the contortions I had to endure while clinging for hours and days to the cold iron of railroad car undercarriages, I had to exhort myself not to complain. I changed my focus to being grateful that I had made it to the safety of the château, and for the comforts it offered. First and foremost among these comforts was running water. Although it wasn't heated, it was warm in comparison to the air temperature and therefore felt wonderful.

All of a sudden, I again heard steps coming down the hallway, but this time they were different. I immediately hid behind the door. Whoever it was, I would take care of him. The person passed the utility room and continued on. The guard had said that nobody was at the château except him. Who, then, was this other person? I stood there in my briefs. I wasn't going to put on those awful, dirty clothes again. Since there were some closets in the room, I started opening them. In one, I found a raincoat. That was better than nothing, so I slipped it on.

Fifteen or twenty minutes later, I heard more footsteps coming up the hall, lighter, less-hurried steps this time. Again I jumped behind the door and waited. When the door opened, a little voice said, "Monsieur? Monsieur?" I stepped out from behind the door and saw this little woman carrying a tray. On it was a terrine of soup and dark bread. She said, "My husband will be here soon with some clothes for you. Sit down now, and try this white bean soup. Don't pay any attention to me, just go ahead and eat. You need to." The soup warmed my insides. Another half hour passed while I ate. Then the guard returned with some clothes for me.

"Thank you both for your kindness," I told them appreciatively.

As it was Sunday, the couple left to go to mass. While they were gone, I waited in the utility room. After church, the guard came back to check on me and to supply me with food for lunch and dinner. After eating, I decided to wrap myself in a rug and lie down on a couch. I slept all day long. That evening the guard took me to another building near the stable.

"Tomorrow is Monday," he said. "Nobody will be coming to this building, but just in case, I'm going to lock you in so that no one can open the door. There's nothing to fear. I have already locked the château, and I am the only one who has the keys. Sleep well," he said, and bid me good night.

I went to bed in my new "home," which was infinitely better for me than the château. Here, there was a bed, blankets, pillows, plenty of towels, and a bathroom with a bathtub and handheld shower spray. "Why didn't he bring me here earlier?" I asked myself. I was still extremely tired and sore, so much so that I wasn't even tempted to take a bath. I fell right to sleep and slept through the night.

It was morning when I heard the key in the lock. The guard set my breakfast down on the table and left. I ate right away and then took a sponge bath. It did me a world of good. I got dressed in my new clothes and went back to bed.

The guard came again that afternoon to bring me more food for the day. "I'll be back before daybreak," he said, "and I'll take you into the city. Your contact is a barber who owns an exclusive salon where the high-ranking German officers go for their haircuts and shaves."

Early the next morning, we climbed on his motorcycle to go to the city. He dropped me on the corner where the opera house was located. What a magnificent building! "There is the salon," he said, as he pointed. "When you think it's relatively safe, go to the back door. It will be unlocked."

People were not yet out on the streets. I needed to find a vantage point with a good view of the barbershop. Then I needed to make my way to the back entrance without attracting attention. I thought, *My only possible cover is to be a beggar.* I dragged my leg as if I couldn't use it and kept my head down low. I found a good place to watch from, the building across from the opera house. The barbershop was on the far side of the building. Large command cars were beginning to arrive, bringing German officers, one or two at a time, to the salon.

Stealthily, I made my way down the street and to the back door of the salon. I partially opened it to peek in. I was sure the barber had been expecting me for a long time. I entered the back room and peeked through the door. I saw that each chair in the salon had blue curtains to pull around for the privacy of the customer. Perfect. Then the barber spotted me and gave a slight nod in recognition of my presence.

At an opportune moment, he looked at me and pointed to a chair. I moved quickly. He immediately closed the curtains around me, draped me with a long cloth, and put a warm towel over my face. He whispered, "Don't move from this chair. I'll get back to you as soon as I can. I need to finish with my clients. You'll need to stay in the chair till my lunch break. We'll talk then." He was careful to hide my appearance even from under the curtains. He rolled my pants up to my knees, took off my shoes and socks, put them away, and put my feet into a basin of water.

When he left, I whispered to myself, "I'm sure he doesn't have another client who looks like I do!" A while later, he changed my damp facial towel for a fresh, warm one.

"Sleep if you like," he said. "You'll be fine here. I

know you must be hungry, but I'll be busy till lunch. I'll come see you whenever I can."

The warmth from the towel felt soothing on my face. My feet were blissfully soaking in warm water. I fell asleep, waking up now and again throughout the morning.

After escorting his last client out before closing for lunch, he came over to my chair. "Now I have time to trim your beard and cut your hair. You are a mess, young man," he said. He had a reassuring touch and an air of self-confidence. As soon as he finished, a client knocked at the door even though it was locked for the noon break.

He glanced out the window. "Ah, it's a regular customer. I have to let him in. That will take care of my lunch," he said as he covered up my face again and drew the curtains. I soon fell back to sleep.

After the final client of the day left, the barber woke me up and took me to the back room where I could wash up and change clothes. "I have new clothes for you so you won't draw any attention to yourself," he told me. The barber was in his sixties, Jewish, small of stature with a beautiful head of white hair. He looked like an angel to me. He was gentle and extremely kind. He seemed to be as totally dedicated to the cause as I myself was.

I cleaned up and put on the clothes while the barber tidied and locked the shop. Someone must have let him know my size in advance because the clothes fit me well. The "angel" gave me some bratwurst and sauerkraut. He had most certainly saved his lunch for me. "Now we'll go by alleyway and side streets to the place where I'll hide you," he said.

The package I was to pick up would originate in Poland and be conveyed via Polish messenger. What I was to receive was so highly confidential that they only trusted the messenger to pass it directly to the barber, who was also of Polish descent. Once the barber received this package, he would in turn have to personally hand it to me.

About forty-five minutes later, we arrived at our destination, a bombed-out building. Much of the outer structure was destroyed, but the staircase was still intact. I followed him as we stepped over the debris and climbed the stairs to the fifth floor. "This is where you'll be staying until the messenger arrives with the package. I had to wait for your arrival before contacting him."

As we entered, he said, "Welcome to my property, such as it is. A mattress and blankets are inside the bathtub. At least, we know you'll be safe here. The whole neighborhood has been bombed. Only the remnants of buildings remain. Do not leave under any circumstances. I'll bring you food and anything you need. Rest well. We'll talk tomorrow."

The tub was too confining for me, so as soon as he left I put the mattress into the kitchen, the only other place that wasn't demolished. As I looked around, it appeared that others had stayed here before. This is where I was to wait for the messenger from Poland.

I stayed longer than I expected. The barber brought me fresh water, eggs, sausage, cheese, olives, bread, butter, chocolate bars, and pastries. At this time in Austria, the rationing system allowed each person very limited amounts of food, but the barber was in a very privileged position, dealing with influential German officers, and was generously rewarded. When he brought the food supplies, he would stay with me to talk and keep me company. He would eat quite a few of my olives—he adored olives—before leaving with my waste in a bucket.

While I waited in the bombed-out building, I made myself useful. The barber had shown me what to do. There were about thirty carrier pigeons on the roof. I took care of removing messages from arriving pigeons and of attaching outgoing messages to the departing pigeons' legs. They were being sent to a short-wave radio station located a few kilometers away. The information collected at the station was forwarded to England.

It took the messenger three more weeks to arrive from Poland. One night, the barber arrived, puffing hard after climbing the steep stairs. "Here is the package," he said proudly. "It is extraordinary!" he said, as he told me about it. "My compatriots"—he still considered himself Polish—"found this machine that the Germans left behind when the Russians invaded. Somehow, the Poles got it from the Russians. Nothing was done with the machine because the Russians didn't know what they had. The Polish officer who found it turned it over immediately to the Polish underground, who contacted London right away. They described their find and emphasized its importance. This machine, called Enigma, can decode messages from German headquarters."

The barber handed me the package that was about

the size of a typewriter. "Be ready for departure before dawn," he said. He handed me a brown and beige angora scarf. "My wife knitted this for you. Wear it in good health," he said with a smile.

I slept well that night, the scarf around my neck. I was happy to be leaving my three-sided residence.

Early the next morning, while it was still dark, an ambulance came to pick me up. The partisans had arranged everything. I was a very sick patient who had to go see a specialist in Geneva. All the papers were excellent forgeries, and they expected to have an uneventful trip. Once in Geneva, I was sent first class on a commercial flight to London via Morocco. At the airport, I was picked up by the military police and brought to the prime minister's country residence. Mr. Churchill was in the midst of a small dinner party when I arrived. The valet escorted me to my room. Soon afterward, Mr. Churchill came to welcome me back with a heartfelt hug to remember. Then he said, "Well done, *mon petit*."

Acquiring the Enigma machine was a great victory for the Allies. From that time forward, they would know much of what the Germans were planning. This information would determine where they would send their troops and where they would concentrate their greatest efforts. German messages could now be quickly decoded.

Years later, in the summer of 1958, I, now a citizen of the United States, was able to locate the barber. I invited him and his wife to stay with me at my horse property in Harrisonville, south of Kansas City, Missouri. To my great joy, they accepted. I sent them round-trip tickets along with my address and directions, though I had no intention of having them take a taxi the almost forty miles to my house from the airport. I just wanted to set them up for a surprise. I owned, among other classic cars, a 1937 Rolls-Royce limousine. I hired a chauffeur to drive and a valet to open the doors and dressed them elegantly in riding breeches, jackets, tall boots, and white gloves. I wanted to do something out of the ordinary for this couple. When I spotted them coming out of the terminal, I told the valet to go greet them and tell them that the limousine was there to pick them up.

"There must be some mistake," the barber responded.

"No, sir, there is no mistake. Monsieur Marc sent me and the chauffeur to pick you up."

When he heard my name mentioned, he realized that it must be true. I had fun watching the entire scenario. As they made their way toward the car, I got out to welcome them. The barber took off his glasses, and his eyes filled with tears. I was thrilled to see him, but at this stage of my life I still had my feelings well under control. I wasn't aware of the emotion hidden deep within me.

The gentle man took me in his arms. He was just over five feet tall. He introduced me to his wife, whom I belatedly thanked for the scarf she had knitted for me, and we all got into the Rolls. I could see that they were amazed by their reception. When we arrived at my fifty-nine-acre property, I was tickled by the look of astonishment in their eyes. I was excited about giving them a memorable experience and took them to all the best restaurants in Kansas City. At that time, I was treated especially well because I was a prominent executive chef and business owner in the community.

I took the two of them sightseeing to some of my favorite places. The barber loved to ride horses, and I gave him my favorite saddlebred to ride every day. I enjoyed watching this wisp of a man riding next to me on the tall, elegant high-stepping horse.

I really respect and admire this man, even if he did eat a lot of my olives, I thought, chuckling to myself. "He had so much courage working for the Resistance out of his little German-infested barbershop in Vienna."

A few years later, during the Christmas holidays, I received a card from the barber's wife saying that her husband had passed away and that he had never forgotten his extraordinary trip to the United States.

As I pondered the painful news, I remembered the sudden change of plans announced to me after I parachuted into that field near Lyon and the struggle I had endured to get to this fine man's shop.

SEVENTEEN

Saving Thousands of Jewish Children

"I am horrified, Marc!" Mr. Churchill paced as he spoke. "The situation is beyond belief. The French Militia is treating its own people worse than the Nazis are." He was as furious as an angry mother bear protecting her young. "We must find a way to save as many Jewish children as we can. It's just too painful to talk about. My secretary will fill you in on the deplorable situation. I'm sending you to Die to talk to the commander, whom you already know, to see if the youth camps can take some of the children. This is assuming that you can find a way to get them out of Paris. See what you can do. May God be with you." He stomped out of the office. He was too upset to waste time on pleasantries.

I went into the secretary's office. She was a little

woman, on the plump side, an older, motherly type, very kind and extremely bright. She always hugged me. This time she said, "You are the only ray of sunshine in England."

"That's easy. There isn't any sunshine in England," I retorted. She laughed. I knew she liked me a lot because I always made her laugh. That was something Mr. Churchill had always done for me, from my earliest memories of him.

When I was a child, my tutor would take me for a few days at a time to visit my godfather, Monsieur Duvernay, who lived only a few houses from where Mr. Churchill vacationed in Cap d'Antibes. This is how I originally came to know Mr. Churchill. I was a very shy child and had very little access to playmates in Monaco. So, when staying in Cap d'Antibes away from the eyes of my father, my tutor found families with children in the neighborhood and got them together with me so that I had someone my own age to play with. At home in Monte Carlo, my father would not allow me to play with other children.

Regularly, I would see Mr. Churchill sitting in front of his easel, painting in his garden. He would call us kids over to him. "Wait right here," he would say. Then he would call a servant to bring us some Petits Beurres LU, cookies that we all loved. Often, I would see him drive off with his chauffeur, cigar protruding from his lips, his car filled with canvases in search of new landscapes to paint. I thought that he always looked so serious unless he was talking to us. When he did, his whole demeanor changed.

One time when I was with him at the estate in England, he reminisced about his life while staying on the Côte d'Azur, the sunny French Riviera. "I loved painting the scenery, especially on the Mediterranean coast. Sometimes I painted on the coast of Italy as well, where I would paint all day and go to the casino of San Remo at night. I also enjoyed taking the *train bleu* to Biarritz, where I could paint during the day and enjoy their casino in the evening. When I went to Monaco, I'd frequent the casino and the clubs. That's where I met your father, Franck, at his nightclub. You are not like him at all, thank God. There, I saw such entertainers as our dear Josephine, Mistinguett, and Yolanda. When I stayed in Monte Carlo at the Hermitage, I didn't need a car. I would take a horse-drawn carriage to get around. If I decided to go to Nice or Cannes, I would take a limousine and driver. The casino in Nice was fantastic, the Casino de la Jetée. There is a pier that extends out into the water, but what am I saying! You know that. Your godfather was the architect." He chuckled at this bit of absurdity on his part, then went right on with his reminiscence.

"When I had time, I loved to take a limo up the Grande Corniche to have dinner at the Château de Madrid. It was an excellent restaurant, even though it was under your father's direction. But enough of that. I don't want to remind you of unpleasant memories.

Below, I would sometimes stop at the Réserve de Beau-lieu sur Mer where the maître d' spoiled me. I would call him a few hours in advance, and he would prepare an exquisite bouillabaisse for me with langoustes, sea snake, various Mediterranean fish, rainbow wrasse, mollusks, shrimp, and mussels. My dinners would last delicious hours. It was a beautiful life in France before the war, and it will be again," he said with determination, con-cluding his pleasant reverie.

But now he was infuriated about the fate of the Jew-ish children in Paris and Drancy. The secretary told me, confidentially, that the prime minister had sent his son, Randolph, on the very same mission on which he was now sending me. He had become frustrated and angry when his son had come back with a shocking report about Jewish children but no solution as to what could be done.

His son's report had also included information about Joseph Kennedy, who was at that time the American ambassador to England. Randolph had put him under surveillance by Scotland Yard. It was discovered that messages were being sent from the American Embassy indirectly to Berlin, so Randolph planted a false message with Joe Kennedy that Churchill and Roosevelt were going to meet in Bermuda. Scotland Yard was able to determine that the message was put into code and sent from London to the American Embassy in Madrid, then on to Ankara, Turkey, and finally to Berlin.

The secretary went into further detail about Kennedy. "Why is she so free with this information?" I asked myself. "Maybe I'm privy to a lot of information because of the precarious nature of my missions. Who knows? Or maybe it's because they trust I'll say nothing."

"The prime minister feels that it is his duty to inform Mr. Roosevelt of the suspicious nature of Kennedy's dealings," she told me. "It has been discovered that Kennedy has been in touch with several American industrialists asking them to manufacture arms, ammunition, and airplanes for Germany. They will be paid in gold and jewels gathered from the pillage of Europe. This wealth is being held in safety in South America and elsewhere. The suspicions are becoming more and more serious owing to the tracing of the transmission planted by Randolph," she said.

"After being so informed, President Roosevelt ordered that all messages of a sensitive nature should *not* be sent to the embassy in London. Only normal day-to-day business is to be conducted through the London office," she told me.

"Here is the situation that you will confront, Monsieur Marc. Hundreds and hundreds of Jewish children are being pulled from their parents' arms and taken to a transit camp called Drancy on the outskirts of Paris. The report that Randolph gave his father described the sordid conditions and deplorable disorganization of the camp. The only food that he identified was cold cabbage soup. It was winter, and many of the children had no shoes and were dressed in ragged clothes. Most of them had dysentery and had to wash their dirtied undergarments in cold water with no soap, then try to let them dry a little in the cold, wet weather, only to have to put them on again still damp, dirty them again, and then repeat the endless process. The mattresses on which they spent their nights and most of their days were never cleaned."

She continued, "Randolph reported that many of the youngsters knew their first names only and didn't know what 'Jewish' meant, as many Jews were totally integrated into the milieu in which they lived. From the children's barracks every night came cries of desperation, voices of anguish calling for their mothers and fathers. Many were in a state of shock, bewildered and lost. Each of the barracks contained about forty children and a French woman guard. The guards tried to appease the children by telling them that they would rejoin their parents soon.

"And it gets worse," she said. "Two days a week the children, aged from about six to seventeen, would take cold showers outside with no privacy whatever. There was no soap or hot water. For each one hundred children, there were about four towels. Every four days, trucks would come to pick up a load of children and bring them to the train, where they were packed into cattle cars, forty to sixty per car. Minimal ventilation came from the top of the cars. Many children suffocated if they sat or lay down. Once a day, the sealed cars were unlocked, and the children were given soup to eat and water to drink. There was no place to wash, and there was no bathroom.

The children would try to get to a corner to defecate or urinate, but that was not always possible.

"Randolph said that this was their world as they traveled toward the camps in Poland, a trip that lasted five to seven days. Many died on the way. Even the German population who came into contact with the reality of this situation was horrified by the manner in which the French were treating the children. It was the French Militia who took the initiative to round up the Jewish children in this manner, store them in the camps, and send them in boxcars to Poland."

The secretary told me that the proof was irrefutable. This situation was described in a letter written by the chief of police, Jean Leguay, of occupied France to the *commissaire général aux Questions juives* of the Vichy government, Darquier de Pellepoix. Minister Laval, who was in charge of the Vichy government under the president, the *maréchal* Pétain (*maréchal* is a higher rank than general), was quoted in the letter to have said, "Purge France of all undesirables."

Now, as I recount this story, I cannot help but wonder how these people could have lived with themselves. After the war, it was estimated that between 1942 and 1944, almost two thousand children under six years of age, and six thousand between the ages of six and thirteen, were deported from France. The French Militia received one hundred francs per child. As far as can be determined, not one of these children survived. I am still furious about what happened. I should have done more.

Somehow, I could have saved more of them, I tell myself, but how? I still don't know.

The secretary and I were fighting tears when she finished telling me the story.

"I understand why Mr. Churchill didn't want to go into detail. He didn't want to struggle to maintain his composure as I just did in front of you," I said to her. "How could they do such things?" I asked. Visions of vengeance filled my mind, but I would not subject this kind woman to my visions of retribution.

The secretary then gave me the new password: "The Moulin Rouge is open at night." The response was to be, "The Moulin Rouge is always closed during the day."

So my mission was to find a solution to this travesty. There was a small group of good French people who were trying to save Jewish children. They belonged to no formal organization. They were just people who had hearts. Their headquarters was in a bar/restaurant, predominantly lesbian, across from the Moulin Rouge on the place Pigalle. They had gathered well over three thousand children and were hiding them in people's homes and cellars all over Paris. There was great difficulty in feeding and taking care of them all. Food was so scarce. What was to be done?

I was parachuted in near Die, where I was met by the *maquisards*, the partisans belonging to the group *Combat*. A colonel of the group was disguised as a member of the French Militia. He told me that he would handcuff me and that I would pose as his prisoner. We drove to the train station in Die, and the colonel requisitioned an entire compartment for the two of us. He was extraordinarily bold and sure of himself.

"I am not to be disturbed during the voyage under any circumstances," the colonel told the man who took our tickets. With that, he shut the compartment door and pulled the curtains. We changed trains in Grenoble for one to Paris. Once again, the colonel demanded a private compartment. When we passed into the German zone, papers were checked by the German military. The colonel showed his *Ausweis*, which was not questioned.

Once we arrived in Paris and exited the train station, the colonel removed the handcuffs. He hailed a bicycle taxi and gave the driver the address of a home near the opera house. A middle-aged woman opened the door and asked us to come in.

"Madame, this is Michel Carbonell, the man I told you about who wants to rent a furnished room."

"So nice to meet you, monsieur," she said warmly. The colonel said good-bye and left.

As she walked me upstairs to my room, she told me that her husband was a prisoner of war in Germany. "I haven't seen him for more than a year, monsieur. He was a tenor in the opera before the war. I pray continuously for his safe return."

We came to a closed door on the second floor. "This is the bathroom and shower, monsieur, and your bedroom is here right next to it. The colonel had me put your belongings in the armoire and the chest of drawers."

I looked in the armoire and drawers. I found six suits, twelve shirts, an overcoat, a jacket, hats, shoes, underwear, and socks. Everything was the correct size and of good quality. All these clothes! They must have expected me to be there a long time.

"Here are the keys to your car that is parked in front and some coupons for gasoline," she said before leaving my room. Later that day, I took the Peugeot that had been left for me to the bar/restaurant on the place Pigalle. I approached the woman at the bar and quietly said, "The Moulin Rouge is open at night." She responded appropriately and called a young woman over to escort me to the meeting place. Her friend was about twenty years old, blond, pleasant looking, and likable. She took me behind the Moulin Rouge, down into a cellar where there were five men and women. We talked for hours. I mostly listened, asking a question here and there. They filled me in on the wretched situation.

All of a sudden, I started feeling hot and sweaty, like I was coming down with a cold. I drove back to the house and went straight to bed. I had a fever and soon developed a cough. Looking on the bright side, I figured this gave me a lot of time to think. Madame brought me *tilleul*, an herb tea, dry toast, and a syrup that her husband often used before he would sing. Many singers used it because it soothed the vocal chords. I stayed in bed and utilized my time well, reflecting and planning. In two days, not only was I well, but I had a plan of action, too.

* * *

I telephoned the office of the *ministre des Invalides*, the minister in charge of military veterans who had lost limbs in World War I. The *ministre*, Monsieur Paget, was the father of a boy who had been educated with me when I was locked up with the Jesuits at the Athenium in Nice from the age of seven to fourteen.

The person who answered the phone said, "He is not available, monsieur. Would you care to leave a message?"

"Yes, I would. My name is Michel Carbonell. Have him call me back at this number." I left the telephone number of the house where I was staying. Of course, he wouldn't know who I was by that name, but I hoped he would call back anyway. If not, I would go to Nice to visit him personally at his home.

He called back a few days later. I told him who I really was.

"My boy," he exclaimed, "I am so happy to hear from you."

"How is your son?" I asked.

"He is still safe in Nice, thank God." After we talked for a while, I explained to him the awful plight of these Jewish children being shipped off to Poland.

"Monsieur, thousands more are being hidden here in Paris. I have devised a plan to secure their safety. To me, it seems straightforward and quite doable; however, it ultimately depends on you."

"Go ahead, tell me. If it's possible, I will do whatever it takes."

So I began to explain what would be necessary. "I will need two buses painted olive green and black, two bus drivers in French Militia uniform, and documents that authorize the transfer of French children to the youth camps in unoccupied France."

Monsieur Paget was quiet, thinking on the other end of the phone. "Yes, my boy. I know I can accomplish that. Do not worry about a thing. I'll supply what you need. Is this the telephone number where you can be reached when everything is organized?"

"Yes, it is, monsieur."

With much enthusiasm, he concluded the conversation. "I will be in touch, and may God bless you."

I then returned to the bar/restaurant and talked to the woman behind the bar. She was the owner. She called the same young woman, Simone, who escorted me once again to the cellar. This time there was only one man there. I recognized him from the time before. We greeted each other, sat down at the table, and I began to explain.

"Choose sixty children who will be the first to leave. I need a photo of each child like those used for official identification cards. I need to know the birth date of each one. They will need warm traveling clothes and shoes as well as work clothes and boots. They will need as many pairs of socks as possible, as they'll be staying in forested areas." The man agreed to take care of everything.

Then I went to the home of a man I had worked with before, Roland Girard, who made counterfeit papers. His wife escorted me down to the cellar.

"Roland, it is so good to see you," I said as he welcomed me. We sat down, and I explained what I needed. "Roland, I need you for an enormous job. All in all, I need around three thousand *cartes d'identité*, but only sixty to begin with. You will be given the names, information, and photos you need as time goes on." I explained the awful situation, and the man enthusiastically agreed to do the job. All seemed to be progressing well.

From there, I went to the library. What I needed was a book with a lot of names. I selected one that listed all known amateur and professional archaeologists. I sat down at a long, dimly lit table and copied the names down, one by one, skipping any that sounded Jewish.

The next day, I met the same man in the cellar at the place Pigalle. He gave me the birth dates and addresses of sixty children. I drove to each address and gave each child his or her new name and explained to each that this Christian first and last name was his or hers from that moment on. They were to forget their old names for their own safety.

One little girl, eight years old, stands out in my memory. "I don't like that name," she said. "I want to choose my own name. I choose 'Sarah.'"

"That's a lovely name," I told her, "but just for a while your name needs to be Suzanne."

She insisted, "No, I don't like that name."

I asked, "Do you have a friend whose name you like?"

"Oh yes, my friend Ange. Isn't that a beautiful name?" Her eyes were wide with admiration.

"Well, there it is!" I responded. "From now on, you are Ange, just like your dear friend. It's a wonderful name, and you look just like a little angel, too!"

She was very pleased, and I was relieved. I eventually placed this girl with a local family because she was too fragile for the youth camps.

I gave each child a name and explained to him or her what life was going to be like. "But I don't like that name," many complained. Some wailed, "I won't be able to remember that name because I hate it so much!" I worked with each child as best I could and worked out swaps so that each child was more or less satisfied with his or her new name.

It took more than a week to get the papers organized. I used the time to visit the different camps in unoccupied France so that each was prepared for this great influx of children. The commander at Die helped me immensely. More than three weeks later, the first sixty children were on buses on their way to the youth work camps to start their new lives as Christians. The plan worked smoothly.

With the system now in place, I left its continuation in the capable and powerful hands of Monsieur Paget, whose influence extended throughout France. Many veterans who lost limbs in World War I were anxious to help in any way they could to free France from German occupation once and for all.

Later, I got word that all the children concerned had been placed in the youth camps except those who were ill or mentally confused. For those, Paget had found several monasteries willing to take care of them until they were strong enough or able enough, if ever, to go to the youth camps. As the older children in the work camps developed, they were eased into partisan groups and worked for the Resistance.

Before leaving, I went to visit Monsieur Paget on the weekend at his home in Nice. It is truly Monsieur Paget who needs to be remembered for the success of this rescue operation. Without him, this plan would never have worked, and thousands of Jewish children would certainly have perished.

After leaving Monsieur Paget, I decided to go to one of my parents' apartments in Monte Carlo at 52, boulevard d'Italie, since I knew they were staying at their apartment in Nice. The concierge knew me and let me in. I put my things away and went to see some neighbors in the building, the Van Hofs, who lived on the third floor. Madame Van Hof invited me to dinner with her, her son, Claude, and her daughter, Dominique. It was wonderful to see them again.

Afterward, I went down to my parents' apartment and began thinking about the Jewish children as I went to sleep. How could I prove that each child was who his identity card said he or she was? An identity card was

simply not enough. There must be further proof. Each
child needed to have a baptismal certificate. How could
I get three thousand baptismal certificates? I wondered.
It didn't seem possible. Then, out of the blue, the solution struck me.

EIGHTEEN

The Vatican

"What I need to do is get to Rome," I said out loud in a voice of triumph as the idea formulated in my mind. "There, I can secure the proof I need for the children's identities if my plan works."

It was early morning when the answer woke me out of a sound sleep. It came to me that I had an ace up my sleeve because of my father. Thanks to Monsieur Franck's vanity, I had been baptized at the Vatican. When you are baptized at Saint Peter's, you have the right to ask for an audience with the pope. My father had done precious little good for me during my life, but in this instance he had done me a good turn that I could convert to a great turn for many unfortunates.

The first obstacle was to devise a way to get to Rome without putting myself in danger of getting caught by the Nazis. I decided to call my friend Pierre, the owner of the limousine service in Beausoleil. I went upstairs to the Van Hofs to ask to use their phone. I called, and Pierre's secretary told me he was out of the office.

"Please have him call Marc at the Van Hof home," I said and gave her the number.

"Have some breakfast with us, Marc," Madame Van Hof offered as soon as I put the phone down.

As we were eating, another idea came to me. I could call Maurice Chevalier, the legendary entertainer. I had his telephone number from a previous encounter when I had hidden in the cellar at his home in Juan-les-Pins, an hour or so down the coast.

Chevalier's valet answered. "Mr. Chevalier is in the sauna and cannot be disturbed," he said.

"Will you give him a message for me?"

"If that is your wish, I will pass him a message," he responded coldly.

"This is very urgent. Do you understand?" I retorted, adopting a superior tone. "Do me the service of calling him to the phone right away. Tell him that it's Marc, the son of Monsieur Franck, the owner of the Knickerbocker in Monte Carlo. I thank you to get him immediately."

Within minutes, I was on the phone with Mr. Chevalier. I explained to him the precarious situation of these Jewish children and my pressing need to get to Rome. He was horrified at the plight of these youngsters.

"Can you get some time free to escort me to the Vatican under your protection? I know you have all the necessary exit visas, and I can provide the limousine and driver," I told him, assuming that Pierre would help me.

"Certainly, my dear young man, I will work it out. How much time will we need?" he asked.

"One or two weeks, I'm really not sure," I said. "I have all the funds we need furnished by the British government."

"Mais non, mais non," he replied. "I'll take care of the expenses."

"Monsieur, it is already taken care of. Thank you for your great kindness and good heart. These children must be saved. If it is convenient for you, I will send a limousine to pick you up about one o'clock tomorrow afternoon."

"I believe that will be fine," he said. "If I cannot change my schedule to accommodate that particular time, how shall I contact you?"

"Just leave a message with Pierre Embalier at his limousine company in Beausoleil. He will know how to get in touch with me."

I hung up and tried Pierre again. He still hadn't returned.

"Claude, would you like to walk to Beausoleil with me? I have an errand to do near the Pâtisserie Pasquier."

"Yes, that will be nice." Then the phone rang.

"It's for you," Claude said. "It's Monsieur Pierre."

"Marc, what can I do for you?" Pierre asked.

"What I need is a limousine and a chauffeur for a week or two. I need coupons for gas that are good in

Italy and exit visas and papers. Maurice Chevalier will be the person on the lease agreement, but I will be taking care of the expenses. He'll be waiting at his home in Juan-les-Pins for the limo at one P.M. tomorrow. Will that be possible, Pierre?"

"Absolutely. I have a trustworthy driver and limousine available. I will have him at Monsieur Chevalier's at one P.M. with all necessary papers.

"Now, on another subject, young man," Pierre continued, and his tone turned emotional. "I told Cécile of your last visit, and she felt bad that she didn't have the opportunity to see you. Do me the pleasure of coming to our home this evening for dinner. She is dying to see you and hold you in her arms. You know, we both love you so much. You are the son we couldn't have. Do you remember when you were little? You would walk with your tutor on the avenue des Spélugues and through the gardens of the Casino. You never missed stopping at our travel agency to say hello and give your regards to Cécile. You were always so polite and respectful, she couldn't get over it. She would always talk about you. 'I wish we could have a little boy, like Marc,' she would say over and over again.

"I told her that I saw you after you quit dental school, and that you looked so grown up and debonair. I promised her that when I heard from you again, I would bring you home for a visit. It would please her so much to see you. Will you stop by the garage to get me around four or five? Is that possible, or do you already have plans? It would make her so happy to see you, to see the man you have become. You know, she hasn't seen you since you were seven years old."

Though slightly embarrassed by what he had said, I agreed to come over. I hung up and told Claude that I didn't need to do the errand after all. I explained the plan to them both, and he asked his mother to pray for its smooth execution. His mother was a charming woman from Holland. She was in the same line of work as I. She helped Jewish refugees on their route of escape to North Africa, across the Pyrénées, or through Sweden by boat to Great Britain. I had known the Van Hofs before I was sequestered with the Jesuits in Nice. They lived in Monte Carlo on the route to the Palm Beach Club, where my tutor would take me twice a week for tennis lessons. She and her daughter, Dominique, about ten years older than I, showered me with love when I was little.

After visiting with the Van Hofs for a while, I got my things together for the trip and then headed over to Pierre's garage from where he drove us home. When we arrived, Cécile was on the front steps of their villa. She broke out in tears as she ran to the car. She opened the passenger door and jumped back in shock. She couldn't believe her eyes. "This can't be Marc, Pierre!" I got out of the car. "He's a grown man! But . . . yes it is. Now, I see his mother's charming smile, his mother whom we love so much. Come, come into my arms, Marc," she said with tears rolling down her cheeks. I did, and she held me. "Thank you, thank you for coming today." We had a lovely talk over dinner, remembering the old days and filling each other in on what had happened since I had left in 1930. After dinner, Cécile said, "I'm sorry there is no coffee available, as I'm sure you know, but let's enjoy a good cognac or eau-de-vie together."

We continued our conversation well into the evening, and then they drove me back to the apartment.

The following afternoon just before one o'clock, there was a knock on the door of my parents' apartment. It was Claude. "Monsieur Chevalier is on the phone for you." I followed him upstairs to their apartment.

"The limo has arrived, but I'm not quite ready," he said. "Can you wait awhile longer to begin our adventure?" he asked in his cheerful way.

"I'll be ready whenever you arrive, monsieur."

"I should be in Monte Carlo by three o'clock. I'll pick you up at Saint Roman, if that's all right with you. The address is 52 boulevard d'Italie, correct?"

"Yes. Just have the chauffeur ring the bell at apartment D."

Before three o'clock, the doorbell rang. The driver took my suitcases, and I followed.

The car that Pierre had leased to Monsieur Chevalier was an exquisite Delage limousine. It had a unique aerodynamic line that I had never seen before. It must have been a special edition or an extremely limited series. The chauffeur's roof was retractable. I had only seen that once before in a Voisin. The roof of the back of the car was a landau, a convertible top. The interior was of precious woods and of mohair, a fabric of exceptional quality that was pleated and padded. There was a bar and an icebox as well. The carpeting was thick and luxurious, almost covering the shoes of Monsieur Chevalier, who smiled as I got in.

"You'll excuse me, my friend. I seem to have caught a terrible cold last night, and I can hardly talk." His voice had become low and raspy since I had talked to him earlier. "Please give the chauffeur our itinerary, won't you?"

"Of course, monsieur. Take the route toward Sospel via the Col de Tende. You'll cross the border and continue on through the tunnel. As you exit, you'll descend toward Limone where I made reservations for the night at the Hôtel de la Gare."

Monsieur Chevalier slept for the few hours it took us to get there. We were not asked for any papers at either the French or Italian customs. The border guards just looked at the car in awe. I carried personal papers saying I was Michel Carbonell, a textile salesman, but they were really more interested in the car than in us or our papers.

At the hotel, once we had signed the registration, Monsieur Chevalier went straight to his room without dining. He was feeling quite sick, but when we met the next morning he felt much better. After breakfast, we took the road in the direction of Torino, passing through Cuneo. We stopped for lunch at a small restaurant in Moncalieri where we enjoyed a fine little meal. The restaurant owner was a *garde de chasse* (hunting guard) of a private reserve in Valdieri for the king, Victor Emmanuel III. We had a delicious ragout of *chevreuil au vin rouge* (venison prepared in red wine) with *champignons des bois* (wild mushrooms). We didn't ask any questions about where the meat came from but appreciated the meal immensely. Monsieur Chevalier was still hungry and asked for a second portion. He had a big appetite. The chauffeur didn't finish his and didn't seem thrilled with the food. He probably didn't like game.

I had made reservations in Torino at a hotel I knew well, the Albergo Principi di Piemonte. My tutor and I had stayed there when I was a child. There was a fabulous view of all Torino. The surrounding mountaintops were covered with snow. It brought back wonderful memories of the times I spent with my colonel, and I felt a profound gratefulness that he exposed me to such wonderful experiences. He was such a benevolent man, always desiring the best for others. He gave me a wonderful example of manhood to emulate.

Mr. Chevalier appreciated the hotel. We had dinner looking out on the mountains that encircled the city. The next day, we took the road in the direction of Florence, Mr. Chevalier's favorite city. He was feeling well again and had completely recovered his voice.

Once in Florence, he gave the driver directions to his favorite restaurant. I'll never forget the experience, though I don't remember the restaurant's name. He ordered for us, not even asking what we wanted, so confident was he in its fine cuisine. The owner was a cousin of a celebrated restaurant owner in Rome named Alfredo alla Scrofa, who was known for his specialty, *fettuccine alla Scrofa.* His cousin mixed the pasta at tableside with butter and egg yolks that beautifully coated the fettuccine, and then added fresh cream. Just before serving this dish, he grated cheese on the top.

"This restaurant is very special to the Italians," Chevalier told me. "The owner had a serving spoon and a fork in twenty-four-carat gold that he always used to mix the fettuccine tableside. At the time Italy declared war and began the attack against Ethiopia in 1936, Mussolini gathered wedding bands from the people to finance the cost of the invasion. The proprietor of this restaurant contributed by donating these massive utensils of pure gold to the Italian cause. Another of his specialties is angel-hair pasta made with octopus in its own ink covered with a delightful sea urchin sauce. You must try it. We'll get an order of this dish as well," Chevalier said with obvious appreciation. He was right. I never forgot this dish, and to this day, I never go to a Japanese restaurant without ordering *uni*, sea urchin sushi. I never miss an opportunity to eat sea urchin.

After our meal, we went to the hotel. Once we checked in, Chevalier said, "Marc, will you ask the concierge to make reservations tomorrow at the Excelsior in Rome, a two-bedroom suite for us and a standard room for the chauffeur?"

The Excelsior was an exquisite hotel. I called the Vatican from our room to let them know of my arrival in Rome. I talked to one of the pope's secretaries who said he would call back with the day and time of my audience.

"Let's dine in the suite tonight, if you don't mind.

I'm a bit tired from the trip, and I'd rather not have to make conversation with anyone who might recognize me," Mr. Chevalier suggested. We completed the fine dinner with calvados, and after some conversation we both went to our bedrooms.

Several days later, I received a message from the Vatican that my audience with the pope would be the following afternoon.

The next day, the chauffeur drove me to Vatican City. We stopped at the gates where the guards verified my appointment. Once inside, we drove on the cobblestone street until we reached the entrance. It was an entire city inside that included a railroad station for the pope's use, a post office, an observatory, a gift shop, and other buildings. I was received by a priest who escorted me to a waiting room where others were also waiting.

The silence was deafening, almost suffocating. People spoke only in hushed voices. The ambience was austere and cold. A priest came in and took me to another room for those specifically waiting to see the pope. There, the skirts of the women were measured, and material was pinned on if they were not long enough. Their heads had to be covered with a scarf before entering. After a while, I was escorted to yet another room and eventually to a final one where I was the only person waiting.

"You are to enter and kneel before the pope on a pillow that you will see," the priest told me. "Then approach in silence, stop in front of him, and kiss his ring. There will be an armchair for you to sit on. Sit down and wait to be addressed."

Finally, I was instructed to enter. I followed the directions I had been given. All was very ornate, including the very heavy draperies. The room was dimly lit. The pope, dressed in his impressive robes, looked gaunt and rather frail to me. His secretary was next to him to take notes. The pope asked me the purpose of my visit. I was able to state my goal in French because he was fluent in the language. He was receptive and listened attentively, then granted my request. The audience itself lasted only about fifteen minutes though the preliminary protocol had seemed endless.

We were called the following week to return to the Vatican to pick up the documents. It was raining hard, so I decided to wait in the car. I sent the chauffeur to the office to get the papers. It took him quite a few trips to bring the three thousand certificates to the limousine.

The baptismal certificates were printed in French by the Vatican printers as we had requested. Names and birth dates of the children would later be written in ink by each parish priest. After the chauffeur finished loading the documents, we returned to the hotel.

A few days later when we arrived back at Juan-les-Pins, I sincerely thanked Mr. Chevalier, telling him how indispensable his help was to the success of the plan.

"Glad to be of service, monsieur," he said with that unforgettable smile lighting up his face.

Later in life, when I held the position of executive chef at a famous hotel in Kansas City, Missouri, who should come to see Mae West's performance at our cabaret but Mr. Chevalier himself. It was my pleasure to fête him and to inform Ms. West of his help in the successful rescue of so many Jewish children during the war. When she came onstage, she saluted him and told the story of what he had helped me do. When she finished, she ordered champagne for everyone in the large audience and toasted Mr. Chevalier for his heroism during World War II. I know personally how much this meant to him.

When I returned to Monaco, I contacted Monsieur Paget and explained to him what we had accomplished at the Vatican. "We've successfully completed this part of the mission," I told him. "I will leave the baptismal certificates with Pierre Embalier in Beausoleil."

"I'll send someone from my office to pick them up," he said. "Thank you, Marc, for all you have accomplished."

With the plan of action for the Jewish children in place, I now had to figure out how to get back to Great Britain. I quickly decided to contact the chief of police of Monte Carlo, Commissaire Plantier. Maybe he would have some ideas. He had never failed me before.

My instincts and timing could not have been better. He knew of a Swedish diplomat who needed a chauffeur. The man's own chauffeur had suffered catastrophic gambling losses in Monte Carlo and had killed himself as a result. This was, sadly, not uncommon in my hometown.

Luck on my side as usual, the Swedish diplomat hired me as his driver, based on Commissaire Plantier's recommendation and a brief interview. I posed as his chauffeur, driving him first to Paris and then south to Biarritz, where I enjoyed a few days at the seaside while I waited for him to conclude his business. Next I drove him to Lisbon, which was the destination I needed to reach. There, I contacted the British Embassy. As things worked out, the Swedish diplomat was recalled urgently to Sweden. The British authorities arranged for my return to England by plane where I soon rediscovered the comfort and safety of Mr. Churchill's country home.

After some time back at the estate, Mr. Churchill summoned me to the library to share a cognac. We talked for quite a while, as he enjoyed his cigar and I relaxed with my pipe.

"Some of your solutions to the tasks at hand are truly original, *mon ingénieux*. Your next mission may require all your resourcefulness," he said, "and it certainly will be your most vital undertaking so far. What you'll bring back is invaluable to the ultimate survival of Great Britain."

PART THREE

MARC, L'INGÉNIEUX

In War: Resolution.

—WINSTON CHURCHILL

NINETEEN

Crossing Europe on Foot

The last thing Mr. Churchill said to me before he saw me off on this latest assignment was that I should expect all my missions to increase in degree of difficulty and in level of danger from here on out. After saying the danger would be greater, he told me he would not hold it against me if I chose not to continue as an agent. He said he now regarded me as a professional but felt guilty for having assured my godfather he would see to my safety. If I stayed on, I was going to be in jeopardy, sometimes doubly and triply so. Far from ensuring my safety, he could only assure the opposite, "imminent peril." That's how he so aptly phrased it.

There was no question that I was going on, danger or not, promises to my godfather or not. I would see France free again—of that I was certain. But I appreciated immensely, and still appreciate today, that Mr. Churchill said I had spoiled him with my successes. But I'm no hero. When he explained the latest mission to me, I didn't know right away how I was going to pull it off. Everything hinged on extracting a brilliant scientist from Bulgaria.

Mr. Churchill had gathered intelligence that the Germans were planning to launch short-range missiles from Calais, France. The missiles would be slow enough that, *if detected*, the Royal Air Force would have time to shoot them down. Without a good detection system, however, Great Britain could be annihilated.

"The scientist is essential to our defense," the prime minister emphasized. "He has already been approached by the Russians but would prefer to bring his family to a free country rather than to a dictatorship. The man is Jewish and is actively seeking asylum."

Mr. Churchill continued to brief me. "The man refuses to leave without his family. We can promise to send another plane, or two more planes if necessary, to get his loved ones. But we cannot risk sending a plane large enough to carry all of them at once. It would be too slow moving and easily detectable in flight. To get him out safely, we have to get in and out quickly."

"How am I going to do it?" I asked myself. "Should I drug and kidnap him? Mr. Churchill wants me to get him out of Bulgaria and to England as soon as I can because he has invented a device that can detect incoming V-1 and V-2 missiles. Whatever I have to do, I will. But how?"

As I listened, I considered every possible solution I could think of to get him out. I thought of something my tutor, the colonel, used to say, *"Sometimes when attacking a difficult situation or problem, jump in, familiarize yourself with the details, and devise the solution as you go along."*

That, I decided, was what I would do now.

When I parachuted into the valley of Samokov in Bulgaria, the King of the Gypsies and his entourage were waiting for me, eager to help in any way they could. They gathered the huge parachute, made of black silk, and stuffed it into one of their wagons. They would use it later to make shirts and skirts. The Germans prohibited them from traveling at night, but that didn't deter them in the least. They were a brave lot. Although I was already dressed in Gypsy clothing, and had that torn and tattered look of a vagabond, the King highly disapproved of the British interpretation. "No one travels with the King of the Gypsies dressed like that!" he exclaimed when he saw me.

They took me directly to their camp and dressed me like the rest of the men. I had never seen clothes like these! The deep golden shirt had billowy, bouffant sleeves, the ochre color of villas in the south of France. Over it, I wore a small black velvet vest, left open in a jaunty fashion. I wore a ruby red scarf on my head and another around my waist. The warm, soft black pants fell just below the knee and were tucked into knee-length socks. The total look was quite dashing, I thought, as I finished dressing.

I joined the King for dinner, and he smiled, approvingly, revealing a mouth full of gold teeth. "Now you look like a member of the family!" he said as I sat down on the ground with the others, already sitting on their colorful blankets and cushions. To my delight and surprise, I was served moussaka, a dish I was very fond of. I wondered how this Greek dish had come to Bulgaria. It gave me an insight into the close communication system among the Gypsies. They were one people. Political borders had no meaning to them. We ate a leisurely meal while they told me how to play the role of a Gypsy.

"My mission is to get a Jewish scientist out of Bulgaria," I told the King. "Mr. Churchill prefers to pick him up in a plane but suspects he will refuse. It is imperative that I meet him in Sofia within the next few days. Whatever day I arrive, I need to be at the synagogue at noontime. The scientist and his family are staying with the rabbi at his home until I get there."

The King was a very good-looking man, with an air of mystery about him. His entire being exuded intrigue. He was massive, rugged, and well over six feet tall. His face, framed by long, wavy black hair, was full of character and suggested a man in his sixties. It was apparent that *he* was the person in command. He wore a burgundy jacket, trimmed with black tassels, and from his ears hung beautiful gold earrings. His enigmatic smile made me wonder what he was really thinking. The man was extremely valuable to Mr. Churchill because of his widespread influence and contacts throughout Europe. He supplied Great Britain with critical information about the movement of German troops.

"Monsieur," he said to me over Turkish coffee, "you will be our bear trainer. Tomorrow you will learn what to do." He smiled. "Now it is late. Let's go to bed." I slept in a wagon with the three men in charge of the bears.

The next morning, I woke up with a jolt. We were on the move. There were about twenty wagons, each one pulled by a single horse. This was the King's court on wheels. All of a sudden, German soldiers appeared on the road in front of us and ordered us to stop. I was in the rear wagon just in front of the bears. "What do they want?" I wondered. "Why are they stopping us?"

One of the French-speaking Gypsies came over to our wagon and whispered, "You are mute. You can hear, but you cannot talk. Go to the bear cages with the handlers. They will show you what to do. The Germans probably just want some entertainment. And don't be concerned. Our King knows how to handle them."

We followed the military car into the woods where there was a Panzer division, complete with about twenty tanks. They wanted a show that evening. The same Gypsy came over to me again. "Pay close attention to the bear trainers so that you'll be able to handle the bears tonight. Tomorrow, our King said we will go to Sofia. No one will ask you for papers if you look like you know what you're doing."

We circled the wagons not far from the Nazi encampment. The Germans were celebrating the return of one of their officers from the hospital. We began practicing right away for the evening's show. As rehearsal began, the variety of simultaneous sounds from the violins, accordions, concertinas, balalaikas, tambourines, and the essential gourds created a huge racket. Singers and dancers were interspersed among the musicians, practicing their numbers. Outside of the musical group, talented gymnasts practiced their pyramids and other acrobatics, while a knife thrower and a flamethrower prepared their stunts. The women were kept safe inside the wagons.

The head bear trainer, a short middle-aged man, motioned for me to stand next to him. He brought out the oldest and most docile female bear. I watched intently as she responded to his signals. She was about six feet tall, about my size. She danced and pirouetted on command. She had her act down pat. All the bears had rings in their noses with chains coming from them to keep them under control. The two males were muzzled because they had a tendency to fight. I held a stick about a meter long with a sharp, metal point on the end, just in case a bear caused trouble.

After dinner, the Gypsies put on the show. My bear did her routine perfectly. The Germans showed their appreciation with a resounding applause. After an encore, we went to our own camp to eat. The German commander summoned the King to his quarters.

When he returned to camp, he told me why the commander had wanted to see him. "He graciously thanked me for the wonderful show and asked how much would be a satisfactory amount to compensate my people," he reported. "I told him that as compensation I would appreciate an escort through Sofia because, as he knew, Gypsies were normally not allowed to travel through the cities of Europe. He agreed to my proposal."

What a great idea. This man was clever. This would cut down our travel time enormously. Over dinner, I discussed with him the plan of escape. "Since I don't think the scientist is going to accept our preferred plan, I will most likely have to accompany this family from Bulgaria to Lisbon, Portugal. What are your suggestions?"

"Nighttime is the only time safe enough to travel. Tomorrow will be our first step. The Germans will escort us through Sofia. This will make it easier for you to get to the synagogue. You're at the end of the wagon caravan, so just drop off at an opportune moment. As we travel along Sofia's main street, you'll see the synagogue on the left across from the Catholic church."

"Will you be able to organize a system of guides across Europe?" I asked.

"I'll need a few days to organize the trek, where each set of guides will begin and end. It's a big undertaking, but I know our people can do it. There will always be six of our men with you, but I need to organize the other Gypsies along the route to arrange for local guides and provisions all the way to the foot of the Pyrénées in France. From there, the Basque partisans can take over. You know, it's about thirty-five hundred kilometers to Lisbon, depending on your exact route. There may be changes, depending on circumstances, but I'll formulate the plan, segment by segment. We'll need to locate good hiding places for you during the daytime. I'll get in touch with you at the rabbi's house when I've completed the initial arrangements."

This one man, the King of the Gypsies, did so much for the Allied effort throughout the war. He was always dependable, shrewd, and inventive—a magnificent human being. Survivors of the war and their descendents owe him a great deal.

At dawn, we were on the road to Sofia accompanied by our German escort. The journey took the entire day. When we arrived inside the city, night had already fallen. As we neared the synagogue, I jumped off the slow-moving wagon and disappeared into the darkness. I tapped on the door of the synagogue. I knew this was an awkward time to arrive, but I thought I would try to make contact anyway.

When no one answered, I wasn't surprised. I really hadn't expected anyone to answer at this time of night. And dressed as a Gypsy, I knew I wouldn't be welcome anywhere, and then there was the question of papers. I realized that I had better look for a place to hide till morning.

On a street just behind the synagogue, I saw a wagon filled with hay next to a fountain. That looked inviting for the night with one exception. Behind the wagon, there was a large doghouse, outside of which was its inhabitant on a chain. I asked myself what I was going to do now. I thought for a moment and remembered that I had put some sugar cubes into my pocket after drinking my last cup of coffee with the Gypsies. Since I always had a great rapport with animals, I decided to take a chance with this big dog that was staring at me but not yet barking. I took one sugar cube from my pocket and tossed it gently toward him. He sniffed it, looked up at me, looked back at the sugar and took it in his mouth. He looked at me again, this time with a softer eye. I decided to approach him slowly. This time I offered the sugar from my hand. The dog didn't hesitate.

Now I had a decision to make. I knew the dog was my friend. Should I sleep in his house and curl up next to his warm body, or should I sleep in the wagon underneath the hay? I decided on the wagon and dug myself into the hay so that I was completely hidden from view. I put a sugar cube in my mouth to suck on and fell asleep. I awoke to the sound of scratching. It was daybreak, and my new friend wanted breakfast. I reached into my pocket for another sugar cube. Good thing I had taken quite a few.

I climbed out of the wagon, brushed myself off, and went to the door of the synagogue. Even though it wasn't the designated time, I decided to try anyway. After all, it's safer to be inside a building than out on the street, I reasoned. An older man opened the door. I spoke to him in French, but he didn't understand. He gestured for me to come in. He showed me to a bench where he indicated I should sit down. He went to the telephone hanging on the wall, talked for a couple of minutes and hung up. He gestured that I was to wait.

A while later, another old man, broom in hand, entered the lobby where I was waiting. He began sweeping the area right in front of me. The man wore the traditional long side curls of Orthodox Jews. He did not take his gaze off me the entire time he was sweeping. Unlike the other man who had opened the door for me, this one had a sour expression. He just stared at me, a miserable grimace on his face. His constant stare made me furious. I got up to look out the window. The man jumped in front of me, holding the broom horizontally in both hands and signaled for me to sit down. Reluctantly, I sat. In those days, it did not take much to make me angry. Later, when I thought about the situation, I realized that this man knew that Gypsies often meant trouble. He probably didn't want anyone to see there was a Gypsy in the synagogue.

As I sat there, I thought, *If only this scientist would have accepted the original British plan, a small plane could have been sent for him, and the mission would have been finished. Then I wouldn't have to put up with this malcontent staring at me.* I was about nineteen years old at the time, and nobody had ever dared look at me like that. I felt ready to do battle, but I contained myself. I did not like this old guy.

I reviewed the situation in my mind. Maybe if I got lucky I could convince the scientist to take the plane. He had refused to take it because they could only take him on board. He would not accept being separated from his family, so this complicated scheme to get him out of Bulgaria had to be developed. I had to admire him for insisting on keeping his family together. It was a simple truth that a plane large enough to take them all was too dangerous, and any other sort of transportation was too risky. And he couldn't afford to trust that we would come right back with another plane to get the rest of his family. How could he? It was his family at stake. He had a right to be doubtful. Anything could have happened in the interim between flights.

So I had to accept the situation, including putting up with this cranky guy and his piercing stare. Hours went by, and the man kept on sweeping. He also kept on staring every chance he got, and every time I looked up our eyes locked. No doubt he saw me as a threat. This annoyed me, and I wondered if he ever had anything else to do. I was so aggravated my jaw was clenched shut. It was crazy on my part to focus on this old man, so I decided to close my eyes and think of something else. It worked. I even dozed off for a while. I was awakened by another man's voice.

I opened my eyes to a radiant smile. The room was transformed. *Now, this is a face to wake up to,* I thought. *The old man should take some smile lessons from this angelic being.*

"I'm Saul Rothstein," the rabbi said, introducing himself. "I am grateful that you've arrived safely," he said softly, with sincerity. A certain peacefulness dominated his being. "You know, I haven't had the opportunity to speak French since the German invasion of Bulgaria. I was raised in Paris and came to Sofia as a grown man." His voice exuded calm. He was young, in his thirties, enthusiastic, optimistic, a breath of fresh air. "I became a rabbi in Paris," he continued. "After I finished my studies, I felt called to return to my own country." That explained why he was living here.

"It is a pleasure to meet you, Rabbi," I replied.

Emotion still fills me when I think of him. Today, tears come to my eyes because I know what happened to this wonderful man. Rabbi Rothstein was later caught by the Gestapo as he was helping Jews get out of Bulgaria. He was tortured but would not talk. He was put on the wheel of torture, attached by his ankles and wrists. It was cranked until he was dismembered. Unbelievable cruelty and such a horrible waste. This dear man sacrificed his life.

"Why don't you change into these clothes?" he suggested, handing me the traditional clothing of the Orthodox Jew: long black coat, black pants, white shirt, black shoes. Since the clothes were big and baggy, I just slipped everything on over the Gypsy clothing. He was taller and bigger than I, so there was no difficulty.

I accompanied him to his home, about a ten-minute walk from the synagogue. We entered the small ground-floor apartment. The walls were bare. The furnishings were very simple. Though it was midday, the room was very gloomy and lit by kerosene lamps. In the middle of the room was the dining table around which the scientist, his wife, daughter, and son were seated. There were places set for the rabbi and me. Lunch was prepared and waiting.

The rabbi introduced us. The scientist, in his midsixties, had gray hair with a receding hairline and was very tall and slender. He had a nose similar to that of Charles de Gaulle. His wife, around sixty, was small, about five feet tall. She also had gray hair that she wore in a short style. She was plump and appeared to be in poor physical condition. On the other hand, the scientist seemed quite fit, as was their nine-year-old son. But the walk would be long and difficult for any adult. How would the wife handle it? What about a nine-year-old boy? And then I looked at his twenty-year-old daughter. She must have been seven or eight months pregnant. She would risk her life—all of our lives, including that of her unborn baby.

The scientist spoke fluent French, and the others understood enough to get along. After the traditional niceties, I reiterated the original plan to the man—we could put him on an airplane the next day and his family would follow shortly afterward on another plane. I told him bluntly, "Monsieur, I have strong doubts that your family is strong enough to make it all the way to Portugal on foot. The trip is well over three thousand kilometers." I enumerated several of the risks involved and then suggested, "You know, monsieur, I could simply kidnap you."

The scientist responded without a moment's hesitation, "Yes, you could, monsieur, but if you do, I will not help the English at all. You see, I'm afraid to leave my family here without me. The Russians have already asked me to help them, and I put them off. I'm afraid that either the Nazis or the Russians will take my loved ones, and we'll never see each other again. My daughter's husband has already died in prison. I simply will not leave without my family."

How could I fault him? I didn't. That wasn't the issue. Getting them all to Portugal alive was the mission that had to be accomplished.

"All right, then," I said. "We will walk most of the way from Sofia to Lisbon. This trek will be extraordinarily difficult on a daily basis. If you commit to take the journey, there will be no quitting. We will be walking at night and hiding during the day. I figure the trip will take between two and three months. There will always be six Gypsies accompanying and protecting us along the way, as well as additional Gypsies guiding us for short distances along the route. If you weaken and hold the group up, you will be endangering every one of us. If you have problems walking, someone will drag you along. If no one has the strength to drag you, we will be forced to leave you behind. This is an important decision for you. These are the conditions that you must agree to. So, monsieur, I suggest you reconsider. Take an airplane tomorrow and allow us to hold your family in a safe house and send them to join you afterward."

The scientist did not waver. "I have already considered every possibility," he said. "This is the only way. I want my family to accompany me. I am positive that we can make it together," he responded, passionately. "I would not try if I didn't believe we could succeed."

And, so it would be. We spent the day discussing the

possible problems that could arise and the trip in general. We ate dinner and continued discussing the details.

"On this journey, there is one law: my law. I will not tolerate any questions. You must simply obey instantly when I tell you to do something. We are not only risking your lives, we are risking our own. Each of the six men accompanying us as well as every partisan along the way has his own family and life ahead of him. They are risking everything for you. They could die if you forget the law as the days go by, so keep it fresh in your memories. In case we are captured, the less you know, the better. Once we cross the Yugoslavian border, there will be no danger until we leave the country." (I expected no problems at all in Yugoslavia because Tito was Communist, and though he had no use for the Russians, he was totally against the Nazi regime.)

I continued, "The trip to Dubrovnik will take about two weeks or so. We will be going through mountains, but they are not too high. There will be a lot of ascent and descent. There is no established road or path that we will be following. We will have neither skis nor snow boots. We will only be equipped with mountain boots. Tomorrow morning, when I return, I want each of you to have all that you want to take placed in front of you. I will tell you at that time what you can take. You will each be supplied with an empty flour sack to put your belongings in, but more about that tomorrow."

So, under these conditions, I agreed to take them. Late in the evening, the rabbi walked me back to the synagogue, where I would wait for the Gypsies to contact me. He showed me to a small room where there was a narrow straw mattress on the floor. "Thank you, my friend, for the great risk you're taking. Have a restful night's sleep," he said as he shut the door.

TWENTY

Deliverance

The next morning, I woke up to some noise in the next room. I got up and opened the door. It was the old man with the bad staring problem. He gestured for me to follow him. In the foyer was Andre, the Gypsy who spoke French. "Tomorrow night we can leave on our journey," he said. "We'll travel about twelve or fifteen kilometers to a location where the men and one of our wagons will be joining us. The two women will be able to ride for a while. From that point, we'll take the wagon in the direction of Breznik as far as we can until the terrain prevents it from continuing. Before we arrive at the border of Yugoslavia, one of our men will take the wagon back to our camp. After that, the terrain will get rugged. We'll continue on foot. We'll have to avoid the Bulgarian border guards, of course. We'll hide in the brush and

descend a kilometer or so where we'll cross into Yugoslavia."

Later that morning, when the rabbi came to the synagogue, I told him the news about our departure. Together,
we walked to his home. There was luggage everywhere.
I explained sternly, "You will only be able to take what
is absolutely necessary. Select wisely. No one is going to
carry your belongings for you. Here are your flour sacks to
pack. Be at the synagogue, ready to travel, at six o'clock
tomorrow night." Then I left, accompanied by the rabbi,
and returned to the synagogue.

That afternoon, several Gypsies came to explain in
detail the next part of the journey. None of them spoke
French, and neither the rabbi nor Andre was there. One
of the men pulled out a map and, using gestures, made
himself understood. Once in Yugoslavia, we would walk
about two hundred kilometers through the mountains
to Pristina, where some kind of vehicle would be waiting. Optimistically, at about twenty kilometers a day, that
leg of the journey should take about ten days, I figured
as I considered the terrain.

The moment of departure arrived. We were all gathered at the synagogue, bundled up and ready to leave:
the family, Andre, and I.

"Good-bye my friend," the rabbi said to me. "May
God protect you." Then he said good-bye to the family.
I explained to them that the first stop would be between
twelve and fifteen kilometers from Sofia where we would
be met by the wagon. We left the city on foot. All too
soon, the walking became difficult for the wife. I was

looking forward to finding the Gypsy wagon. It was hard to watch her suffer.

How was she going to do it? How would I ever convince her husband to leave her behind if she couldn't continue? What other option did I have? I decided I just wouldn't focus on any of that right now. I trudged on in silence, keeping my own counsel and suppressing my doubts.

Before leaving England, Mr. Churchill had advised me, "If the scientist still refuses to take the plane, I suggest you walk through Yugoslavia to Trieste, then cross northern Italy into the Basses-Alpes of France." He added nostalgically, "When you arrive in France, say hello to my home away from home in the distance, on the Mediterranean. You'll be my guest on the Côte d'Azur when we return at the end of this war." He had such a love for France. Returning to the task at hand, he instructed, "You'll cross the Basses-Alpes, which you know like the back of your hand, continue through France and Andorra where the Pyrénées are not quite as high, and then enter Spain. If they accept, the Gypsies will be your guides until you reach the Pyrénées, near the Spanish border. After that, only one Gypsy will remain with you, Andre. He'll be accompanying you back to England."

About six hours later, we met the wagon. The older woman had needed to rest a lot. Six Gypsies had set up camp while awaiting our arrival. They were gathered around a campfire. The two women and the boy immediately climbed into the wagon, but the energetic little one kept jumping in and out all night long. As it turned out, he was frenetic the entire trip. Although he was aggravating, I let him be as long as he was quiet, spoiled brat that he was.

We headed toward Breznik. It was almost daybreak when we arrived. At that time, the wagon and six Gypsies left us, and other Gypsies replaced them. We hid for the day and continued our journey that night, hiding in the brush along the Bulgarian border so as not to be detected. About a kilometer beyond the guard post, we began crossing into Yugoslavia. At that point, the mountains were about twenty-one hundred meters high. We were guided through a pass to a farmhouse where we could eat, sleep, and rest for the day.

Our next destination was Pristina. When we arrived, there was a truck to take us as far as Titograd, around 200 kilometers over bad roads filled with potholes. At that point, the mountains were much too rugged for the family to climb on foot, a reality the King understood. We continued by bus to Dubrovnik, another 150 kilometers. We arrived at night and went straight to the docks where a Gypsy was waiting with a message.

He spoke to Andre, who translated for me. "The plans have been changed. We've received orders from London that we are not to go through Italy. You will hide on two Turkish tugboats and, under the guise of helping an Italian ship in trouble off the coast of Yugoslavia in Korcula, you will take the group to the port of

Blato, Korcula. There, you will join up with the ship and resume the voyage. You'll refuel in Reggio, on the boot of Italy, and then continue up the west coast to La Spezia, where the ship will be put in dry dock." When the man finished talking, Andre explained the new plan in more detail and answered my questions.

The trip to La Spezia took about three days. It was an unpleasant journey because we had to stay in the hold behind the fuel tanks where it was filthy and foul-smelling. The family and I stayed in one tug, and the rest of the group stayed in the other. That little boy put up a fuss several times, but at least the noise couldn't alert the enemy while we were on the boat, so I didn't say anything.

Upon our arrival in La Spezia, we learned that the ship was too large to be put into dry dock. We would have to go to Genoa where the port could accommodate her. When we docked, there was an ambulance waiting for us. It was driven and escorted by "Fascists," dressed in their all-black uniforms. One of them identified himself immediately to me as a member of the *maquisards*, the partisans.

"There has been a change in plan," he informed me. "We'll take you in the ambulance on the route to Mondovi. Before we arrive in Cuneo, an Italian doctor will join us. He'll be waiting at the side of the road just before we enter the city. The British are providing him passage to London." As we approached the city, we spotted the man. He quickly got into a car, and we continued on.

The ambulance was escorted by three "Fascist"

cars. The car in front had all the appropriate papers. The ambulance followed. The grandmother-to-be was instructed to lie down on the stretcher just in case anyone checked. Behind the ambulance were the other two "Fascist" cars. Two Gypsies, besides Andre, rode along in one of the cars.

In a little more than an hour, we arrived at the Col de Tende, a very arduous pass to drive because of all the hairpin turns going up one side and down the other. On the top of the pass is a tunnel that goes into France. Before the entrance to the tunnel, we confronted the Italian border guards. We had no problem with the Italians or with the French guards at the other side of the tunnel. A French ambulance met us, escorted by "French Militia," actually partisans dressed in the pro–Nazi Militia uniforms. They transferred the "patient," the family, Andre, and me to the large ambulance, and the rest of the group climbed into a black and green "militia" bus and a black Citroën car. We continued along the pass and arrived in the village of Allos. From there, we took the road toward Saint-Martin-Vesubie, where we picked up provisions and then went to the gas station on the outskirts to fill up the vehicles and use the bathrooms. One of the "militia" stayed behind at the gas station, and the caravan headed toward Draguignan.

After several hours on the road, the caravan arrived in Draguignan, where it was stopped by a militiaman who turned out to be a partisan. He asked to speak to me.

"We must change the plans," he explained to me. "Go to the *gendarmerie* in Brignoles, about a half hour's drive from here, and ask for Victor Bonelli." I knew of him, as did everyone deeply involved in the fight against the Germans. Victor, a Corsican, worked closely with the anti-Nazi gendarmes of France who were fighting on the side of the Resistance.

As per instructions, we stopped in Brignoles. A man approached the ambulance and asked that Michel Carbonell step out. I got out to talk to him.

"Carbonell, I am Victor Bonelli," he said. "You have a spy in your group, the doctor. You need to get rid of him before you cross the Spanish border."

I nodded and replied, "Bonelli, you know this region better than I. Where would be a good place?"

He thought for a moment. "When you cross the bridge over the Rhône River near Istres, it should be around midnight. That will be a good time and location for you to take care of the matter. I'll have two men on motorcycles following you just in case any problems arise. Do you have any arms on you?" he asked.

"No, my instructions were to carry no weapons."

"I'll get something for you. Wait here." Victor returned minutes later with a hunting knife. "You can use this," he said as he handed me the knife. "Afterward, you can use it for a razor," he added, alluding to the razor-sharp blade. I walked over to the lead vehicle and told the driver to stop when we reached the bridge. Then I climbed back into the ambulance.

It was past midnight when we approached the bridge.

The bus stopped, as did the ambulance, the Citroën behind, and the two gendarmes on motorcycles. I got out and went to the bus. The two "militia" got out, as did the doctor.

I asked the two partisans, "Would you mind leaving me alone with the doctor for a few minutes? I need to talk to him in private." Without a word, they left us. After distancing ourselves from the vehicles, I asked the doctor, "Do you know how to swim?"

"No, I don't. But why are you asking me such a question?"

"If you don't know how to swim, I am going to help you learn." I took his cap off and tossed it into the Rhône, grabbed a fistful of hair, turned him toward the river, and stepped behind him. The doctor started screaming. I leaned him over the railing, and said, "This is your first and last swimming lesson." I slit his throat easily with the well-sharpened blade, waited over a minute to be sure he was dead, and then pushed him into the river.

That was the second man I killed, and I did it with no hesitation. My training had been effective. The two gendarmes were waiting nearby to make sure everything went well.

"We don't know what information the doctor passed on," one of them said, "so the plans have to be changed again. You are to go to Narbonne and then on to Perpignan. We will leave you now, but you'll be provided an escort who will accompany you from Perpignan to the foot of the Pyrénées at the border of Andorra. The three of us returned to the caravan. I got into the ambulance, and we continued on toward Narbonne, followed by the gendarmes, who left soon thereafter to return to Brignoles.

A few kilometers down the road, the ambulance pulled over, and the caravan stopped. Andre, who had been seated next to the ambulance driver, opened the back door and asked me to come out.

"One of my men has to leave us now to take a bus back to the Camargues," he said. I nodded in agreement, and he walked over to the Citroën. The Gypsy got out and waved us farewell. Andre and I got back into the ambulance, and the caravan started up again.

We avoided Perpignan because it was too big. The larger the population of an area, the more likely we were to encounter French Militia. We took the road toward Prades. I noticed that two new gendarmes were behind us. I knocked hard on the partition between the back of the ambulance and the cab. The driver stopped. Andre came back to find out what I wanted. "Tell the driver to stop at the main square in Prades."

When we arrived, I got out and went up to the gendarmes to ask if they knew the hotels nearby. We could always trust the gendarmes.

"Of course," one replied. "There are several."

"Well, let's start with the closest one," I said. "There is a man waiting in the lobby of one of them close to the square whose name is Claude Marron. He will have let the manager know that he is waiting for someone. Once you find him, ask him where he was born. If he says 'Casablanca,' put handcuffs on him. That means he's in danger and cannot talk there. If he says 'Marrakesh,' that means all is well. I need you to bring him to the bus." They nodded and left. The gendarmes had told me to contact this man.

Soon after, I saw them returning with a man, headed toward the bus. The man with them wore no handcuffs. That was good. I was waiting and watching beside the ambulance. When I saw them approaching, I quickly hid behind the ambulance so that Marron would not know what I looked like.

"Andre, tell the two *maquisards* to get out and tell them privately to ask Marron what his profession is and where he lives. If he answers that he is from Nîmes and owns the Hôtel Cheval Blanc, all is well. If not, let me know and I'll decide what to do."

All was in good order, so we could safely move on. These precautions were necessary because the German Fifth Column, the Gestapo, had infiltrated everywhere. Marron would let Churchill know where we were on our route and estimate the amount of time necessary to arrive at our final destination. There were other "Claude Marrons" stationed in different towns.

We left and headed for Ax, which we passed a couple of hours later. We then continued on until we reached a farm at the foot of the Pyrénées. Partisans directed us to the barn where we were all to stay. We shared the barn with at least fifty cows. While everyone took turns going to the outhouse, the partisans went to the farmhouse and returned with cheese, Bayonne ham, fresh-baked bread, wine, milk, and water. Everyone was hungry and tired. Daylight was breaking when we went to sleep. A large group of partisans guarded the barn while we slept.

The Pyrénées were only about eleven hundred meters high at the point where we were to begin the climb on foot. But already there was a lot of snow. It was the beginning of November, and not only was it very cold, but the wind was whipping, howling, and gusting as well. We would have to pass under the noses not only of the French patrols but also past Spanish and possibly German patrols. The partisans knew the approximate circuits and routines of the patrols and wanted to leave at 11 P.M., but the family was completely exhausted. I knew how grueling the trip was going to be, so I worked it out to leave at 4 A.M. That would give the family more time to rest. The small paths we were going to take were those used by smugglers going to and from Andorra. The journey would be very difficult for those who didn't know how to climb, but there was simply no other choice.

"Everyone, wake up," I called out. It was after 3 A.M. "Dress warmly. The wind hasn't let up." I waited for them at the foot of the mountain. "We'll walk single file. Monsieur, follow this man, and lead your family. I'll walk behind them," I told the scientist. We successfully got past the French patrol units and had the good fortune to come upon an abandoned farm where we ate and rested till night.

About 11 P.M., we headed out again. The paths were covered with ice and snow. The weather worsened, and the mountains got steeper. I attached everyone with a long rope so that no one would get lost. When some-one stopped, we all stopped. What made it even more difficult was the number of ascents and descents. They seemed never ending. To those with experience, this posed no problem. My fitness saved me, but the physical draw-backs and the inexperience of the family members made it more dangerous for us all. We climbed this type of terrain for two days or more. At its end, we found a huge boulder and a cluster of trees under which we could hide and sleep.

Night arrived. "Everybody up, it's nine thirty and time to leave," I announced. The family had been fairly good about not grumbling and had followed directions the entire trip. If they did complain, it was in Bulgar-ian and remained only among themselves. The boy had caused several minor problems, but I just ignored him as best I could.

We commenced the trek again. After a short while, we heard the sound of dogs in the distance. This was not good. I figured it was probably a German patrol that had picked up our scent because it was unlikely that the French patrols would have dogs.

"We need to move more quickly," I encouraged, and they all made an effort. At that inopportune moment, the pregnant girl's water broke. The partisans, being well prepared, began spreading cayenne pepper all around because this would numb the dogs' sense of smell. "We cannot stop, continue on," I insisted.

After another hour or so, the mother-to-be began to moan and shake uncontrollably. There was no choice.

"Everyone, stop. I'll deliver the baby, and then we must move on quickly. Spread some jackets out over here on the snow," I told some partisans. "Lie down on the jackets," I told the girl. Her parents helped her lie down. I could see the baby's head already. "Hold her down," I told the partisans while I brought the baby into this world under these strange circumstances.

The child slipped out quickly, not knowing what he was getting himself into. The mother and I worked well together. She was thrilled that he was a boy. I cut a piece of my shoelace to tie off the umbilical cord. I took my shirt off, wrapped the baby in it, and put him on my chest. I put my jacket on again and closed him inside.

"I need a big piece of your slip," I told the new grandmother. She came next to me, and I took what I needed. I stuffed the cloth in the mother's vagina. "Get up now," I told the new mother. "We must leave right away."

She didn't complain at all as I helped her to her feet. The partisans spread more cayenne pepper all over the area of the birth, picked up their wet jackets and we left immediately. We could still hear the dogs barking.

I was covered with blood and there was no way I could clean up the baby or myself. What a mess! The air was frigid, and the wind, icy. I was afraid the baby would catch cold. He was crying. Of course, he wanted to nurse. I could feel him shivering. My body heat did not seem to keep him warm enough.

Everyone was thirsty. "I know it's tempting, but do not eat the snow to quench your thirst," I told them. "It will only irritate your tongues and make them swell." We needed water. But to have water, we needed to make a fire. To make a fire, we needed dry wood. In any case, we could not make a fire right under the nose of the enemy. "Bear with the thirst and stay strong," I told them. "People don't die of thirst during the winter," I invented.

The baby was screaming for nourishment. We had to stop. I handed him over to his mother. She put the child to her breast, but he kept screaming. I said to her, "Hand me your baby." She did as I said. I then passed the boy to the grandmother. I took the girl's right breast in my hand and pulled on the nipple with my thumb and two fingers. It was as I thought. I felt a waxy substance that was blocking the flow of milk. I had seen the same thing happen to dogs, cows, and horses. I put the large nipple in my mouth. I sucked hard and spit out the wax. I could see that she was stunned. Her mother looked horrified, but no one uttered a word. I then took the other breast and sucked the wax coating off. I took the baby from the grandmother and handed him to his mother. The baby tasted his mother's milk for the first time. Everyone was grateful for the quiet.

All was silent—too silent. There was no more screaming, true, but it was eerily quiet owing to the absence of the dogs barking. Apparently, the Germans had lost our trail. That was excellent news, if true.

Fifteen minutes later, we began a long, difficult descent with the snow at waist level. Then it began to rain. Being so cold, the rain turned to sleet. We walked the rest of the night, but by morning the snow was becoming very wet and slippery.

"It's too dangerous to continue. Let's stop here under these protruding rocks and trees and rest for a while," I instructed.

The baby wanted milk, it seemed, every half hour. Everyone felt the cold more since we weren't moving. Of course, the soles of everyone's climbing boots were paper thin. My right sole was attached only at the heel and the shoe had only part of a shoelace. I had wrapped the front of the shoe with wire to keep it closed. I was really fortunate that I didn't get frostbite.

After about twenty minutes, the weather cleared. "Now the sleet has stopped, let's move on," I said. We didn't stop for the next four hours.

"Soon we'll arrive at a clearing where there is a cabin," a partisan told me. About a kilometer later, we spotted what appeared to be a cabin in the distance that was engulfed by snow. Everyone's pace picked up. When we arrived at the place, our hopes were answered. It *was* the cabin! The partisans dug a pathway to the door, opened it with some difficulty, and we all piled in.

We were packed like sardines, but that was all right. We were inside. The cabin was not well stocked. There was a pail made of zinc, a Spanish-style stove made of clay, a good number of potatoes and kernels of corn. The potatoes and corn were for the animals that were probably there during the summer. Happily, there was a good stock of wood behind the stove. The leader of the partisan group said that they had brought the dry wood to the cabin earlier in preparation for our eventual arrival. "Too bad you didn't stock it with food as well," I reflected in silence.

Now, we could heat the snow and have some water to drink. There were a few mess tins that the partisans passed around while I started the fire and began to melt the snow. I used the potatoes and corn and prepared an awful slop. Though it was not appetizing, it warmed everyone's insides.

The partisan in charge said, "Don't worry about any Germans coming here. They don't patrol this area. And don't be concerned about the Spaniards either. They are too sensitive to the cold to venture out this far."

The stove warmed the little room, and that was a welcome change for us all. There were about fifteen people in the group at this time. The new mother fed her baby again. We all filled our mess tins and ate. After the mother drank and ate, I said to her, "Take your baby behind the stove where the temperature is the warmest. I put a straw mattress there for you to lie down on." The two of them fell asleep immediately. The rest of the group lay down on the floor, and soon all were asleep with the exception of one *maquisard* who took the first watch.

* * *

In the middle of the night, something woke me up. A flash of light! I went to the door. The guard was asleep. Perhaps it was someone from the Spanish Guard. I woke our guard, then everyone else, and quickly explained what I had seen.

One of the partisans spoke Spanish and said, "Let me orchestrate this. I'll put some men behind the door. Carbonell, invite them in to protect themselves from the weather. If they don't understand French, I'll invite them to enter in Spanish." He told three of the men to take their submachine guns behind the door. I opened the door and shouted, "*Venez, venez,*" gesturing with my hand to come in.

There were indeed men approaching. They had skis that they leaned against the cabin as they arrived. One of them had a submachine gun and responded in French, "Send one unarmed person out of the cabin. If you don't, we'll begin shooting!" So I went out with my hands in the air. Since the man spoke with an accent, I decided to answer in Italian. "We have two women and one newborn child with us. We don't want any trouble. Come in and warm yourselves."

I understood they were French Basques after speaking with them for a short time. I convinced them to come in, but I entered first. To immediately ease everyone's mind and to avoid anyone pulling a trigger, I enthusiastically said, "We have a pleasant surprise. These three men are part of the Communist partisan group in the area of Perpignan. They're on their way back home." The truth was that they were smugglers, but no one needed to know. What was important was that they were no threat.

I took out my pipe and pouch of tobacco and lit up. A little wind was coming out of the north. It found its way into the cabin and blew the smoke throughout the room. Delicious odor! It was this benevolent wind that had blown the snow around and erased our tracks. What a wonderful moment this was! Relaxing, I puffed on my pipe, thoroughly content for this reprieve. The Germans were no longer on our trail. The mother and child were sleeping comfortably. Everyone was protected from the weather. Suddenly my feelings of relief were interrupted as the mother of the child began to cough. I quickly snuffed out my pipe.

The Basques left early, but we rested the entire day. The head of the partisans discussed the next leg of the journey with me. "A few hours from here," he said, "is a large sheep farm owned by a Basque woman who is strongly anti-Fascist. We need to climb another mountain and then descend into the adjacent valley where the farm is located. I am sure that she will let us stay a day or two. Her husband disappeared about nine months ago while on a trip to market to sell his sheep. The woman is sure that her husband was taken by the Spanish Fascists on his way to sell the animals."

I was certain, conversely, that the Franco police, the Fascists that the woman referred to, would not venture into this valley because they knew that most Basques were Communists. If they dared to travel through, especially during the harsh winter, they would most likely disappear for good. Her husband's disappearance was a puzzle.

Since there was no more danger from the Germans or from the French Militia in these mountains, and no threat from the Spanish, from this point on we could start traveling during the day. This was a relief to me and to the other partisans because it was so easy to lose someone at night. That is why we had used the cord so often during our long trek.

We rested all day, and our journey began again at sunrise. The day's climb was nothing for this group of hardy souls. I was very proud of them. Two and a half hours later, we arrived at the farm. This short day of travel was welcome to all. Our boots couldn't take much more wear.

"Welcome, welcome to all!" the Basque woman called out, greeting us warmly. Other partisans were waiting for us at the farm. "Go kill a sheep, and we'll prepare it together," she said to one of the *maquisards*. The sheep cooked slowly for the next six hours on a spit over an open flame, one partisan or another next to it the entire time, continually basting and turning it slightly. Everyone was willing to help with the task. When we sat down to eat, the Basque woman held the baby. The Bulgarian family spoke Spanish and had nice, long conversations with her during the meal and for the next three days.

During our stay, we mended our boots any way we could with anything we could find. The Basque woman helped us with the repairs. She couldn't do enough for us and provided a welcome rest for all. It was evident how much she enjoyed having the company. She must have been so lonely and tired, taking care of the farm all by herself, especially during the winter.

At dawn on the fourth day, we left to continue our climb, our boots, bodies, and spirits in much better condition. We walked on for days until we finally reached level ground near Torrente, a town southwest of Valencia. Even though no danger was expected, we still hid in the brush as we traveled. One could never be too cautious.

Suddenly, one of the partisans shouted, "Stop!" An instant later, we saw a bus approaching. A British flag flew on the driver's side.

"Safety, thank God!" I shouted deep within. I had been holding on to so much tension for so long. I could finally let go. The responsibility would now be on British shoulders. The journey had even started wearing on the scientist. He hadn't been looking good. All the while he seemed to be fading fast, I had kept saying to myself in mantralike repetition, "I have to get him to England alive." The family got into the bus that had come from the British Consulate in Lisbon. Andre and I climbed in after them. Once inside, we were all on "British soil." I was relieved to be home.

The family must have been grateful, but no one showed any emotion. The daughter and her father had been gems the entire trip, but the little boy had been such a demon and the wife had been a whiner, although she hadn't complained in French. The Gypsies and partisans had dealt with the boy most of the time. All was forgiven in that moment that I laid grateful eyes on the British flag. The partisans wished us well and left in the direction of Barcelona.

There were two drivers who took turns so that we would not have to stop, except for gas and to go to the bathroom. There was plenty of food and drink on the bus as we headed toward Madrid, where we stayed on the outskirts at a luxurious hotel. It all seemed surreal. We slept, ate, and departed in the morning on the road toward Trujillo, Spain, where we stayed the night. The following morning, a car arrived from the Portuguese Embassy. A doctor had come to examine the mother and child and determined that both were in good health.

The tension was gone, and we were all more relaxed. "Doctor, please join us for breakfast," I offered, after he completed the examination. The boy no longer annoyed me as much, as I didn't have to be concerned about being captured because of his antics. And the wife wasn't complaining. "How does the scientist put up with her, anyway?" I wondered, as we made our way to the dining room.

Immediately after breakfast, the wife, the daughter, and her child left with the doctor to drive directly to Lisbon. Soon after, the rest of us got into the bus. The British government was in a hurry to get this important man to London.

* * *

When we arrived at the British Embassy in Lisbon that evening, we walked through a large room filled with about a hundred beds, all occupied, to an examination room on the far side where we were all asked to remove our boots prior to being examined by a medical doctor. After the lengthy exam, we returned, barefoot, through the same room. By then, only about half the beds were occupied.

We went to the waiting room where the women of the family greeted us, along with the newest and youngest male member. They looked refreshed. We men then went to shower and get haircuts. Fresh, clean clothing was brought to us in the dormitory along with new shoes to put on. Now, only about twenty beds were occupied. I asked one of the employees where all the former occupants had gone. "Two buses just left for Gibraltar," he told me.

We were all reunited in the waiting room. As we were talking, the British ambassador entered. He introduced himself and walked over to the scientist. "I welcome you and your family, sir, on behalf of Great Britain. Mr. Churchill has asked that I personally accompany you to the airport. You will be taking an airplane directly to London."

When we arrived at the airport, the ambassador escorted us to a private VIP room where we sat down to eat while we waited for the flight. One of his aides interrupted the meal. "Sir, there is an urgent telephone call for you." When the ambassador came back to the room, he told us what had happened.

"The British minister of aviation gave me bad news. The plane we were to take has been shot down. Mr. Churchill has requested an airplane from the Turkish government to pick your group up in Gibraltar. I'll arrange for a Portuguese plane to take you there. You'll wait a day or so in Gibraltar for a Turkish flight to London."

He stayed with us at the airport until our plane left Lisbon. When we arrived in the air space above Gibraltar, we had to circle about thirty minutes before we were able to land because the small airport was extremely busy. We were greeted by the governor as we disembarked. He nodded to me in recognition. I had met him before with Josephine when she had driven with me to Gibraltar for my extraction by plane back to England. The governor asked the scientist and me to join him in his limousine, and everyone else got into the car waiting behind the limo.

"Sir, it is a pleasure to meet you," he said to the scientist. "My wife and I will have a dinner in your honor this evening. We would like you and your family to stay with us at the governor's mansion while you're in Gibraltar."

As we all entered his home, the governor's wife welcomed us. Because it was late, we were shown directly into the formal dining room where a lavish table was set. "Everyone, please begin without us," the ambassador said, as he indicated I should come with him. "We have a few minutes' business we must take care of before we join you."

We walked to his study. "Welcome back, monsieur. How is our charming Josephine?" he asked.

"Sir, I have not had the pleasure of talking to her for quite a while."

"Please send regards from my wife and me when you speak to her, won't you? Now, to the business at hand," he continued. "Mr. Churchill asked me to call as soon as your group arrived safely at the mansion. Please sit down." He dialed and was able to get through to the prime minister right away. He gave me a bewildered look. Apparently, Mr. Churchill was speaking to him assuming it was me. The governor interrupted him to let him know that he was going to put me on. "*Monsieur, prenez le téléphone,*" he said, as he handed me the receiver.

"*C'est vous, Marc?*" Mr. Churchill asked.

"*Oui, monsieur, c'est moi,*" I replied. It felt so good to hear his voice again.

"Was your mission accomplished without any great mishap?"

"There was only one," I said, "but I couldn't call it a mishap. I have an extra traveler."

Churchill burst out laughing, "So I heard, so I heard. And how is the little urchin?"

"He's in excellent health. He's a strong little boy."

Changing the subject, he said, "Let me explain what will happen next. As you already know, a Turkish plane will pick you up in Gibraltar and bring you to England. I am going to send three Spitfires to protect you when you enter British air space to make sure that you arrive safely. We will direct your plane to the private airfield at the base where you sometimes stay. That night, everyone will stay at the base *except you*. We'll bring the scientist to London the next day where he'll begin his work immediately. Andre will accompany him.

"I congratulate you. Another job well done, *mon petit!* I fully expect that England will be safe from missile attacks. On another note, it is urgent that you come directly to my country home."

I thought, *Aha, another mission.*

But he totally surprised me when he said, "You'll spend the Christmas holiday with my family and close friends. We have only two days left till Christmas, and we must get to work on getting some game on the dining table. You and I must take good care of our guests, mustn't we? My car will be waiting for you at the airfield. Ask to see me as soon as you arrive."

TWENTY-ONE

Christmas with Churchill

I was extremely touched by Mr. Churchill's invitation to spend the holiday with him. I knew we'd be going hunting and riding, and I thought of it with great anticipation. Then my thoughts traveled to Christmases past. A "family" Christmas—I had never experienced a family Christmas. My father had never permitted it. I ached inside as I remembered how much I loved my mother and had wanted to spend Christmas with her—or any time for that matter. But my father forbade all contact. I sometimes wondered why I couldn't have had a real family and a normal father.

Mr. Churchill didn't know that I had never had a family Christmas before. In fact, my father didn't believe in *any* holiday celebrations, let alone Christmas, with its heavy family and religious meanings. Even if he had, he certainly wouldn't have included me in any family celebrations. In any case, he didn't seem to believe in religion either, as he forbade my mother to go to church.

While I was locked up with the Jesuits for those seven years, I did celebrate Christmas but not with family. Usually three boys out of the twelve were left at the monastery over the holidays, two others and me. With our Jesuit teachers, we would decorate the monastery's sailboat with Christmas lights and take it for an annual outing off the coast of Nice. That was really fun, but it never replaced the family I didn't have.

When I arrived at the estate, the property was adorned with decorations of all colors on the house and on the bushes and trees. The chauffeur honked his horn and pulled up to the main entrance.

"Monsieur, come into the foyer. Mr. Churchill is expecting you," one of the servants said as he took my bag from the car. As I entered, the grand man was coming down the staircase from his bedroom. He was wearing a beige chenille robe, fluffy slippers, and a nightcap with a pom-pom on the end. I was astonished. There was no cigar between his lips. I couldn't remember ever seeing him without that cigar. He came bounding down the stairs, full of energy with a huge smile lighting up his face. He was coming down so fast that I was afraid he would fall. He was so adorable. I felt that he was the father I never had. It felt so good just to see him again.

When he reached the bottom of the stairs, he pulled

me into his arms and hugged me tight. "My boy, it is so good to see you," he said as he cradled me back and forth. That must have been a sight, my chin resting on top of his head. I was so moved by this show of affection, but it felt strange. The emotion I was used to feeling most of the time was anger. I asked myself what were emotions like this all about, anyway? Whatever they were, this warm hug and huge welcome felt extraordinary.

"Would you like some tea?" he asked, holding me out at arm's length for a quick inspection.

"No," I replied, "but I would like some ice cream, if you have any."

"Chocolate or vanilla?"

"Chocolate," I said, decisively. He sent the butler to the kitchen. I sat down in an office next to the entry, and Mr. Churchill left the room. When he came back, I was already finishing up the ice cream, and the hot tea was waiting for him on the tray along with a carafe of eggnog.

When he entered the room, he had a full bottle of whiskey in his hand. "We'll baptize this one together," he said. He asked the butler to pour the eggnog. "Not too full," he said. It seemed as though the butler was used to this because the spoon was already next to the glass, ready to stir the mixture. We drank the spiked eggnog together out of large cut-crystal glasses. He wasn't interested in the tea. "Let's go to sleep now," he said. "We must be ready to leave the house by five A.M., and it's already one."

The valet escorted me to my room. It was not the one

I usually stayed in. He opened the grand door for me to precede him and then, once in the room, opened the armoire. In it was a silk robe, a hunting outfit including boots and hat, a new uniform, two suits, a tuxedo, shoes, and all the accessories to go with them. He showed me the bathroom, in which I saw a chenille bathrobe and slippers and all the toiletries one could possibly think of. It was as if I had lived there for ten years already. "I think you'll find everything you need, monsieur," he said, and closed the door behind him.

Suddenly, I realized how exhausted I was. I took off my clothes, put on the nightgown that had been laid out for me, and slid into the turned-down bed. It felt oh so good to lie down.

Two and a half hours later, I was up and in the shower. I was downstairs just after 4 A.M., to be early, but Mr. Churchill was there ready and waiting with a thermos of café au lait. He smiled and said, "Good, I'm glad you're up early. Are you ready to go, Marc?"

"Oui, monsieur."

His two gamekeepers were waiting in the foyer, so we left right away. Four horses were saddled in front of the house. The gamekeepers mounted their horses, each taking six hunting dogs along. Then Mr. Churchill and I mounted our horses, ready for the hunt.

We hardly entered the forest when we saw a female boar, her four babies, and the male. He made his attack on me immediately. I was loaded up and ready, and shot him in the heart. One of the gamekeepers strung him up to a tree and disemboweled him. "Congratulations, that takes care of the big game," Mr. Churchill said with a smile. "Let's dismount and continue on foot."

The time went by quickly as we gathered the game for Christmas dinner. I shot two ducks, and the prime minister shot two pheasant and seven quail. On the way back, we picked up the horses and returned on horseback. We were home by ten o'clock. Breakfast was served upon our return. There is nothing like an English breakfast, especially at Mr. Churchill's home. We began with porridge and condensed milk, followed by double-thick rare lamb chops, veal liver, bacon and sausage served with sautéed potatoes and onions cooked to a golden brown, and croissants, which we dunked in our café au lait. It was good to be back "home."

After breakfast, he told me, "Go shower, and then we'll take some steam and discuss your recent mission. Afterward, I've arranged for massages."

After the steam and massage, I relaxed for the rest of the day, taking leisurely walks around the property. In the late afternoon, Mr. Churchill sent for me. "Come, we have something we must do." We climbed into the limousine. One of the servants came along with two huge bags of Christmas packages. "We'll distribute presents at some orphanages and hospitals. At least the children will have some momentary happiness."

When we returned home, we went to the library where a servant poured us each a "fine" Napoleon cognac. It was smooth as velvet on the throat. I lit my pipe, and

Mr. Churchill continued smoking his cigar. We relaxed and talked. The two of us had a light supper and went to bed rather early that evening.

Though I stayed at this country home many, many times, I rarely saw Mr. Churchill's wife, though I know she was often there. I mostly stayed in a section of the house that she didn't frequent. She seemed to like to maintain a low profile.

The next day, family and friends began arriving for Christmas dinner in the early evening. It was a black-tie affair. There were about twenty people at the table. I wasn't seated next to Mr. or Mrs. Churchill, who were the only ones at the table who spoke French. No one spoke Italian or German either. I, more or less, just observed the party. I watched the guests as they enjoyed themselves.

The dinner was delicious. Mr. Churchill had a fine cook in the kitchen and had developed a French palate, so there was nothing at all bland about the meal. We started with a madrilene, a cold tomato consommé. Then the wonderful fresh game was served accompanied by potatoes Champs-Élysees, which is sautéed potatoes layered with black and white truffles. Salad was then served, a combination of watercress and Belgian endives in a hazelnut oil and lemon dressing. The meal was completed with English trifle for dessert.

After-dinner drinks and coffee were served in the salon while presents were handed out. Mr. Churchill got up and walked in my direction. He reached into his vest pocket and pulled out a small satin pouch that he handed to me. He said, "It isn't much, just a sign of affection." On the outside was written Van Cleef & Arpels. I opened it and pulled out a lovely pocket watch. I felt awkward. I had never received a Christmas present before. Besides that, I had nothing to give him in return. *"Merci, monsieur,"* I said, not knowing exactly what to say.

I watched as everyone opened their presents. Not understanding English, I felt like an outsider. Then it dawned on me—I *was* an outsider. I didn't quite feel as if I belonged in a family. Such thoughts made me uneasy. Wanting to escape my malaise, I went over to Mr. and Mrs. Churchill. "Thank you for the lovely dinner," I said, and excused myself from the party. *"Joyeux Noël."*

The next morning, the horses were ready, and off we went for hours through the forest and around the small lakes. It was just the two of us—Mr. Churchill and me. I felt exhilarated and renewed as the cool wind blew in my face. We raced along, passing sweet little houses, scattered here and there, with their roofs of straw. I told myself it didn't matter if I didn't have a real family. But I was only protecting myself from the unidentified feelings of the night before. I had to keep my mind on what my life now involved. We were going to free France. We were going to save the Jews and the Gypsies from being slaughtered. We were going to rid the world of the Nazi infestation.

Thinking like this, I suddenly wanted to get back to Europe. Not wanting to wait as usual for Mr. Churchill to take the initiative, I planned to ask about my next assignment as soon as the time felt right.

My inner strength and sangfroid were restored as we flew across the picturesque countryside. I would never forget that Christmas with Mr. Churchill.

TWENTY-TWO

Paying the French Communists

A few days later, when we returned hungry from our exhilarating morning ride, another sumptuous breakfast was in store for us. Mr. Churchill was in a very good humor. The U.S. entry into the war had buoyed his spirits. For so long he had worked and dreamed of it, and now the moment was here. He sensed the impending shift in the war that would surely occur in the new year. He was certain that the change in the balance of power would manifest just as it had when the Americans had entered the world war in 1917. I had seen him burdened in the earliest days when England was alone in the tense and grim Battle of Britain. That was when I first joined him, the summer of 1940, only eighteen months earlier. That now seemed like ancient history because so much living, dying, and danger had been crammed into the intervening period. Now this great man seemed not just happy but jolly, just like Father Christmas.

"I must tell you something that happened a while back, Marc. My friend Baruch was visiting me. My valet was serving us breakfast, and he tripped. The tray flew and landed in the chest of my friend. My valet didn't know what to do. He was so embarrassed and horrified that he couldn't move. My friend took it well. He reached into his pocket and took out his wallet and handed my valet a large sum of money and said, 'I am only giving you this much money because the next time, you mustn't miss my pants. If you succeed next time, I'll double the amount.' The look on my valet's face was priceless. Baruch broke out in laughter so hard that my valet started to laugh as well. Then I burst out laughing, too. There we were, the three of us, almost rolling on the floor. When we finally got ourselves under control, Baruch said to my valet, 'You know, you're a good man. Why don't you come spend the holidays with me in South Carolina.' He was quite an exceptional man, my friend Baruch." As he told the story, I experienced so much pleasure seeing him relaxed, his face radiant with joy—for the moment not stressed by his war responsibilities.

"I have another story about Baruch," he said, obviously enjoying reminiscing about the man. "One night, we stayed at one of your father's clubs till around five in the morning. Then we left to go to the Casino to gamble. After a couple of hours, Baruch left to get some sleep, but I was feeling lucky, and I stayed. I wound up winning a lot of money, so I stopped at Van Cleef & Arpels and bought him a watch similar to the one I bought for you, but I had time to get his engraved. After that, I went back to the hotel. Baruch is a good friend. He's given me a lot of sound financial advice. He has a great sense of humor and likes to joke around like you do. He sometimes calls me 'the King of Nitrates of Chile.'" He laughed. "Before he left to go back to the United States, I picked up the pocket watch to give him. What it said was, 'To the best friend in the world,' and he has been a dear friend." He nodded and smiled for emphasis, appreciating the memories, then resumed talking.

"Well, you've let me go on and on. Did you enjoy our little ride this morning?"

"Very much, but I'm ready to get back to work. Do you have something in mind for me?"

"As a matter of fact, I do," he responded with a smile. "I thought you might want some extra time off. That was quite a walk you took, after all," he said, with that twinkle in his eye.

"I can be ready to leave at a moment's notice," I responded, anxious to get something positive accomplished.

"I do have some funds that I need you to personally deliver to someone who will get it to the Communist partisan group for us. But I want you to take off some more time until after the New Year. A little more rest won't do you any harm, *mon petit*. When the time is right, I'll have my secretary fill you in on all the details.

Now let's go clean up. Then I'll take a little snooze, and you do as you like."

A couple of weeks later, I was on my way back to Europe. To avoid detection, we were flying very low into France in a light German airplane that had swastikas painted on the wings. After we left England, I had handed the pilot the written flight plan from Mr. Churchill. He spoke English only, but the copilot spoke German and French. If they were intercepted on the radio by Germans, the copilot would say they were on a secret observation mission.

I was readying myself to make the jump into a long valley located between Sisteron and Carpentras, a region I knew very well. It was an isolated area, far from any roads, villages, or farms. As I awaited the signal, I made sure my overcoat was well fastened. It was a critical piece of clothing. Now came the signal! I jumped into the dark, cold night.

It was an easy jump into an alfalfa field surrounded with rocks that had been cleared by the farmer while plowing. After landing, I unhooked myself from the chute and buried it under a small boulder. The pilot immediately headed in the direction of the Mediterranean Sea to fly to the military base in Gibraltar to refuel. He was not allowed radio contact until he neared Gibraltar. At that time, he would send a coded message so they would know he was not the enemy.

This valley brought back memories. When I was a student at the Athenium in Nice, the Jesuits brought me here for wilderness training. Armed only with a hunting knife, I had to survive for three days with a loaf of rye bread, a small piece of cheese, an onion, and a half liter of water. I learned then that there were a lot of streams and natural springs in the area.

Three million francs had been given to me to personally deliver to a certain policeman who would pass it on to the PPF, the Parti Populaire Français, the Communist partisans who were stationed in the Basses-Alpes. The money was well placed and well deserved, for the group was united with all the other partisans and England in one common cause—to harass and kill the enemy and create as much confusion and turmoil as possible.

I began the forty-kilometer trek to Sisteron, where I was to go to the *gendarmerie* located in the center of town. I had to remind myself to walk slowly in keeping with my cover. I figured the walk would take about twelve hours. That meant I should arrive in Sisteron about 3 P.M.

I was disguised as a very poor, sick man wearing worn and dirty wool clothes—brown pants, a long-sleeved beige shirt, a faded jacket, an old brown overcoat, a Russian sock on the left foot and none on the right, and oversized old brown shoes. I had a yellow Star of David sewn onto the pocket of my jacket and on my coat. Embroidered across the star was the word *Juif.*

* * *

That afternoon, I entered the two-story governmental building that had a tiled roof typical of the region. There was a sergeant sitting on the left at his desk.

"May I see Sergeant Decoste?" I asked.

"What is the purpose of your visit?"

"Some of his friends asked me to come to see him. They told me I could always find him in his office at the end of the week."

My instructions had been to come to see Sergeant Decoste either Saturday at his office or Sunday at his house. It was Saturday.

"He happens to be sick today. If you want to see him, you can find him at home."

"But I don't know where he lives."

"Just follow this street past the church, then pass the main square, and you'll find his house right there on the corner."

I arrived at Decoste's home and knocked at the door.

"Hello, monsieur. What may I do for you?" Madame Decoste asked politely.

"*Bonjour, madame*. Excuse me for disturbing you. I know your husband is ill, but the sergeant at the *gendarmerie* suggested I come to your home to talk with him, as it is rather urgent."

She called out to him, and he came to the door. His wife disappeared and left the two of us alone.

"What may I do for you, monsieur?"

"*Savez-vous qu'il pleut en Allemagne au printemps?*"

He replied correctly, "Yes, I know it rains in Germany during the spring, and it also rains in France. Go out to the garden and around the house and back toward the street. You'll find a wood door. Open it, and go down to the cellar. I'll meet you there."

Sergeant Decoste had an olive complexion and wore a handlebar mustache. He joined me as I was descending the stairs.

"Do you have a coat for me?" he asked.

"I have your coat," I said. Once in the cellar, I took off my overcoat and handed it to him. Decoste went outside and called for his wife to come down. He handed her the coat and asked her to remove the Star of David from the brown one and sew it onto the old navy blue overcoat he had brought from the police department. Madame Decoste brought the coat upstairs to do the work while we sat down at a small table to talk.

"Sergeant, someone from the PPF will pick up the coat in a few days." He must have questioned the significance of the coat, but I didn't mention that there were three million francs sewn into its lining, which was made of newspaper and cloth, effectively hiding the sound of crackling franc notes. He offered me a glass of wine, some goat cheese, and fresh bread. The bread was a treat for me. I could never get bread often enough. While partaking of this small feast, I explained that the coat with the Jewish star was part of my cover. I was posing as a man with tuberculosis on his way to a camp for Jews where his illness could be treated. The camp was in the vicinity of Avignon, and I had a letter from the Gestapo—forged, of course—explaining my condition and destination.

Decoste commented, "Who but the English would think of hiding a spy behind a Jewish star?"

I carried the letter written in German as well as my normal papers that identified me as Michel Carbonell. My picture was in the upper left corner and embossed on it was the Nazi swastika so there could be no chance of forgery.

"Is there something else I can do?" he asked.

"Yes. Will you handcuff me and take me to the train station and hand me over to the *chef de gare* personally so all appears to be in good order?"

"No, I am truly too ill, but I can call the police station and ask for another officer to pick you up and take you to the train station in Nice."

About a half hour later, his wife came down and handed me the blue coat without saying a word. Shortly after, I was picked up by a gendarme who handcuffed me and led me to the police car. It was almost 5 P.M. Across the street, a group of locals was playing *boules* (bocce ball) on a flat, hard dirt surface in front of the church. When they saw the officer putting me into the backseat of the car, one of the men shouted, "Look, look. They've arrested another Jew."

The policeman put the car in gear, but before leaving, Decoste shouted to him, "Stop. Come over here!" The young man put on the hand brake, got out, and headed toward the front door to find out what the sergeant wanted. Decoste handed his younger colleague a paper bag to give me. When he returned, he handed me the bag.

It took a few hours to drive to Nice. The gendarme removed the handcuffs and delivered me to the station-master, who then turned me over to the German police. As Carbonell, sick with tuberculosis, I was coughing and doubled over in pain. Not asking me for any identifi-cation whatsoever, speaking French, they told me to sit down on the bench. The stationmaster was very kind and told me that he would ask another railroad worker to find a cattle car that had straw on the floor to make me a little more comfortable on my trip to Avignon.

The train arrived. The weather was cold and rainy. Two German officers approached and said, *"Identité, s'il vous plaît."* I coughed as I handed them the letter. They took their time reading it, and then one of them turned to face me. He addressed me gruffly in German. "I have some questions to ask, and I want the truth."

Though I understood what he said, I replied, *"Je ne comprends pas,"* indicating that I didn't understand Ger-man.

The two continued looking at the letter and study-ing my identification papers. One was more sympathetic than the other. He said in German, "Oh, let him go. He's going to die anyway." The other reluctantly relented, and they gestured toward the railroad employee waiting next to the boxcar.

Irritated, the stern Nazi officer threw my letter on the ground. As I slowly bent over to pick it up, the man kicked me in the rear and said, *"Schwein!"* I stayed on the ground, went into a fit of coughing, and acted very sick.

As the Germans left, the railroad employee came over and helped me climb into the boxcar and closed the door behind me. I was alone in the car. I was grateful to be a Jew, in this instance. Second class, where I was not allowed to go as a Jew, was packed with people, many of whom would have to stand for the entire trip.

Here in the boxcar I had my own private compartment. It felt good to be alone. As I sat down on the floor of the cattle car, I opened the bag that Sergeant Decoste had given me. I found three apples, a chunk of hard goat cheese, and a piece of bread. *People can be so kind*, I thought, pleased to have something to eat.

I made myself comfortable in the dirty straw, lay down, and fell asleep. It seemed like only moments later the train came to a halt. This train was headed for Aix-en-Provence, where I had studied at the university. From there, I was to transfer to the train for Avignon. The stop was one of several on the way to Aix. The door opened and six men in tattered clothing climbed into the car. All had the yellow star sewn onto their wool coats. One closed the door and the train started up again. One of the men said to another, *"Savez-vous qu'il pleut en Allemagne au printemps, n'est-ce pas?"* There it was—the code phrase. The man did not respond. Apparently, they were waiting for me.

I responded appropriately, *"Je vais à Avignon dans le centre."*

That was the new code phrase. Codes were changed often to protect us from infiltrators.

I asked them, "How do you happen to be here?"

One answered, "We received a message that the Gestapo is waiting for you in Avignon. They know who you are. There's a leak. We don't know where it is, but we've developed an alternative plan. In three kilometers, there is a curve where the train must slow down. At that point, we'll jump off to the outer side of the curve so as not to be seen. There are bicycles waiting for all of us."

These were all men in their fifties and sixties devoted to freeing France. I really admired them. At the time, I was nineteen, strong and fearless.

It was a still night and very dark because there was no moon. The rain had stopped. We jumped off as the train slowed down and made our way toward the bushes, where we quickly found the bicycles. We pedaled for about four or five kilometers, passing through a small village. Once outside the village, one of the men said to me, "We'll leave our bikes here and continue on foot."

They arranged themselves in single file, and I was told to follow the man leading the group. We arrived at an intersection where there was a small hotel. There were five or six German military cars parked in front. That didn't stop them. The leader went around to the back, opened the back door, and entered. I followed him in, and the others followed me. The couple who owned the hotel must have been listening for us. They came back and told me that they were going to hide me behind the bar in back of four wine barrels, each about a meter or so in diameter.

"You must not move or make a sound until the Germans leave in the morning, *monsieur*." When no one was around, they motioned to me, and I lay down on the floor behind the barrels. They left me there. About ten minutes later, the woman returned with half a broiled rabbit, dark German-style bread, and a bottle of goat's milk. She said good night and left me to eat and sleep.

I slept on and off. I was kept awake by the noise that the drunken German soldiers were making just on the other side of the bar/restaurant. They were so close to where I was dozing. Strange, but it was only the elevated voices that were disturbing my sleep. For some reason, I felt safe.

I awoke to the smell of a cheese and mushroom omelette brought to me by the woman. She handed me the plate and a tall bottle of goat's milk. This was luxury. Eggs were a rare treat. But this was the countryside, and they were readily available.

"Monsieur, the German soldiers have left. Eat now. You must replenish your strength. There will be someone coming for you in an hour. Here is a straight razor and soap. Use the bar sink to wash and shave." She left momentarily and came back. "Here is a postman's uniform. Most important, here are new forged papers." This would be my new identity, a very good one, I might add. A uniform of any sort looks legitimate, for some reason.

I got ready, and an hour later into the restaurant walks a skinny young girl, maybe twelve years old. The girl had long brown hair and was with her little brother, who was about seven. I followed her out the front door where she got on her bicycle and helped her brother up onto the handlebars. I followed her on another bike, and she led me to the post office, and then to the head post-man who was standing behind the counter. He peered at me through the bars and said, "I'm counting on you to deliver all these letters, including this registered letter for the schoolteacher and this package for Monsieur the Mayor. Thank you for helping us out of this jam. Our mailman is sick today."

I didn't dare say anything because I didn't know if I could trust the man. I stepped away from the counter with the packed mailbag. My mind was eased when the little girl said, "My father is the mailman. He received orders from the *gendarmerie* to be sick today to help the Resistance. Don't worry. I know the route by heart. I'll take you to the farms and the school, but first we need to go to the mayor's house."

When we arrived, the maid opened the door and called for the mayor. He came to the door, greeted us, and asked me to come inside. The two children waited outdoors, and the maid was excused from the room. The mayor, originally from Nantes, told me that he had extremely important news that must reach England as soon as humanly possible.

He began, "One piece of information that I have is bad news for the French. Pierre Laval is returning to a position of power as prime minister of France, joining General Pétain in Vichy. As I'm sure you know, Pétain has been placating the Germans and doing his best to help France. Laval, on the other hand, is pro-Nazi and an anti-Semite as well. The Germans know that he will wholeheartedly collaborate with them to establish a system of forced labor that will expatriate French boys and girls to Germany, where their hands are needed in the German factories."

He shook his head in disgust, then continued, "The good news is that General Giraud has escaped from prison at Königstein. During his imprisonment, he organized a plan for the underground to create an insurrection in occupied France. Giraud will meet General de Lattre de Tassigny and General Frère first in Toulouse, then in Aix-en-Provence, followed by meetings in Grenoble, Vienne, and finally in Lyon to organize the partisans. In Lyon, these meetings will include the heads of large industry and many other civilians in positions of power as well as several important army officers, including General Chambe."

"Will you let the English know that General Giraud is in his hiding place in La Verpillière in the Isère department? The *gendarmerie* will be notified if he has any difficulties. Should he be in danger, they will be responsible for creating a diversion to keep him safe from the hands of General de Gaulle. De Gaulle is well aware that Churchill would prefer that Giraud were in charge of the French liberation army." Churchill disliked de Gaulle, and this was no secret.

"Giraud's next move is to meet the vice-consul, Constance Harvey, of the United States at a château in the vicinity of Lyon." Everyone knew that there was a certain friction between England and the United States. Any time there were English and American military in the same bar, a fight would break out. This was as true in Paris and Casablanca as it was in Singapore and Hong Kong. The only exceptions to this were the American and British air forces. They always seemed to be on the same wavelength.

After leaving the mayor's home, I followed the children on their father's postal route. We finished by noon and returned to the hotel. I changed back into my original disguise and returned everything else to the owners of the restaurant.

One of the men who had met me on the train was waiting at the hotel. "Is there anything else I can do for you?" he asked.

"Yes, there is," I answered. "Contact the group *Combat* and tell them to send a message to London that 'the Russian Sock' wants to come home immediately."

"I will," he said. He returned an hour later with a message. "You will be picked up tonight. I will show you the location. You will stay with me until the plane arrives." I waited at his home until the specified time of arrival. We went to the field, but no plane arrived that evening. We received word of the plane's rescheduled arrival place and time the following night.

At sundown next day, we left his house. He drove a small Berliet truck, fueled by a wood-burning furnace. We drove to a valley several kilometers from the village.

"There are about two hundred partisans hidden in the hills watching the roads for any intruders," he told me. There was a sliver of a moon. Otherwise, the night was black, and the skies were filled with dark clouds.

When we arrived, three piles of wood were prepared. They would be lit as soon as the sound of the airplane engine was heard. The plane was to arrive from Gibraltar.

A cable upon which a simple rope harness was attached was stretched between two trees in front of the leading woodpile, the triangle of the three forming the shape of an arrow. The pilot knew how low he had to come in, that he had to come in against the wind and reduce speed so that he could catch the steel cable onto which the harness was attached.

We heard the sound of the plane. I got into the harness, the fires were set and the airplane made its pass to grab me. Too high—the hook missed. The pilot circled and made another pass. With a painful jolt, I was airborne. The crew cranked me up to the door as the plane made its way back to safety. Once in Gibraltar, I was told that an English submarine was on its way to pick me up.

"No, that's not acceptable. I have an urgent message for Mr. Churchill, and I must get back immediately,"

I told them. So the plan was changed. A plane would pick me up later that day. Relieved, I thought how glad I was to have this significant information from the mayor to pass on to the English. Besides its importance to the cause, it had saved me from that awful confined trip on yet another submarine. This way I'd be at Mr. Churchill's and on a horse's back before I knew it.

TWENTY-THREE

Stealing a Submarine

I answered the knock on my door. "*Bonjour, monsieur*," Hughes said. "Mr. Churchill wants to see you in his office right away."

"Thank you, Hughes," I said as I left with him to go upstairs.

"Marc, in a few days you'll be flying to Malta. There, you'll get on a submarine that will take you to Cap Martin. An Italian submarine has been discovered, caught in a fishing net near the Italian-French border. I'll give you the phone number of the retired British agent who came upon this interesting information. Call him when you get there. He has lived in Cap Martin for several years now. He notified the British Consulate yesterday about the entrapped submarine, and they contacted me right away."

I couldn't seem to avoid these submarines. I'd deal with it somehow.

I arrived in Malta without incident and was driven to the harbor where the submarine was waiting. We left at night at surface level and plunged before daybreak. I truly did hate these English subs. They smelled of diesel and battery acid. Of course, it didn't help matters that I was more than slightly claustrophobic. I encouraged myself silently to just keep my purpose in mind, and I'd get through this challenge, too.

"Monsieur, we've resurfaced," one of the men came to tell me. "The commander wants you to meet him on the bridge." After two days of being submerged, it was wonderful to smell the fresh air again.

"We've arrived in the gulf of the Ligurian Sea," the commander said. "Take my binoculars. Directly in front of you are the lights of San Remo. To the left is Ventimiglia and to the left of Ventimiglia are Menton and Cap Martin. You will be transported by rubber boat to the coast. You'll signal me from there with a light when you are ready for us to pick you up. We will be watching for your signal."

I climbed the rocks where the boat dropped me off, and walked a few blocks to the Hôtel du Cap Martin from where I called the British agent. It was about four in the morning. He had been expecting me around one, but the trip had taken longer than expected. He gave me directions to his home, which was not far from the hotel.

"I am so pleased to meet you," he said animatedly. "Come in. Come in." I think he was very excited that his information was significant enough for England to act on it. The retired agent had a lovely little villa facing Menton-Garavan, well situated on a hill overlooking the harbor, with a view of the French-Italian border.

He began as I entered, "My friend is a fisherman from Alassio, a little city in Italy not very far from the French border. While checking his fishing nets a couple of days ago, his crewmen were unable to pull one of them up. It was stuck on something. When they dove down to try to get it loose, they discovered that the prop of a small submarine was tangled in their net. Apparently, the Italians had abandoned it because they could not get it free."

He went on and on in great detail, not even suggesting that I sit down. I finally just sat, at which time he realized that he had not even offered me a seat.

"Excuse me, monsieur, I didn't even offer you a seat or something to drink or eat. Would you like some coffee or tea or perhaps something stronger?" He hardly paused for a breath. "Let's see. I have ham, salami, goat cheese. That's all I have in the house. I eat all my meals out, you see. I live alone and find it easier that way. Why don't I open a bottle of champagne? I want to celebrate." Giving me no chance to answer, he took out a bottle of Veuve-Cliquot and popped the cork as he continued talking. He poured two glasses and toasted: "To our great success!" He must have forgotten about the food because nothing appeared.

He started posing some questions. He must have been surprised that I gave no answers, or perhaps he didn't notice. I brought the subject back to his friend, the fisherman.

"He's out fishing now. Then he'll go to the fish market in Monaco to sell his catch. He has his regular customers there and gets a good return on his efforts. After that, he'll come to meet us. He should be here by two o'clock this afternoon. In the meantime, if you like, we can go to the hotel to have breakfast after sunrise. I find it very convenient to live so close to the hotel. Would you like to take a little nap? I can put you in the room at the back of the house. That way, the sun won't wake you."

He continued, obviously beside himself with excitement, "Would you like another glass of champagne?"

"*Non, merci,*" I responded, and he poured another for himself and downed it quickly.

"I'm going to take a nap. Ta-ta," he said, and walked toward his room. "Make yourself at home."

I went to the guest room and lay down in bed. I didn't really sleep, but I dozed a little while listening to Radio Monte Carlo. I remember the Coco Cabaña Boys were singing on the radio. I got up and tried to organize the rest of the day in my head. I thought to myself, *The way to transport the small sub would be to attach it with chains to the side of the English sub. If we tow it behind, we risk losing control of it should the weather turn nasty.*

* * *

It was about eight thirty when the former agent came out of his room. I was sitting in the living room. "Let's go have breakfast," he said, obviously in good humor. We took the short walk to the hotel and went to the dining room. There were about a dozen people having breakfast when we entered. We found a table near the window, overlooking the Mediterranean. It was a glorious day, accompanied by the sweetest of sea breezes. The pines nearby were a rich green. The deep blue sky contrasting with the deeper blue of the sea was an extraordinary sight for my eyes.

The waiter came to the table to take our order. He faced the Englishman. "What may I get for you this morning, monsieur?"

"I'll have two eggs, sunny side up, with two pieces of toast and an order of sautéed chicken liver. I'll have a cup of tea, right away, as always."

"Of course, monsieur. And for you, monsieur?" he asked, as he turned toward me.

"I'll have three eggs scrambled with tomatoes, two *pistolets*, fresh orange juice, and a café au lait. Do you have orange marmalade from Seville?"

"Of course, monsieur. Will that be all?" I nodded, and the waiter left to place our order. He returned with the tea and café au lait. Fifteen minutes later, he brought our breakfast to the table. The only criticisms I had were the terrible coffee and the absence of butter. The so-called coffee was made of burnt grain, the new "specialty" of

France. During the war, coffee was a difficult commodity to come by.

When I finished breakfast, I was still hungry. "Waiter, will you bring me two more *pistolets*?" I asked. I excused myself to get away from the talkative man. "While you finish your breakfast, I'll take a walk," I said without giving him a chance to respond. "I'll be back shortly."

When I returned, he was waiting for me on the terrace. "I enjoyed my little walk. It is so beautiful here among the pines," I remarked.

"I signed for the breakfast," he said. "I have an account with them."

"Thank you, monsieur, I appreciate it."

"Let's go back home. I have some calls I need to make."

It was about ten thirty when we got to his house. I made myself comfortable on his terrace overlooking the harbor. After completing his telephone calls, he came out to the terrace.

"I'm going to go pick up my laundry. I'll be back in a jiffy." He took off at a good rate of speed on his bicycle. At the time, I thought he was very old, probably around seventy. He came back with two *flutes* (bread loaves about half the diameter of baguettes) and a small bag of real coffee.

"He must have noticed my reaction to the café au lait at breakfast," I mused to myself. "That was very kind of him."

"I'll make some sandwiches for lunch with a cup of real coffee," he said proudly. The phone rang.

"My friend will be here before three o'clock."

It started getting chilly on the terrace, so I went inside. Soon afterward, the fisherman arrived. He was a good-natured man, quite jovial, in fact. He had a package with him that he promptly opened on the kitchen table.

"Come take a look at these!" he said proudly, as he released the two fish from the package. I had never seen more beautiful mullet in my life.

"I'll prepare them if you like," I said. "I saw some capers in the cupboard, and I'll just need flour, parsley, and butter, if you can find any."

"That's sounds wonderful. I know where we can get what you need. We'll be back as soon as we can," the fisherman said.

"While you're away, I'll gut and scale the fish," I told them. I intended serving them with their tails in their mouths, a beautiful presentation I had learned as a boy with the Jesuits.

The two returned with everything I had requested plus an apricot tart for dessert. We had a lovely meal, and the fisherman recounted his tale of discovering the sub.

It was around eight thirty when we finished dinner. "We'll go to my fishing boat," he said, and explained to me the approximate location. I went out on the rocks of Cap Martin and signaled the commander. A sailor came for me in a rubber boat, and I returned to the submarine. We spotted the prow of the fishing boat, pale green in color, and we followed the fisherman to a spot where he dropped anchor. The commander hid the profile of the sub by putting it parallel to the coast to partially blend in.

"Three sailors and an engineer will dive with you," the commander told me. We put on wet suits, scuba gear, and oxygen tanks. I was anxious to take a look at the situation to see what we needed to do to steal the submarine. Two of the men carried battery-powered lamps. Just before diving in, the former English agent boarded the sub, eager to talk with the commander. The scene was comical. I saw the captain's reaction to this talkative, though sincere man. He left the agent alone on the bridge, saying, "Excuse me, sir. I must take care of something down below."

We used the fisherman's boat as a cover, just in case the coast guard came by. His men placed their wooden frame afloat on the sea. Should they see anyone approach, they would turn on the lanterns at each corner of the wood plank to pretend that they were fishing.

The submarine was larger than I had imagined, although it was only for two men. It was entangled in a fishing net that was supported by a stainless steel cable.

I found that the cable was wrapped around the prop several times. Now I understood why the Italians couldn't get it out. The water was very deep at this spot. When we released the sub from the cable and net, it would need to be attached to something. If not, it would sink below the level of possible recovery. At present it was between twenty-five and thirty meters below the surface.

Gesturing, I indicated for us to return to the surface.

I told the men, "The sub must be attached and secured before we free it. We will need to cut the cable with an acetylene torch. If we just try to tow it, we'll certainly have problems keeping it under control. Instead of attaching it to the side of the boat, as I pictured earlier today, I think we can secure it to the deck of your submarine with stainless steel chains. Afterward, we can work on untangling it from the net."

The four of them nodded in agreement, climbed back aboard the sub to retrieve what we needed, then dove down again. I was already on the minisub underwater, where I had checked the electric panel and found that the electricity was not working. When the engineer came back, I motioned that he should come over. He checked the panel and found only a little bit of life left in the battery. We needed to recharge the cells by connecting the generator of the English sub to the battery of the Italian sub. I showed him the plug, reminding him that the European plugs were different from the English. He was able to do the job by connecting bare wire to the back of the panel. We needed to get the battery working so that we could release some of the water from the ballast to allow the trapped submarine to rise up. Then we could maneuver the English sub underneath and attach the Italian sub to the aft of the deck. All went well as we worked away, taking breaks to resurface and take on new oxygen tanks. Six hours later the small Italian sub was secured to the deck of the English submarine.

Churchill was anxious to get the sub delivered to England as soon as possible so that the design could be duplicated. This was a suicide submarine, a torpedo submarine with all the guidance instrumentation on the top. England could use these two-man submarines for exploration or as suicide subs.

"I congratulate you on the ability of your men," I told the commander. We left immediately for Malta with the "small package" attached to the deck. From Malta, a military plane took me to Gibraltar and then on to Great Britain, where I returned to Mr. Churchill's estate, relieved that my submerged journey had been so short.

TWENTY-FOUR

The Bank Robbery

"We have a very delicate mission on our hands in Amsterdam," Mr. Churchill told me. "I don't have total confidence in the partisans involved owing, essentially, to the enormity and value of the fortune we will be recapturing. It is a temptation for most, I'm afraid. We will be repossessing containers of pillaged treasures. Our sources have determined that the boxes are filled with diamonds and other precious stones, thousands of kilos of gold and silver, and all forms of valuable jewelry and art that has been confiscated by the Nazis throughout Europe. The plunder is estimated to be worth millions of pounds sterling. It is too much to expect that no one will succumb to the temptation to make just a few cases disappear. Marc, we must be certain that each chest is counted and numbered. This will be your responsibility.

The agent going with you is our invaluable link to the city of Amsterdam. It is due to his connections in high places that we have the possibility of carrying out this mission. But don't mind him too much. He's a bit full of himself."

He continued, "We have reliable information that the Nazi officers involved will soon transfer the wealth to their individual accounts and vaults at banks somewhere in South America. We urgently need to take possession of these treasures and get them to England before the transfer.

"Of course, the substantial presence of Nazis in Amsterdam is a great threat to our mission. You must make sure that the local partisan military leader organizes several diversions that will totally preoccupy the German troops. We want to keep them away from the city's center. The military segment will be part of the same group of Dutch partisans that picks you up when you parachute in. You can have confidence in them."

He paused, his eyes fixed with a stern and troubled look. "Marc, I sincerely pray that one day the treasures can be returned to those from whom they have been stolen, but I know this is doubtful. Your mission is to supervise and make sure that all goes according to plan. I know you'll guard the treasures well. See my secretary tomorrow for the rest of the details, and return to us safely, *mon petit*. May God be with you." He pulled me into his arms.

* * *

Early the next morning, I went to see the secretary. "You'll leave for Amsterdam this evening," she announced. "You'll be traveling with another agent who has close connections with the Department of Street Maintenance in Amsterdam. Here is the flight plan for the pilot that indicates the coordinates where you both must jump. You'll land outside the city where partisans will be waiting for you.

"I'm sure Mr. Churchill told you about the cases filled with the valuables stolen from those arrested throughout Europe. As we speak, the partisans are digging a tunnel to the bank's sublevel vault where the containers are being stored. The point of the tunnel's inception is in a large building across the street. The plan is precisely organized, as you will see when you get there. Good luck, and return to us safe and sound."

Early that evening, I was picked up and taken to the airfield where I met the other agent. Though we didn't converse much, I figured he was Belgian by his accent. He was rather aloof, which greatly limited our conversation, as I was not one to initiate and pursue communication.

It was a foggy, wet night. I knew we were to land near Amsterdam, which caused me to experience some anxiety. I knew that anything could happen so close to a large German-occupied city.

"You'll be landing on a vast uncultivated plain quite a distance from Amsterdam," the pilot told us. When we were given the signal, we jumped. As I've said, the parachutes of the day were uncontrollable. Once your chute was open, all you could do was to pray to land safely. I barely missed landing in the water because my parachute caught an air current and drifted toward water's edge, but I was fortunate and managed to land safely, as did my colleague. As planned, the partisans were waiting for us.

They took us by car to Amsterdam. It was a Friday. When we arrived at the site in the center of the city, we were escorted into a building and taken straight down to the basement. About thirty partisans were in the process of digging the tunnel.

This process was far more complicated than I had imagined. They had been working for five or six weeks already. Simultaneous work aboveground masked any noise from underground. I could see that the work was slow moving and physically tiring. Besides the digging, an extensive steel framework and beams had to be erected to support the street above. Lights had been installed as well as a system of ventilation. The dirt and debris that was removed was dumped in the lowest level of the building across from the bank, bucket by bucket. The men rotated shifts every eight hours. The smell of sweat filled the dank tunnel and the busy base quarters of the building.

The tunnel, which would end at the wall of the bank, was almost complete when we arrived. The agent who parachuted with me had been chosen because of his connections with the Department of Street Maintenance in Amsterdam. Besides French, he spoke Flemish and Dutch.

"Will you ask the person in charge of the project to report to us," he asked one of the partisans in Dutch.

From the street level, a middle-aged, tall, slender man entered the basement of the building where we were waiting.

"Welcome to Amsterdam," he greeted us in French. "I'll just get to the point. We are nearing completion of the tunnel. We'll arrive at the wall of the bank within a few hours. We'll blast it with plastics to gain entry."

He continued, "The plan is to set off explosions on the street synchronized with the group's blasting of the bank wall underground. The supposed reason for the detonation aboveground is a necessary repair of the sewer system. The entire project zone is barricaded. It is off-limits to all and will remain so until early Monday morning. Police guards are posted to ensure that no one enters the area. They are not aware of what is going on underground.

"We are planning three blasts unless we need more. We will give the signal to our men aboveground to blow dynamite at the precise moment we blow the plastics in the tunnel."

"Do you have plans in place to keep the German troops occupied while we are loading the trucks to transfer the goods?" I asked him.

"Yes, monsieur, we do. You can be assured that our diversions will keep their attention focused on our activities in the suburbs of Amsterdam while our partisans work on this project in the center of town."

"For our part," I shared with the partisan organizer, "we will be responsible for making sure that each chest is numbered and accounted for, one by one, as they are removed from the vault, brought to the building, and then loaded onto the trucks. After that, we'll make sure that the trucks stay together in a group, that one doesn't disappear from the others on the way to the harbor. The two of us will stay in the last truck to observe as we drive to the docks."

The Belgian agent added, "We'll need Street Maintenance uniforms to travel in the trucks."

"Absolutely, you'll have them and rain slickers as well."

The basement of the building was teeming with activity. There was a cantina open twenty-four hours a day where the volunteers could get something to eat or drink or wash up and use the bathroom facilities.

The amazing tunnel was completed on schedule that night. As the two of us walked through, I couldn't help but comment, "What an admirable job these men have done. I'd like to meet the engineer who created the plans. The framing is so well built." I had always admired architecture and the construction that supported it. I had gained this appreciation in my youth from my godfather, the master architect I so greatly admired.

Early Saturday morning, the plastics blasts blew through the walls of the bank perfectly synchronized with the blasts on the street. We gained access to the vault. There were several rooms underground stacked to the ceiling with padlocked wooden munitions boxes containing the loot. These rooms were packed so tightly that there was hardly enough room to pass through them. I numbered each box before it was carried to the building on the other side of the street. Once I established my position, I didn't move from there. I didn't eat, drink, or go to the bathroom unless the other agent was there to relieve me.

With the exception of Friday night, we hadn't slept. Sunday morning, in the wee hours, several German transport trucks covered with canvas and driven by partisans disguised as German soldiers lined up on the street waiting to be loaded. It was raining hard—a torrential rainstorm. We were all wearing rain gear. The partisans loaded the treasure one truck at a time while my colleague recorded the number on every box placed in each truck. He was also responsible for tying the straps attached to the canvas securely together with a rope and knotting them before beginning to load the next truck. I was supervising the boxes as they were being removed from the building.

When all the trucks were loaded and secured, the project manager came out to say good-bye. We climbed into the cab of the final truck.

"Open the barricade," he ordered as he gave the signal for the first truck to depart. We traveled closely, one behind the other, as we left for the harbor.

Another group of partisans was at the dock when we arrived next to the Swedish cargo ship that was waiting to take the treasure to England. They unloaded all the chests from the trucks and placed them into nets on the dock. These were lifted by crane and lowered into the hold of the ship.

"That's it," the agent said. "Let's board the ship."

Absolutely nothing went wrong. We were entirely certain that every last confiscated jewel and valuable would be delivered to England. Once the boxes were safe in the hold, I felt I could relax and breathe easier.

We had completed another successful mission for Mr. Churchill. He would be well pleased. We left Amsterdam on the freighter, captured treasure intact.

TWENTY-FIVE

The Port of Saint-Nazaire

I was amazed as I watched highly trained volunteers in Falmouth, England, assault a very large model-to-scale replica of the port of Saint-Nazaire in Brittany, France. This key Atlantic port was essential to the German war effort. The model had been constructed so every movement and detail of the upcoming assault could be precisely choreographed.

One of the commanders addressed me, "You'll organize the partisans to attack and cause confusion among the German troops if anything goes wrong with our plan. Your contact will be the head priest of Saint-Nazaire."

"Why blow up Saint-Nazaire?" I asked him.

His answer made sense. "If a German warship, such as the *Tirpitz*, is in need of repair, a dry dock large enough to accommodate her must be readily available. The only port in France big enough and deep enough to service ships of this size is in Saint-Nazaire. Even the ports of Toulon in the south and Dieppe in the north, though they are deep enough, they are simply not large enough to accommodate ships of this size. The destruction of Saint-Nazaire will dissuade the Germans from bringing their battleships to France."

It was the early spring of 1942. Preparations for this mission were highly secret and took place in the southwest part of England. Knowledge of the mission was very limited in view of the widespread infiltration of the German Fifth column. Each man involved, sworn to secrecy, practiced his task until it was done to perfection. Besides the leaders in this room, there were to be over a hundred commando volunteers with backup support of hundreds of men on barges, torpedo boats, motor launches, and two destroyers. They all knew going in that this was a high-risk mission.

I took a plane from England and was parachuted close to Saint-Nazaire four or five days before the English commandos arrived. A priest and a farmer came in a horse-drawn wagon to pick me up in the field. This was unusual. Normally, a larger group was waiting to whisk me away from the landing site.

The two brought me to the farmer's home. "I have a priest's robe for you to change into," the priest said. "Disguised like this, you can circulate without fear of being stopped by the Germans. They don't bother the clergy too much around here.

"From what I understand," he continued, "we need to organize about six hundred partisans as possible reinforcements. We'll meet with members of *Combat* this afternoon. First, let's have something to eat. Then you can rest for a while, and I'll wake you when it's time to leave."

"I'll welcome breakfast," I said to the priest, "but I'm really not tired." Then I asked the farmer, "Would you mind if I took a look around your property after we eat? I just love animals."

"Not at all, not at all," he said. "For breakfast, we'll have bread and jam, and I can make our war rendition of coffee made from roasted barley, or would you prefer milk?" he asked.

"Milk will be fine. Where can I change into my new identity?"

"Just go into my bedroom," he said, pointing to indicate the way.

The partisan force to be assembled consisted of six companies of one hundred men each. Arms had been parachuted in for them in the area of Nantes. This drop shipment included 1,200 grenades, 36 bazookas, 600 Stein machine guns, 180 mortars, and corresponding ammunition.

In the afternoon, the priest took me to meet with the partisan leaders at an estate outside Saint-Nazaire. We looked over the plans together and split the duties and responsibilities among them.

"I have radios for you," the priest said as he handed me and the others our walkie-talkies.

"I've been instructed to get in radio contact with you if the commandos need our help," I told them. "I'll be in the bell tower of the church where I am to watch and wait."

During the nights that followed, we searched out the areas along the Loire River where we should place the men for attack to be ready at a moment's notice if needed to intervene and support the mission.

I stayed with the priest at his house in Saint-Nazaire, close to the church, and I ate at different locals' homes each day. Oftentimes, I had to drive us both home in the horse-drawn buggy after a meal because he really enjoyed his wine.

On March 27, the night before the mission, I went to the bell tower of the church in the city's center. From there I observed and waited for a radio signal from the commandos requesting our help. I mulled over what might occur. The ship was due to arrive by one thirty in the morning, if all went according to plan. I was to do nothing if not radioed. If I was alerted, I was to radio the partisans, and our supporting attack would begin.

The ship, *Campbeltown*, altered to look like a German vessel, had left the English coast with the plan of arriving early in the morning on March 28, during high tide at the mouth of the Loire River. While at sea, the volunteers placed explosives in the hull of the ship.

When they arrived at the estuary, many of the volunteers got off the boat to prepare themselves to do battle with the Germans as the captain set his sights toward the inside of the lock that he planned to ram at 1:30 A.M.

Suddenly I could hear a lot of gunfire, and I saw big flashes of light from the vantage point of the bell tower where I was stationed so as to have the best radio reception and clearest view possible. *The fighting is steadily intensifying, yet no one is calling,* I thought, eager to do something to help. As the fighting escalated, I told myself again and yet again that I must wait. Doing nothing had never been more difficult. Feelings of helplessness assailed me. I wanted to do something to be of assistance.

The commandos were under attack by the Germans from land. The RAF sent air support. As scheduled, the *Campbeltown* rammed into the side of the lock at 1:34 A.M., doing considerable damage. The explosives on the ship were timed to go off between 5 and 9 A.M. The Germans never expected an explosion on top of the ramming of the lock. When the ship blew, the blast caused irreparable damage to the lock and shipyard.

The mission was ultimately accomplished, though, sadly, very few commandos escaped death or capture. The doors of the locks and shipyard remained unusable for the rest of the war.

As there was no signal for support from my group, I did nothing. I found out later that those in command really expected no one to survive, and all the commandos had been apprised of that before leaving Falmouth. Not one of them backed out of the mission even though they knew it meant probable death. The few who survived returned to England, but many others, most of them badly wounded, were taken prisoner. The rest died while accomplishing this great mission. A few days later, in early June, I was extracted by a tuna fishing boat. It took quite a long detour to drop me in England, but that was all right with me because the mission had left me heavyhearted and feeling useless. I needed the time to contemplate and renew my focus.

Several months later, the Canadians pulled off the same type of attack in Dieppe, unfortunately suffering heavy losses. The ingenuity of the Saint-Nazaire plan and the courage of these men would be responsible for saving thousands of lives as the war continued. No large battleship was able to dock in France till well after the war ended.

I didn't know what a great loss of men we suffered during the mission until I returned to England. The raid was considered a remarkable success despite the cost in human life. I didn't understand why our partisan forces were not called in as reinforcement, but I surmised it was for the best. At least the locals did not suffer reprisals as they might have had we been called in to assist. We also might have revealed too much of the underground network in the effort, which could have compromised the partisans' future usefulness. *Combat* might have been too negatively affected to survive the losses of personnel and secrecy.

While on the boat to England, a lot of questions and thoughts went through my head that would go unasked and unanswered. Disappointed, I thought that maybe I'd be more useful on my next mission. I certainly hoped so. Being a spectator at the slaughter of your comrades in arms and not being allowed to do something was hard, very hard.

TWENTY-SIX

Jailbreak

It was a morning that I happened to sleep late. As I was finishing breakfast, the valet came to tell me to go see Mr. Churchill's secretary in her office.

"Bonjour, Monsieur Marc," she said as I entered. "The prime minister can't be here and wants me to fill you in on the details of your impending mission. It is urgent you leave as soon as possible.

"We have an agent we call Pap who was taken prisoner in Italy. He is an extremely important and effective agent for us. We've gathered information that they are planning to use excessive torture on him. Whether or not he talks, he will be killed.

"Mr. Churchill knows you are very familiar with this region on the Italian Riviera. Pap is in prison at a fortress in San Remo. You need to find a way to free him. He is

Jewish, born in Sóller, Majorca, in the Balearic Islands archipelago. He was a doctor before he became an agent for us. His wife and children were taken from him by the Nazis. The wife was sent to a work camp, and the children were sent on to an extermination camp in Poland. We don't know if they are still alive. It was the French Militia who discovered that they were Jewish and gave them up to the Italian Fascists. Pap was out of town at the time. After that, he offered his services to us and has eluded capture until now.

"Because of his connections, Pap had the privilege and opportunity to be well ensconced in diplomatic circles. Unfortunately, he took too great a risk and put himself in danger. Special secret services in the intelligence departments of France and Italy had suspicions about him and had him arrested."

I was parachuted into a field outside Lyon. I knew a double agent who was a political agitator living to the east in Aix-les-Bains. The partisans met me and drove me there. When I knocked at his door, he answered.

After introducing myself, I laid out the problem. "I've been told you've worked for both the French and Italians. Do you know someone who can help me with breaking out an English agent imprisoned in San Remo?"

"As a matter of fact, I do. I can arrange a meeting for you. She is the most influential of all Italian partisans, Madame Wally Toscanini Castelbarco. She lives in Campione on Lake Lugano. You probably have heard of her."

"Of course I've heard of her. She is well known for her integrity, courage, and cunning. She has helped the English many times already by infiltrating influential groups of military and civilian personalities. She's gifted in the art of counterespionage and has the loyalty of many capable Italian Communist partisans." I was thrilled that he could put me in contact with her.

He told me more about her. Most of what he said I already knew, but out of politeness I let him finish. "She *is* legendary in our circles, isn't she? She works with all the different factions of partisans in northern Italy. She even works with the Mafia to accomplish her goals. She has crossed the German and Italian borders many times and has never been caught. She has used her position to great advantage, as she is the daughter of Maestro Arturo Toscanini. She is in contact with General Badoglio's Royalist forces and the Count Ciano himself, the son-in-law of Mussolini. Did you know, the count contacted Great Britain for political asylum for himself and his family but ended up doing many good works while still in Italy? He's responsible for establishing partisan meetings in a small, remote village in Switzerland called Les Diablerets."

"I'm sure she will be perfect for this mission. Where and when can I meet with Madame Castelbarco?"

"I have a small studio apartment at Thonon-les-Bains on Lake Geneva. You can stay there while I arrange the meeting."

* * *

Madame Castelbarco came to meet me at Thonon-les-Bains as arranged. My contact had already told her that we needed a plan to free the British agent. She came right to the point.

"I'll organize a convoy of Italians to pose as Fascists. They will enter the prison at San Remo with orders that I will have forged. The orders will specify that Pap be transferred to another prison where he is to be condemned to death. I'll send a small van and a military truck loaded with partisans dressed in Fascist military uniforms to the prison with orders to take possession of the prisoner. I can have them ready to go in two days' time."

As Pap later related the story to Mr. Churchill's secretary, he heard these men talking near his cell but didn't know what was going on because he didn't speak Italian very well. What he didn't realize was that most of them were from Piemonte and spoke a dialect that he wouldn't have understood even if he had spoken Italian fluently.

"What's going on?" he asked one of his guards who spoke some English.

"The German government has condemned you to death. You are being transferred to a prison in Nice run by the SS called Lynwood, which was originally a fine villa but is now used for extreme and inventive ways to torture its prisoners. The reputation of the place is that you either tell the SS what they want to know or they will remove your body parts, limb by limb, as they continue to torture you. I suggest you tell them what they want to know quickly, s*ignore*."

Pap had continued to tell the story to Mr. Churchill's

secretary, as she subsequently related to me. "I was taken from my cell and put in a van. Inside were more Italian Fascists. At least, that's what I assumed. They talked animatedly with each other. They seemed to be in good spirits and didn't treat me badly.

"We crossed the Italian-French border at Menton-Garavan. That same night, the van arrived in Cap Ferrat. Still handcuffed, I was taken down a narrow, winding road that led to the sea. Two men were waiting in a rubber boat. One of the supposed Fascists handed the key to my handcuffs to one of the men in the boat. He indicated that I should step in. Then, to my astonishment, the man with the key reached over and opened my cuffs."

"We're taking you to a submarine that will take you to Gibraltar," he explained to me in English.

"This was the first indication that I was being saved and not condemned. What an unbelievable relief! Inconceivable—a real miracle," he expressed to her, still emotional about being alive.

The escape had gone so smoothly that it surprised everyone. The Italian partisans followed the plan to the letter. There was no need for improvisation. They quietly removed Pap from the prison at San Remo with no opposition and transported him to the south of France. The submarine took him to Gibraltar, and from there a military plane took him to Great Britain.

Later, Mr. Churchill's secretary shared with me Pap's description of the prison and his escape from it. "In Pap's words," she said, "the fortress seemed not to have been cleaned for over a century. The massive walls were at least a meter thick and full of humidity that ran from ceiling to floor. The dungeon walls were encrusted with filth, human waste and vomit. The guards would put buckets in the cells once a week for human needs. When the buckets were emptied, they were not rinsed. And sometimes, it took a couple of days to get the buckets back to the cells. During that time, the floor had to suffice.

"He said there were two or three floors underground. He described the place as 'the innards of hell on earth.' The passageways were narrow and lit with dim lamps. Of course, there were no windows. Each cell had an iron door, heavily rusted by the humidity. The door was attached by hinges to the granite rock. The cell itself was the shape of a vertical bottle and had barely enough room for one person. He could not completely stand up in it. It was so narrow at the top that he could hardly move at all. When he did stand up, his head would be bent over and he could barely turn his face. His shoulders and knees were against the rock itself. Only once during the hellish days he spent there did he remember getting a hunk of bread and a tin of water. It was like being starved in a coffin of damp stone.

"As he was being walked down the pathway to the Mediterranean Sea, he remembered thinking that this place of torture they were taking him to must be on an island. Why else would they be putting him in a boat? He knew this would be the last time he saw the outside world, so he really treasured the beauty. As he steeled himself against the torture that was to come, he made a firm decision to never reveal the truth. He is a wonderful man. I hope you have the chance to meet him one day, Monsieur Marc.

"I just want you to know that the prime minister is thrilled that you were able to generate a plan to free this man. He appreciates your ingenuity and speaks of you often when you're away. He has another mission in the works for you that he'll explain when he comes to the estate this weekend. At least, that is the plan," she said with a wry smile. "One can never be sure."

TWENTY-SEVEN

Atomic Bomb

"Someone is with the prime minister right now, Monsieur Marc," the secretary said with kind eyes. You might have to wait awhile. Why don't you sit down?" I took a seat.

By chance, Mr. Churchill came into the secretary's office, saw me, and said, "Oh, you're here. Come with me into my office. I have someone I want you to meet." When we entered, I saw an older man sitting at Mr. Churchill's desk, striking because of his mass of gray tousled hair.

"Marc, this is Monsieur Albert Einstein. You'll excuse us as we finish our conversation, and then I'll tell you what's going on."

Since they continued in English, I was not privy to what was being said, but they both spoke with passion. Afterward, the prime minister explained to me, "Mr. Einstein suggests that all physicists working on splitting the atom be organized to work together in the laboratories located in London, Oxford, Cambridge, and Liverpool. He emphasizes how important it is that the research be kept out of Nazi hands. If the Germans somehow get it, they will make a huge leap forward in their own research toward developing the atom bomb. We're ahead of them now, and we want to keep it that way," Mr. Churchill said adamantly.

He looked at me with those piercing eyes. "I need to send you immediately to Norway with special instructions and explosives to destroy a certain production plant that is supervised and directed by the Nazis. The employees are Norwegian, forced labor working under Nazi control. They are producing 'heavy water' needed to make the atom bomb. Their project will be crippled no matter how close they get once we succeed in destroying the factory.

"I am sending a scientist/engineer with you who knows where to effectively place the explosives near the machines to disable the plant even if they manage to reconstruct it. He knows how to ski and speaks Italian and Norwegian. Since you are such a good skier, you'll join him and a group of six Norwegians on the mission.

"I want you to know, my boy, that our last attempt to blow up the plant failed. It is vital to totally stop this production."

He continued, "King Haakon will keep us updated because he stays in contact with all developments in Norway through the Norwegian Resistance. Good luck and a safe return, *mon petit.*" I left the two of them in his office as they continued their conversation.

When I arrived at the airfield, the scientist/engineer with whom I was to travel was already there. After introducing ourselves, he explained in Italian, "Here I have all the explosives and detonators necessary for our mission. I have our white ski suits that are reversible and are camouflaged on the inside. We also have white ski boots and white skis. All is in this cart, ready to go."

It was early evening. We would fly over Norway and jump with all the equipment. The plane's engine turned over, and one of its crew came out to help us load.

The pilot had his flight plan already. We left right away. Hours later, over Norway, he spotted the landing fires. He circled and turned on the red ready light in the cabin. The plane's other crew member opened the door. When the light turned green, he threw the equipment out, hooked to a parachute. Then the light turned red again, and the pilot circled. When it turned green, the scientist said, "Let's go," and jumped, and I followed suit.

We landed in a snow-covered valley where about thirty partisans were waiting for us. They buried our chutes as we changed into our white protective clothing. We put on our boots and skis as they explained, "We'll guide you from here to the mill where you'll meet with the rest of your group. If you hear an airplane, throw yourselves flat on the ground and don't move. Let nothing be seen

that is not white. Let us help you carry the equipment."
The scientist translated for me and further explained,
"We are meeting in the forest at a deserted sawmill that
is closed for the winter. It'll take us about two hours to
get there."

The scientist was not physically prepared for the trek,
and we had to slow down for him to keep up. When we
arrived, six tall, strong, well-built Norwegian military
men working for the Resistance greeted us. An entire
bivouac had been set up at the mill. Someone heated up
food while we discussed the mission ahead. There were
kapok mattresses ready for us where we could lie down
after breakfast if need be.

The scientist told them, "We have to get into the factory and place the explosives in the precise places where
they will totally destroy the machines that are producing
the heavy water. For precaution, the explosives and detonators are packed separately."

One of the officers opened up a military map and
spread it on the floor. "We have to be careful and take our
time," he cautioned. "German planes patrol the skies. It
will take about two days on skis to reach our destination," the scientist translated for me. "We'll travel mostly
at night, when we'll reverse our tunics so as to blend in
and disappear into our surroundings. When we're traveling in the forest by day, we'll reverse our tunics again."

It was a long, difficult trek, especially for the scientist.
During the day we hid, rested, and ate. When we finally

approached the factory, we took the long way around, climbing the mountain behind so that we could approach the immense structure from the rear. We followed the water supply that led us a long way behind the building. This is where we hid until the next day.

When night fell, I was directed to stand guard on a hill above, where I could see everything. I had a radio in case of trouble. The scientist said, "You'll alert us should anything irregular occur."

It took them about an hour and a half to place the explosives. The German barracks were next to the factory, on the one side. At that hour, everyone was asleep. There were no undesirable interruptions. No one had spotted us.

When they returned, the scientist told me, "The bombs will explode in two hours' time because they're on time-delayed detonators. Now, we'll all get out of here. You and I will separate from the others except for one Norwegian who will guide us to the harbor where a British submarine is waiting to take us back to England. This area is more populated, so we'll travel only at night and sleep during the day. It'll take two or three days to get there. The skiing will be easy though, as it's all downhill."

We left right away. Three days later, when we arrived at our destination, we signaled the submarine. A rubber boat came to pick us up.

When we arrived at the camp at Folkestone, England, the colonel in charge received us warmly. With a sly smile he announced, "Your operation was a great success. The factory was totally destroyed." This was a time for celebration. The scientist was especially pleased. He had placed the explosives perfectly. The next day he and I said our good-byes, and he left for Liverpool. I never saw him again. Later I learned that they were somehow able to repair the plant, much to the dismay of all.

The following year, in early 1944, a message was intercepted saying the Germans were planning to transfer by train what remained of their heavy water because it was needed to complete construction of the atom bomb in Germany.

This was grave news indeed. Mr. Churchill assigned me to go again to Norway, this time by submarine, to meet with a Norwegian group at a port.

He told me, "What is necessary to accomplish is to find a way to get aboard the ferry that is to transport the heavy water to Germany. The Norwegian partisans are developing a plan. You will be there to observe and report back to me. The ferry is guarded by a troop of SS. The containers will arrive by train and will be labeled 'no commercial value' in German. Come home safe, sound, and successful!"

Again I had to travel by submarine. Once near the port, one of the seamen took me to shore in an inflatable dinghy where a German-speaking Norwegian partisan was waiting for me. Our language in common was German, so we were able to communicate when no one was in earshot. He took me to a pub where I met the others. These men were Norwegian electricians working for the Resistance. Not one of them spoke French or Italian, and I wouldn't speak German in public. They were all dressed like workmen. My guide whispered, "Under the guise of checking the electricity, these men will be allowed to board the ferry. A couple of them know some of the crew and the captain personally."

He explained, "They will place the explosives in the hull of the boat as soon as they receive the message indicating the transfer of heavy water is imminent. They'll set them to go off a few hours later when the boat is well out to sea."

I watched from a distance as the heavy water containers arrived on the dock and were pushed onto the ferry. Whoever was on board, innocent of crimes or not, had to be sacrificed because it was too dangerous to risk warning anyone.

The explosion occurred at sea as planned. Nothing was left of the ferry. This was confirmed before I left Norway. The German-speaking Norwegian accompanied me to a point on the coast from where he signaled the sub. From there, I was transported back to England.

Unfortunately, in this top-secret sabotage operation, innocents were sacrificed for the Allied cause. These courageous Norwegian patriots saved the world. Without the heavy water, the Germans were unable to build the atomic bomb. I could hardly wait to get home to tell Mr. Churchill.

TWENTY-EIGHT

Patton in North Africa

Softly, the secretary knocked on his door. "Come in!" roared Mr. Churchill. Glasses perched on the tip of his nose, he was perusing the papers on his desk. When he eventually glanced toward the door and saw me, he jumped up and rushed over to take me in his arms. And he was strong. He grabbed me with great force and held me for a long time. After he sighed a couple of times, he let me go. I could feel his happiness and relief to see me. It felt good that he cared so much. When he sat down, I also took a seat.

A car had picked me up at the camp where I was staying at Folkestone and had brought me to Mr. Churchill's estate. Smiling, the secretary had given me a cheerful welcome. "It feels wonderful to be back," I had responded.

After discussing the details of the mission in Norway,

Churchill announced, "On your next mission, you'll wear your French military uniform. You will be the liaison and communication officer between the American and French troops in North Africa. Because of the French animosity toward the English, we will hold our troops back for a while and have the Americans go in first.

"You'll have about three weeks here before it's time to leave. Ride the horses. Take Hughes with you if you want company on your rides. If you want to go to town, just ask him to take you in the carriage." He reached into his pocket. "Here is some spending money. I'll see you one of these evenings if I return early enough. Don't hesitate to ask the cook to prepare whatever you feel like. Remember, you're at home, *mon petit*," he said with a smile. "I am so very proud of you!"

At this point in time, writing down what happened so long ago, I feel what I was not conscious of in those days. I am so moved by his trust in me. This compassionate, loving, and brilliant man is so close to my heart today. Now that I'm older, I can appreciate all he did for me personally, not to mention what he did for the entire world.

"I want to explain to you the importance of what you'll be doing," he continued. "I've already talked to President Roosevelt about this. We are planning a landing in North Africa, probably beginning with Morocco and Algeria. Since England is in a state of war with both of them because they are pro-Vichy, it will be useful to have you assigned to General Patton's immediate staff to play the part of liaison between the Americans, the French, and later, the English. It is Patton who will be in charge of the landing.

"It's a very sensitive situation. We know that Algeria and Morocco will accept the American presence more readily than the English. I am sure that the intelligence we have received regarding the state of mind of these two countries is accurate. When they see Americans arriving, and *not* the English, we will have a better chance of avoiding needless opposition and slaughter. I know my countrymen will be firmly opposed to the Americans going in first, but this will save lives and make the conquest much easier."

Pausing, he knitted his hands across his waistcoat and then resumed: "After the landing, the second wave of soldiers may be English. I've already talked to General Patton. You will stay close to him. He speaks French very well, and I know you two will get along. I have great respect for him. If he encounters resistance from the pro-Vichy Algerians or Moroccans, now and again, just your presence in his command car wearing your French captain's uniform will have a positive psychological and political effect on their troops."

"But *monsieur*, I'm a first lieutenant, not a captain."

"Don't be concerned about that, *mon petit*. We'll need to give you a temporary promotion for the sake of appearance." I understood his motivation. He needed to add a gold bar to my uniform to impress people.

"So, to promote the general public's acceptance," he continued, "the English army will stay in the background, in the beginning, as much as possible. This simple tactical move will provide a partial victory in itself."

"I understand," I responded.

"You'll be transported to Gibraltar by plane. From there, you will board a submarine that will take you out to sea where you'll join the Americans. If we English could put on American uniforms, were it acceptable to the Americans, we would be proud to do so; however, you know that Eisenhower doesn't like the English much, so I don't think that will ever happen," he said with a wry smile.

Then, thoughtfully, he added, "We'll see how things play out. You'll meet Patton at sea between Africa and America. You'll be joining 24,500 men who are being transported by the Western Naval Task Force. The armada coming directly from the United States will consist of 102 vessels. Twenty-nine of these will be boats specifically dedicated to the landing. They will be carrying the troops. The rest of the ships will be carrying arms, ammunition, and supplies. Following will be 18,500 troops coming directly from Scotland and Northern Ireland under the command of Major General Lloyd R. Fredendall. They will be escorted by British naval forces under the command of Commodore Thompson Troubridge. They'll be departing from the Clyde, Scotland.

"President Roosevelt and I, among others, have grown discontented with the poor judgment and arrogance of General de Gaulle. We believe that General Mast, the associate of General Giraud, would be the best candidate to be at the head of French North Africa. I know you recall that our British secret service aided the partisans in freeing Giraud from prison, where he was being held for being anti-Nazi. Now we need to transfer him from the southern coast of France to the coast of Algeria. I've given this assignment to General Mark Clark. If all goes as I predict, the Americans will approach the coast of Morocco in less than four weeks, and you will be with them.

"Roosevelt needs to convince certain American politicians to support the planned landing in North Africa, because whether they like it or not, there is no other choice if we want to win the war. The Americans want to invade the south of France first, but I am trying to convince them that the Germans are too strong in France to initiate an attack against them there at this time. What we must do is gather all our forces in North Africa. Then we will have the strength necessary to invade Sicily, then the rest of Italy, and finally France. Like this we can push the enemy back toward Germany while giving the Russians the opportunity to attack from the north."

He reflected a moment and took a puff from his cigar. "So, enjoy yourself, Marc, and rest these few weeks. Not a word to anyone, even here, about the mission because none of my staff knows anything about it. I have only conferred with President Roosevelt, General Patton, and you. I have already ordered two uniforms for you, a kepi, boots, short leggings, and new gloves. And don't forget to wear your medals."

I got up to leave when Mr. Churchill said, "Oh, by the way, your godfather sends his best regards. I just talked to him a few days ago. Unfortunately, he's suffering from a terrible bronchitis right now. To pick up his spirits, I told him about some of your accomplishments, and I could just feel him beaming over the phone. He told me that he went to see your mother in Nice and that she is in good health. If she knew what you were doing, she would be very proud of you. Your godfather certainly is."

That provoked a reaction in me. My poor mother. France would be free one day, but would my mother ever be free of my tyrannical father?

Without my knowing it, Churchill had changed the design of my uniform and the color as well. When the uniforms arrived, they were blue like the French Alpine Ski Troop but a much deeper hue, and they had a modernized jacket, the new waist-length "Eisenhower" style. He included a number of medals along with the extra stripe.

During my extended stay at the estate, I rode horses almost every day, sometimes with Hughes and sometimes alone. Hughes looked to be about thirty years old, tall, very slender, and quite fit. His father was English and his mother, Italian. They had also worked for Mr. Churchill. Most of Churchill's employees had been with him a very long time. Every day, I would get up early and ride, rain or shine, and it was raining much of the time. Sometimes I went out for as long as six or eight hours. When Hughes came with me, he carried knapsacks with lunch and snacks inside. We always had our raincoats with us.

I was tireless, and Hughes never complained. Often he would suggest, "Why don't we stop for a beer and a chat with the boys?" I wouldn't protest when he wanted to stop at the pubs, even though I would have preferred to keep on riding. I knew how much he loved the camaraderie.

He was a very pleasant fellow, and we got along well. He showed me the beautiful countryside surrounding the estate. It was magnificent, interspersed with rolling hills and lush meadows. "Let's let them have their head," he would say when we reached a spot that inspired him. Then we would ride at a full gallop, up and down the hills. There was hardly anything I liked better in the world than being on a horse's back in the countryside.

After an entire day's ride, we would get back home. Hughes would take care of the horses and go to bed exhausted. Famished, I would go into the kitchen. The cook would always be waiting up no matter the time.

"Do you have any veal liver?" I would often ask. She would either nod or offer some other wonderful choices. "Will you prepare the liver extra rare with sautéed onions, three duck eggs, and a whole baguette with butter?"

She was a wonderful cook, and her preparation of veal liver was superb. She soaked it first in cream. It just melted in your mouth. She was a really nice woman and understood a little French. She often prepared meals in the French style but also made wonderful English muttonchops, slicing away the bone, tying three together, and wrapping them in bacon. Mr. Churchill appreciated her fine cuisine.

While she was preparing dinner, I would usually go to my room to shower and change clothes. After the meal, I would often go into the library to read. There was a wonderful collection of French books. I needed only three or four hours of sleep a night, so I had a lot of time on my hands.

During these weeks, I rarely saw Mr. Churchill. Most of the time, he stayed in London. One night, after the great triumph by Montgomery and the Eighth Army at El Alamein, he came home elated by the victory, though his joy was tempered by the loss of life. It always was. His exuberance, however, continued throughout dinner as he focused on our next step toward ultimately winning the war. That goal was his obsession. When at the estate, he was usually working in his study or sleeping. He would frequently take catnaps, just a few minutes at a time. He worked tirelessly and, like me, required very little sleep.

One morning, he summoned me to his office and greeted me warmly. "Get your gear packed. This afternoon, there will be a car to take you to the airfield. May God protect you, *mon petit*."

I spent the morning walking around the property and visiting with the horses. After lunch, I put on my uniform and packed the other two. I was ready to go. I went to wait in the library, my favorite room. There was a knock on the door. A "little gray mouse" came in and took my luggage. I went to the secretary's office. "Good-bye, madame," I said. "Take good care of him."

The large twin-engine military plane had a machine gun mounted at the rear. "I have no envelope for you this time," I said to the pilot. "You must know where we're going."

"I do indeed," he replied. I had flown with him before.

The crew consisted of the pilot, copilot, navigator, radioman, and gunner, a larger crew than was normal for my flights, but it was also a larger airplane. I speculated silently to myself that they were perhaps expecting some trouble.

"Here, put on this parachute," the copilot told me. Each of us was given a parachute to put on. There were no incidents, however, and we landed safely in Gibraltar.

After landing, someone came to take my bags and hurried me to a waiting car. I was taken to the submarine base where I boarded the British ship that would take me to join General Patton in the Atlantic, well below the Canary Islands, which were, at that time, occupied by the Germans.

We left after dark and traveled through the Straits of Gibraltar to the Atlantic Ocean, heading southward. I held on to the thought that it wouldn't be long before I was let out of this metal capsule, heartening for someone who hates to be confined.

In the early morning, we came upon the impressive armada that would constitute the invading force of

North Africa. The horizon was filled with boats of all sizes traveling in our direction. The closer they got, the more monumental they appeared.

It was the eighth of November, 1942. Standing on the bridge with the commanding officer, I commented, "This is the most awe-inspiring sight I have ever seen." Shortly afterward, four men in a torpedo boat drew close to the submarine. Members of the crew handed them my luggage, and I climbed down the ladder. They took me to a large warship where I was taken directly to meet General George S. Patton.

What an impressive man! He had an air of self-assurance and carried himself like a gentleman. I introduced myself. He graciously welcomed me. "Did you enjoy your trip in that sardine can?" he asked, chuckling.

"I avoided going inside," I answered. "I stayed on the bridge as much as I could. I hate those submarines."

"As do I, as do I," he responded. "Give me the wide open spaces on Mother Earth any day. And how is Mr. Churchill doing these days?"

Patton's French was excellent. Without waiting for a response, he continued, "We talked a few weeks ago about our strategy in North Africa. That is when he told me that he was sending you to be my liaison officer to interact with the French. He is very proud of all that you have accomplished, you know. When the French, Algerians, and Moroccans see us together, they will realize that we are all on the same side. He is confident that this tactic will diminish the amount of resistance we encounter.

"My orderly, Meeks, will put your bags away. We will

land on the coast of Morocco in a few hours. If you need anything, just ask for it. For now, come with me to take a look at the battle plans. My officers are waiting for us."

There were about ten men surrounding the large table covered with a map of North Africa. One of the officers spoke French and translated what General Patton was explaining to the others.

"Today, November 8, 1942, I solemnly promise you that within one week, we will be victorious in North Africa. Our first objective is here at Cape Fedala, not far from Casablanca. I have chosen this spot because there is plenty of open terrain where we can deploy our troops and also because there will be little or no resistance to our deployment." He pointed to the map and explained further. "We will take positions to the south, as well, at Mehdia and Safi." He explained the entire plan to his staff and then dismissed them. He was confident the plan would be successful.

As we approached the coast of Morocco, the Atlantic was calm. While the landing was taking place, General Patton was talking to his commanding officers. Knowing that I didn't understand English, one of the American officers who spoke French was kind enough to explain what Patton was saying. His words were approximately, "Never in the history of the Romans or the Greeks did it truly matter the day or time of day when a battle took place. What was of ultimate importance was the first five minutes of battle. If we land close to Fedala, I promise that within a week we will be victorious." In actuality, the Americans were victorious within two days.

The landing took place behind a screen of smoke produced by smoke bombs dragged along by antisubmarine torpedo boats that traveled about thirty-five to forty knots, considered very fast in those days. The smoke hid the ships' approach. Despite this, three destroyers were sunk because the French military in charge of the cannons defending the coast of Morocco had not been convinced that they should not fire. There were also some mines along the coast that caused some damage to the armada, but, all things considered, the landing went extremely well.

The officers in charge were well trained and precise in their maneuvers. As Mr. Churchill and General Patton had predicted, opposition was minimal. Patton confided in me that Eisenhower had directed him to land on the beaches of Casablanca. After doing his own research, he found that the area was too well defended, so he chose to ignore the directive and devise his own plan. He was usually in disagreement with Eisenhower.

Our ship followed some of the smaller landing boats. Ours carried larger equipment, such as jeeps and tanks. I got in the command car with General Patton along with several other men. The car could hold nine people. He and I stood behind the driver. Everything was eerily quiet where we landed. There were no fortifications whatever. The locals were offering oranges for sale. Patton told the driver to stop.

"Ask the woman for a couple of dozen oranges," he

said, as he handed me the money to give her. I asked the price in French, and she understood. He turned toward her and said in Arabic, "Go with God." I could see the awe on her smiling face. His stature made an impression on people.

On the horizon, I beheld a remarkable sight: three graceful gazelles, quietly grazing. As I was appreciating the extraordinary beauty of the scene, Patton broke my reverie by saying, "I hear you appreciate fine cuisine. You must taste a camel-meat stroganoff. Unforgettable!"

Patton told the driver to go into the village and had him stop in front of a small boutique. "We'll go inside and find a robe for you to wear this evening while I have your uniforms cleaned and pressed. Your uniform must be impeccable for tomorrow. I have mine cleaned and pressed every day. You'll need to accustom yourself to this. It will be a daily routine. We must set the standard for others."

We entered the boutique. General Patton addressed the owner in Arabic. "We are looking for a robe. What is your name, sir?"

"Said al-Hilaly," he replied. Smiling, the owner approached me and, taking the collar of my uniform between his fingers, said in French, "Ah, monsieur, this is excellent wool." He went to the back of the store and returned. "Now, touch the material of this robe," he said, as he proudly showed us the handsome piece of merchandise. "The material is of the highest quality, and it is only one hundred seventy dirham."

Patton replied in Arabic, "Very good, but really too

expensive." Then he made a counteroffer: "One hundred ten."

"No," al-Hilaly retorted. "One hundred fifty."

Patton replied in French, "One hundred forty, take it or leave it."

The owner shrugged and nodded. Patton turned to me and said, "Accept it as a gift from me." He paid the man, thanked him, and we left.

The following day, General Patton suggested, "Let's take a walk around the city. I've noticed that our soldiers are negligent about their uniforms. I must teach them a lesson." We got in the car, and he told the driver to take us to a popular area for soldiers.

"Stop right here," he ordered. The driver immediately pulled over and stopped. The city was calm. The residents were going about their daily business. After a few moments, Patton got out of the car and approached three American soldiers who were walking in our direction. They saluted. Patton said, "Stop! Come to attention. Do you know who I am? I am General Patton. Button your shirts properly and straighten your ties accordingly."

Two other soldiers were passing and saluted as they did. Patton snapped, "You two, there. Come over here. Attention!" The two came to attention.

"Your shirts are unbuttoned. Do you think you're at a county fair? From now on, any soldier caught dressed improperly will pay a fine of one week's wages. The second time he has an infraction, the fine will be doubled.

The sum will be deducted from your salaries. This gross neglect must stop. You're showing a total lack of respect for yourselves and your country. You'll give your names to my orderly. From this moment on, your uniforms will be immaculate in public. Report back to camp immediately and report your fine and the reason for it to your immediate superior." With that, we left and went back to headquarters.

A couple of days later, we returned to town. All the soldiers we encountered were impeccably dressed and groomed and comported themselves well. Patton had made his point and had obtained the results he desired.

While in Morocco, I spent much of my time appeasing the French officers, explaining to them what the Americans were planning. They didn't like the Americans. They found the soldiers offensive, especially when they got drunk. I explained that they were new troops, very young, far away from home, and not educated in the traditions of other countries. I tried to keep peace among them all.

I needed to take control of the Communication Bureau. It needed to be controlled with an iron fist, especially in Algeria. Morocco was easier because the soldiers were better educated, and the troops that were there were not fighting as much among themselves.

In Algeria, it was a mess. There were some soldiers for de Gaulle, others for Giraud, and the old school that was pro-Nazi. These three factions were in constant battle among themselves. To keep order, I went to small villages outside Algiers with a group of Touaregs, the local tribe that served as the Sahara desert police force. One American sergeant accompanied me. This elite police force was very disciplined and did an admirable job of protecting the nomads of the desert.

We traveled on camelback, dressed in the black uniforms of the Touaregs. My camel was white and was good looking as far as camels go. I whispered to the sergeant, "I've never encountered a nasty animal until now." He agreed with me. All of the camels were bad-tempered and ill-mannered. We had to keep them muzzled to prevent them from biting us and each other.

I had a lot of difficulty in maintaining the peace among the Algerians. I had to remain neutral, and that was truly difficult. I saw crosses of Lorraine painted on some walls, the sign of pro–Free French. There were groups that were armed and totally against the government of Vichy, and there were others adamantly pro-Nazi. Still others among them did not want to submit to the English or the Americans or to the command of General de Gaulle. We called the various groups "les Giraudists (for Giraud)" or "les Pétainists (for Pétain)" or "les Gaullists (for de Gaulle)" or "les Brits (pro-British)" or "les Amerlots (pro-American)." Each group detested all the others.

In the midst of all this chaos, I would often muse that if Churchill, Roosevelt, and Stalin were able to find a way to agree, why couldn't these Algerians?

We had to patrol the desert south of Fez and Rabat,

the capital, to the foot of the Moyen Atlas Mountains to the high plateaus of the Sahara. It was a huge territory to cover, especially on the back of a camel.

I often felt while riding my camel like I was going to vomit because the movement of these animals gave me the sensation of seasickness. But I kept this discomfort to myself. I needed to show no sign of weakness.

In Morocco, I established communication posts with French officers in charge. Then I preceded the troops into Algeria to establish landing bases and posts of communication before the rest of the military arrived.

I continued to work on my own objective. I sent French officers to establish more posts along the coast of Algeria to direct the Allied forces from these points of control. At these military posts, we would establish telephone and radio communication stations to transmit the orders of General Giraud and, of course, to thank the Allies for the support they were giving France so that she would be able to free herself from German occupation.

We did our best to keep peace among the warring factions. Then, out of nowhere, after about seven weeks on the back of a camel, I was thankfully recalled to England by Mr. Churchill, right after the holidays, in early January 1943.

The last time I had contact with General Patton, he had extended an invitation. "I have a fine stable of horses at my ranch in California. You must come spend some time there. I think you'll enjoy riding them more than the camels," he remarked facetiously. Though I never thought of it again until recently, isn't it strange that I wound up living in Southern California?

So my work with General Patton was finished. After my departure, Patton attacked the coast behind the enemy and continued into Tunisia. Then Bradley took over the command of these troops, and Patton returned to the headquarters of the Sicilian Invasion Deployment Division to plan the invasion of Sicily.

As for me, I was grateful to get aboard a British plane that picked me up at an airfield in Algeria. I dreamed of riding Mr. Churchill's horses again across the green landscape in that welcome wet weather. It would exorcise the agonizing memories of swaying and jouncing across the sweltering beige dunes on the back of an ornery camel.

PART FOUR

RETURN FROM HELL

In Victory: Magnanimity.
—WINSTON CHURCHILL

TWENTY-NINE

Captured

Threatening black clouds covered the skies. There was almost no visibility. As we approached the target area, rain was coming down in sheets. "I can't see the torches in the landing field," the pilot shouted. "I'm taking the plane up higher. Then I'll descend for another approach. Jump when I give you the signal."

We were supposed to be just south of Nancy, above the valley near Neufchâteau, north of Châtenois. I thought to myself that if he couldn't see the landing field, and neither could I with all this foul weather, would we be close to the right landing spot? After takeoff, I had given him the letter from Mr. Churchill indicating the destination and the route to take. For safety's sake, we were allowed no radio communication even under these circumstances.

I was ready, braced in front of the door. The pilot gave

the signal, and I jumped. A blast of cold air and sideways rain hit me. I was wearing only a three-piece brown business suit with a shirt and tie, shoes and socks. Every piece of clothing had a label showing that it was made in France. I was carrying letters of recommendation in my pocket and, of course, my identification card stating I was Michel Carbonell.

The ground raced toward me. "I'm heading for the trees. There's nothing I can do!" The thoughts sped through my head just before I crashed into the branches. And there I stayed, stuck high up in the trees, suspended from my parachute, which was tangled and twisted. It was about four thirty in the morning. The night was black. What little I could see was due to the phosphorus pills I had been taking for several days.

Wet and hopelessly tangled in the branches, I couldn't reach the trunk of the tree. I needed to grab it to release myself. Struggling as best I could, I pushed myself back and forth again and again, trying to jostle myself free. That didn't work, so I decided to contort my body enough to reach the hunting knife strapped to my calf. By stretching, I was able to pull it out of its leather sheath and cut the right strap of my chute. *Now,* I thought, *all I need to do is get closer to that trunk, wherever it is.*

Suddenly, I heard a voice from below say, "Do you need any help, monsieur?" He spoke in French with a pronounced foreign accent. I couldn't see him. "Can we do something for you, monsieur?" he asked.

I quickly responded, "Yes. You can get me out of this tree and then give me directions to Neufchâteau."

The voice coming from below asked, "But what are you doing here?"

"I am a tourist. My travel guide, who is a pilot, dropped me here because he couldn't see where a clearing was located."

The voice replied, "Stay there. Don't move. I'm going to help you."

I just couldn't resist retorting, "Don't hurry. I'll wait."

After a short while, I heard the same voice ordering in German, "Bring the tank over here so that we can help this wayward traveler."

At that moment, I stiffened. I understood where I had landed—right in the middle of a German encampment, probably a Panzer tank division. I heard several voices speaking German in the distance. One of them said, "The lieutenant has captured a spy, an English one, I think." I wasn't surprised. Of course, it was obvious the "tourist" line was a joke, but what else could I say? Admit the truth? I decided I would do the only thing I could—play for time.

One of the young soldiers climbed a neighboring tree and yelled down in German, "Tell him to swing himself toward me." I waited for the translation. I didn't want to let on that I spoke German.

After the lieutenant translated into French, I made several attempts to swing myself over to the soldier, but my chute was too tangled up. One of the soldiers cut two of the culprit branches. I still couldn't free myself. *Maybe I can reach the other parachute strap and cut it now*, I thought. *Then gravity will solve the problem.*

"Wait a moment, wait a moment," the lieutenant shouted as the sound of an approaching tank reached my ears. "Everyone stop. The tank is in position."

The formidable machine pushed against the tree and as it groaned, it gradually began to fall. I freed myself and descended from my perch onto solid ground. The lieutenant appeared to be a likable fellow and seemed to find the entire situation hilarious. He dismissed his soldiers.

Now the two of us were alone. He opened the conversation. "I couldn't sleep tonight, so I decided to take a walk and smoke my pipe. I was enjoying the silence of the night. Everything smelled so fresh in the rain. Then I saw your parachute coming toward the trees."

I interrupted him. "Would you mind, Lieutenant, if I reach into my pocket to take out my pipe and tobacco so I can join you?"

"Certainly, go ahead," the man responded kindly. He reached into his own pocket, removed his tobacco pouch, and offered me some of his.

"I thank you, but I really enjoy my own blend," I said, and then added, "Would you care to try some of mine?"

"Yes, thank you. That would be nice."

We both stood in the darkness and silently stuffed tobacco in our pipes. I had a great hurricane lighter that didn't go out in the wind. He tried repeatedly to light his pipe with matches and just couldn't do it.

"Try my lighter. You'll be surprised," I said.

I handed it to him, and he lit his pipe in one attempt.

"What a great lighter!" he marveled. "Where did you get it?"

"In Nice," I answered.

"How is it that you're obviously coming from somewhere else, and yet you have a French lighter? he asked.

"I am in France because I live here. Would you care to see my identification card?"

"Yes, of course. Let me see it."

I handed the man my card. "As you see, my name is Michel Carbonell. I'm a tourist in Nancy and the surrounding area. My travel guide told me to jump at the wrong time. He had no visibility whatsoever!"

"You do realize, monsieur, that I must put you in the hands of the Gestapo. I have no choice in the matter, amiable fellow though you are. I must transfer you to Paris, to the Gestapo headquarters on avenue Foch. That's the street you French call avenue 'Boche,' your disparaging term for Germans. We have a name for you French, too. I guess that's the way of war. I really regret having to send you to headquarters, monsieur. You seem like a nice man."

I made no reply but told myself, "I must avoid that at any cost." On a recent mission to the vicinity of Lyon I had seen Wanted posters depicting a likeness of me, a sketch of a young bearded man who precisely fit my physical description. I had barely managed, with the assistance of prewar friends, to flee to the Côte d'Azur and the safety of Monte Carlo. There, I hid in the apartment of friends from childhood whose mother was a countess and whose father had been captured and taken prisoner when France was defeated in the spring of 1940.

The officer was going on about his life before the war as I was searching for a way out of this situation. I certainly had to avoid Paris at all costs; but of greater urgency was finding a way to escape before this officer turned me over to the Gestapo. If descriptions of me had circulated in my wake in Lyon, then it was probable the same thing had happened all over France. I knew the solution to this predicament would come to me. It always did. I just needed to be patient.

My captor, the good-natured lieutenant, was enjoying my company. I knew how to *appear* to be listening, and apparently I had done that quite well, for he had not stopped talking. Finally, he said, "Excuse me for going on like this, but I love to speak the French language. My wife is French, from Alsace. Our son is going to school in Strasbourg right now until we return to Germany. What will be, will be. Maybe we have another year here in France, at most."

Silently I asked myself, "Where is he going with this?"

"Just between us," he said, "and for some reason I trust you to say nothing of our conversation, very soon we Germans will lose the war. You were very lucky to fall into my hands. Let's go into my tent and have a cup of coffee. I am sure you will not have real coffee again for a very long time."

We entered his tent and sat down. While he was making the coffee, he continued in a philosophical vein. "Who knows? Perhaps one day you will have the opportunity to

do some kindness for me. I am not the SS. I am an officer of the German cavalry. Since we were forced to use
our horses to feed our men during the war effort against
Russia, I was transferred to this tank unit." He paused,
then took a long draw on his pipe. We sat for a while in
silence, peacefully puffing on our pipes.

He handed me a cup of coffee. Then, in a soft voice,
he continued. "May I show you photos of my family?"
I nodded. He showed me a photo, obviously handled a
lot, of his dear ones. "On the right are my mother and
father. Here, on this side is my wife next to her sister,
and this is our precious child in my wife's arms. He was
sixteen months old when that photo was taken. Now he
looks exactly like my father. When the war broke out, I
was in Paris studying to be a veterinarian. Of course, I
had to return to Germany to serve my country."

He became quiet and thoughtful again. "As I was
saying, it was truly necessary to sacrifice the horses. We
needed to feed the millions of men who had been mobi-
lized. Yet I feel it was such a disgraceful thing to do. I
know that I must continue to do my duty, but if we were
totally alone and my troops hadn't seen you, I would tell
you to stab me and tie my hands behind my back and get
out of here. Circumstances force me to do otherwise."
Then he stopped for a moment and stared at me. "I have
an idea. I'm going to call a sentry to guard you. He's
an older man, in his fifties. I don't think he would do
you any harm, and I ask you not to harm him either. He
has five children and adores his wife. He's about your
size. Take his uniform. You will see motorcycles about a

hundred meters from my tent. The keys are in the ignitions. I wish you good luck, monsieur."

That was a shocking bit of good news! The lieutenant called the sentry, who moments later entered the tent rather casually. His pipe was resting between his lips. He, too, had been enjoying a smoke. As he came in, the German officer turned to leave and ordered, "Guard the prisoner."

I was sitting in a chair, and the guard stood near the table. I seized the moment immediately. "Would you mind handing me the matches next to you? My pipe has gone out." He looked at me quizzically. I realized he didn't understand French. I gestured to make him understand that I needed the matches on the table.

The guard turned ever so slightly to look and spotted the matches. As he reached for them, I quickly jumped up and put a hammerlock around his neck and my hand on his mouth so that he couldn't yell out. I removed his bayonet. "If you want to see your wife and children again, do not make a sound. I will kill you if you do." Again, I realized he didn't understand a word. So I just gagged him and removed his clothes with one hand as I held him with the other. I left his underwear and shoes on. I gestured for him to sit down. I tied him to the main pole of the tent. I put his clothes on over my own and left soundlessly.

Everything was quiet in the camp. I left the tent and moved toward the motorcycles. Without slowing my pace at all, I greeted several people as I passed (in German, of course), including the soldier who was guarding all the vehicles. Then I adopted a very nonchalant demeanor as I went from one to another motorcycle removing all the keys. I got on the last one. It was a Zundapp with a sidecar. I turned on the ignition and engaged the starter with my foot. It turned over immediately. I moved out extremely slowly on the bike so as to draw no special attention to myself.

I didn't take the road. Why ask for trouble? I went through the fields and forest. Because of the river, I knew which way to go. I just followed it downstream. I saw no one for about an hour along this route. Then I began seeing French farmers and their families up and about. I stopped when I saw two children playing marbles near a bridge. "Hello, children. My compliments on your beautiful marbles. They're agates, aren't they?"

The children politely responded, "Yes, sir."

"What is the name of this river?"

The older of the two answered, "It's the Moselle. If you continue a little farther along the river, you'll find a lot of your buddies at Épinal."

"Thank you, kids." I took the first path I came to. It veered to the left away from the river. I didn't want to find any German buddies. "I need to get to the woods where I can take off this uniform. They'll be looking for a man dressed like a German soldier on a motorcycle. It's time to get rid of all this."

I came upon a small forest beside a lake. I removed the uniform and tied it securely to the back of the motorcycle.

Then I got on again, revved it up, and started it in the direction of the butte above the lake. As it picked up speed, I jumped off and all vestiges of the German military went sailing into the sky and then gracefully fell toward the water, finally disappearing in the lake. I stood and watched, happy within myself to be the French Michel Carbonell again. Even playacting as a member of the Wehrmacht left me feeling violated and disgusted.

I walked out of the forest and took the path in the direction from which I had just come. It was still lightly raining. I had passed a farm that had a lot of chickens, goats, and sheep. As I came close, I saw a woman playing with her little boy. He looked to be between two and three.

"*Bonjour, madame.* Terrible weather we're having! But the rain has finally stopped. Is your husband at home?"

Her eyes saddened, and the smile left her face. "No, he isn't home, and he'll never return. The Germans took him prisoner and sent him to Germany. I was told that he escaped, was captured, and then shot to death about a year and a half ago. He never even knew his son."

The woman was very young, nineteen or twenty years old. She asked, "Did you know my husband? What did you want of him?"

"No," I replied, "I didn't know him, but I am sorry for your loss. It is only out of courtesy to the lady of the house that I asked after your husband. Since you are now the head of the household, I would like to know if you have a few days' work that I could do in exchange for food and a place to stay. I would be happy to sleep in the barn. I've come a long way, and I'm hungry and very tired."

"Gladly," she responded. "Come into the house and I'll get you something to eat." She turned and headed toward the door. I followed her into a very large room. It was the kitchen, dining room, and living room all in one. There was a massive fireplace with two benches inside that could easily seat four people. An enormous copper pot was hanging in the center of the fireplace. In the middle of the room was a long, traditional farm table with bowls carved into it. Beautiful large wooden beams crossed the ceiling. One wall had low windows with narrow, rectangular panes framed in wood.

She pointed to a photo on the buffet. "That was our wedding photo. He was handsome, wasn't he? And such a good man," she said nostalgically. "He was kind to everyone. He was a blacksmith and a very good one, too. He was a very hard worker and a good provider. But I've gone on long enough. Please, sit down, monsieur. Would you like a bowl of goat's milk with some bread?"

"Yes, I would," I answered instantly.

She continued, "Sorry I have no coffee to offer you. As I'm sure you know, it is very difficult to come by these days. I do have that substitute coffee made from burned grain, if you like, but it's really not very good. I don't care for it myself."

"The goat's milk will be just fine," I said, "and I thank you for your kindness."

"Would you like it cold or warm?"

Still chilled from the rain, I replied, "Warm, please. It will heat up my insides."

She warmed and served the milk with a half loaf of

bread. As I ate, she continued talking. "Enough of this formality. My name is Emma. What's yours?"

"My name is Michel. Michel Carbonell. At least, so it says here on my identification card," I said half jokingly as I pulled it from my pocket and handed it to her.

"Hmm," she mused. "I see you are a farm animal salesman by profession in the Free Zone. Of course you are," she said suspiciously.

"After you finish eating, go into the first bedroom on the left. I still have all my husband's clothes. I'll bring you something dry to put on."

She reflected, "He loved me so much, and I fell hopelessly in love with him the first time we met. Within two months I was pregnant. I'm sure you know how it is in small towns. They all turn their backs on you if you're pregnant and not married. Well, I told him that I was pregnant, and he suggested we marry right away. A few months later, he left to fight against the Germans. That was it. He never returned. I am all alone—well, not really. My child and I have each other. I have no other relatives. My husband's family was killed when France was occupied."

She directed me toward the bedroom. "Take off your wet clothes. I'll hang them by the fire and get you something to put on. And don't worry about a thing. You are hired, even without references. My closest neighbor is the mailman who lives three kilometers away. I rarely see him because I don't receive any mail." Of course, she told me that to make me feel safe from intruders. She obviously wasn't afraid of me at all.

As I entered the bedroom, the bed looked so fluffy and inviting. "The bed looks very comfortable. Would you mind if I took a nap?"

"Not at all. I'll bring you the change of clothes right away."

"Would you have a razor in the house? I'd like to shave." I wanted to change my look because of the Wanted posters.

"Of course, I do. I'll bring it along with the clothes. Oh, it's such a pleasure to talk to someone! Tomorrow, if you will watch my child, I'll take my bicycle to the village of Mirecourt, which is fifteen kilometers from here. I need to buy some supplies. Oh yes, a change of clothes and the razor," she reminded herself. "Just leave your things right here by the door, and I'll put them by the fireplace."

She returned with dry clothes and placed them on the chair next to the door and called to me, "Rest well, now. I'll wake you for dinner. Perhaps, you'll tell me what's happening out there in the world. If you're thirsty, we have a wonderful spring in the back. I could bring you some water, if you like. It's delicious and icy cold."

I called back, "For the moment, I'm just fine, and thank you for everything."

Though the bed felt wonderful, I couldn't sleep. I thought about the day to come and the one after that. I knew I was near the Vosges Mountains and that I needed to go toward Melun to the east, or toward Nogent-sur-Seine where I knew some members of *Combat* who could help me. I was sure that all the roads were being searched for my whereabouts. Thank God, I had had the knowledge to take the motorcycle with the sidecar. It was equipped with the traction to take me along those muddy pathways and through the wooded areas where the Germans were probably not searching. I had put quite a distance between the encampment and the farm where I was staying, about a hundred kilometers or so.

Since I couldn't sleep, I figured that I might as well get up. I went to the door, opened it, and picked up the dry change of clothes. Extraordinary! It was as if they were made for me—except for the shoulders, which were too narrow, the sleeves, which were too short, and the pants, which would barely go over my muscled thighs. I dressed as best I could and went into the kitchen, where Emma was preparing dinner. She turned around when she heard my steps and burst out laughing. She woke the boy with her outburst. He started crying. She excused herself right away and ran over to comfort her child from his fright.

"I'm so sorry for laughing. Please excuse me. My husband's clothes are way too small for you. I just didn't think. I have my father-in-law's clothes here as well. They'll be too big, but at least you'll be able to get into them. As soon as my baby quiets down, I'll go get something for you to put on. You'll keep an eye on the rabbit while I'm gone. I'm preparing a stew in white wine."

When the youngster calmed down, she left the two of us in the kitchen and went to search for clothes. The boy seemed very good-natured. Emma returned with a bathrobe, slippers, corduroy pants, a shirt, and hand-made virgin wool socks. "I'll put these in the bedroom so you can change right away."

I went back to the room and put on the robe and slippers. The robe was big, but it was just fine and the slippers fit well enough, too. "For someone who was raised so formally," I said softly, chuckling to myself, "I seem to be wearing bathrobes to meals a lot during this war."

When I returned to the big room, she said, smiling at me, "That's much better."

"Your little boy is adorable. He seems to be a very happy child. He was showing me his toys while you were gone."

"Yes, he is wonderful. I am really very lucky. I'm raising him without any help, so I'm grateful that he is such a delight. He has no one to talk to except me, which makes it extremely difficult. We listen to the radio and to the records I have of Tino Rossi, Edith Piaf, Jean Sablon, and Caruso, but we don't have the opportunity to see people too often."

The young woman talked nonstop. Of course, she did, and I understood. She was starved for human contact. I listened politely as she talked about everything. In the early evening, I excused myself to change into her father-in-law's clothes. The little boy was playing with his toys on a thick rug in the corner of the kitchen that was fenced off for him.

When I came back, she said, "Michel, come over and sit with me on the sofa. I can watch my boy from here." I went over and sat down.

"What do you want to know about the outside world?" I asked her.

"I listen to the radio every day, but I know it goes through German censors. Since we're located at the very bottom of the valley, we cannot receive signals from radio stations like Brazzaville or the BBC from London. The BBC in English wouldn't do me any good, anyway"—she laughed—"since I don't understand the language. I can't receive the BBC in French, either. I do understand some German, though, since my parents were from Alsace. At home, we always spoke Alsatian."

"What I can tell you, Emma, is that soon there will be an Allied landing in France. The war should be over within a year."

"That's wonderful news! Tell me, Michel, where did you come from today?"

"I parachuted into Neufchâteau and planned to go toward Vesoul, taking the Saône or the Rhône Valley. But assessing the situation, with so many Germans around, I'm in no hurry to leave. If I'm caught, they will probably send me into forced labor in Germany."

"Oh, you're right to stay here. Stay as long as you'd like. You'll be safe with us," she urged with a tone of desperation.

"Does any military traffic pass by?"

"None at all. This road doesn't lead anywhere. It just ends at the bottom of the valley. You'll be just fine. Thank you so much for stopping at my home. I needed some human contact. You have no idea what your presence means to me. I have a feeling that you are strong and determined and will succeed in all that you do."

She had suffered incredible loss, and her great need for love and caring was evident. She was so sweet and sincere, so simple and naïve. She had never been out of this valley. Her knowledge of the world was so limited. She was totally innocent and trusting. What a breath of fresh air in a world filled with cruelty.

THIRTY

Sanctuary

We chatted for a while, and then all of a sudden Emma jumped up and announced, "Dinner is ready!" It smelled so good. She had made the rabbit with potatoes, carrots, and onions. I sat down at the large table and the young girl put a serving in my carved-out bowl. I tasted it and generously complimented her on the dinner. In truth, it needed a lot of help in its seasoning. Some red wine would have made it so much better. We ate for a while in silence. Then I asked, "What work would you like me to start with tomorrow? I always wake up before dawn, so you really need to tell me tonight."

"You don't have to get up that early here, but the rooster crows before daybreak, and he would wake you anyway," she laughed. "I'll be up to fix you your breakfast. We can talk about what needs to be done then. After dinner, we need to go look for some work clothes for you."

When we finished dinner, she led me to the other part of the house where her father-in-law used to live. "After work, if you'd like, you can rest in my father-in-law's side of the house. The only drawback is that the walls are very cold, and I'm not heating that side right now. Our only heat comes from the fireplaces. So, probably, you would be more comfortable staying in our side of the house after all. Anyway, the company would do me good, if you don't mind."

As we approached the door leading to the other side, she said, "Here's the key. Go get some clothes and come back to warm yourself by the fire."

I opened the door and entered, but I couldn't find any light. I returned to her kitchen right away. "Where might I find a carbide or an oil lamp?" I asked.

"Of course, I should have thought of that!" she replied and brought me a carbide lamp right away. I checked to see if there was enough water in the reservoir. There wasn't, so I went over to the kitchen pump to fill it. The blue flame was really beautiful. I then went back to her father-in-law's side and entered one of the bedrooms. There was nothing in the armoire. Then I opened the door of another room and found wall-to-wall clothing. There were several military uniforms from the artillery unit with the stripes of captain as well as a huge selection of other clothing. I tried on a hat. It was a little big, but I could add a strip of something on the inside to make it fit. The jacket was huge on me but over a shirt and sweater, it would be just fine. The pants fit perfectly. What I really needed were short pants to work in the mud, several shirts, overalls, and a straw hat. I tried on the shoes. They were too big, but I would make do.

I gathered the work clothes and a pair of pajamas in my arms and returned to Emma's. I showed her what I had chosen. She was so happy that I was able to find something to wear. I could see it in her sparkling eyes and pleasant attitude. What an angel!

Now that my stomach was full and I had found the clothes I needed, I asked, "So, what work would you like me to begin with tomorrow?"

"We need more wood cut for heating and cooking," she said. "The fences for the sheep have fallen over. I've lost all control of the animals. The cages for the chickens and the rabbits need to be repaired. I am sure you will find plenty to do. Start where you would like. I hope it is not too much to ask."

Changing the subject, she said, "Let's listen to the radio now. I'll put my boy to sleep and then join you. Make yourself comfortable on the sofa."

I turned on the radio and found Radio Toulouse that was advertising, at that moment, "Herbes Zan," a catchy commercial for herbs. It made me think of Josephine. She liked the tune and would sing it a lot. And Radio Toulouse was her favorite radio station.

Emma came over to the sofa and sat down. I told her about Josephine Baker and how nice she was to me when

I was a little boy. I told her about my childhood, about my tutor retired from the Austrian cavalry, about riding horseback with him almost every day. She interrupted, "Oh, you ride! My husband and I used to go riding all the time! We have two horses. We can go riding together."

"But what will you do with the boy while we go riding?"

"I don't know yet, but I'll think of something. Could you trim the horses' hooves tomorrow so that we can plan to go riding? Their hooves haven't been trimmed in such a long time."

She talked on and on, jumping quickly from one subject to another. "My neighbor, the mailman, came over to cut the hay for us, and I gave him as much hay as he wanted in exchange. I still have a lot left over because we don't have the number of animals that we used to before the Germans occupied France. I sell the hay that is left over. We used to have twenty cows whose milk we sold. We had a lot more goats and sheep as well as two oxen, a donkey, and a mule. My husband worked with those animals to run the farm besides working as a blacksmith. We didn't do badly at all. When the Germans came, they took almost all of the animals. If I had only known what was going to happen, I would have fed them arsenic so that the Nazi troops would have been poisoned while they ate," she said with anger in her voice.

Suddenly, she was in a fury. She had lost so much. I said to her gently, "You know, all the Germans are not bad. They were called to serve their country as we were called to serve our own."

"Well, they didn't have to kill my husband, his parents, my parents, the two oxen, all the cows, the donkey, and the mule," she blurted out. She was visibly shaken. She had had to overcome so much alone and at such a young age. She had probably been sixteen years old or so and pregnant when France was occupied.

As we listened to the radio, she calmed down and eventually fell asleep next to me. After a while, I got up very quietly so as not to disturb her and went to the bedroom to go to sleep myself. I awoke during the night to go to the bathroom. I checked on Emma. She was sitting up reading on the sofa. "You're not tired?" I asked.

"Yes, I am but . . ." She hesitated. "This is difficult for me to say, but you're sleeping in my bedroom."

"Oh, excuse me, I didn't know. I thought you had another room," I explained.

"It was my fault. I didn't tell you," she said. "The other room is the baby's room. If you don't mind sleeping on the sofa, I'll bring you a pillow and blankets. I sleep so much better in my own bed."

She brought me two blankets and a pillow, then went to her bedroom. During the night, I heard the child calling out. I went to his room, picked him up, and held him in my arms. Once again, he was all smiles when he saw me. After a time, I put him back to bed and returned to the sofa. It was still dark outside. Soon after, she passed by the sofa to go to the bathroom. She must have noticed that my eyes were open.

"I thought I heard my little boy a while ago. Did you?" she asked.

"Yes, I did. I went to his room to quiet him down so that you could sleep. Again, I saw that wonderful smile of his. He is such a good boy. After I held him a few minutes, he was ready to go back to sleep."

"Thank you so much," she said, with an endearing look on her face. "Michel, may I sit down next to you? As long as you're awake, I'd like to talk to you about something."

"Why yes, of course."

"Do you think you'll be staying any length of time with us? I ask because I have a pension that goes directly to my bank owing to my being widowed during the war. I would like to go get some money to pay you for your work. I really cannot accept that you work without getting paid."

"I'd like to stay for a while, if you don't mind. I missed meeting some friends because of the German patrols all over the place. If it's all right with you, I would like to stay three or four days."

Suddenly, she became very emotional. Her face turned red. She exploded, "But I don't want you to leave at all!"

I tried to calm her down. "Perhaps I can stay longer, but I cannot promise how long. I'll chop the wood later this morning. I'll fix all the fences. I'll try to stay till the end of winter, but I really cannot say right now. I simply do not know."

She seemed calmed by the possibility of a prolonged stay. "I'm going to bed now. Good night, Michel. I'll see you at breakfast," she said. I wished her a good night. I had noticed the desperation in her reactions. Her age, raising her boy alone, the responsibility of the farm, losing all her loved ones—it had all been too much for her. While considering all her difficulties, I eventually fell asleep.

As she said, the rooster crowed before daybreak, but I was already up. I was washed, dressed, and outside cutting wood when she came to the door. "Good morning, Michel. Did you sleep well?"

"Yes, I did. And you?" I asked.

"No, not really," she said. "I could hardly wait to talk to you again this morning. I just kept thinking and thinking and couldn't fall asleep. You're such a good listener."

"I've been wondering, how is it that the Germans didn't take your horses?"

"As good fortune would have it, they were out on the range, and the Germans never saw them."

"You were lucky."

"I know, and I'm grateful," she said. "My husband and I shared some wonderful times together on horseback. It brings back good memories just to see them."

"Now, come on inside," she said. "I've made an omelette for you with duck eggs, potatoes, and onions."

After breakfast, I went back outside to finish cutting wood. After neatly piling it up, I began repairing and putting the fences up again. It took the entire day to make new posts and dig new holes to place them in. I didn't stop to eat lunch. I worked until three in the afternoon.

Then I went into the house to take a shower and change my clothes. I put on my brown suit and opened the door to go outside. Suddenly, I heard sobbing from behind me. I turned and saw Emma in tears. She screamed, "You're leaving! You're leaving!"

I walked over to her and took her by the shoulders. "No, no, I'm not leaving. I had nothing else that was clean to put on. That's all. I didn't want to put on your father-in-law's uniforms."

"Oh," she said, apparently relieved, wiping the tears from her cheeks. "Go into the storage room. I'm sure you'll find everything you need."

As I went to get the key for the back of the house, I said to her, "Promise me that you'll calm down." She looked into my eyes and said, "Swear to me that you're not leaving today." I returned her gaze and said, "I swear."

I went to the back of the house and found the storage room. I found several pairs of pants, shirts, socks, and sweaters. Then, I went back to the kitchen. "Tomorrow, I'll take care of your horses' hooves," I said. "Then I would like to take a ride through the woods and in the immediate area to get an idea of where the roads and paths are located."

She was heating up the rabbit stew for an early dinner. I'm sure she knew I hadn't eaten lunch and would be hungry. She poured me a glass of goat's milk to go with it. I devoured the meal. As soon as I finished, I felt extremely tired. "Do you mind if I lie down on the bed?"

"Please do," she said.

* * *

I slept through the night till morning. I found Emma next to me in her bed. I was careful not to wake her when I got up. I washed and dressed. Then I heard her boy chattering to himself, so I went to his room to let him know I was going to heat a bottle of pabulum for him. When I came back, the sweet little boy was smiling as usual. I gave him the bottle and went out to trim the horses' hooves and begin working on the fence again.

After a couple of hours, I took a break and walked around to the front of the father-in-law's house. The day before, I had entered through the connecting door. From the front, the building was enormous. I had had no idea just how big it was from the little bit I had seen inside. There were other structures as well. The stables were about a hundred meters long. They included a dairy barn with hay storage above and a ramp for taking the feed up to the second floor. This was clearly two properties.

After seeing this obvious wealth, I did not understand. This was no ordinary farm. I went back to the house to ask Emma about it. She was still in bed. It must have been a treat for her to not be awakened by her son early in the morning. She heard me come in and called out, "Come in. Come in." I entered the bedroom.

"You must have taken care of my son. Thank you. Did you sleep well?"

I smiled at her. "I slept very well. And you?"

Obviously rested, she said, "I slept quite well, too."

I decided to broach the subject right away. "I took a walk around. This is no ordinary farm, Emma."

She responded, "Ah, yes, well, why don't you go sit down on the sofa? I'll put on my robe and we can sit and talk." I went and sat down, and she joined me right away.

"My father-in-law bought the properties in 1935. He was a career officer in the military. He had inherited huge sums of money from his uncles and then from his father. The property includes about eight or nine hundred acres. I'm not exactly sure. Then he built this house for his son, who was the blacksmith of the village. When he learned that I was pregnant, he insisted that his son marry me. For our wedding gift, he put both parts of the property in both of our names. This part of the property has always been used to grow potatoes and wheat. There is a sharecropper who does the work and takes sixty-five percent. He pays me the rest in crops and money. So, now you know the whole story."

Changing the subject, she said, "I want to get to the village so that I can take some money out of the bank to pay you for your work. Now that I know you a little better, I want to confide in you that I need some guidance. This property is a big responsibility. I know very little about business or about life in general. You see, I really need your assistance. I don't want you to leave. If you have to, I understand, but I ask you to return when you can. I trust you and pray that you will help my son and me."

"I understand," I said. "Let's get started right away. I need a pencil and some paper." She jumped up and brought them to me. I began to sketch and draw some plans. We spent several hours working on the project and discussing potential sources of income.

"If I cannot come back, I want you to follow this line of planning, which will take care of you and your son for your whole life. If I can, after the war is over, I will come back to help you for a time."

"Now, let's go saddle up the horses and take a ride. I took care of their feet early this morning. Do you have a backpack?" I asked. She nodded. "Bring it to me. I am going to cut two holes in it for your son's legs and put him on my back. I want you to show me the extent of the property before it gets dark. I'll have a better idea of what we are working with if I see it with my own eyes."

She was excited. "This is wonderful," she said, "but first you must have something to eat."

"No," I replied, "we must get back before it gets dark. Get dressed and get your son ready. Take some bread and cheese for us and whatever you need for the boy." While she was getting ready, I cut two holes in the backpack and saddled the horses. When they came out, I put the backpack on and told her to put him in. We mounted our horses and left for our tour of the property. When we returned, it was almost dark.

The following morning, the boy didn't wake either of us up. We had all been affected by the wonderful, long horseback ride, and we all slept late. We ate breakfast together and then walked over to her father-in-law's house.

First, we entered his office. There was an amazing stillness in the room. One could picture him there, a learned man, reading one of his leather-bound books in the comfortable armchair. The war had canceled his retirement and was responsible for his premature death.

"Here is a portrait of my father-in-law. He looks very proud, don't you think? Look at all the medals on his uniform," she pointed out. "Just after his son and I were married, he shared with me that he had long looked forward to the peace that he would enjoy here during his retirement. His days were cut short, right here in this house," she said sadly.

I really liked the house. "The Spanish brick gives the building an austere façade," I said, "yet somehow it welcomes you. The exterior contrasts with the sweet harmony of this beautiful room. Anyone would be surprised to discover such a beautiful library in such a remote region. Look at these rare editions!" On several glassed-in shelves were very old editions of famous books. "It's amazing to find a collection like this intact, especially during these troubled times. This is a moment to remember. I'll never forget this experience my whole life. It is such an important lesson in this short visit to your father-in-law's home. Without warning, all his expectations came to an end. We discuss life with each other, what the future holds, and then it can end abruptly, dashing all our dreams."

She showed me more of the house—the entry hall,

the small salon, the living room, the billiard room with its beautiful wood paneling. There were fifteen bedrooms on the second floor, each with its own fireplace and bath. It was impressive.

Then she showed me the kitchen. "Ah, this is a wonderful kitchen! If I see what a person eats and how he prepares it, I can tell you who he is. The copper pots and pans are of excellent quality. And these ovens! It's unheard of! There are four of them, all with burners on the top." I paused in appreciation, then continued, "You could feed an army from this kitchen, Emma. There are four sinks and look! Look at this huge pantry! This kitchen must be twelve by sixteen meters and the dining room must be ten by twenty. You could easily convert this house into an *auberge* and organize vacations on horseback. You could call it 'Les Chevauchées.' The possibilities are tremendous."

While I was savoring this fabulous home, my mind was actually focused elsewhere as well. I was thinking that I had to find a way to get in contact with the *gendarmerie*.

As we concluded the tour of the big house, I asked, "Do you know any of the gendarmes in your region, Emma?"

"No, personally, I don't know a one. But why do you want to know?" she asked, suddenly tensing up.

"Oh, I just have something I want to ask them."

She pleaded, "But I want to know. What is this about?"

"Emma, I need to get in contact with the gendarmes so they will contact the partisans in your region and in the region just south of here." Then I counseled myself and remained silent, thinking that I couldn't tell her any more. She had lost too many people close to her already. If the Germans came and interrogated her, she'd have nothing to fear if I told her nothing. Besides this, it would be dangerous for me if she knew anything more.

She responded, "Why don't you talk to the mailman? He's a veteran of World War I and, of course, despises the Nazis. His son and nine others were captured and killed about four months ago after trying to inhibit the German transport of people and arms by blowing up railroad tracks. The boys were brought to the central square and shot." She shuddered at the horrible memory. "You can take my bicycle to go see him, if you want."

"Emma, it's too dangerous for me to be on the roads. Would you go to his home and ask him to come here? I'll watch the boy."

"Of course I will." She went out, got on her bicycle, and left right away. Forty-five minutes later, she and the mailman returned on their bicycles. They came into the house where I was playing with her son. The mailman said, "*Bonjour, monsieur.* I hear you want to contact the gendarmes."

"That's right," I said. "Can you help me?"

The mailman replied, "There are no gendarmes close to us in this region. The closest *gendarmerie* is in Neufchâteau, about fifteen kilometers from here. We never see them around here because we are far from the main national highway. But in my profession, I know everyone—the good and the bad. I am on a first-name basis with most of the citizens in the area. Normally, I just mind my own business and don't get involved in other people's affairs; however, I do know the mayor and the leader of the French Forces of the Interior."

"I think you can help me, if you're willing. If Madame will excuse us, why don't we take a walk in the garden," I said as I walked toward the door, indicating that he should follow. "Please, don't be offended, Emma. I am only thinking of the welfare of the two of you," I said as I looked at her and the boy. She nodded.

Once outside, I said to the mailman, "Since you know the leader of the FFI, would you be so kind as to tell him that I would like to meet with him personally. I need to give him some confidential information regarding the Allied landing in the south of France. It may happen in the days to come, next month or next year. I would be grateful if you could contact him within the coming twenty-four hours. Each moment is valuable because we need all the preparation time we can get. I was parachuted into the vicinity of Vittel three days ago and was taken prisoner by the Germans. Aided by a German officer, I was able to escape."

"I can help you," he said. "I'll be in touch."

After his departure, I went into the house. Dinner was on the table. Emma didn't say anything. She was pouting because she had been excluded from the discussion with the mailman. It was already 8 P.M. We ate in silence. After finishing, she quickly did the dishes. Then she took the boy, put him to bed, and went to bed herself. I went to the living room, lay down on the sofa, and fell asleep.

About one in the morning, I heard a tapping on the window. I went to the door and opened it. In front of me was a little boy, maybe ten years old, standing on the porch. He whispered, "We must be very quiet so that Madame doesn't hear us. Put on your shoes and follow me."

I put on my shoes, grabbed a jacket, and followed the little boy. We went around the barn and then to the other side of the big house. There, the boy tapped on the basement window. He turned and whispered, "Everything's all right. Follow me."

About twenty meters farther, there were five stairs that led to a door. The boy went down first and knocked. "All's clear," he said and indicated that I should follow. Another ten meters beyond was another door, which opened abruptly. There stood a massive man dressed in a gendarme's uniform. He motioned for us to come in and said as we entered, "Watch your head. The entry is very low."

The room was dimly lit with candles, but I could see that there were four other gendarmes seated at the table and another man standing to the side who wasn't in uniform. To my great surprise, it was the mailman who stood there on the right as I entered the room. He nodded and asked me to sit down. Then he left for a moment and returned with a bottle of eau-de-vie and seven glasses.

"I know you must be surprised," he said. "Madame does not know that her father-in-law's basement is our general headquarters."

One of the gendarmes said, "We have heard about you and your escape. The Germans have placed a price on your head and have mounted a widespread search. They are powerful in this region. Last week, a Jesuit priest was captured. He was waiting for an English plane to pick him up but was taken prisoner before it arrived."

I sat down at the table, and the mailman began speaking. "After you give us the instructions about the landing, you'll need to place your confidence in us. We'll arrange for your return to England. We'll do our very best to help you in any way we can. We don't want you to end up a prisoner of the Gestapo. After you leave, I'll call a general meeting to implement your instructions."

"By the order of British Intelligence and General Giraud," I began, "we need to keep the enemy busy in the south. We need to blow up bridges, gas and diesel stations, to derail trains and create as much destruction and havoc as we can in the train stations themselves. We want to propagate the information that the Allied landing will take place in the south of France. Our goal is to encourage the enemy to bring more troops here to the south. Urge those who work for the railroads in any capacity to leave their jobs for a time and join the Resistance because there will certainly be a backlash against the railroad workers. You also must contact the Post, Telegraph, and Telephone Office and encourage them to stop all communication and leave their homes to join with the Resistance. Tell those in charge of the electrical stations to destroy the generators and those in charge of the radio stations to blow them up. You need to create as much disorder as you can. That is my message. Do you have any questions?"

Since there were no questions, I asked, "When do you think you'll be able to secure an airplane for my return to England?" The mailman said, "We'll let you know in the morning." Everyone got up and left.

When I returned to Emma's house, I entered quietly so as not to wake her or the boy. I lay down on the sofa and went to sleep. I woke up to the clatter of pots and pans. Emma was preparing breakfast. When everything was ready, I walked over to the table. She still wasn't talking to me. Just as I sat down, there was a knock on the door. It was the mailman. "Please, come in," she offered. "Join us for a bowl of warm goat's milk."

"Thank you, but no," he replied. Then, turning toward me, he said, "The rendezvous is set at four o'clock tomorrow morning. You'll need to say your farewells today. You'll be picked up at nine this evening." He quickly said good-bye and left.

Emma turned pale. There was a long silence. The first words spoken were hers. "Where are you going?" she angrily demanded.

"As I said before, the less you know the safer it will be

for you and your son." Then she raised her voice. "We really don't need you, anyway, you know. You can leave now for all I care!"

After a few moments, in a softer tone, she added, "If you decide to stay, you can make a life with us. We can move to the big house. We can create a new business together, an equestrian center and lodge. It will be wonderful."

Grasping the meaning of the look on my face, she stopped talking. I said nothing. There was nothing to say. The child was chattering away. We finished our breakfast in silence. She cleaned up the kitchen, dressed her boy, and the two of them left for the village on her bicycle.

I spent a peaceful day walking around the property, taking in its beauty. Now I was satisfied that my mission had been fulfilled. I felt good about my achievement. I had successfully started to spread the rumor that Mr. Churchill wanted to circulate, to fool the Germans into expecting an Allied invasion in the south of France rather than in the north at the Pas-de-Calais or in Normandy.

When Emma and her son returned late in the afternoon with the groceries, I asked her, "Did you have a nice trip to the village?"

No response. I approached the bicycle. "I'll take the groceries in for you." I lifted the little boy off the back of the bike and put him on the ground, then took the two sacks and walked toward the house. The two of them followed. The boy was quiet, tired after the long journey. I put the bags on the counter.

All of a sudden, she spoke, "Don't touch a thing. Leave everything as it is. I want to talk to you. I'll put my son down for a nap, and I'll be back in a few minutes."

I went to the living room and sat down on the sofa. She joined me about ten minutes later.

"He fell asleep as soon as his head touched the pillow. Now we're alone. I have something for you. I stopped at the bank while I was in the village. I took out ten thousand francs for you just in case you need some money. Since you won't tell me where you're going, I figured you might need some funds for expenses along the way." I didn't say a thing. Of course, I would not accept the money but said nothing about it. I just listened and let her talk. She spoke of how our life together would be after the war. I didn't respond. Somehow, she had it in her head that I would return. I had never meant to give her that impression.

We shared a few drinks and went to bed around eight o'clock. I put my travel clothes on and gathered my few things together. Emma fell asleep right away. I dozed off and woke up just before nine. No one had arrived. Again, I nodded off.

I slept fitfully through the night, expecting the partisans to come at any moment. I got up before daybreak and went out to milk a goat. I came back inside, poured some warm milk into a bowl, and made some toast. No one had showed up the night before to pick me up. What did this mean?

As I was eating, the boy wandered into the kitchen. "Shhh," I said, putting my finger next to my lips. "Your mother needs to sleep this morning. Shall I give you some warm milk and toast?"

"Yes," he whispered. The two of us ate in silence. Then I went upstairs to help him get dressed. It was cold and windy outside. We went out for a walk. We looked in on all the animals and talked to the man who took care of the property while he was feeding. I told the boy some stories as we walked along. He was very bright and talked a lot.

When we returned to the house, it was about nine thirty. There was a truck parked in front. It was filled with bales of straw. There were two young men inside the cab. The man in the passenger's seat shouted, "Come over and get in!" There was no explanation as to why they had not arrived at the designated time the night before.

Emma was standing at the door in her bathrobe. Bad weather had led to this strange saga: a wayward jump into the trees, a kind German officer who let me go free, and then this affectionate and very needy young woman who took me in. She called to her son with arms outstretched, "Come here." Immediately, he took off at a run toward his mother. She picked him up in her arms.

She called out, "Michel, I have your bag."

I went to the door. "Thank you for your hospitality, Emma. I know you and the boy will be fine. I must go now." I went to the truck, climbed in, and shut the door.

The little boy shouted, "Michel, Michel! We'll see you after we win the war!"

I shouted back to him, "Take good care of your mother!" The truck drove off. I was on my way to safety in England.

THIRTY-ONE

Interrogation

Abruptly, the driver stopped the truck. There was no one around. Why then was he stopping? We had just left Emma's house only five minutes before. Had he spotted German soldiers?

"Climb up on the hood, then onto the roof of the cabin, and pull up the canvas that is covering the straw. The truck bed is empty in the center. You'll find two men armed with Hotchkiss antiaircraft machine guns inside. Climb in, and I'll tie down the canvas behind you."

I got into the back of the huge truck, an eight-wheel, double-axle Berliet. There was a lot of available space inside the truck bed. "The driver will avoid main arteries and national routes because they are blockaded by the Germans who are still searching for you," one of the two heavily armed partisans told me. "They are stopping every vehicle to search and requiring each person to get out and show his identity card. That's why we're taking secondary roads. We're heading toward Vittel. It's longer this way, but we intend to get you out of the country alive."

After a few hours, the truck came to a gradual halt. The man riding shotgun pulled back the canvas. "Get out now. We've arrived at the farm. We'll leave the truck in the barn and continue on foot through the mountains. We have about a six-hour trek in front of us, so let's get going."

Hours later, we reached the top of a hill that overlooked a beautiful valley about four or five kilometers long. This was a perfect flat landing area for the airplane that would be picking me up. The mailman was there waiting.

"*Bonjour*, my friend," he greeted me, and nodded at his colleagues. "You must be hungry after your little hike. Come sit down. I have plenty of bread and cheese for all and some wine to wash it down."

The last of the sunset was glorious beyond the mountains. "Do you see all those silhouettes in the valley?" I looked down into the valley and saw shadows of more than a hundred men surrounding the proposed landing site. "They are all here to protect you in case the Germans discover what is going on."

We ate and talked and waited. At exactly eight o'clock, we heard two cries of an owl. Three bonfires were lit to form an arrow to indicate the landing field. As soon as they were lit, a red flare was sent up. "That's the signal *not* to land," the mailman whispered. "Lie down. Don't move. We'll take care of everything."

At the end of the proposed landing strip, there were four German trucks with searchlights, illumined well by the light of the fires. They were creeping slowly forward. I could see an entire company of German soldiers, well over a hundred men. In front of them, in their black helmets, were about fifty French Militia. I could hear the droning of the airplane circling. Then I heard a voice shout out in French, "It sounds like we have company." Right after, there was a shot. A scream—someone was hit. Then a barrage of gunfire rang out. The Germans fell like flies. They were totally surrounded by the partisans who were well armed with lightweight machine guns. Mortars were being shot at the trucks. The Germans and French Militia began to retreat but were confused about which way to go because the mortars were coming from behind. They retreated toward the mortars—they had to choose one direction. A small group of partisans ran past us. "Stay flat on the ground behind those rocks and bushes," one of them whispered as he hurried past.

The shooting intensified. The machine-gun fire was coming dangerously close to our small group. All of a sudden, we heard an engine that sounded like a German plane. The trucks were firing their machine guns in the direction of the mortars. It had become a really intense battle. About twenty partisans appeared behind us. They hadn't known we were there. They took position in front of our group to protect us. Suddenly, we were surrounded by the French Militia. The gunfire was continuous. Our men started dropping. Almost all the partisans protecting us were shot, but before they died they must have killed about thirty of the French Militia. The mailman and I and a few others had no choice but to surrender. It was a very dark moment.

The Germans and French partisans were still fighting down in the valley. The French Militia took prisoner other partisans besides those in our small group. They forced us down the hill, loaded us into trucks, and took us to their camp near Vittel, where they had a prison. We were unloaded, about forty prisoners in all, and were each thrown in a separate cell.

Quite a while later, the colonel in charge of the French Militia gathered us all in the courtyard. "If it were my decision," he announced, "you would all be shot here and now. I would have the pleasure of killing the leader of your group myself but not with my revolver—with my knife, to be sure that he would have a slow and painful death. And for every ten of my men that were killed in this battle, I would cut off one of his fingers or toes. And for him to avoid this suffering, he would have to give up the man who was supposed to leave on that plane." My mind was working fast and furiously, but as yet no plan had come to me.

He continued, "As I am sure you know, last month we caught one of your spies, a Capuchin priest, who was waiting for his plane to England. I don't know why this piece of dirt would interest the British. I want you to know that he was tortured till he died. You are all being taken to the Gestapo in Paris. I wish you all a slow and painful death."

This was disturbing news. Escaping from the Gestapo would not be an easy task. As we were being reloaded into trucks, I was searching for any possibility of escape before being handed over to the Gestapo. No solution so far. We had been given nothing to eat or drink since our capture and were not allowed to talk to each other. Seven or eight hours later, we arrived in Paris. It was nighttime.

The trucks pulled up in front of an impressive, beautifully built fourteenth-century building made of granite. We got down from the trucks and were ordered to go up the stairs to the second floor. The steep stairs were beautifully carved of the same granite as the façade. One of the militia led the way. In all, we numbered about a hundred prisoners. He turned left and strode down the hallway to its end. We followed.

"Face the wall and kneel down. Listen to me!" he instructed. "You will now be interrogated. There is one man among you who was going to take that plane. The first one to denounce him will be given his freedom. We give you our word," he said in a sincere tone. "Now, the first man in line, get up and enter the interrogation room—the door to my right."

The man obeyed without question. There was an overwhelming silence that filled the hallway. A couple of minutes later, we heard a shot. Two of the Gestapo came out carrying the body of the first prisoner. "He didn't want to answer our questions," one of them said as they dropped the dead man on the floor. They had killed the first man for effect. After this, they would probably torture the remaining men, one by one, until they had the information they were looking for.

"Next in line," one of the Gestapo said. The next man got up and entered. Again the silence lasted about two minutes, broken by the sound of a revolver going off. One of the Gestapo opened the door. Another body was dropped on the floor. "Next," he ordered.

"I was wrong about their method," I realized. "They must be under a lot of pressure from their superiors to quickly find out who I am."

The third man went in, and the door was closed behind him. A couple of minutes passed, and again a shot was fired. A different man from the Gestapo came out. He looked like the one in charge. "This is ridiculous!" he said. "You all want to die for nothing! We will change our methods to make you talk." A large group of SS arrived. It was about six thirty in the morning. The sun was up already and making its way through the shutters. They began separating the prisoners into groups of four. I was in a group with the mailman and two men I didn't know.

"All right, get moving," someone ordered. We were shoved forward with rifle butts, and many of us received blows to the kidneys to try to make us move through the hallway and down the stairs more quickly.

Thoughts were racing through my mind. Primarily, I was hoping to find an opportunity to escape. At that moment, there was no possibility. Once outside, my group was told to get into a commando car. There were two SS in front of us and two SS behind us in the car. I strategized to myself silently, "What should I do? Denounce myself and tell the SS that I have a cyanide pill that I can use at any time, so it makes no sense to torture me? No, giving them that information would do me no good. Denounce myself and 'confess' the rumor we want to spread about the Allied invasion coming in the south? That sounds pretty good. The false confession would only further serve our cause. That's the purpose of my mission, after all, so maybe this is the perfect opportunity. Since I'm in this predicament anyway, I might as well use it to our advantage. When the interrogation starts, I'll pretend to be very strong, to have no fear, say nothing, and slowly I'll show weakening. I'll begin responding to their questions and finally, I'll confess, and they'll totally believe my story. It sounds good in theory. We'll see how it works."

As soon as everyone was loaded into cars, we were taken to another Gestapo center. Our car stopped, and we were ordered to get out. The instant my two feet hit the ground, two huge men came toward me. Each grabbed me under an armpit, lifted me up, and took me toward the compound, my feet dangling. *This must be a tactic to make me feel small and powerless,* I thought, keeping my thinking removed from the situation and my mind clear. They shoved the others together into a group with the butts of their rifles.

The building looked like a prison from the outside with bars on all the windows. We took the stairs down. The two men holding me changed their grip. One lifted me by the belt and the other by the collar as we went to the basement level. My feet were still not touching the ground. After going down a few steps, they tossed me to the bottom. Trying to humiliate me, one of them said in a mocking tone, "Oh, isn't it a shame that a guy like this wants to play war. Look, he can't even stand on his own two feet!"

This is another way to impress me with their force, I thought, ignoring the pain.

They walked down the remaining steps and picked me up under the arms again, opened a door, and carried me inside a small room containing only a wooden bench that was attached to the floor. There was a steel-mesh window in the center of the wall in front of the bench. "Sit down!" one of them ordered.

On the other side of the window, this huge, bulky woman with a shaved head appeared. She must have been at least six feet tall. *What a horrid-looking woman,* I thought to myself. *How do the buttons on her uniform hold those enormous breasts inside? She looks like an over-sized stuffed sausage.*

In German, she dismissed the two men in a very stern, deep voice. They shut the door behind them. She remained standing and addressed me in French. "Do you know which Gestapo center you are coming from?" she asked.

"My name is Michel Carbonell."

She interrupted, "Yes, I see your name here on my list. You're coming from the sorting center, the *centre de triage*. It's about time they sent me a nice young man! Usually they're too young or too old. Why don't you help me and give me the information that we want to know," she said in a sickly sweet tone. "If you do, I'll have you taken from your cell tonight and brought to my room. You'll be able to order whatever you'd like to eat and drink. I have a pencil and paper here. Just tell me what we want to know."

Inside my head, I was saying, "How am I going to get out of this one?" The response that came out of my mouth was, "I must tell you that I have had diarrhea the last four days and also have difficulty holding my urine; however, I am very flattered by your offer but feel morally obligated to tell you that I have crabs."

With an air of disappointment, she responded, "Well, I am going to help you, anyway. Instead of your being sent from one office to another, I will send you directly to the person who will handle your case."

Hmm, I thought, *she's really being quite nice. I didn't think she'd take rejection that well.*

"The only recommendation I have is that you *must* collaborate or you will certainly suffer the consequences. Good luck," she added. Two soldiers entered and escorted me out.

* * *

Next I found myself in an office, unlike the others. A very bright interrogation light was facing my direction that made it impossible to see much. I couldn't make out anything on the walls. In the middle of the room, I could make out the legs of a table. That's all.

Suddenly, I heard a lot of noise coming toward me. Two men wheeled a steel chair on a platform in front of me. "Sit down!" The two soldiers grabbed me and shoved me into the seat. They tied me to the chair with leather straps at the waist, each shoulder, each forearm, each wrist, and then put a steel collar around my neck to restrain my head to the back. They placed a basin of water on the floor in front of me and removed my shoes and socks. "Aha," I surmised. "The friendly and amorous Amazon wasn't that nice after all. I know what the water means." They put my feet in the basin. Now the circus would begin. I mentally prepared myself for it. I knew I was to be the star performer. In silence, I readied myself for the torture to come.

A voice, amplified by a microphone, came from behind the light. "What is your last name?"

"Carbonell," I answered.

"How do you spell it?" the voice asked.

"C-a-r-b-o-n-e-l-l."

"What is your first name?"

"Michel."

"Where were you born?"

"In Oran."

Then the voice asked, "Where is Oran?"

I decided to provoke the man to test what he was made of. "Monsieur, you don't know your geography."

In a furious voice, the man blurted out, "Answer the question!"

"Since you don't know, I'll tell you. It is in Algeria, North Africa."

"What is the closest city?"

I adopted a patronizing tone and replied, "Since you don't know where Oran is, what difference does it make what city is closest to it?" Not giving him the time to respond, I said, "All right, I'll continue your geography lesson—no charge. The closest city is Algiers. Algiers is just north of the Sahara desert. And all of this territory is a *département* of France."

The man reacted to my answer and said sarcastically, "You think you're funny, don't you? What is your religion?"

"For me, your questions are not 'catholic,' but I am."

He asked, "Where are your parents?"

"I have no idea."

"Why don't you know where your parents are?"

I was getting exasperated with these questions. "Because I left the house at the age of seven," I responded.

"Did you return?"

Then I said in Italian, "You're breaking my balls."

He reprimanded me. "Speak clearly."

I retorted, "You should ask for a translation from your friend Mussolini!"

The man was not rattled. "Answer the last question."

I mimicked him. "Answer the last question. Oh, excuse me, for a moment I thought I was a parrot. No, I didn't return."

"How old are you?"

"I was born in 1922. How is your math?"

"Where were you born?"

I was trying to irritate him. "You have a short memory. I already told you, I was born in Oran."

A man approached with a very thick bath towel in his hands. He dunked the towel in the basin of water, backed up, and with a lot of force, whipped me on both sides of the face, hard enough to dislocate my jaw, but it didn't. What it actually did was to knock the cap off my tooth. The cyanide pill was loose in my mouth. I had to catch it with my tongue! I kept trying to get it as they were talking. I wasn't concentrating on what they were saying. I just kept trying to get that pill back into the hole in my tooth with my tongue.

I could hear the words of the interrogator again. "Have a little respect. You know better than to talk to me like that! Where are your manners? You're not in a position to be joking around because *you* are the prisoner here—not me. We can do whatever we want with you. We can kill you right away, or we can torture you slowly until you are ready to give us the information we want." While he was lecturing, I was able to get the pill back into my tooth, and then the cap. Whew!

Another voice came from behind the light ordering two soldiers to get the battery. "We're going to change tactics now," the voice said. "We'll see if he becomes more willing to talk. We'll also see if he loses some of his insolence. I believe he will become a little less jovial when we put the electrodes on his testicles and turn on the battery!"

They wheeled over another table with a six-volt battery on it. It looked like the rheostat on the Lionel train set that the raja of Kapurthala gave me at the age of five while visiting my parents. He gave me a lot of presents and, more important, kind attention. I never forgot him for that.

"Cut off his pants!" jolted me from my reverie back to reality. Two men took out knives and cut my pants off. Another man took the two electric wires in his hands and held them in front of my face, his eyes gleaming with pleasure. He touched the two wires together, which created a lot of sparks. "This burns the eyes very effectively," he said, fiendishly. "Should I try?" I said nothing. I decided to make no more jokes.

"Spread his legs apart and attach them with leather straps so I will have the pleasure of easy access to his testicles."

I was thinking back to my training. I had been given a course on how to withstand electric shock. The instructor had us all join hands, himself included. Then he put his hand on the battery wire and told his assistant to turn the battery on. The current went through us all and we shook uncontrollably. Slowly, the assistant increased the intensity of the current until the instructor told him to stop. Then that would be it for the day. The next day, the intensity was increased so that we would become more accustomed to it.

"Now we are going to have a good time," said the man with the wires. He clipped a wire to each testicle, turned, and walked toward the rheostat.

I was thinking, "I'd better exaggerate my response." So, when he turned on the battery and gave me a small charge, I shook especially hard, and yelled, "Stop, stop, stop." After a few seconds, the Gestapo increased the charge. I screamed louder and shook more. "Tell me when you've had enough," he said.

I yelled, "Now! Now! Stop! Stop!"

The sadist continued anyway and said, "I will augment the charge every ten seconds just to increase our pleasure in watching you squirm." He increased the intensity again and came and stood in front of me and grinned. At that moment, I truly lost control. I felt as if I were going to pass out. A stream came out from my penis with such force that the urine went all over the Gestapo man, covering him from head to toe as I shook. He stomped off, muttering to himself.

The battery was turned off, and another man took over the position. This one had a nicer demeanor. "Very good," he said. "We are beginning to get good results. I'll start from the beginning again so *I'll* have the pleasure of watching your body jump around from close up." He turned on the battery again. I decided that I would not yell this time. The man turned up the charge after a few seconds. I didn't make a sound. Abruptly, he stopped the battery and asked, "Are you ready to answer some questions now and tell us who among you was going to take the plane for England? If it was none of your friends . . ."

I interrupted and began the false confession that I had prepared. "I'm going to tell you everything that I know. If you don't want to listen, I'll spray you like I did the other guy. The reason I'm here is that one of my French friends in England had a mission to tell the partisans to begin sabotage tactics in the south of France because there was going to be an invasion soon on the southern coast. I had met this man and his sister in Paris in 1940 after we were defeated. The three of us became close friends. The way to escape back then was to take any boat we could to get over to Great Britain. On the trip, he and I got to know each other. When we arrived in London, we went our separate ways but stayed in touch. His sister stayed in France with their parents, who had a home near Vincennes. She needed to stay to take care of them because they were older and not in good health."

I drew a deep breath, underscoring my discomfort and pain, then continued, "My friend, who is very wealthy, was able to hire a private plane and pilot to parachute him back into France to spread the word about the landing and to find his family. He said it would be easier to locate them if the two of us searched together. He was certain that they were no longer in their house because the Germans were taking over all the nice estates. He asked if I wanted to parachute near Neufchâteau with him. He probably sensed I would be interested because he knew that I was in love with his sister."

The Gestapo man interrupted, "What is his name, this friend of yours?" I didn't hesitate a moment. "His name is Paul Maas." Then I thought quickly to myself, *I haven't created an address for him yet. I'll make it in North Africa, if the Gestapo asks. The Germans have not yet occupied North Africa, so they won't be able to verify.*

Sure enough, the question came. "Where exactly is he from?"

"I think he's from North Africa."

"Where does he live?"

"I have no idea because we never talked about it. We always met in the park for lawn bowling. All I know is that we both were wearing our parachutes and that the pilot told me to jump first. I suppose he jumped soon after I did. He must have landed quite a distance from me because I didn't see him."

"Did you ever find him?"

"No, I didn't. In fact, I was taken prisoner when my parachute caught a tree and I was stuck among the branches. I am sure you know the rest. I was able to escape, and the partisans hid me and took care of me. The evening when we were caught, we were waiting for the plane that was going to take one of their men to England. The French Militia took us all prisoner. That's what happened."

A voice speaking in German from behind the light said, "Take him off the battery."

I understood but, of course, didn't let on. I thought to myself, *They believed my story.*

The voice continued, "We'll take him to the prison at Compiègne for a nice long stay. If we can confirm his story, we'll send him to Germany to work in a munitions factory. If his story is a lie, we have other methods available to encourage him to tell the truth. If he is lying to us, we'll get the truth out of him and then let him rot in prison at Compiègne."

It was helpful understanding German. I had begun learning the language at the age of three when my father hired the retired Austrian colonel to be my tutor. The colonel had formal instructions from my father to speak only German to me. I was to be given only onion soup to eat for the whole day if I answered or asked a question in French. (My father knew that I detested onion soup.) Since I knew nothing of the German language, it was actually an effective method to learn it. At the beginning when I knew no words at all, my tutor, the cooks, and other servants sneaked other food to me in secret and threw away the onion soup, which I refused to eat. I was very angry with my father, and I wanted to take revenge against him. Since he spoke French, English, and Italian but not German, I decided that if he spoke to me, I would respond only in German and say, "I do not understand." I planned then to turn to my tutor and ask him to translate what my father had said into German, and then, and only then, would I respond accordingly. I learned quickly and spoke rather well within five months, and I was fluent by the age of four. But now, as a German prisoner, I thought it best to continue pretending not to understand their language.

THIRTY-TWO

Torture

Once back in my cell, I was able to verify that my cap was well in place. Early the next morning, two Gestapo came to get me. Accompanied by several soldiers, we left the building on avenue Foch. The blinding daylight hurt my eyes. Handcuffed to one Gestapo and accompanied by another, I was escorted by German soldiers from the building and put into a large vehicle. In the front seat was the driver with two soldiers beside him. The Gestapo climbed in behind me and sandwiched himself between two more soldiers. I was in the center seat squeezed between two other Gestapo.

They certainly are generous with their personnel to guard one person, I thought to myself, wryly. There was no chance of escape in this situation. I had a hard time even walking and sitting because of what I had just been through, but my morale was still intact.

As we pulled away, I assumed we were headed toward the infamous prison of Compiègne. It took a long time to get through Paris and then a couple of hours to get there. The *fourgon* finally pulled up in front of a huge stone fortress—Compiègne. At the entrance, the Gestapo that I was handcuffed to flashed his papers and commanded, "Open the gates, we have a prisoner for you." We drove through a long alcove built of stone that led to a large central square, at the end of which was a large iron gate, guarded by two soldiers.

The Gestapo ordered me to get out as he yanked on me, pulling the handcuffs. That aggravated me. Getting out of the seat was not easy. I moved slowly. My testicles were so swollen that I had to walk with my legs spread apart, and I was in a tremendous amount of pain. We walked toward the iron gate and entered the prison building.

The Gestapo told one of the soldiers to put me in a cell. The stone walls and floors of the building were dripping with humidity. The cell was approximately a meter square and about a meter and a half in height. There was a bucket inside. That was all. I couldn't lie down. I couldn't stand up. If I pushed the sanitary bucket to one side, I could comfortably squat. There was very little light. I was two or three floors underground. The only lights were on the ceilings in the hallways, spaced about thirty meters apart. I hadn't eaten for days. I was given a can of water and a thick, hard cracker.

After a few hours a guard came to my cell and informed me that I was being taken for a medical visit. We stopped at the communal showers, where I was told to undress and wash.

It was a good thing my pants had been cut open because my testicles were the size of grapefruits and they wouldn't stop throbbing. The water was icy cold and there was no soap. I was given no towel to dry off but was told to get dressed again.

I told myself that I needed to find a way to escape, but right at that moment I didn't see how. Perhaps during the medical visit, I could steal a military uniform or, for that matter, a doctor's or male nurse's uniform. There had to be a way to get out of here, there just had to be.

"Follow me," the militia guard told me. There was a bunch of keys hanging from his belt. I was walking very quickly behind the guard, trying to make him feel uncomfortable. It worked. "Walk in front of me!" he ordered. The rats were running around in packs all over the place. I had to be careful to avoid them because they would bite if touched. They were almost tame and had the run of the place. *They* seemed to have nothing to fear here.

We arrived at another hallway, which crossed ours. "Turn left and go in the first door on the left. I'll come back to get you after the visit." This man seemed nicer than all the others I had met since I had been taken prisoner.

"Maybe I can overcome him and steal his uniform when he comes back to get me." On second thought, I knew he was too small. I hoped the doctor or the male nurse would be my size.

I stepped into the large room. One of the walls consisted simply of iron bars. Behind the bars, in the adjacent room were work uniforms and overalls. The woman in the uniform room said, "Undress completely, including your underwear and socks, and hand me your clothes through the bars." I took off my clothes and handed them to her. "Try on these overalls," she said. I tried, but I couldn't get into them.

"They're too small. I can't get into them," I told her.

"Try these," she said as she handed me a bigger size. "They're too big," she said, "but they're the only ones I have that will fit you. Just roll up the pants and sleeves." I had to roll the pants up three times so I wouldn't trip over them. "Sit over there on the bench."

I sat on the bench for around three hours, listening to screams. I wondered where they were coming from. People were surely being tortured. Or perhaps some were just going insane from wanting to get out of this nightmare. My imagination sought reasons and invented stories as I sat there. Finally, the doctor appeared from behind the closed curtain. He motioned to me to come in. He examined my lungs and heart with a stethoscope and gave me a shot of something.

After being in front of the extremely bright light while being interrogated, I could no longer see very clearly. My whole body was in pain after being in that damp cell for so long, where I could neither stand nor stretch out. My testicles and lower abdomen ached. I felt weak because in those few days all I had drunk were three ladles of water, and all I had eaten was that one cracker. Of course, there were also the effects of the electric shock, sleep deprivation, and the interrogation process. I asked myself to what extent they had affected my state of body and mind. And I speculated about what was in the injection the doctor had given me. The last thing I wanted to do was to give them the satisfaction of knowing how terrible I felt. I didn't want it known that I was weakened by their methods in the least.

It was difficult to pretend that the constant screams, the dampness, the odor of rotting rats, the lack of sleep and nourishment, and the physical torture had not affected me. Indeed, it had. I knew that this was all part of their methods to weaken the prisoner. Thanks to the training I had received at the compound in Great Britain, I was well prepared. Yet seeing the rats eat each other while still alive made me think that it was only a matter of time before they would start eating human flesh—mine!

As I was considering my circumstances, the examination came to its end. Not a word had been exchanged between the doctor and me. I supposed they would return me to my wretched cell. But the doctor drew open the curtain, and an unwelcome sight appeared. The tall, bald woman from that first interview entered the room and spoke to me. "I came to see how you're doing. The doctor reassured me that you are in good health. I even asked if I could bring you back to my division. Since that's not possible at this time, I am hoping that once they have verified your story, they will give me the opportunity to take you back with me."

To my great joy and relief, the militia guard entered the room to take me to my cell. I could only imagine what this Amazon wanted to do with me. "I hope we'll see each other very soon," she said as I was escorted out of the room. "I'll think of you every night till then," she added.

As the man was leading me down the hall, he said, "I'm going to transfer you to a different cell so that she will not be able to find you."

I knew he was a good man, I thought to myself, *and this confirms it.* He put me in a cell that faced a large room, obviously used for torture. In the room was the requisite equipment: a bathtub, a large wooden wheel on which to stretch the limbs of a person, two three-meter posts with over a meter between them with requisite chains and large metal cuffs attached.

When I arrived at my new cell, I felt that it was late at night, but really there was no way of knowing. I had lost my sense of time. This cell was a little bit bigger. I could almost lie down with my legs bent. I took off one of my shoes and used it for a pillow under my head. That was certainly more comfortable than the damp stone floor. After a while, I felt some gnawing on my big toenail. I looked down. A rat! I jerked my foot away and scared him off. I managed to put myself in a sitting position very quickly. I immediately decided to leave my shoe on. I chose to put my head on the humid stone floor rather than have the rats chew on my foot while I slept.

* * *

My attention was drawn to the torture room when two guards entered with a woman prisoner around thirty years old. They chained her up to the two posts. She was about five foot four, maybe 120 pounds. A few minutes passed, and I watched as she tried to bend her knees a little but could not. The chains had her attached close to the poles with no room for any movement. Two other men entered the room wearing black leather coats. The Gestapo. They moved toward her until they stood directly in front of her.

"Are you ready to tell us what you know about the German officer?" they asked.

"I met him near the opera house. I was having coffee on the terrace of the café directly across the street. He turned to talk to me. He seemed nice and was very polite. We had a lovely conversation. He invited me to dinner at a restaurant called Le Boeuf sur le Toit, where they had a burlesque show in which men took on the personages of famous women entertainers. We enjoyed dinner while watching the show. We hardly talked to one another during the performance.

"At intermission, he asked me if I was married. I told him that my husband was a career officer and was a prisoner of war being held at a camp for officers near Mulhouse. I told him that just before being captured he had been promoted to the level of captain of artillery in the cavalry. I shared with the officer that I had received only one letter since his imprisonment, which had been mailed by an unknown third person. Apparently, he was not allowed to write to anyone or to receive any mail. I told him that since my husband was taken, my life had been extremely sad and difficult. That is everything."

At this moment, two SS came into the room and dismissed the other two interrogators. I could tell they were SS by the insignia on their collars. The men took positions on either side of her. Each was holding a leather strap. They began whipping her back, alternating between the two about ten times in all. Her dress was torn up, and she was bleeding badly. She did not scream even once during the beating.

"Did the German officer know that you were Jewish?"

"Yes, I was wearing the yellow Star of David on my jacket. The officer didn't do anything wrong. He just talked to me. I told him that I was married to an army officer who was a prisoner at Mulhouse."

I watched the scene unfolding before my eyes. I was incensed. I listened as the two men conferred in German. One said, "She's not telling the truth. Let's release her and make her talk." Then, in French, he yelled at the woman. "We're going to drown you in this bathtub!" They unchained her, dragged her limp body over to the tub, and shoved her face in the water. One picked up her head for a moment and said, "When you've had enough to drink, maybe your memory will be refreshed." Then, each holding an arm and a leg, they lifted her up and submerged her in the tub. They held her under for what seemed like an eternity to me. I was furious! The woman was resisting. Water was splashing everywhere, and the tub was overflowing. The water was turning red from her wounds.

It was impossible for me not to react. I needed to defend her. My whole life, it had enraged me to see someone strong pick on someone weaker. Such cowardice! And this, this was too much to take! Finally, I could no longer control myself. I screamed out, "You bastards! You are inhuman to relentlessly torture this poor woman, guilty or not. You are so degenerate that you are probably proud of yourselves! If I could, I would make you eat your own excrement! I would rub your noses in it! You're nothing but cowards!"

They stopped suddenly and looked at me. One of them picked up a dried bull's penis and angrily ran toward me. He thrust his arm through the bars of my cell and tried to hit me. With one hand I yanked him by the hair and pulled his head through the bars. With my other hand, I grabbed his forearm, pulled it all the way through the bars and broke it. I took his nose between my teeth and tried to bite it off by twisting his whole head. He screamed out in pain and pulled himself out of my cell, leaving his nostril behind between my teeth. I spit it out on the floor and yelled, "Would someone bring me some water to rinse out my mouth. I don't want to catch their disease!" The man with only three-quarters of a nose was swearing in German. The other one was yelling in French, "We will make a report about this incident to our superiors!" In German, he said to his injured SS cohort, "Don't worry. We'll take care of him!"

While this exchange was going on, a major general of the German army walked into the torture room. Alarmed, he asked, "What happened to your nose and your arm?"

He pointed across the hall toward my cell, about eight meters away. "He did it!"

The major general demanded, "What were you doing outside this room? You're supposed to be a professional! Explain this to me—now! *He* is not your prisoner. He has nothing to do with you, and you have nothing to do with him! He has already been interrogated. From now on, just mind your own business and mind it well! I believe you have enough to do with your own prisoners."

He looked around as he was talking. "Why is there blood all over the place? And why is this woman lying in the tub with her back and bottom torn up and bleeding? We want results, but we want no trace of force. We don't want you to drown the prisoners, either. Ask them questions. If we're not happy with the answers, we'll investigate further. And I don't want you to use the wheel at all. From this moment on, if I see a mark on any prisoner, I will send you to the Russian front. I hope you have understood me well. I will have your superiors as well as your colleagues report your behavior to me. Now, send this poor woman to the hospital. Have them send me a report immediately after she is examined!" he ordered. "And get your nose taken care of!"

The major general turned, left the room, and approached my cell. He stopped a safe distance away and said, "I promise that this will not happen again under my command.

We do not approve of these Gestapo methods. I know that your case is in the process of being investigated. Then he noticed the bull's penis on the floor of my cell.

"Would you tell me how you happen to be in possession of *that* in your cell? Do you have difficulty walking? Do you use it like a cane? It's too flexible. I must get you a cane." I could see the comprehension in his eyes. "Give it to me now. I want to use it right away." I picked up the appendage and handed it to him. "Watch me well when I return to the room. I understand what must have happened, so I won't use it on that one. I've decided. He will get what he deserves. He'll become a simple soldier on the Russian front as soon as his wounds heal. I offer, once again, my apologies for him. What he did is unacceptable in the German army."

The officer turned and went back to the torture room. He addressed the SS man who was not injured. "I have decided not to wait for any further reports. I will send your colleague to the Russian front, but now I want you to keep him company at the hospital. Attach yourself to the poles with the cuffs!" he ordered. The man looked at the major general in astonishment but followed orders. With the smaller end of the penis in his hands, he whacked the SS officer four times with all of his force on the back of the legs, just above the knee. The man screamed out in pain. "You will not walk for a long time. This way you can keep your friend company during his convalescence. When you both recover, you can take the trip to Russia together where you can both freeze your feet off!"

The major general then turned and called the jail keeper who held the keys. "I have ordered these two SS to take this woman and admit her to the hospital. Since they are no longer officers, they cannot give the orders to admit her. I want you to have this woman admitted and taken care of immediately. These other two can wait their turn. I want a report on her condition as soon as the doctor has finished his examination. Write on your report that these two are officially demoted. They are now privates in the German army. They will be sent to Russia together as soon as possible upon their recovery. The report and appropriate paperwork will follow."

This admirable German officer had appeased my fury. I lay back and fell asleep. What had just passed before my eyes was absolutely the worst experience I had during the war.

When I woke up, the guards were at my cell door. They opened it and told me to get up. It was difficult to straighten up. My body ached everywhere. I had slept scrunched up on the humid, stone floor. Of course, I couldn't stand tall in the cell, but once out I was able to stand up straight, little by little. I had no idea of the day or the time. The guards were French Militia. One of them said, "We have special instructions for you. I'll put a chain around your neck, which will go from there around your waist, your wrists, down your legs to your feet and around your ankles."

The chain was very heavy. It was difficult to move

at all. They both seemed to have an air of compassion, unusual for the French Militia.

"It's not your day today," one of them said.

"You said it!" the other added.

The first continued, "The group of Gestapo that is going to interrogate you now is the most vicious of all. I suggest that you answer their questions as fast as you can. They torture the prisoners more if they answer slowly."

The hallways were gloomy. I could hardly see anything. It was a real labyrinth of passageways going every which way. "I'll let you walk with your shoes on till we arrive. After that I'll take them with me because you will not be able to use them on the way back."

I wondered what that meant but remained silent.

It took the three of us about a half hour to get to our destination. In the chains, I could only shuffle my way along. We stopped in front of a door. The guard took off my shoes. That left me barefooted because my socks had been taken when I was issued overalls.

"Be courageous," the one guard said.

With a look of compassion on his face, the other said, "We'll come back to take you to your cell. The quicker we can get you out of this room, the sooner we'll be able to get you medical treatment. Before the war, my friend here was a veterinarian. He specialized in cats. Now a cat cannot be found in the streets."

The former veterinarian said, "I joined the militia to avoid being sent to the factories in Germany. I still have some medication from the old days that I keep aside. If you are suffering too much, I'll give you an injection that will calm you." He opened the door to the interrogation room, and I shuffled in as best I could, restricted as I was by the chains.

"Sit down on that table," one Gestapo said. Then they chained me to a stone pillar. I'll have to tell the Brits to add this situation to the training. I could have used some practice. My plight was more difficult than it sounds because the tension I experienced made me perspire. The sweat went into my eyes and burned, and I couldn't do anything about it. I also had an itch that I couldn't scratch. Relative to the predicament as a whole, it may seem entirely insignificant. But obviously, I was totally helpless. The itch and my burning eyes became separate tortures in and of themselves.

Suddenly, a floodlight glared in my eyes. I couldn't see what was going on because of the blinding effect of the light. What I smelled was smoke. A coal furnace? It seemed to be moving closer to where I sat on the examination table. To my right, I could barely see a man in a white smock. He pulled out red-hot branding irons, along with an array of instruments, which he laid out on a side table. Was this yet another test to add to our training, a scene producing drama and anxiety in the prisoner? They've created an operating room—a meticulous setup indeed! I was becoming impatient. When was their play going to start? I knew I was still the leading man. Out of nowhere came the thought *Does Mr. Churchill even know I'm here?*

A man smoking a cigar appeared on the left. Behind the floodlight, a loud voice spoke to me. "What is your name?" Textbook—same old routine. "Michel Carbonell," I answered. The smoker, dressed entirely in black, walked up and slowly put out his cigar on the bottom of my right foot, twisting it slowly between his fingers—right, left, right, left. All my nerve endings screamed. This classic torture was far more painful than I ever expected.

A man appeared on the right, swinging a red rubber hose less than a meter long. *Probably buckshot inside,* I thought. Churchill's team had familiarized me with the standard tools of torture.

"You must excuse me. When I asked you your name, we were interrupted by my friend who needed to put out his cigar. Will you repeat your answer, please?" I considered how grave my situation was. Though agitated, I restrained myself and replied evenly, "Michel Carbonell."

The hose whipped across my thighs, ripping flesh that splattered blood. "If you come out from behind your screen and show me your face, I'll tell you all that I know! If you'd take the time, you could read it in your dossier. I'm sure the facts are all there. Maybe I have a hard head, but if you don't stop these barbaric tactics, I will refuse to open my mouth."

At that moment, my rage was greater than my pain. I felt like Samson in the Bible. My chains felt as light as sewing needles that I could have broken with a mere contraction of the muscles of my torso. A small fat man, bald, white-skinned, and slimy, came out from behind the light. He was dressed in black like all of the Gestapo.

"I will tell you once more," I said, "and this will be the last time." The man stood in front of me, slouching, his fat lips partially opened. He looked slow and dumb. Strange as it may seem, I felt extremely powerful, even more so, after seeing this little nothing appear from behind the light. He was a disgusting little man. His body odor almost overwhelmed me to the point that I thought I would vomit.

So again I confessed the lie I had prepared. "Listen carefully," I said. "I was parachuted outside of Neufchâteau, as you can read in the dossier. I already told this to your colleagues. I had become acquainted with a French man and his sister in Paris during the time of France's defeat. The three of us became close friends. When it was clear that France was defeated, he and I took the opportunity to take a boat from Dunkirk to England. His sister stayed with her parents near Vincennes. He and I saw each other regularly while we were in London. One day, he told me of his decision to hire a private plane and parachute back into France. Not only did he want to find his family, but most important, he needed to contact the French partisans to let them know of the proposed Allied landing somewhere on the coast of southern France. He asked if I wanted to join him. He was wealthy and money was not an issue. I didn't really have to think twice about it. I accepted right away. You see, I was in love with his sister—and still am—and I wanted nothing more than to see her again. That is all."

"*That* was why you parachuted into France?" the ugly little man queried. He suddenly became furious and started yelling. "You take me for an imbecile?"

Yes, I do, I thought, but didn't say.

"You think I'm going to swallow your little story? Not a chance!"

The stunning pain of the hose again, this time on my thighs and chest. I gasped for air. This was an opportune moment to pretend to faint. I faked passing out. A bucket of ice water was thrown in my face to revive me. Actually, that did me some good, but I didn't move. If I could feign an unconscious state, maybe they'd stop the torture.

"Drag him to a cell and hang him by his thumbs! Let his toes barely touch the floor. If he isn't conscious by the time you reach the cell, throw another bucket of ice water in his face. Before you hang him, remove all of his clothing. I plan to visit him often. I have a special way to make him tell the truth."

The pain was unspeakable. I asked myself, as I was being dragged along the filthy, icy floor, what this repulsive little man was going to do to me next. Abruptly, the movement stopped. They opened a cell door, picked me up by the arms and legs, and tossed me inside. I landed facedown with a thud. The floor was covered with excrement and urine. I did not move so they would think I was still unconscious. That was a good idea, but it didn't stop them from doing what they had been ordered to do. They threw another bucket of ice water on me before lifting me up. One held me while the other tied leather straps to my thumbs. They hoisted me up to the ceiling and tied each strap to a small ring. I could barely reach the floor with my toes. I did not give away that I was truly conscious. After they left, I tried to get some of the shit off my face by grimacing while keeping my mouth closed. I tried to get it off my lips by blowing out several times. Nothing worked. The more I tried, the more of it seemed to seep into my mouth. I needed to change my thoughts and *not* think about this at all.

Then—the sound of steps advancing toward my cell! Two German soldiers were talking about two Gestapo higher-ups who had discovered a better way to make prisoners talk. The method was to gather roaches and ants, put them in boxes and bring them to the interrogation room. Without warning, they would dump the roaches on the head of the prisoner and observe his reaction. Sometimes the prisoner would break, sometimes he wouldn't. If he did not talk, they would take the other box filled with red ants and dump it on his head. This was always more effective because the ants would crawl into the nose and the ears. As they passed my cell, I didn't move or make a sound. I thought to myself, *At least I know what's coming next.*

Or did I? Despite the pain and biting cold, I had only one thought: *Escape.*

THIRTY-THREE

Breakout

I'll push off the cap, bite down on the cyanide pill, and be out of this unbearable pain. This thought screamed in my head, over and over, as I helplessly hung by my thumbs, stark naked, my toes barely grazing the floor. For days, I passed in and out of an unconscious stupor. Sometimes the cold would be as overwhelming as the pain I felt in my thumbs, arms, back, neck—oh, everywhere. Thank God for the long periods of comatose oblivion. Then, coming to now and again, I would say to myself, "Hold on, Marc, just hold on. What good will come from dying?"

The Countess Hannah von Bredow, a leader in the German Resistance and a descendent of Otto von Bismarck, received an urgent plea from Churchill to somehow get "the man with the Russian sock," my code name, out of prison. Earlier in the war, I had delivered bombs in the form of attaché cases to her group in the vain attempt to assassinate Hitler.

The countess devised an audacious plan to get into the prison at Compiègne. A group of her German anti-Nazi volunteers would pose as a sanitary detachment responsible for cleaning the prison. She would provide intricate instructions, uniforms, trucks, and all the appropriate equipment necessary to successfully deceive the officers in charge. As a pretext, they would announce that a German military health inspection was scheduled later that day.

By the time the "cleaning crew" arrived at the prison door, I had been hanging by my thumbs for several days and nights. The countess had organized five German military trucks, each with four men inside, to clean this labyrinth of a prison. They arrived at about five in the morning. Everyone at the prison was taken by surprise.

"We have orders to clean the prison and remove all the garbage," said the captain responsible for the cleanup brigade, as he presented the orders to the guard at the gate. "There is an inspection this afternoon." The guard looked at the orders with suspicion and went to look at his log. "There is no inspection scheduled this afternoon, Captain," he responded curtly.

"Of course there is, soldier. The notification was sent to your commander a week ago," he insisted.

"I'll call my commander, sir." He stepped away, and

when he returned, he said, "The officer in charge received no orders to prepare for a health inspection. My superior is coming right away to inspect these documents."

The commander soon appeared and examined the paperwork thoroughly. The orders looked exactly like an official document with all the requisite stamps and signatures needed to satisfy those responsible for making decisions.

"Open the gate and allow the trucks to enter," he ordered brusquely. "Have all the cell doors opened immediately; however, those prisoners chained or otherwise restrained are to be left as they are. Have the guards shine their boots and change into fresh uniforms before noon," he commanded the officer at his side. Then, addressing the captain of the cleaning contingency, he ordered, "Begin at the bottom floor where all the garbage is gathered."

My cell was apparently located on the floor above that, but the countess's group didn't know where I was. I woke up to voices and doors clanking as they opened and shut. At each cell, someone asked, "Are you the man with the Russian sock?" When they were a few cells away, I heard the question and softly answered, "I am here."

Two men entered my cell while two waited outside. "We are here to help you escape," one said as he reached up and cut the leather straps. Gratefully, I was on the floor. At that moment, a guard passed by. "What's going on here?" he demanded, as he reached for his sidearm. One of the men responded in German while another poked a needle filled with poison in his neck. He died instantly.

The men continued their cleaning and casual conversation as if nothing had happened. They put the guard in a barrel and put it to the side. I looked at my hands. My right thumb was elongated by a centimeter and the left by a little less. They put a blanket over my head and upper body. One of the crew gave me a shot of morphine. They lifted me up and stuffed me into a garbage barrel and filled it with excrement and other garbage. The agony was unbearable. I didn't want to be awake. I kept trying to turn my thoughts to something else, but it was futile. The pain was consuming me.

One of the crew said in a loud voice, "What should we do with that barrel?" Later, it was explained to me that they were trying to figure out whether to take or leave the dead guard. Another responded, "Just leave it. We have enough garbage for this haul." The barrel in which I was hidden was placed on the dumbwaiter. "Wait," someone said. "We have enough room for that other barrel after all." I found out later that they decided it was safer to take the dead German guard with them. The barrels of garbage were sent up to the first floor and lifted up onto the truck. Someone whispered, "How are you doing?" I answered, "Give me another shot."

From that moment on, things happened quickly. I am so impressed with the daring and courage of this group of Germans. Just thinking of the sacrifice these men made, putting their own lives in such jeopardy, amazed me.

Today, I gratefully realize that without the countess's help, I would not have survived.

Much later, when I finally returned to England, Mr. Churchill's secretary told me a secret and made me promise not to tell the prime minister. "When he learned you were in Compiègne, he dictated a message to the Countess von Bredow that ended in words to this effect: 'Dear Countess, I beg of you to somehow rescue this man because he is close to my heart. I know that this prison has a particularly brutal reputation.' It was put into code and sent urgently to the countess."

She went on, "Mr. Churchill suffered throughout the time that you were taken prisoner. He ate very little and drank too much. He told me that he wanted to be contacted the moment I received any news of you, no matter the time of day, where he was or with whom. He said, 'The most important thing is that they rescue Marc. I've been informed that he is being tortured, and it's breaking my heart.'

"He reminisced about your youth. He told me you were a little boy when he first met you playing with your friends in front of the villa where he sometimes stayed in Cap d'Antibes. He thinks of you with such fondness, Monsieur Marc," she said. "I am telling you this because I want you to know that he loves you like his own flesh and blood. But you must not tell him what I told you. He would be furious with me. I just feel it's important that you know. May God bless him. We are so fortunate to have him as our prime minister."

The commandos worked very quickly. Within about

an hour from the time I was lifted up onto the bed of the truck, all the garbage was loaded, and the trucks were ready to move out. The commando who had given me the two injections kept me up with what was going on. I felt some relief from the morphine. It had dulled the pain. I was very groggy.

"We're completely loaded and ready to move out," he said. "Our truck is third in the line of five trucks." I heard the sound of another truck moving, but we didn't. "There's a problem," he said, "but don't worry. They can't start the truck in front of us." Some time passed, and then I heard his voice again. "They attached a chain to the front of the second truck so the first one can pull it. We'll be starting any time now," the commando said. I dozed off. It must have been the effect of the morphine.

The trucks pulled out of the fortress and made their way to the dump outside Paris. That took a few hours. Finally, I heard the words, "We've arrived." The commando explained, "We have to stop at the gate for permission to go through. Then we'll drop you off at the home of the dump manager. She's trustworthy."

The truck stopped momentarily when it came to the gate and then moved on. Suddenly, it came to an abrupt halt. I felt my barrel being lifted out and put on the ground. The cover was removed, and they pulled me out. "There is something that's burning my eyes," I told them. They pulled the blanket off my head. "We will take care of your eyes soon," one of the commandos said kindly. "There may have been some live ashes from cigarettes or cigars in the garbage."

The pain in my hands was becoming unbearable again. I was naked and very cold. They tried to put a sweater on my body, and I screamed involuntarily. The pain was excruciating. My hands and arms hurt. So did my testicles and thighs. "My eyes are burning. I can't see. I am blind," I murmured as I realized this alarming truth with sudden heartbreak.

"Don't touch my hands or arms," I told them. They carried me inside the manager's little house. Many hands were supporting my neck, head, torso, and legs. They lay me down on the floor. One of the commandos asked the woman, "Do you have any men's pants in the house to put on him?"

"Yes, I do. They'll be too big for him, but they'll work for now. Let's get him washed up before we dress him. He's a mess. Go outside. You'll see a bucket next to a large container of water. Fill it up, and bring it here while I get some washcloths and towels."

I know she tried to be careful as she washed my body, but it was a painful process, especially when she handled my arms and hands. Then a couple of men pulled the pants on me and asked her, "Do you have a belt or a rope to hold them up?"

"No, I don't," she replied, "but I have a strap that I use to tie things on my donkey." She returned with the strap, and a commando tied it around me.

The woman took over after that and began giving instructions. "Move the bed over to the right and pull up the rug. Push the lever that's at the head of the bed. You'll see a trap door." One of the commandos asked,

"Where's the trap door? I don't see it." She retorted, "That's as it should be. I told you to push the lever. When you do, you'll see the door pop up." He did as she said, and the door opened.

Apparently, the sandy floor underneath the house was partially covered with a pile of empty flour sacks. It was basically a crawl space less than a meter high. The area equaled the size of the house. The little house was mobile and was moved from one area to another on the dump site.

One of the Germans jumped down into the space. "Do you have the nerve to say that this man is going to lie down in the sand surrounded by these old jute sacks after all he's been through?" She didn't reply. "I'm going to give you a chance," he said to her. "Find an extra mattress for him or for you because *he* is not going to lie down on that sand for long."

I was lowered into the space by the men. The commando who was already in the space caught me by the legs and helped lay me down. Someone said, "I'm going to give you another shot of morphine. We'll be back in a couple of hours." Then he addressed the woman, "Take very good care of him, or we'll take care of you." They left abruptly.

As soon as the door closed, she came down to see what she could do for me. "I've only eaten two crackers in four days as best as I can remember. I would appreciate something to eat. Also, I really need something to help me eliminate." She replied, "I'll go upstairs and make you some herb tea. That will help."

"But, madame, I'm going to have a problem. I can't use my hands to lower the pants." Then I joked, "I can't even scratch my nose much less reach the rest of me." In good humor, she retorted, "Don't worry about a thing. I'll take care of any scratching you need." Then, changing the subject, she said, "I'll go get you a bedpan, and I'll be right back." When she returned, she began, "Here's the plan. I'll cut open the back seam of your pants. I'll bury the bedpan next to you in the sand. I'll help you roll over and open the seam when you need to go."

"Now I'll get you a bowl of Ovaltine to give you some strength. Then I'll bring you some herb tea, and I'll find my boyfriend's razor blade so that I can cut your pants."

When she came back, she started talking again. "Since we'll be spending quite a bit of time together, I want to introduce myself. My name is Yalena. I am French now, but I'm Russian born. I don't understand what's going on. Will you explain something?"

"Before I explain anything to you, isn't it time to give me a shot?"

"No, it isn't. The men only left twenty minutes ago. They'll be back in two hours to give you a shot. Now, will you answer a question? My boyfriend told me that Germans would be bringing you here and that we needed to hide you from the Germans. I know I'm old, forty-nine, and time seems to speed up after the age of forty. But why did these Germans who are occupying our country want to hide you from other Germans? This is really beyond my understanding."

Her naiveté was astounding. She didn't understand that not all Germans were in favor of occupying France. I told her in a simple way, "These are good men. They disagree with what Hitler is doing."

"My boyfriend, David, said to do anything I could to make you comfortable. I have the razor. Turn a little if you can, and I'll cut your pants. No, wait. I completely forgot your Ovaltine! Let me go up and get it for you." Up she went again. She seemed to have a good heart but was not at all organized.

She returned with the hot Ovaltine. "And now, finally, for the third time, I'm going to cut your pants." Then, changing her mind yet again, "No, first I'll help you to drink. Be careful, in one hand I'm guiding a glass straw to your mouth to make it easier for you. In the other hand, I have David's razor and it's open." I had no idea why she didn't put the razor down first. I guessed that she was simple or nervous. I took the straw in my mouth. "Finish the Ovaltine. Then I'll go fetch something for your eyes. Pus is seeping out."

A while later, she returned and held two warm compresses on my eyes. They smelled like *tilleul*. Just the smell alone was soothing. Then she gave me the tea to sip. "I have a hard time moving around in this space. The ceiling is so low," she complained.

"Yes, I know about cramped places," I reflected as recent memories raced back to me.

Interrupting my not-so-pleasant reverie, she said, "I'm not sure how I'm going to do what I need to do for you because I'll have to do some things lying down. I'm not a young chicken anymore. All right now, I'm beginning. Roll over totally on your side. Don't make any quick movements. If I see any blood, I'll stop and try again. I don't see any blood, so I'm continuing. Now, I have a beautiful view over the courtyard. There is a lot of merchandise here." She was speaking of my inflamed testicles. "I'll be careful not to cut anything off," she said with humor. Then she changed the subject again. She must have been uneasy. She talked so much. "I need to warn you that we have about two dozen cats and two fox terriers. We really need them to take care of the enormous number of rats."

I shuddered and mumbled, "More rats."

She continued, "David is coming over tonight. He'll get a mattress down here with the help of his friends. He is meeting with the head of the Resistance group *Combat* and the leader of the PPF. I am very proud of him. He's very active in the Resistance. His wife and six-year-old little girl were among the thousands of Jews taken prisoner in the raid of the Vel' d'Hiv. He never saw his family again. He was informed that they were taken to a camp outside Paris, at Drancy, where his daughter came down with pneumonia and died. His wife was sent with the others to a camp in Poland where she was killed. So many heartbreaking stories."

* * *

After a few hours, the herb tea had an effect on my system and I was able to eliminate. I called for Yalena to help, and she came right away. She wiped me and cleaned me up. I was so grateful for her help. She was truly very kind. As soon as she left, I fell asleep, soon to be wakened again by someone giving me a shot of morphine. I fell back to sleep.

Later, I woke up to the sound of male voices. Men were in the house. Who were they? The trap door opened. It was then I met David and his patriot companions. They spoke to me with concern in their voices. Though I couldn't see them, it felt wonderful to speak to Frenchmen who were not pro-Nazi.

"Thank you. Thank you for your kindness and your work for our liberation," I told them gratefully. It had so sickened me that the French in the militia were working *for* the Nazi occupation. How could they? It was incomprehensible to me.

Soon, the others left, but David remained. He came down and explained what had been decided regarding my recovery period. "There will be a doctor who will come here twice daily. We'll get you up on your feet as soon as we can. Through the British, we'll arrange an identity for you with the government of Switzerland. You'll be a Swiss railroad brakeman who has been burned by steam and is returning home to Villeneuve, located a couple of hours from Geneva. They'll provide you with a temporary Swiss identity card with your photo showing you in bandages."

He continued, "In about three weeks, depending on

your recovery, someone will come to pick you up, and we won't see each other again. I'll be going to the south of France because the English will be landing there soon."

Good. The rumor has spread. I can rest easy now. I've accomplished my mission.

The French doctor who visited me worked closely with the Swiss. "Monsieur," he said, "we are going to bandage up your head, your eyes, and both hands for the trip to Switzerland. Then we'll take a photo for your identity card. We must hide your face," he continued, "because posters are up all over Europe offering a reward of a million francs for your capture, dead or alive."

Every day for three weeks, this doctor came, once in the morning and once in the evening. He gave me anti-inflammatory injections between the thumbs and forefingers and gave me pills for something, I don't know what, which made me nauseous. He injected me with shots of morphine for the pain. Yalena always brought me something to eat before I took the pills because I would vomit if she didn't. I probably also threw up from the pain itself. My hands burned all the time. The bones in my arms felt like fragile porcelain that would break with the smallest of movements. It felt like the muscles were going to burst and melt. My neck ached. In fact, everything hurt. I could not find a position on the mattress that did not hurt some part of my body.

During the entire time I stayed with her, Yalena gently took care of all my needs. The pants became a problem because they became soiled each time I eliminated. "Michel, it's just not worth the effort to wash and dry your pants every day. Anyway, it hurts me to put you through the agony of putting them on again. I'll cover you with a sheet and a blanket, and all will be fine," she said.

"You know, Yalena? I'm not feeling cold anymore, though the weather is still chilly. I think it's a good sign. Normally, I'm not cold at all. In fact, I even wear shorts in the snow."

"That is good news," she said with a lilt in her voice. "Now you need to eat more." During my recuperation, I didn't have much of an appetite. Yalena gave me an easily digestible diet of soups, mashed potatoes mixed with minced chicken, Ovaltine, herb tea, and lemonade. She fed me with a spoon, and I used a glass straw for the liquids. She read me the newspaper every day. She was dedicated to giving me exceptional care. As I became stronger, different men from the group would lift me out of the crawl space and walk me around the house. I was impressed with their strength. I was dead weight.

About three weeks after my arrival, the doctor came in one afternoon and told me, "I am going to wrap your head, eyes, and hands in bandages so no one can identify you as you travel. Then I'll have a photo taken. Two men from the Swiss Embassy will come very late tonight to take you with them."

That evening, Yalena was exceptionally tender. She fed me my dinner and stayed to talk a long time. I was asleep when I heard the trap door open. "*Bonsoir, monsieur. We* are going to put a cape around you first and then help you out of the crawl space." The two Swiss guys must have been built well to get me out of there. Usually the task required three men. When we were out of the crawl space and starting for the car, they said, "We'll cross our arms and make a 'chair' for you to sit on. Now sit down. That's it." They brought me out to the car and helped me onto the front seat. *"Au revoir, Michel,"* Yalena said as she kissed me affectionately on the cheek.

"I don't have the words to thank you, Yalena," I said, feeling so moved by all that this dear woman had done for me.

As we drove off, the driver began talking. "We're in a diplomatic car, and we have all the appropriate papers. We don't want you to worry about anything; however, should something unexpected happen, don't say a word. We're taking you to the Swiss Embassy in Paris."

The entrance to the embassy was on the ground floor, so I was able to walk inside on my own. That felt good. Two staff members took me to get cleaned up. They removed my bandages, gave me a shower, and put a hospital-type gown on me. They brought me to a bed on which I sat down. The same doctor who had visited me at Yalena's came to see me at the embassy. "Do you want to eat something before I give you your injections?" he asked.

"Only a glass of milk, thank you," I said. Someone brought it to me and held it as I drank. The doctor gave me medication for pain and for sleep. My eyes still burned terribly. The medication relieved the burning a little, and I fell asleep.

The next morning, the doctor was there when I awoke. He washed my eyes and put drops in them. "I can vaguely see shadows passing over there," I told him.

"That's a wonderful sign," he said. "You're pointing toward the window."

Someone came into the room and announced that the tailor had arrived to fit me for my railroad employee uniform. I got up from the bed and leaned against a piece of furniture, lifting first one leg, then the other. The tailor marked the pants for altering. He was going to put the shirt on next but I stopped him. "Let's skip the shirt for now." Surely recognizing the amount of pain I was in, he said, "As for the shirt and jacket, I can see that the sleeves are too short and that I will have to make the sleeves and cuffs wider to accommodate the inflammation of your hands and arms. I'll take your measurements now, and we'll have an initial fitting after I make some adjustments. You don't need to try anything else on right now."

A man helped me go to the bathroom. I needed to have someone lift up my hospital gown so I could sit. Then he would have to come back to wipe me off. Someone brushed my teeth, combed my hair, and of course trimmed my beard. Others fed me. The tailor returned in the afternoon, having adjusted the sleeves. They were wide enough now, and he stitched them by hand as he sat across from me chatting. He was very gentle when he tried the shirt on me.

"Thank you for your kindness, monsieur," I said.

With satisfaction, he responded, "I'm quite pleased with the fit."

An officer from the Swiss Embassy came to my room to tell me of a change in plans. "There are an increased number of trains descending toward the south of France due to the belief that the Allies are going to land at any time."

I was thrilled. I loved knowing that the lie I confessed was spreading quickly about the false landing. This would relieve the Russian front of some of the German troops and also draw military tanks and artillery away from the Pas de Calais and Normandy.

The embassy officer continued, "The trains, especially at night, are filled with German military troops. During the day, they are mostly occupied by civilian travelers and merchandise shipments. For this reason, you'll travel by day."

He went on, "They must have taken a photo of you during the time you were prisoner. You're worth a fortune, monsieur. You look like a pirate on the posters. We're going to alter that look completely. We decided that it was too suspicious to bandage your head. Instead, we'll remove your mustache, your beard, your eyebrows, and your eyelashes, and we'll leave your hair about a half centimeter long. To change your physiognomy, we'll stuff your cheeks on the inside with a gummy substance that will give you puffy cheeks.

"We'll be leaving first thing in the morning, and we'll only bandage your hands," he added. "In fact, we want them to see your face because it will be obvious that you are *not* Michel Carbonell. We will adjust your identity card tonight with a new photo that will be ready before we leave in the morning." That evening, the barber and others came to my room to create the new look of the railroad man.

THIRTY-FOUR

The Monastery

Early the following morning, I was fed breakfast, washed, and dressed in my new uniform. My eyes were tearing badly and had to be wiped often. The doctor came to wrap my hands and provided me with a wheelchair. I was lifted into the ambulance, wheelchair and all. Four men accompanied me as well as a driver. It was a short trip to the train station. I was lifted out of the ambulance, still in the wheelchair, and placed on the ground. A voice said, "We are from the Red Cross. We'll take over from here. There is a compartment reserved for him."

By the noise level, I could tell the Gare de Lyon was crammed with people. Another voice commented, "We always take good care of our railroad employees. We have a comfortable traveling space for him in the car reserved for the Swiss Post. He won't even have to get out of his wheelchair." Then my wheelchair began moving. I was lifted into the Swiss postal car. By the number of voices speaking, I could tell there were several people in the car. Then I heard the door shut.

From behind me, a familiar voice spoke. "I am here with you because of *Combat*'s participation. Do you recognize my voice?" I said nothing. "Two days ago the partisans derailed a German military train on the way to the south of France. There is a rumor that there were a million German parachute jumpers prepared to invade Switzerland. Now, owing to the widespread knowledge of the imminent Allied invasion in the south of France, these men have been diverted away from Switzerland to concentrate on protecting German-occupied France."

It was David with the news. Evidently, the plans had been altered again. Focused on my suffering, I responded, "I recognize your voice, David. Will you give me something for my eyes and hands?"

"Don't you worry," he said. "I have everything you need. It looks like an entire pharmacy is here. If we give you shots, you can yell as loudly as you want because we're in the last railcar." He joked around, trying to lift my morale, I suppose. He didn't realize that my morale was just fine. It was the incessant pain that was driving me mad. David put compresses on my eyes, gave me pills, and then gave me injections in both hands.

The wheelchair was moving around a lot. David said, "I'm going to move you to the side of the car and tie the chair to it so that you won't be jostled around quite so much." It was difficult to have a conversation with him because the panels of the car were not insulated and they made a racket. Soon the injections took effect, and I fell asleep.

The train stopped abruptly, and I awoke airborne. I flew from my chair and smashed into a dog cage. Oh, the pain! The dog started barking. Several men came right away to help me up. The top of my head was torn open by the corner of the cage. Now they *would* need to bandage my head. I was helped back into the wheelchair, and then someone cleaned the fresh wound. This time they tied me into the chair.

"I'm going to see what's going on," David said as he jumped out of the car. He came back right away. "Everything is all right. Looks like our partisans have been overzealous." He chuckled. "They've tampered with the tracks. They will be repaired shortly, and then we'll be on our way again."

It took over an hour to fix the rails. As soon as the workmen finished, the train slowly began to move, and I fell asleep. I awoke to David making an announcement: "We are approaching the silk capital of France, the city of Lyon." He was speaking as if he were a tour guide. He was a jovial guy with a lot of heart.

The train began to slow down and finally ground to a stop. There were passengers who got off and passengers who began their journey here in Lyon, headed for Grenoble or for Switzerland. "German troops are surrounding the train," David warned. A voice came over the loudspeaker. "*Attention! Attention!* Everyone have your papers out and ready to present," the voice blared in French with a heavy German accent.

"Hmm. I don't like that," David muttered. The door of the car opened.

"Let me see your papers," a young German officer demanded brusquely.

Another voice responded, "I represent the Swiss Postal Service, and I'm in charge of this car. Here are the documents." After inspecting the papers, the officer said, "Now I will enter the car."

"This car is the national property of Switzerland. You do not have permission to enter," the Swiss government employee responded.

The German curtly replied, "Don't you dare tell me what I can and cannot do. *We* are in charge in France, not you."

The Swiss official was not daunted. "I demand to speak with the officer in charge." The young man acquiesced and shouted instructions to go get the German commander. He waited outside at the door of the railcar without saying another word.

David whispered to the Swiss employee, "Don't leave the car for any reason without me. I'm going to make a phone call."

About thirty minutes later, David returned with the German officer in charge of the Lyon Railroad Station. He was in mid conversation with him explaining the situation as they approached the Swiss postal car. The German SS officer acknowledged his arrival with a "*Heil, Hitler*" and then began to explain. "Sir, I have requested entry to verify the interior of the railcar because I heard other voices inside."

The commander responded, "What is inside this car is the property and the concern of the Swiss government. Even if a Russian spy or, for that matter, Stalin himself were inside, there is nothing you could do about it."

David got into the car. "I've talked with the officer in charge of the station, and he has refused entry to the SS officer. *This* man is an honorable German career military man." Outside, we could hear the young Nazi blowing off steam.

"You'll see who really is in charge here. In a few days, we'll occupy Switzerland and all of Europe. We will reign supreme!" he shouted.

We heard the career officer's response to the youngster. "Perhaps, you'll reign supreme in your dreams. That is why I, a Prussian, am in charge here and you, you have only six men who report to you. Now enough of this ridiculous behavior. We will allow the train to depart immediately. It is already an hour behind schedule, thanks to you."

The insolent young man shouted, "I'm going to make a report about this and send it to my superiors." David told me that he angrily turned on his heel and strutted off. Then the train flagman waved the red flag, signaling for the train to depart.

When we were well en route, David explained to us what he had learned from his phone call. "Resistance sabotage is becoming more and more effective. The Germans are very nervous. They rarely dare to travel on the highways now. On the call, I learned that the area from Lyon to Grenoble is now all pro-Gaullist. Civilians, farmers, and city folk alike are defying the law and are openly carrying rifles and other weapons. All Germans and known French Militia who dare go outside the cities are openly fired upon when they are spotted."

David had to practically scream to be heard, the train made so much clatter. "I want to explain something else to you all. As soon as we begin our approach to Grenoble, I gave the order to the conductor to have the locomotive slow down at a certain place where these tracks cross some others. At this point, the tracks that the train crosses descend to the right. When we reach this intersection, I'll get out of our railcar and release our car from the rest of the train. We will follow the descent of the rails. It will take a few hours. Then we'll enter a tunnel that is blocked on the far side. It is the entrance to a former lime mine. Michel, I'm so happy the plans have been changed. We're not taking you to Switzerland after all. Crossing the border is too great a risk at this time."

There was much discussion after the announcement, but I could hardly discern a word. Hours passed. The train began slowing down. Just before the train came to a complete stop, David jumped out. He disconnected the car and jumped back inside. The car began rolling downward on its own with the force of gravity determining its speed. He reassured everyone.

"Everything in this area is under the control of *Combat*, so we expect to encounter no problems whatsoever. The whole region is on the alert. More arms and munitions are expected to arrive by parachute this evening."

It took a long time for the car to coast to its destination. Then, without warning, David jumped out to put the brake on. Everyone started talking at once. The car came to a complete halt inside the tunnel.

"No one leave the car until someone comes to talk to us," he said. "On the other side of this tunnel is the lime mine. The partisans will be coming up from that side to meet us."

About twenty minutes later, three cars arrived escorted by two trucks filled with members of *Combat*. David went out to talk to them. He came back to the railcar and said to me, "Monks from the monastery will come pick you up in two or three hours. You will be staying with them. We are well protected here while we wait." They untied the wheelchair and lifted me down to the ground. David told me that it was already dark outside.

Suddenly, I was famished. I mentioned it to David, and he said he would take care of it. A half hour later, a car arrived with food, including milk, cheese, bread, and wine. David fed me as soon as the food arrived. My appetite was surprisingly robust. David was talking to another *Combat* member while he was feeding me. The other man said, "We blew up the electricity supply to the south of France. Practically all of southern France is in the dark right now."

A while after I finished dinner, I heard a vehicle arriving. David described the large yellow van that was approaching, a Berliet with LA GRANDE CHARTREUSE written on the side. Three monks got out. One of them was carrying packages in his arms. One of the *Combat* officers pointed them toward David and me. They introduced themselves, and one of the monks began talking to David.

"We'll have to put the cassock over his clothing. That will be the easiest for him," the monk determined. David helped me stand up. The burning in the testicles made it hard to move after being squished into that chair for so long. Someone put the robe on me and helped me to sit again. Then someone took off my shoes and socks and put leather sandals on my feet. "He already has the haircut we need. We only have to shave a circle on his crown," one of the monks said.

Someone wet my head and shaved the appropriate circle. "You are now Father Francis. You don't need an identity card or any other papers. We'll give you more details during our trip back to the monastery, so say your farewells now." I called out for David. He put his hand on my shoulder.

"Thank you for all your care and help and for being my eyes," I said, "and good luck on your trip to the south."

His voice was filled with warmth as he replied, "And good luck to you, Father Francis." David and someone else helped me into the back of the car. Another adventure was about to begin.

The winding road was filled with potholes. It was an uncomfortable journey. I felt every bump and hole. The night was frigid, but the heater was on in the car.

"The trip will take us about five hours or so," one of the monks told me. "They gave us your medication, and we are well supplied at the monastery. It's our responsibility to get you back to good health again. When we get home, your rehabilitation will begin. You'll be safe with us. We have never had any problems with the Germans or the French Militia. We'll take good care of you," he assured me.

When we arrived, they helped me out of the car. It smelled moldy on the way to the building and inside as well. The monastery was probably built of stone, and the humidity caused the mold. I was shown to my cell. Someone helped me change into a nightgown. Before I went to bed, someone gave me a shot for the pain.

"There isn't much in the room, so it shouldn't be complicated for you," he said. "It is a monk's cell, after all. There's a small window to the left as you lie in the bed." I felt the narrow bed and kapok mattress. "A cross is on the wall above the head of the bed, and there's a nightstand on the right with a bedpan underneath," he described. "Good night, brother," he said to me, and I heard the door close. The trip and the pain had worn me out. I went to sleep as soon as he left.

One monk or another took care of all my daily needs. I still needed injections twice a day and was given pills as well. There was a common dining room where I was fed my meals. The communal toilet facilities were down the hallway and consisted of Turkish-style toilets. Those are the kind where one stands up to go to the bathroom. There are two tile areas on which to place the feet with a hole in between them. Next to the toilets were the showers.

After a couple of days, the monk who acted as my main nurse began to take me for walks around the property. He held me by the rope that was tied around my waist. He controlled me from the rear, telling me when there was a step or uneven terrain. He took me all around the property even though I couldn't see. He showed me the location of the chapel and told me about the well-kept vegetable gardens where the other monk who took care of me worked as a gardener. He described the architecture and explained the monks' way of life at the monastery.

One day, after a few weeks had passed, the monk came to my cell to take me for my daily walk.

"I can see your shape," I told him excitedly. I was thrilled, and so was the monk. "I can see shapes slightly, if they are close to my eyes. I can see the cross, the bed, the nightstand—everything!"

That day he took me down a pathway to another building. It was the distillery where almost all of the monks worked in one capacity or another. He brought me close to the huge copper vats. In the immense room built of stone, there were about thirty or forty vats, each with a fire underneath. I could actually see their forms when right next to them. Inside were roots and herbs from the surrounding mountains from which the monks produced their wonderful liqueur, Chartreuse. Clear, spiral tubing descended from each vat to another container. The vapor produced in the process would pass through the tubing and turn to alcohol in these containers.

From the distillery, he brought me over to the other monk who was working in the garden. He was elated by the news that my sight was returning. It was about two o'clock when the doorbell rang out at the front gate. Immediately afterward, the bells of the monastery sounded two times. The gardener said, "That's the signal for trouble. Hide your hands underneath your robe. Get down on your knees and bow your head in prayer. Do not move. If someone talks to you, do not respond. You are mute. I'll speak for you. I don't want you to be concerned. We have nothing to hide here *except you*. We'll let them enter and search if they wish. When they find nothing, they'll leave."

The gates were opened and about two hundred Germans entered the monastery at a run. The search lasted about thirty minutes. They did not approach me at all. They left as rapidly as they had entered. The bells sounded two times and then once. The gardener told me that the first two rings indicated "all clear" and the single ring meant we were all to meet in the chapel.

The three of us walked toward the chapel, as did all the monks. Once inside, a voice from the front said, "Do not kneel down. Remain standing. It will take up less space." The chapel seated only about two hundred persons at any one time. By the time everyone arrived, there must have been four hundred of us.

The brother who was speaking from the front of the room said, "I want to let you all know what is going on. We received a message from the Grand-Saint-Bernard Monastery about an hour ago that they had been inspected and that nothing was found. Of course, nothing was found here either.

"We feel the reason for the sudden increase in German searches is that they are becoming agitated by the impending Allied landing in the south of France, as well as being very disappointed that their rumored invasion of Switzerland was called off. They have closed all the borders to Italy, France, Switzerland, and Austria. This is why our guest could not go to Switzerland. It would have been too dangerous. Let us all pray for the complete recovery of our guest."

I enjoyed the hospitality of the monastery for two more months, during which time I learned a great deal about gardening through daily observation as my sight continued to come back. I regained some of my strength owing to the daily walks that I took with my "nurse." I wore dark glasses because my eyes couldn't take the brightness. To everyone's delight, especially my own, I eventually fully regained my eyesight.

One day, the gardener brought the news. "It's time for you to leave, Michel. Can you ski without poles?"

"Yes, I can."

"Good. Then, we'll leave tomorrow at daybreak. After a few hours' skiing, we'll pick up a car we have in storage in the next valley. You'll be in Switzerland tomorrow night. The Swiss will get false identification papers for you."

This was great news. To be on skis again breathed new life into me. Three monks accompanied me on the mostly downhill trip. It was a good thing that I could ski without poles because my hands were still useless. But I knew they would heal eventually. I had made excellent progress since my escape from Compiègne. Skiing down the hillsides, I asked myself how I would ever be able to thank the countess, Yalena, David, the monks, the partisans—everyone who had contributed to saving my life. I had come back from the dead. I skied jubilantly down the slopes with the brisk, cold wind blowing in my face and freedom within "sight."

The weather was rather mild, and the landscape thrilled my senses. We left the skis at the storage where we picked up the car. Arriving in Thonon-les-Bains, we waited for nightfall. Then we followed the southern shore of Lake Léman, passing Evian. Just before the Swiss border, a rowboat was waiting to take us across the lake to Vevey, Switzerland.

When we arrived, a small produce van was parked and waiting. The driver and two women climbed out to help me. My heart was full as I thanked the brothers for their devoted care. They hoisted me into the back of the van where one of the women helped me into civilian clothes as we drove toward a new chapter in my recovery, the Hotel School of Lausanne.

THIRTY-FIVE

Convalescence

The driver started the van and drove off. One of the women said, "Monsieur, you can sit on one of those sacks of potatoes after you change your clothes."

I had the feeling these women were nuns, but I asked no questions. I carefully slipped the pants on but had difficulty taking off the monk's robe.

"Here, let me help you," the same one said as she assisted me with the shirt and jacket. "We'll be at the hotel school before you know it."

When we arrived, the driver opened the door and helped me out of the van. He looked at me curiously for a long moment, then removed his cap. "Here, put this on," he said as he handed it to me. I must have looked like a convict with my hair cut so short. Most Swiss men at that time wore their hair a bit longer than we do today, so I must have looked exceptionally odd. Switzerland was very conservative in all ways, including dress, hairstyles, and politics.

"Thank you, monsieur," I responded as I put the cap on and said good-bye to the three of them.

I entered the building and walked toward the director's office. Seated behind the desk was a lovely Swiss Italian woman, about twenty-eight or twenty-nine years old.

"Hello, madame. Though I've stayed here several times, I've never had the pleasure of making your acquaintance. My name is Michel Carbonell."

"*Bonjour, Monsieur Carbonell.* I've seen your name on our occupancy list before. What has happened to you?"

"I had an accident and have difficulty using my hands. Would it be possible to stay with you again and perhaps just observe some classes?" I asked. My hands were still wrapped in bandages.

"Absolutely. We'll work something out, monsieur."

"Could I use your phone to call one of my friends in Geneva?"

"Certainly, I'll call our operator for you." I gave her the telephone number, and she placed the call. Once there was a ring, the director handed me the receiver, which I balanced in both hands. The phone rang and rang, but no one answered. I was about ready to hang up when I heard the voice of a woman.

"May I speak to Monsieur Toby?"

"He's not home right now. Would you like to speak to his father?"

"Yes, I would, madame."

"Be patient. He has difficulty moving. I'll call him to the phone."

When he came on the line, I asked him to give a message to his son. "Please tell Toby that his old friend has returned and is staying at the Hotel School of Lausanne and ask him to return my call. If I'm not available, just have him leave a message for Michel Carbonell, and I'll call him back."

"Monsieur, I believe I will see him within a couple of hours, and I'll give him your message."

I hung up and thanked the director. "Would it be possible, then, to have a room and a bowl of soup or something that I don't have to cut? I can't use my right hand at all nor the thumb and index finger of my left hand. I can use a fork, though with some difficulty, with the other three fingers of my left hand. Soup will really be the easiest thing for me to eat."

She looked at me with intensity, then relaxed and smiled. "Don't worry about a thing. I'll take care of you. It will be my personal duty. Now, about a room. Let me look at my chart. There are two available on the first floor and several on the second. One of the rooms on the first floor is larger than the others. If I were you, I would choose that one."

"You have made my choice, madame."

"Would you like your meal served in your room or in the dining room? No, wait a minute. Since I need to stay in the office, I can help you eat right here."

She made a phone call and asked for a particular

person. She explained my situation to the person in Italian and said that she was going to help me eat.

"Thank you for your generosity," I said in Italian. She looked surprised.

"Where did you learn Italian?"

"I skied with the Italian Alpine Troop accompanied by my tutor when I was a child."

"My parents are from Piemonte, near Torino," she told me. "Italian is my first language. My mother still lives there, but my father died a while back."

About twenty minutes later, a man around fifty years old came in with a tray holding a large bowl of lentil soup with sausage cut into small pieces accompanied by a bottle of vinegar and a covered plate. He placed the tray on the table. She thanked him, and he left.

"Come sit down at the table, and I'll sit next to you." She put a napkin on my lap and added a little vinegar to the soup and mixed it for me. Then she started teasing me in Italian as if I were a child, "Now, open your mouth. That's a good boy."

For some reason, I didn't feel too embarrassed with her little game. She seemed so kind and caring. After I finished the soup, she removed the dome from the plate. The smell that flew into my nostrils was exquisite. A risotto with octopus similar to what I had eaten with Maurice Chevalier in Florence so long ago.

"I want to try to serve myself," I said, but she insisted on serving and feeding me. Before finishing the meal, however, I insisted again and didn't back down.

"Truly, I must do all I can so I can recover quickly." She understood and placed the fork in the fingers of my left hand. It took some time, but I finished the meal. Then she ordered espresso for both of us.

I got up to go to my room, but before getting to the door, the phone rang. "Monsieur, it's for you. Why don't you go to the bar, and I'll pass the call to you there."

It was my contact, Toby. He was a British agent caught in Switzerland when the Swiss closed their borders. He worked for the English and indirectly for the Americans through Allen Dulles, who was in Berne. I explained to him my injuries and limitations without explaining the details. "I've been receiving injections in my hands daily. Can you arrange medical help for me?"

"Certainly, Michel. I'll bring a doctor to see you this evening."

When they arrived, I explained to the doctor what I had been receiving. He gave me shots for the pain and gave me another to sleep. Though I didn't need one for sleep, I didn't say anything. The two of them undressed me for bed, leaving just my underwear on. The following morning, Toby returned with pajamas, a bathrobe, slippers, and socks.

"Tomorrow, I've made an appointment with a tailor to come take your measurements and make you some clothes," he said. "I noticed that the clothes you're wearing bind your thighs and arms."

After he left, I put on my robe and went to the director's office.

"Excuse my attire, but I don't have any appropriate

clothes yet. A tailor is coming tomorrow to take my measurements."

"I see. And, how do you like your room?"

"Very comfortable, thank you."

"You know, my brother died a couple of years ago. He lived with me at my house. He was a soldier in the Swiss army and was killed in an avalanche. All of his clothes are still in his room upstairs. Maybe some of them will fit you. If you like, tonight I can drive you home, and you can try some of them on. I'll make a soup for the two of us, a specialty of Piemonte. I love the cuisine that I was raised with, though I rarely take the time to cook. I work six days a week from seven A.M. to six P.M., and it's much easier to just eat here. My time away from work is very limited. Of course, there is the housework, washing, and errands to do. Sunday morning I go to church, and that is my life. So, is it agreed? We'll go to my house after work tonight?"

"Yes, agreed. It's very generous of you." The woman was patient, thoughtful, and caring. I was fortunate in that people generally treated me with kindness and respect.

"If you have any needs, you must not hesitate to ask. I will help you eat, get dressed, whatever you need. All right?"

"Yes, yes. I understand," I said, hiding my discomfort in accepting yet another person's help.

The dining room of the hotel school was open to the public. It was a learning experience for all those attending the school. Guided by professional chefs and hotel personnel, the students learned the art of cooking, serving, greeting, and pleasing the public as well as the intricacies of hotel management. The hotel school restaurant offered its clients fine cuisine at reasonable prices. Over the next few months, I would eat either in the dining room, my guest room, or at the director's home. The food was excellent at the school as was the attention to detail. The director took care of my every need, and the students and staff accommodated my every request.

I was also fortunate that Toby would visit frequently to take care of anything else I needed. He arranged for the doctor to check on me regularly, and he in turn scheduled regular visits by a nurse. As my recovery progressed, I no longer needed to see the nurse daily. She would look after my hygiene and administer any medicines I needed, including the injections so crucial for recovering the use of my hands. My rehabilitation was an excruciatingly slow process. Young and independent by nature and education, I was impatient to get back to work.

Cherished memories of the time I spent at the Hotel School of Lausanne have remained with me all these years. The three-month stay gave me time to develop a strong relationship with the director like that of a loving big sister. It was a pure and honest friendship, a truly beautiful experience.

Every so often, I think about my extraordinary saga of capture, escape, injury, and recovery and realize just how amazing it is that I am still alive.

While in Lausanne, I worked intensely on my physical recuperation. As I got stronger, I joyfully began running and climbing the surrounding mountains greater distances every day. I also took advantage of my time at the school by taking as many classes as I could. At the time, I had no idea how this education would later fashion my destiny as an executive chef in the grand hotels of the United States of America.

Finally, one bright and beautiful day, I said to myself, "I'm ready to get back into action. I'm exceptionally grateful to be alive and in good shape again. It's a miracle that I am still drawing breath on this earth. What is waiting out there for me to do?"

I was fully recovered, physically and mentally strong again. I felt ready for any challenge, no matter how daunting.

THIRTY-SIX

Return to Combat

As the plane took off from the airfield headed toward France, I reflected on my triumphant return to England. The secretary, the cook, her assistants, and even Hughes made such a fuss over me. Evidently, they knew something of my imprisonment and escape. I continued my exercise regime perfected in Lausanne as soon as I arrived at the estate—walking, running, and working out every day besides riding the horses every morning. I did not want to lose the gains in strength and fitness I had achieved in the past months. A few days later when Mr. Churchill came to the estate, I was called to the library. It was a greeting to remember. He stood as I entered the room. The look of warmth in his eyes filled my heart.

"Mon petit, mon ingénieux," he began, "may God continue to protect you," he said as he held me close. "I

know this has been a difficult passage in your life. I have been kept apprised of your progress in Paris, Chartreuse, and Lausanne. And finally, here you are, alive and in one piece. I'm surprised how fit you look. I know you've worked hard to make such great progress in your recovery. I am so grateful you have survived this ordeal. His voice was filled with compassion. "Come, let's have a cognac."

He asked me to tell him all that had happened. Although he knew, I'm sure, he wanted to hear the story in my words. We sat together for a long time as I shared my near-death experience, my escape, and miraculous recovery. "I'll never be able to adequately thank the extraordinary German partisans who saved me from the bowels of hell and all the wonderful people who nursed me to health again. I would certainly have died without each of their efforts."

"You will thank them by continuing on in the fight," he said, suddenly animated. "We are making great progress. We will win this war—I am sure of it. After a prolonged rest, I want you to parachute behind enemy lines again. I'll give you a large sum of money to deliver to *Combat*'s commander in charge of the Basses-Alpes. And I want you to continue where you left off in spreading the rumor of the fictitious Allied landing. I want everyone to be convinced that it will take place in the south of France. We need every advantage we can get to conquer the Nazis and bring this war to a close."

In readied position at the door as we approached the target area, an unexpected fear came over me.

"I just can't jump," I said. "I just can't do it this time." The fear totally enveloped me. I didn't know where it came from, but I felt paralyzed faced with what I had to do. The green light was staring at me. "You must jump, Marc," I urged myself silently. "You must." What came out of my mouth was, "I just can't."

"You have to jump—and right now!" the navigator said as he approached me. I was standing at the door, holding on to the side of the plane, frozen, looking into the blackness. Then I felt the push, and I was freefalling. The fear vanished, and instinct took over. I pulled the cord at the right moment and landed as planned near Le Vernet in the Basses-Alpes, not far from the Col d'Allos.

The sky was totally black that summer evening in 1944. The gendarmes and members of *Combat* came to pick me up in the field where I landed.

I knew the area well. Two years in a row, when I was five and six years old, my colonel and I stayed in the small village of Allos during the summer so that we could go hiking in the mountains. We stayed at the Auberge d'Allos, but we'd leave for a few days at a time to go camping. I knew this time I wouldn't be going camping.

"Our commander was arrested last night by the French Militia," one of the members of *Combat* told me as he helped me hide my parachute.

"That's not good news," I replied.

"Yes, but it's all right. We have a replacement, and we'll take you to him."

I was to contact *Combat*, the organization that included all partisan groups with the exception of the Communist PPF. When the Communist partisans first joined together, the PPF had no equipment, no direction, and little consideration for the welfare of their fellow French citizens. As time passed, however, the group began to achieve significant victories for the Free French. Unfortunately, the French people often suffered repercussions from its ill-thought-out offensives.

I met with the members in an outbuilding behind a house. Though the new leader was a dedicated man, I felt that he was too old to accomplish what was necessary.

I pulled aside the officer who had met me at the field. "We need a seasoned organization with an established leadership for the task ahead, monsieur. Can you direct me to another group of partisans?"

"I'll put you in contact with the leader of *Combat* in Tulle, department of Corrèze. You'll like him."

I met the man in Tulle two days later. Indeed, he seemed organized and capable. It was evident that he commanded a lot of respect from the other members.

"I need you to call a general meeting," I told him. "Gather together as many area leaders as you can."

Several days later members of *Combat* gathered together at Tulle from Puy-de-Dôme, Haute-Vienne, Lot, Béziers, and Montpellier along with the mayor of Sisteron, Haute-Provence. On the way to the meeting, I stopped at the city's small grocery store. The owners, whose daughter was an active partisan, gave me a couple of big, beautiful round loaves of country bread to bring to the meeting.

I addressed the group, "We must plan for the arrival of arms, munitions, food, radios, and other supplies by parachute to prepare for the landing in the south of France. We need to sabotage all the hydroelectric equipment supplying all the main cities, such as Brive-la-Gaillarde, Tulle, and the hydroelectric plants in the region of Dordogne. When you're contacted, you'll need to gather everyone you can at Beaulieu-sur-Dordogne to pick up the supplies."

To distinguish themselves from the noninvolved French citizen, the members of *Combat* wore armbands imprinted with the cross of Lorraine and sometimes uniforms in accordance with the Hague Conventions. In case of imprisonment, the Germans would be able to identify and respect the prisoners as military fighters according to the rules of the Geneva Conventions. In theory, this identification protected the noninvolved French citizen from retribution.

The next day, I left for La Turbie, over eight hundred kilometers from Tulle, escorted by the gendarmes. The trip took a day and a half. Mr. Churchill had given me a large sum of money to give to Commander Guillaume, the officer in charge of all the Basses-Alpes, for distribution among all the partisans of *Combat* in his area.

A couple of days after our initial meeting, two young German soldiers, in a blockhouse below La Turbie on the Grande Corniche, began talking to a couple of partisans walking by. The two soldiers were from Alsace, in France, and had been forced to join the German army. They were anti-Nazi and were complaining about their dilemma.

The partisans suggested that they desert and join them in the fight against the Nazis. The two soldiers agreed and accompanied the partisans to the terrace of the café where I was having a drink with Commander Guillaume and a partisan named Captain Charley.

"What is going on here?" Commander Guillaume whispered as the men approached. I immediately got up and stood a distance away.

"May we sit down?" one of the partisans asked as they arrived.

"Yes, of course, pull up some chairs," Guillaume replied. "And what can I do for you?"

I could see that Charley was unsure of the situation, understandable with two armed soldiers in German uniforms coming to join them at their table.

"These soldiers are really French from Alsace. They were forced to join the German army and would like nothing better than to desert and join the war effort against the Nazis," one of the partisans explained.

"Hmm, that could be possible," Guillaume said, "but let's talk for a while." The four sat down at the table. The two soldiers had the butt ends of their rifles on the floor while the barrels rested against their thighs. I could see that Charley held a 9-millimeter Beretta in his lap, and his finger was on the trigger.

All of a sudden, the younger of the two soldiers, still

seated, lunged forward to catch his rifle because it had slipped off his thigh. Charley, being on edge, thought the man was trying to shoot the commander and tensed up. The revolver in his lap went off and Guillaume, seated directly in front of him, was shot. Charley, shocked, threw himself on his knees in front of Guillaume.

"I'm sorry, I'm sorry, Commander! The gun just went off. I didn't mean to . . ."

Guillaume stopped him, saying, "Don't worry about it. It's nothing. I'm sure it's only a flesh wound."

I hurried to the cashier inside the café and asked if there was a doctor in the area.

"The closest one is in Beausoleil," she answered. "What happened?"

I ran back to the table without answering. Guillaume was slumped in his chair. I saw a tiny whole in his shirt and tore it open. The bullet had gone into his stomach.

Charley told the partisans, "Carry the commander to his home. It's only about three hundred meters from here."

They lifted him up, and the bleeding increased. One of them said, "The wound doesn't look too serious. We'll get the bullet out and bandage him up at his house."

I left, thinking all would be fine. After the liberation, I learned that Guillaume had died from that wound.

Soon after this incident, I was traveling in the south and central parts of France, still spreading the rumor among the partisans about the Allied invasion in the south. The more people who believed this was true, the better.

The partisans were blowing up bridges and railroad tracks, and generally doing anything they could to harass the Germans. One small group would fire on the Nazis and then disappear. Then another group a few kilometers away would launch a sneak attack and run. Their goal was to create confusion, and they were quite successful.

I went to Aspremont to talk with the members of *Combat.* "Come rejoice with us, monsieur, and stay the night," one of the partisans said as I entered the city. "The south of France is free after almost two years of German occupation," he proclaimed with joy. "Paris and the north have been dominated by those despicable Boches for four years now. Let's toast to the freedom we have regained in the south and for the freedom we will soon regain in the rest of France!" Everyone was celebrating, opening up their houses to everyone else. All the Germans had been chased out or taken prisoner.

"I happily accept your generous invitation," I replied to the man as he handed me a glass of wine. We talked for hours of continued victory and of reclaiming France for the French. Most of us who shared that wonderful meal in that breathtaking moment had never seen each other before.

One of the partisans at the table shared one of his encounters: "We attacked the German troops from all sides. The Germans were forced to retreat toward the Italian border. We deprived them of their shipments of food, clothing, gasoline, and arms. Some of the German officers and their troops fled by way of Mont Saint-Bernard and the Petit-Saint-Bernard, the passes leading to Italy. Some stopped on the way to protect themselves in old fortifications in the Haute-Savoie, where, I suspect, many are still hiding."

With all of the south free, I decided to go visit the farrier near Drap, next to the the Paillon Bridge. I had visited him when I was clandestinely inspecting the youth camps early in the war. The following afternoon when I arrived, he was shoeing a horse. It was wonderful to see he was still there and that some things had not changed. All of France would soon be *la belle France* again.

"*Bonjour, monsieur,*" I said, and he looked up from his work. At first, he didn't recognize me. "Remember me? You shod my oxen a few years ago."

He put the horse's leg down and screamed with joy. "Come, come to the restaurant. This is a blessed occasion. You've survived the war. Let me offer you a drink. Have dinner with me."

He took me to the same bar/restaurant next door, and we talked and drank till the wee hours. I stayed overnight at his house, and we had breakfast together in the morning. Then we both took the tramway to Nice to see how the beautiful city was faring. And who do we see on the tramway? The animal trader who had bought my pair of oxen! Elation was in the air. Everyone was feeling that the liberation of all of France was near.

When we arrived in Nice, we each went our own way. I went to meet with the regional commander of *Combat*. He was a real estate agent and had his offices just off the place Masséna. I stayed at his home a couple of nights. I asked him how things were going.

"It's a triumph in itself to have the Germans on the run, but we have a serious problem. Many of them are escaping into Italy by crossing a bridge over the Var River. The Americans have tried to blow up the bridge several times, without success, because for some reason they have been instructed to fly their planes at such a high altitude, it is impossible for them to hit their targets. Will you ask the English to help us? The destruction of the bridge is crucial."

"I'll see what I can do about it tomorrow, Commander," I replied.

The next morning, I went to see one of my contacts, a British agent who lived at the Hotel Ruhl. I told him about the bridge. "We'll take care of it," he said. "By tomorrow, there will be no bridge." He was true to his word.

Without the bridge as a means of escape, the Germans were stranded in the Var region. Some tried to swim or walk across the river in areas that were not too deep. They were taken prisoner if they gave themselves up. If they tried to escape, they were shot. There were those who did escape by going up through the mountain passes; however, all the trucks, tanks, armaments, and supplies they could not carry on their backs had to be abandoned.

With the Germans on the run, Nice was liberated. "*Combat* is organizing a parade to celebrate the liberation of Nice," the commander told me. "Would you do the honor of carrying the French flag leading the parade flanked by two of my sergeants?"

"Why, of course, I will. Thank you for the privilege," I responded, astonished that he asked me. Why me? I wasn't even a member of *Combat*. I suspected the invitation was the result of my part in getting the bridge blown up.

The following day, the partisans gave me clothes to put on like the rest of the members of *Combat*. The parade began at the train station, where I was given a white belt to wear to support the flag. I had a sergeant on each side of me, and we were followed by all the *Combat* troops and the Communist partisans. There must have been between six hundred and eight hundred participants in the parade, which came to its end at the promenade des Anglais. The place Masséna and the whole route of the parade had been crowded with joyous citizens, thrilled to have their homeland back. All members of *Combat* wore their blue, white, and red armbands. Trumpets and drums added their raucous contribution to the exciting festivities. People's smiling faces filled the crowd. The whole day was the embodiment of joy and the appreciation of freedom. It was a day I'll never forget. Our determination to never give up until France was French again was finally being rewarded.

"Marc, Marc Crovetto!" I heard my name being shouted after the parade had ended. It was Alain Le Favre.

"What a wonderful surprise, Alain! How are you and

Suzanne?" His younger sister was still as timid as she had always been.

"We're on the reception committee. We have a local house where you can stay, eat, rest, and get cleaned up."

"Wonderful. I'll just pick up my gear. Wait here for me."

Getting through the crowd was difficult, but I picked up my duffel bag and found them again.

"We'll take you to the house of some wonderful people we've met." The couple couldn't do enough for me. I was lodged, included in all family meals, and made to *feel* like a real member of the family. It was a special moment in history when everyone felt a close kinship, one to another.

In Nice, I found a few other members of my original Alpine troop, the Third Division. After days of celebrating, I contacted army headquarters in Nice. They directed me to Saint-Martin-Vesubie, where I would join with others in setting up local headquarters for the Alpine Ski Troop Division and would begin to re-form my own company. It proved difficult, as always, to find men with the ability to be good soldiers who were already good skiers. And, of course, so many of my compatriots had died.

After a month's searching, I had found only sixteen men and one sergeant capable of filling the positions. There was no lack of enthusiasm and willingness to do what was needed, but most men lacked the skills and experience. We sent most of them on to the infantry.

"We'll have to try another area to recruit because there aren't enough men here who know how to ski," I told my sergeant. "We'll move to Grenoble to form our company. We'll take several trucks with us and recruit along the way. We need an additional one hundred sixty skiers. I'm sure we'll have better luck in the areas of Grenoble, Megève, and Chamonix. Once we find at least two hundred, we'll begin the process of elimination and training."

At Grenoble, we picked up the equipment for my company: uniforms, boots, skis, sealskin—everything I thought that we would need. Though it had taken some time, we were able to find the men we needed. I chose Chamonix to be our first center of training because of the excellent snow. It was very deep with an icy crust on the top. We would make camp near each particular skiing area so our new recruits could train on different kinds of snow. We eventually arrived at the foot of the mountains of Chamonix.

"Sergeant, give the order to attach the sealskin to their skis. Explain that they'll ascend the steepest slope, four at a time, and that the skins will provide the traction necessary for the climb. Then tell them you'll demonstrate what I'll be judging as they ski down the slope. First, do a pattern of six half circles of thirty meters each, alternating right and left, followed by a slowdown of one hundred meters, then coming to a complete stop. I'll keep sending others up, four at a time. Tell them that everyone should imitate what you do. After they execute it well, I'll give you another exercise."

I had them repeat the same exercises from morning till nightfall day after day. Then we moved on to

Megève. There we utilized the cable that pulled us up between the other mountains to the highest summit. We all assembled at the top for the long descent.

"I'll take the lead and you'll all follow, single file, until we reach the bottom," I explained. "The descent will take between thirty and forty-five minutes. The slope is steep, and we'll be going for speed. As soon as you reach the bottom, take the cable up again."

We stayed at Megève several weeks until I felt they were ready to move on to the greatest challenge: Peira-Cava. Peira-Cava was icy and rocky, the ultimate test and judge of excellence. Here, the skier had to be vigilant, agile, and flexible because there wasn't a lot of snow. Each man followed the man in front of him, maintaining a distance of thirty meters. We climbed to the highest point. I knew these mountains intimately from childhood. The drop was steep, and the slope was very rocky toward the bottom. One had to be an excellent skier to avoid the rocks. Suddenly, at the bottom, there would be no more snow, so each man had to remove his skis and climb to another mountain to find some snow. Then he would have to put on his skis again and begin another descent on a new slope. This would continue until we all finally reached the bottom. Then immediately, we would begin our climb again to the top. Small injuries were plentiful because of the rocky terrain, but it was an excellent learning ground. We continued our training there for many weeks. Those who survived it well were able to continue with the rest of the course.

After I found enough competent candidates, we

continued the course for the new group of Chasseurs Alpins at Saint-Martin-Vesubie. From the 175 men I needed to fill the ranks, I would select the top 35, the best of the best, for my elite group of shock troopers.

After they became proficient in skiing, we taught the new troops maneuvers, the climbing and military tactics that would be necessary for our success. The course was intensive. When my men were fully trained, I would plan the offensive on the fortifications occupied by the Germans and Italians on the French-Italian border. Of these the most formidable was the nearly unassailable mountain fortress at l'Authion. Trying to devise a strategy by which we could attack it was causing my superiors many a sleepless night. The fortress seemed impregnable. The attack on l'Authion would play a large role in my destiny, but I had no way of knowing it just then.

THIRTY-SEVEN

Attack on l'Authion

My commander called me to his office. "Lieutenant, as you know, the fortress at l'Authion has all its artillery pointed toward France, although the actual front of the underground stronghold faces Italy because it was built long ago by the French to protect themselves from Italian invasion. When the Germans took possession, they dug trenches at the foot of the fortress on the back side where they set up their defenses facing France. Their soldiers are heavily armed with mortars and machine guns.

"This is one of the last bastions of German resistance along with other fortresses at the French-Italian border. We have not yet been able to work out an effective plan to get them out. Up till now, l'Authion has been virtually impenetrable," he told me. "Lieutenant, I want you to formulate a plan of attack that will successfully oust the Germans and Italians holed up inside. Officers from the First Division will present their ideas on the subject as well."

It was early 1945. The Germans had been entrenched in the fort since 1943. Normally, the strategy for attack on German-occupied fortifications was to approach on foot at night as close as possible to the blockhouse and to shoot flames inside with flamethrowers. In this situation, there was no way to approach without being seen and gunned down.

I met several times with the high command of the Chasseurs Alpins. Everyone studied the terrain on the map and threw out their opinions and ideas. The plan of a massive offensive was put on the table, but the Germans were so well protected because of the way the fortress was situated that it would have been suicidal to approach in this way.

A plan had come to me. At one of our meetings I explained to the other officers, "The attack I've devised will be an effective offensive owing to the element of surprise. It requires getting my ski troop to the top of the formidable mountain above the fortification. The Germans will never expect an attack from there because the ascent is deemed impossible. I've been training my company in rock and mountain climbing for months now on a similar terrain, though not as treacherous, and I know they can do it."

I paused to let the audacity of my plan sink in, then continued, "Using 'wings' made of white silk, my shock troopers will fly on skis from the mountaintop over the German trenches to the foot of the fortress. Once we land, we will attack the dug-in German soldiers from behind their trenches while the rest of my company, one hundred forty men, will engage them in a frontal assault after they ski the few minutes it will take to reach the bottom of the slope; however, before we take off, the legionnaires on my right will show themselves and draw the German fire. They'll advance as they are able. Then, opposite them, to my left, the Senegalese sharpshooters and machine gunners will begin shooting from their position, effectively trapping the enemy in cross fire. The remainder of the Senegalese company will advance, rifles in hand, toward the trenches. With my troops in front and behind them, the Germans will be surrounded.

"If all goes as planned, we will kill or take prisoner all soldiers in the trenches. We will then wait for nightfall, at which time we'll use our flamethrowers and grenades to attack the blockhouse. We have the building plans of the fortress in our possession, so we'll be able to place tear gas inside the ventilation systems and force the enemy inside to surrender."

After a lengthy discussion, my plan was adopted.

One day I pulled my sergeant aside to let him know I'd be gone for a few days. "Sergeant, our company is making good progress in their climbing and skiing skills.

Continue the same exercises while I'm gone. I know our offensive will be successful. I am leaving you in charge while I find someone to make thirty-five silk 'bat wings' for my fliers. The wings need to be sturdy but light-weight because we'll have to carry them on the climb as well as our machine guns and ammunition. You and the other men will be armed with paratrooper machine guns. You'll ski down the mountain at the same time we jump."

I had picked up the wing idea from a ski school in Grenoble in 1940 just after joining the Alpine Ski Troop. The instructors connected the silk with a cable from the tips of the skis to the tips of the wings at the end of each man's outstretched arms. Bamboo stays strengthened the wings that were attached to the arms with three straps. This contraption allowed the skier to fly up to a hundred meters farther than he could without them. I would have my men practice with the equipment in the mountains above Chamonix, where they could ski down the slope to a ridge from which they would jump over a small valley.

When I returned, I orchestrated the attack and I coordinated the timeline with the foreign legion and the Senegalese. Thirty-five of the finest marksmen from Senegal, along with the rest of their company, camped next to us. Most of them were tall, over six feet in height. Their ebony-colored skin was smooth and sleek. They watched us practice and called us *les chauves souris*, the bats, because of the wings that we used to gain distance when we made our jumps on skis.

"Ask the Senegalese corporal to come see me, Sergeant."

The corporal and two of his soldiers reported to me. "Guard our camp and let no one pass while we're away," I ordered. Late in the afternoon, when we approached the camp, my sergeant fell into a fit of laughter. "What's going on?" I asked. Hardly able to contain himself, he pointed to the entrance of the camp. There, at the gate, was a colonel detained by the guardsmen who refused him entry. The Senegalese followed orders to the letter.

Being on skis again brought back memories of childhood. My tutor happened to be friends with the commander of the Italian Alpine Ski Troop in Limone. Each winter from 1926 to 1929, we often skied together from the Maddalena Pass in Italy, often crossing the border into France, where we would spend the night at Saint-Martin-Vesubie. My favorite place to camp was Lake Terrasole above Limone. It was a cirque, a perfect ring made of granite. The water was warm in the midst of the snow and ice, and steam rose from it. On the border of the lake on the opposite side from our camp, edelweiss grew wild. In the spring, the Italians would swim over to pick them and put them in their hats. This flower was the emblem of the Italian Alpine Ski Troop. The experience was enchanting and is one I'll never forget. After camping for a night, the following day we would continue toward the Col de Tende, passing by Roquebillière and Sospel before arriving in Limone. It's hard to express my feelings about these mountains. When I was there, I was truly at home. These mountains belonged to me.

* * *

It was a clear but chilly day in April 1945, the day we began our climb, two days before the planned attack. Early in the morning, I met with the leaders of the foreign legion and the Senegalese at the camp at Saint-Martin-Vesubie. I spread the map of the area out on the table.

"It will take us two days to get to the top of the mountain overlooking the fort. The day after tomorrow at sunrise, we will be ready to descend toward l'Authion."

I directed my words to the legionnaire commander. "Just to review, you'll climb up here. It's about a half kilometer to our right and then down into the valley. I received the report that you totally demined the area last week using German prisoners to precede you, so we won't have any surprises. Upon my signal, before my company descends, you'll make yourselves visible and draw the Germans' fire."

Then I addressed the Senegalese captain. "You'll climb this ridge to our left, where you'll remain with your sharp-shooters and machine gunners. The rest of your men will descend when I radio you. Are you sure your men cannot use the boots, Captain? It's so rocky and icy, I don't see how . . ."

"Lieutenant, the boots hurt their feet. They just can't get used to them. I assure you, they will be fine."

"All right, but I don't understand how you'll keep your feet from freezing." The Senegalese were tough soldiers and never complained. They had incredible endurance and a high tolerance for pain. They were humble, respectful, trustworthy, and had a healthy pride in themselves.

"Let's get going." The mountain was very rocky and extremely difficult to climb. Even goats would have had a difficult time, the terrain was so rugged and icy. There were no paths and no trees. The higher we got, the greater the accumulation of snow. It was an intense ascent, especially since we had to carry all our ammunition, machine guns, mortars, grenades, water, and food. My special flying skiers had to carry their bat wings as well.

We climbed up and down the mountains until dusk. That first night, many of the men were able to sleep among the rocks, but I couldn't fall asleep because of the excitement. I was eager to carry out the mission and achieve our objective. The next morning at daybreak, we resumed our climb. In the late afternoon, we reached the summit. The mountain facing the fortress was blanketed in white. There was a great accumulation of very icy snow created by the snowdrifts from the direction of Italy. The scene was breathtaking, the moment intense.

"Sergeant, tell the men to spread out among the rocks and sleep. Tomorrow is the day we've been preparing for all these months. Tell them we'll wake them in plenty of time to get ready."

I couldn't even think of sleeping. My mind went over everything again, every last detail of the attack, every crucial aspect of its tight coordination. Throughout this rugged climb, the morale of my men had been great. Their training had been intense, and I was proud of them. Victory was just ahead—I could feel it. Soon we would triumph. We would finish this war in glory. But I also felt such agony about killing the human beings that I would have to shoot—good German soldiers I didn't even know. These considerations led me to thinking about the people I had killed.

I had never felt comfortable killing another human being. When I killed that member of the militia who was selling out his son and the Jews in La Turbie, that act had saved human lives, and I felt good about it. When I killed the traitorous doctor on the escape through the south of France with the Bulgarian scientist, I saved many lives again, including my own. So I did what I was trained to do, not considering their humanity.

"And proudly, I will do the same thing again in a few hours for the righteous cause of freedom from tyranny," I said out loud to the Universe.

Then, totally focused on our plan, I felt calm and completely confident that we would be successful. I knew the Senegalese sharpshooters never missed. Even if the Germans spotted us, our descent would be rapid and they'd be caught in cross fire. At my signal, the foreign legion would make themselves visible, attracting the attention of the Germans. The enemy would become anxious, surprised by the legionnaires' advance. The Germans would be blinded by the rising sun and diverted by the legionnaires as we flew over them. While we were in flight, the Senegalese marksmen would open fire, holding their position while the rest of their company would descend toward the trenches.

"I think the plan is good. The fortress at l'Authion will be recaptured by the French today! Yet I have an ache deep inside when I think of all the men who will no longer be alive this afternoon. It's heartbreaking, such a waste. I look forward to this day being a distant memory. France will be liberated, the world will be free of this Nazi menace, and World War II will finally be "the war to end all wars."

My solitary contemplation came to an end as the moment of battle approached. Now I got up and walked toward my sergeant.

It was still dark. "Sergeant, wake the men."

Finally, the moment was here. We were ready. I waited for the call from one of my men, a Basque whose code-name was Le Coq. He was crouched on a peak a distance away from our group. As soon as the sun was about to appear, he would radio me.

Finally, I got the call. In moments, the sun would rise in the east, blinding the Germans' view of our fliers. "Call the legionnaires. Tell them to show themselves and attack," I ordered my radio man.

"Alert the Senegalese to start shooting as soon as we're airborne."

Instantly I shouted, "*Allons-y!* Let's go, men! Follow me!"

We took to the slope, picked up great speed, then jumped. I felt like a bird. I soared through the air like a mountain hawk on a thermal. It was exhilarating.

Then suddenly—searing pain! It tore through my whole body, causing a spasm. I lost control of my wings. I had been spotted in flight and shot through the knee.

I fell quite a distance short of the trenches. Several of my men skiing down the slope stopped and shielded me while my shock troopers continued in flight. They landed safely on the other side of the front line, beyond the German trenches, as planned.

The pain was overwhelming. I couldn't move. My orderly had seen me go down and had stopped the forward motion of his flight by raising his head and lowering his wings. Soon he was at my side. He had a radio and called the medic. I was bleeding profusely from the right knee where the bullet had entered and from the thigh where it had exited.

Because of their huge number of injured and dead, the Germans in the forward trenches put up the white flag of truce in order to get help for those shot. This briefly allowed me protected passage as well. Eight or nine legionnaires took charge of getting me to the first-aid station. Additionally, around twenty Senegalese had the burden of taking turns carrying me on a stretcher, taking shifts four to six at a time, up and down the rocky and treacherous terrain.

The white flag stayed raised until we reached the top of the first mountain. From that point, the bumpy journey took around seven hours. The medic gave me blood transfusions and morphine along the way.

"Stop the pain. It's burning me up inside!" I shouted. Apparently, I began screaming uncontrollably, so they gave me more morphine, too much in fact, and I became delirious. I have no memory of this at all.

Later, I found out that these German soldiers occupying the fortress, many of them Bavarian, had used copper bullets rubbed with garlic. So that if the bullet didn't kill you, the gangrene caused by the corrosion would poison your body. The Bavarians always prepared their bullets well in advance so that verdigris had already formed on them.

I was bounced around owing to the rough terrain on that long trip to the first-aid station above Saint-Martin-Vesubie. I was incoherent when we arrived. I didn't know where I was.

"I have to get up, I have to get up," I kept repeating over and over, I was told. They had to tie me to the stretcher. The doctors cut off my pants, rebandaged the wound, and gave me more injections. From there, I was taken by ambulance to the Hôtel Majestic in Cannes, which was serving as a military triage hospital. I was in a room with three other men. The doctors came over to see me.

"No sense in wasting time trying to save this leg," one doctor said to the other. "The condyle is cracked open. It can't be repaired. I recommend the leg be amputated," another suggested, never addressing me.

Two or three days later, I was transferred, leg still intact, to the Hôtel Eden-Roc overlooking the Mediterranean in Cap d'Antibes, which was serving as a hospital for officers. I was put in the two-bedroom suite of Colonel

Passy, who had been in a jeep accident and had broken his hip and leg.

"Why would a lieutenant be placed in the suite of a colonel?" I asked myself. I believe that this was somehow especially arranged for me. If not, it was incredible luck. Passy's orderly, a very tall man from Cameroon, picked me up and placed me on the bed as if I weighed nothing at all.

Several doctors came to see me. "Let's try to save the leg," one of them said. "Let's bandage the condyle as tightly as possible and put a cast on to immobilize the leg." They took me to the operating room to do the procedure.

After that, someone came to my room every day to give me injections. A few days later, they saw that pus was seeping through the cast. When they opened it, the smell was putrid. They analyzed the secretion and found that I had developed gangrene.

"It looks like we've done all we can to save the leg. This gangrene makes it impossible. We'll have to schedule an amputation right away," one of the doctors concluded.

"Wait, doctors," Colonel Passy interrupted. "I know there's an English hospital ship, the *Pearce*, in Toulon. Let's have the English take a look before you cut off the lieutenant's leg. They have medicinal products that we don't. I'll make a phone call."

As the result of the colonel's intervention, the hospital ship came to the Bay of Cannes. Men from the *Pearce* came to the suite, put me on a stretcher, and loaded me on an ambulance in front of the hotel. From the pier, I was transferred to a motorboat that had come from the ship. I stayed on the *Pearce* for eleven days. They placed a board from my right heel up to the middle of my back. Of course, this meant that I could not sit up. The bandages were changed every three or four hours. The wound was covered with an antibiotic powder and then the leg was rewrapped with gauze because they could not use plaster again owing to the infection. The flesh smelled awful, but little by little the gangrene began to disappear. They were able to save my leg, but the condyle of the knee was cracked. There was nothing they could do about that. I was sent back to the Eden-Roc to recover. The board was removed a couple of months later, but I stayed at the hospital in recovery for well over a year.

EPILOGUE

In Peace: Goodwill.
—WINSTON CHURCHILL

One day during my convalescence at the Eden-Roc, I received such a surprise visit. Who should show up to see me, but four of the Senegalese who had carried me down from l'Authion on a stretcher. The guard at the gate would not let them in. He called me on the phone. "Lieutenant, I have four visitors who want to come up. They are from Senegal. They have no right to enter the grounds without passes."

I replied, "What are their names?" The guard asked them and told me. I didn't know their names, but I responded, "Of course, I know them very well. They are responsible for saving my life. Direct them to my room."

When they entered the suite, I could see that Colonel Passy was uncomfortable with their presence, but I didn't care. He told his orderly to shut his door. I loved these men. Their smiles were radiant when they saw me. They told me that the battle had continued a long time after I was wounded. Eventually, the Germans and Italians who were still entrenched within the fortification surrendered, but we lost a lot of men. The Senegalese corporal was wearing a necklace of copper wire with ears strung onto it.

"Lieutenant, these are all ears cut from the Germans killed at l'Authion," he said as he placed the treasured necklace around my neck. I was truly touched. This was an invaluable gift that represented personal pride and honor. Still, it made me uneasy. I pictured my nearly amputated leg as someone's treasure of war and didn't like the image. Defeating the Nazis and bringing an end to the war was all that was important to me. There had been enough maiming and killing.

Another surprise came shortly thereafter in the form of a visit by my mother and father. I remember it vividly. They both stood at the end of my bed. They did not approach. My mother wasn't allowed to come close to me, and my father didn't want to be. My father remarked with a smirk on his face, "Well, at least they didn't shoot you in the back while you were running away!" My mother glared at him but said nothing. The orderly offered my mother a chair, but my father blurted out, "Don't bother. We can't stay long." They were in my room for only about five minutes before they left. That was their only visit.

The war ended while I was still in the hospital. Late in 1946, a few days before I would finally be released, I heard a commotion out in the corridor. Next thing I knew, two sentries flanked my doorway. A cacophony of excited voices grew louder as they neared my room. I recognized the sentries' uniforms. The men were British Royal Marines.

Suddenly, in the doorway stood the most recognizable man on the planet. Dressed in his habitual dark blue suit, with waistcoat and gold watch chain stretched across his ample stomach, he tipped his bowler to me in tribute. In the same hand he held a lighted cigar. The head nurse was loudly imploring him in French to put it out. He wheeled on her and politely said in English, which he knew she probably wouldn't understand, "Madame, I have only a minute. Then I'll be gone and, with me, my offensive cigar."

Turning back to me, he thrust his free hand into the air. The index and middle fingers formed a big V. He winked and said, *"Mon petit, la belle France est libre. Vive la France!"*

"Vive la France, mon commandant," I replied, an overwhelming joy filling my heart.

"Merci beaucoup, mon lieutenant." He bowed toward me, sweeping his hand in a wide arc.

"Monsieur, je vous remercie, vous, le peuple britannique et tous nos alliés" (Sir, I thank you, the British people, and all our Allies.)

He strode toward my bedside, kissed my brow, and put his calling card and one of his signature Montecristo cigars into my hand. "We have a lot of fine restaurants to try together and a lot of catching up to do, *mon petit.*

I've written my private number on the card. Call me at the villa as soon as you escape!"

He turned and left. The last thing I heard was the frantic head nurse yelling as she chased the greatest man to live in the twentieth century down the corridor. "No smoking! *Il est interdit de fumer! C'est dangereux! Il est interdit de fumer!*"

Max Ciampoli was seventeen years old and a lieutenant in the French army's elite Alpine infantry on skis when France was invaded and swiftly defeated by Germany. Through his godfather's friendship with Winston Churchill, Max was invited by the Prime Minister to come to England for training as a special agent, which launched his heroic wartime career. After the war, Max moved to the United States, where he found success in a number of professions, including chef/executive chef (in New York, Houston, and St. Louis); horse breeder in Missouri; owner of an exclusive car dealership (Classic Cars) in Beverly Hills; and luxury yacht dealer in Marina del Rey, California. Max became a U.S. citizen in 1956.

Coauthor **Linda Ciampoli** (née Rhodes) studied at the University of Bordeaux and the Sorbonne in Paris and is a graduate of the Department of French at UCLA. Also accomplished in many fields, Linda was pursuing a career in the hotel industry when she and Max met in Marina del Rey. They married in 1991 and are now working on their second book, which relates Max's fascinating life in Haiti and the United States following World War II.

You can contact Max and Linda Ciampoli via their website at www.churchillssecretagent.com. Or you can e-mail Max at max@churchillssecretagent.com and Linda at linda@churchillssecretagent.com.

M14G0610